The ball was already in full swing when a subdued commotion on the staircase heralded what the company assumed was the arrival of the Imperial party. Couples stopped waltzing and turned expectantly toward the door.

A gasp of astonishment rose as a female figure swathed in pink and lemon saris rode through the doorway on a jet black horse in cloth of gold and with a golden egret between the ears. At a word from its rider, the Arabian reared to its full height and remained for a moment poised in mid-air with the splendor of an equestrian statue.

A burst of spontaneous applause rang through the ballroom. Therese was the indisputable success of the evening . . .

THERESE LACHMANN
A WOMAN AGAINST THE WORLD

Also by Evelyn Hanna
Published by Ballantine Books:

STOLEN SPLENDOR

A WOMAN AGAINST THE WORLD

EVELYN HANNA

BALLANTINE BOOKS • NEW YORK

Library of Congress Catalog Card Number: 82-91080

ISBN 0-345-28931-5

Manufactured in the United States of America

First Edition: June 1983

Contents

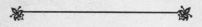

Prologue

*I*N APRIL, 1910, *a lawsuit was scheduled for hearing in the Berlin Supreme Court. It promised to be one of the most sensational within living memory.*

The plaintiffs were the heirs of the two sisters of the last Prince of Oppeln-Piast. They were, on the one hand, the three Princes of Baden-Oldemburg—Maximilian, Otto, and Sixtus—and, on the other hand, the Marquess of Hadley and his sister Lady Honoria Fitz-George, children of the Dowager Marchioness of Hadley, who was not considered competent to appear. She was mad by any accepted standard and was kept under surveillance at the Dower House at Hadley Hall. These distinguished persons, represented by a regiment of lawyers, were contesting the Will of the late Prince Augustus Lothair Boleslaus Miesczko Lobachevski of Oppeln-Piast, Duke of Brieg and Liegnitz, Count of Breslau and Katowice, Count of the Holy Roman Empire, and a number of other resounding titles.

At stake were the Piast estates at Radoom, on which flourished the Silesian Coal and Fuel Company, the largest coal fields in Europe; large blocks of shares in the Berlin-Baghdad Railway, with its tributary lines that stretched to important industrial centers throughout the Balkans; shares in the Russo-Turkestan Railway, which ran from St. Petersburg to Tashkent; shares in the Zaharoff armament industries with their subsidiary companies in France, Germany, Sweden, and England; real estate in New York City, comprising the four corners of Fifth Avenue and Forty-second Street, on one of which the new Public Library had been built, and two entire blocks on both sides of Park Avenue between Sixty-eighth and Seventieth Streets;

1

*a long stretch of coastal property adjacent to Rio de Janeiro,
on which the resort town of Petropolis was rapidly expanding;
several hundred thousand acres of jungle in the vicinity of Sao
Paolo; and cash deposits amounting to millions in various
American, Swiss, and English banks. And last, but not least,
the Piast Museum in Berlin, containing the Prince's library
and his unique collection of porcelains and paintings.*

*The defendant who had amassed this staggering fortune was
the Princess of Oppeln-Piast, a legendary figure now rumored
to be in her fifties. She was represented by one lawyer and two
clerks, whose duty it was to produce any one of a vast pile of
documents at any given moment. As it transpired, they would
seldom be called upon to do this, as the Princess's memory
was as remarkable as her genius for making money. She was,
in all probability, the richest woman in Europe, with the possible exception of the Queens of England and Holland.*

*Very few people in Berlin had actually laid eyes on this
female Midas. All that was certain was that, somehow, she had
amassed an incredible fortune, all of which the plaintiffs, who
had done nothing in life but take the precaution of being born
into noble families, intended to appropriate.*

She had a good many surprises in store for them.

*The case opened on the twenty-fifth of April. The visitors'
benches were packed with the cream of Berlin society, foreign
diplomats, and the international press. The three Baden princes,
wishing to make it plain how distasteful they found these proceedings, took their places with haughty formality among their
black-coated entourage of lawyers. They bowed condescend-
ingly to their English cousins who had fewer lawyers and were
at the disadvantage of not speaking German; their mother, the
demented Marchioness, had neglected that side of their education.*

*There was a flurry in the courtroom when the Princess made
her appearance. She was tall, dressed in a long black cloak
lined with sable and a black cartwheel hat that partially hid
her face. She moved with a lurching gait, assisted by an ebony
cane. Those on the left of the courtroom glimpsed a classic
profile, chiseled as an intaglio, and unmarred by time. Those*

on the right saw a frightening wreck with a scar that had twisted her cheek into a livid knot, the right eye partially closed by another scar that sliced at a right angle down her forehead.

She made her way to a small table and sat down. Her lawyer stationed himself at an adjoining table, with the two clerks behind. They took some time to arrange several piles of documents. She drew off her black gloves, revealing strong hands unadorned except for one ruby ring, gleaming like a clot of blood.

The judges at last took their places. The preliminary procedures followed, and the trial began.

Part One

The Muranov

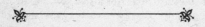

*F*OR NINE MONTHS of the year Warsaw was a city of mud, for the remaining three a city of dust.

During the interminable rains the unpaved streets turned into swamps through which carriages and carts, horses and pedestrians, splashed and slithered and slid. When the snow fell the city was briefly purified, but the mud worked its way through like a subcutaneous disease and, in a day or two, the white mantle was discolored. Then the mud froze and the carts and horses and pedestrians slid and splashed more dangerously, breaking limbs and axles. The carriages of the nobles skidded to the doors of the palaces on the Ujazdov and the Krakowskie Przedmiescie where flunkies waited to carry the guests indoors. The mud oozed in with them and spattered the marble floors and the Persian carpets. The guests would be carefully deposited on chairs where the gentlemens' boots would be pulled off and their evening pumps put on and the ladies' overshoes removed to be replaced with satin slippers.

From October to June Warsaw battled the mud.

In June the mud dried up and during the brief hot summers a reddish dust blew along the streets and through the parks, choking and smarting. In the crazy twisted alleys of the Muranov, clouds of flies buzzed and sometimes in the afternoon of a particularly drowsy day the old Jewish quarter steamed and sweated like one great droning, drumming hive.

No one had ever planned the Muranov. It had proliferated in its own haphazard way. The hovels huddled like derelicts seemed always on the point of collapse. But they didn't collapse. They clung on. They clung together, matching the in-

7

explicable endurance of their occupants. The alleys twisted and
twined in a labyrinthine muddle. Every hut and synagogue and
tiny ill-lit shop lurched and leaned and decayed beside its neighbors. But they survived. The ghetto was a displaced mid-East-
ern slum on the outside, evil-smelling, murky, bitter with
deprivation and suspicion. But inside, behind the morose little
windows, sometimes paned with coarse glass, more often stuffed
with rags and oiled paper, it sustained an intense, secretive life
of its own. A narrow life but, according to tradition, a rich
life. What it lacked in money it made up for in dreams. The
dreams of the Muranov went back for thousands of years to
Babylon and Egypt and, before that, to the Land of Promise.
The dreams of the Muranov coursed slowly but persistently
through the arteries of all who dwelled there. On the Sabbath
the dreams became a glory in the synagogues and briefly even
the poorest were rich as kings.

It was an encampment of Jobs and Jeremiahs.

Solomon Lachmann lived in what, from the outside, was
scarcely even a hovel. It was a tumbled down chicken coop
with a roof that slanted at a crazy angle and two little windows
squinting like eyes with cataracts. There was a wooden palisade
to one side, enclosing a tiny yard. The palisade, seven feet
high, propped up the hovel.

Very few people ever crossed that threshold. Certain mysterious visitors, heavily cloaked and armed, found their way
through the Muranov maze, bearing mysterious bundles. After
a careful scrutiny of the alley, they were admitted to transact
mysterious business and then to depart as furtively as they
came.

Solomon Lachmann's place of business was deliberately
dingy. The heavily barred door opened into a small chamber
that betrayed nothing. It contained an old table and a brass
lamp, two rickety chairs and a threadbare rug on the dirt floor.
The front room confirmed Solomon Lachmann's pretense of
being a hermit on the brink of destitution who had never had
anything and never would have anything and who only wanted
to be left alone to lament the miserable fate which the Lord
had visited upon him. Those mysterious transactions were ac-

companied by a whining lamentation about his poverty, the bad times, the tragic past and the awful impending future. What could he, an old derelict with no one, do about it? Nonetheless, while he was bewailing providence, he was unwrapping the mysterious bundles and shaking his head dubiously and weighing and appraising and denigrating and repeating again and again that he couldn't be expected to do business when he was down to his last few sous. Then the bargaining would begin and the complaints and protests and accusations and denials would rise and rise like a bow scraped across the string of an ancient fiddle. Solomon's head would wag miserably to and fro. The mysterious objects would be rejected and wrapped up and then, after more complaints and protests, unwrapped and reconsidered and finally the lowest possible figure would be offered and, of course, refused. The bargaining would go on for half an hour until by dint of exasperation a deal was made.

Old Solomon Lachmann would unbolt and unlock the inner door, huddling over the lock so that his mysterious visitor wouldn't get any mysterious notions of what he was doing. He would open the door just wide enough to squeeze through and then the relocking and rebolting would be repeated on the other side. The visitor would be left there tapping his heels and thinking what a time the infernal old wretch was taking and that some patriotic Pole should burn down the Muranov once and for all and get rid of these infidel moneygrubbers. After a long wait the process of unbolting and unlocking and rebolting and relocking would be repeated while the visitor cursed under his breath and the old merchant and sometime receiver of stolen goods would lay out, with groans and protests, the few coins that the mysterious objects had cost him. The coins would be counted and tested and pocketed and the visitor would thankfully depart for some mysterious destination beyond the Muranov.

Then Solomon would bolt and lock all the doors and retreat to the nether regions of his dwelling which opened out, cave by cave, into a ruinous old warren of a house.

The brass lamp which he carried because, night and day, the nether regions were always dark, revealed boxes and bun-

dles and piles and proliferations of merchandise stacked against
the walls, the value of which he had long forgotten, gleams of
brass and flickers of silver, pictures in gilt frames and carpets,
rolled and unrolled, mirrors and monstrances, furs and fire-
arms, a necropolis of objects of bizarre and questionable prove-
nance.

In the blackest of back rooms Solomon would settle down
like an old spider returning to its web beside a tiled stove and
sit for hours, immobile, seemingly asleep. No one knew on
what he pondered. His cogitations were as circuitous as the
alleys of the Ghetto and as secretive. His daughter—if she was
his daughter—in her room upstairs knew nothing about the
workings of his mind. His granddaughter—if she was his
granddaughter—never even knew where he came from. He
was an enigma, as wrapped in speculation as the bundles that
were brought by persons and from places best not inquired
after.

He was rich.

In her carved French bed with its peeling puttis, under a
rotting canopy, the once beautiful Rebecca dreamed and drank
and slumbered and decayed. She was still voluptuous, white-
skinned, with copper hair fine as silk now streaked with gray,
and immense mournful eyes, dark and velvety as pansies. She
dreamed of the past glory that had lasted exactly one year, and
cared for nothing else. Every incident of that year had become
sanctified as Holy Writ. She lived and relived those incidents
each day and each night in the ornate bed in which most of
them had happened. The bed was the crucible, the memorial,
the cathedral, of all that she had been or had ever aspired to
be.

At the foot of the bed was a leather trunk studded with brass
nails. There were occasions when she roused herself from her
habitual stupor and unlocked the trunk and unpacked it, fon-
dling and dreaming over its contents. Her child, Therese, knew
everything that was in the trunk as intimately as one knows
old friends. There were linen sheets embroidered with the initial
S under a crown. There were pillowcases edged with lace as
delicate as cobwebs. There were three dresses, one of honey-

colored silk embroidered with seed pearls, one of sky blue brocade with little birds nesting in branches and one of deep yellow satin like old wine with a bodice stiff with gold thread. The time had long since passed when she could have worn these dresses; she had grown corpulent with drink and inactivity. But she caressed them, her hands lingering over the folds and embroidery as though they were living things. There were white, blue and gold slippers with diamond buckles. There were nightdresses of fine lawn and a silk robe trimmed with tiny feathers like the wings of angels. There were shawls and scarves and bottles of perfume long since emptied that smelled of mold but were to her as fresh as spring. There was a red leather box, stamped with the same S under the crown. It contained a necklace with pendant earrings and a brooch of glittering topazes. Rebecca would gaze at them as though they were talismans. There was a gold mirror and a gold comb which she would run slowly, slowly through her hair. There were two gold brushes and three bottles with gold tops and there were other relics, ribbons, little animals of carved quartz and carnelian, an amethyst ring, a snuffbox and posies of dried flowers that had turned quite black.

Therese grew up in that house. She never went out. Her mother was always sleeping or drinking and her grandfather—if he was her grandfather—was always brooding by the tile stove. Once a day a woman left food at the street door. A pot of stew and a bowl of kasha, boxes of dried fruit and sometimes cakes. She would knock three times and Solomon would lock and unlock the doors and carry the food to the back room. Therese was always hungry. She would gobble up her share and take a plate up to her mother who hardly ever touched it. Therese would eat that, too. Once every few months a man with a cloak drawn up across his face, as though he were venturing into a plague area, would leave an envelope for Rebecca. It contained money with which she supplied herself with brandy. Therese had no clothes and no friends. She was so ragged and unkempt that she might have been a beggar child left in a house of strangers.

She was never taught to read or write.

She was unclean.

Everything in that warren of a house was unclean, covered in dust, crawling with bugs and fleas, rats and spiders. Often as a child Therese was pocked all over with bites and blotches. She taught herself to pick the vermin out of her hair. She had no room of her own and slept in a sort of closet outside her mother's room on a pile of carpets.

She grew up like an animal, wild, fierce and frightened.

When the rains came in the autumn Therese would take off her filthy rag of a dress and stand naked in the yard and let the rain wash off the grime of the summer. She loved the rain that fell like a blessing over her itching body. She let the rain pour through her tangled hair. Better still was the snow. She would scoop up handfuls of the wonderful whiteness and rub it all over her until her body glowed. The third miracle of the year was the almond tree. No one knew how the tree had grown there. There were very few trees in the ghetto, little if anything that was green and living. But each spring the little tree would clothe itself in a veil of lace like a bride. Therese would gaze up into the branches and her soul would be filled with joy like a bird's first taste of flight. She would stand with her face raised and the white petals would float down like imperceptible caresses. She would gather up the fallen petals and scatter them over her bed. The blossoms were gone in a week or two. But then came the leaves, tiny and bright as jade in which sparrows flitted and chattered. The almond tree was a promise of something beyond the foul old prison of a house that was the only world she knew.

She was not exactly lonely as she had never known anyone but her mother and Solomon and had never experienced companionship. But as she grew she became restless and her restlessness turned to rage.

She began to plot ways of escape. She had no idea what lay beyond the high wooden fence and the locked doors. She wanted to escape anyway. She wanted to be free.

Things in the outside world sometimes impinged on that murky backwater. Once plague stalked the Muranov. Solomon went out late at night with a sack and spread lime along the front of the house and along the inside and outside of the palisade. Saucers burned in all the rooms with some substance that rose in a thick and sickeningly scented smoke. The woman who brought the food no longer came. They lived off dried fruit and kasha which Solomon cooked over a brazier. The windows were sealed and the house became suffocating. The Muranov was filled with wailing and the heavy tramp of feet bearing coffins. One night Therese woke screaming. A rat with cinder-red eyes was creeping up her body. She rushed into her mother's room and hid under the covers.

No one came in or went out. They were besieged.

On another occasion, at the peak of an unendurable heat-wave, there were sudden outbursts of firing, screams and the thunder of hooves in the alleys. Solomon pushed boxes against the doors and blocked up the windows with rugs. They cowered in the darkness listening to the muffled tumult and then to the roar and crackle of the tinderbox houses as they went up in flames.

After two days a heavy silence fell. The same high wailing drifted with the black smoke over the ghetto, a sound neither human nor animal that seemed to issue from some abyss of primeval despair. Solomon removed the boxes and the rugs from the windows and did what he seldom did: he went out. He was away for about an hour. He came back and huddled over the tile stove.

"What has happened?" the child asked.

"Much was burned. Many have been killed."

He rocked to and fro, keening in a way that struck cold dread to her heart.

Then everything went on as before. That is to say that nothing went on because nothing whatever happened.

Like a plant struggling to survive without light or water, Therese grew by the sheer obstinate persistence of flesh and bone.

She spent her days dreaming and making dolls. She made little shapeless figures out of rags and straw and scraps of material that she stole from the storerooms. These dolls had names and personalities: Moomo and Dumi and Titchtich,

Grumgrum and Lalilu. She talked to the dolls in a language that only she and they could understand. She shared secrets with them that came to her under the almond tree. They went on long journeys together at night. The dolls lolled and sprawled on her bed but in her dreams they grew tall and walked about and took her great distances to places where houses had wings.

Sometimes when the dolls were sleepy or cross or refused to communicate she would rummage through the storerooms. There were always discoveries, brass candlesticks and strange inlaid boxes and pictures one could hardly make out they were so dark. She would light one of the lamps and peer at the blackened canvases, at the faces and trees and what she supposed were animals. There was a portrait of a beautiful woman in a blue gown holding a child, with tall white flowers growing in pots on a windowledge and a stretch of tender and distant sky.

Solomon heard her and unbolted the door of the back room. "I thought you were the rats."

"Is that my mother?" the child asked.

"No, it's Miriam, queen of the goyim."

Therese had no idea who the goyim were, but she studied the serene and loving face. She made a doll out of a piece of blue velvet ripped off an old cloak. She set the doll up at the end of her bed and whispered, "You are Bubilala, queen of the goyim."

She made many journeys with Bubilala, who always carried her child and her pots of flowers.

On fine days Therese went into the yard and talked to the almond tree. It always had things to tell her and the sparrows gave her news of the outside world. In late summer the tree bore nuts. She would crack them against the fence and extract the kernels. They were bitter, but she always thanked the tree for giving her such fine gifts.

And there was the patch of sky. She would stare for a long time at that distant blue across which clouds drifted and birds flew. The sky changed color according to its moods. Flames burned up there and faded. Yellow swords flashed for a moment and were gone. Rivers of violet flowed into darkness.

She would hurry inside and tell Bubilala and the dolls. They held consultations in their private language about where they would go, all together, one day.

One day!

She became cross with the sparrows because they came and went as they chose. The sparrows made her jealous and sad. She hunted for pebbles in the yard and flung them into the branches. The sparrows twittered and flew away.

Where had they flown to? It made her cry.

One day Therese could stand it no longer. She confronted her mother who was now a shapeless mound of discolored flesh. Her mind had been too long sodden to understand what Therese was saying.

"Why do we live like this?"

Her mother stared. The lustrous velvety eyes were dull and the whites netted with red veins.

"Does everyone live like this?"

Gradually Rebecca focused. Perhaps for the first time she realized that her child was beautiful. She was tall for her age, perfectly formed, with white skin and astonishing yellow-green eyes; *his* eyes, *his* bearing. Her hair was like her mother's during her time of glory, except that there was more gold in the copper. She was a little princess in rags.

Rebecca heaved herself up. A slow astonishment spread through what remained of her mind.

"Come here."

"I want to know if this is how everyone lives or if there is something wrong."

She went to her mother's side. Rebecca managed to sit up. The room reeked of female sweat and the dregs of brandy. Mice had eaten away the hangings of the bed which hung in tatters.

Rebecca pushed back her daughter's tangled hair to reveal a fine high forehead. *His!*

She considered the child in amazement.

Her mother's stench overpowered her. Therese stepped back in disgust. "Why do you never speak to me? Is there something wrong with me?"

A wave of bewildered shame came over the ruined woman.

The girl confronted her like a fury, her eyes blazing. "I hate this house! I want to go out! I want something to happen!"

Rebecca groaned. She was hearing that noble voice which had shouted like that at his servants, which had shouted at her because she was ignorant and lazy.

Therese stamped her foot. "I'll burn it. I'll set fire to it. You'll burn."

Rebecca moved her hand before her face as though brushing away reflections in a dusty mirror.

"Therese—"

It was one of the few times when her mother had used her name. She had a name. She *was* someone. She wasn't just part of the house like the rats, like the boxes and carpets. She had a name like the dolls.

"Wait—"

It was so hard to think. There was such a weight, such a thick cloud on Rebecca's mind.

"He should see you."

"Who?"

The mound of flesh sank back against the pillows.

"I'll take you to see him." She nodded slowly, appalled at the prospect of such an expedition into the outside world.

"Who?" The girl was aflame with curiosity and rebellion. She came a step closer and glared at her mother. "You're horrible, more horrible than the rats."

Rebecca held out her arm. "I'll take you. Help me!"

Therese shrank from touching her mother who was filthier than the filthiest corner of the house, but she dragged her up.

"Get a bucket of water."

Therese was astonished.

"Now?"

Rebecca nodded and groaned.

At least it was something, something out of the ordinary, something to do.

She ran down into the yard where the cistern was. She climbed onto a stool that had two steps and lowered a bucket over the side. A thrilling idea struck her. She could climb on this stool and get over the palisade. It had never occurred to her before. She could get out of the house and vanish. To whatever happened out there.

She pulled the bucket up. She was amazed at her daring. The water was brackish with dead flies.

She lugged the bucket back to her mother's room.

Rebecca was sprawled over the trunk. The three ceremonial dresses lay across the bed. She was hunting for something. Therese knew everything that was in the trunk, the topazes, the sheets, the little carved animals. Her mother was searching for something else.

She found it at last, a small oblong box wrapped in paper. She unfolded it carefully as though it was some great treasure. The box had green leaves painted on it and letters. Inside were three little greenish cakes that had a faint earthy smell.

"What are they?"

"Soap. From Paris."

She took out one of the little cakes and dipped it in the water. Gradually a soft foam formed on her hand.

"Take off your dress."

Therese slipped off her rag. Her legs were gray with grime. Only her belly was pale as alabaster.

Slowly Rebecca washed her daughter. Slowly and carefully as though it was a religious ceremony she soaped her from head to foot. It was the most delicious sensation Therese had ever known.

A wonderful freshness and coolness spread through her. She felt as though she was becoming freer and brighter, like the first bright leaves of the almond tree, like the sky.

Rebecca washed her all over and then washed and rinsed her hair. Therese was too amazed to speak. Not even Bubilala could feel as heavenly as this.

Rebecca reached into the trunk and pulled out one of the embroidered sheets and wrapped her daughter in it. She dried her slowly and with care.

She brought out the gold brush and the gold comb. She untangled the knots in her daughter's hair and brushed it with long, slow strokes until it fell in a dazzling wave over Therese's shoulders. Surely no child had ever had hair as fine and glistening as this.

But this extraordinary occasion did not stop there. Rebecca heaved herself up and slipped the blue dress with the little birds over Therese's head. It was far too long. She looked like a doll dressed up for a children's party.

Slowly, painfully, Rebecca lumbered to a cabinet with many little drawers, filled with all sorts of rubbish and specked with mice droppings. She extracted a pair of scissors and, thudding to her knees, slowly and painfully cut off a strip of brocade from the skirt. Therese's blood ran cold.

"Why are you doing that?"

Her mother was crouched on the floor like an old sick animal, snipping and snipping at the dress.

Rebecca clung to the bedpost and heaved herself up.

The bodice was far too big. Once it had swelled over Rebecca's superb white breasts. She pulled it tight over her daughter's narrow chest.

"Take it off now."

"What are you doing? Isn't it for me?"

"Yes, for you. Bring me a lamp."

Therese sped downstairs. She was breathless with wonder and excitement. She found one of Solomon's lamps and knocked on the door of the back room.

The thin voice wheezed. "Ech! What is it?"

"There's no oil in this lamp. She wants it."

There was the familiar unbolting and unlocking. Solomon peered 'round the door at the naked girl.

"Cover yourself. Have you no shame?"

"She wants a lamp."

"What for? She'll set fire to the house."

"She wants it now. She's making a dress—for me."

Solomon took the lamp and filled it and preceded his granddaughter—if she was his granddaughter—upstairs. Therese could never remember him going upstairs before.

Rebecca was sitting on the side of the bed sewing. Her eyes were watering in the fading light.

"What's this? What are you doing?"

"It's time I took her to see him."

Solomon raised the lamp and the yellow light fell on the wreck of what had once been a beautiful woman.

"Why?"

"He should do something."

Solomon snorted. "Ech! What can he do? She's your shame—and his."

"There's no shame in beauty."

"Shame is to be bidden. He'll turn you away."

"Put down the lamp. I can't see."

The old man hesitated. "You'll set fire to the house."

"I've done nothing for her. That's shame enough."

The naked girl had squeezed into the room and was watching her mother in consternation.

"How will you get there?"

"Walk."

Solomon pshawed and humphed and fingered his corkscrew curls.

Rebecca drew a deep breath. "He always kept his word."

Solomon gave up and shuffled out. Therese edged to her mother's side. "Who is *he*? Where are you taking me?"

"To see a great gentleman." Rebecca sewed slowly, deliberately. "Once I was not like this. I dressed like a princess and lived in my own house. I had furniture and mirrors and carpets. We drank wine from tall glasses."

"Why did you come here then?"

"He married. A noble's daughter."

For the first time Therese considered her mother as a human being. After all she was someone. She had once been someone. In a vague sort of way she felt sorry for her as she was sometimes sorry for the dolls.

At last her mother had finished the back of the dress.

"Try it on."

Therese slipped the lovely blue folds over her head. The skirt just touched the ground and the bodice was smooth across her chest.

"Tomorrow I'll do your hair."

"Tomorrow?" the girl cried in dismay. "Aren't we going now?"

The thought of facing her former lover filled Rebecca with horror and remorse. She sank back against the filthy pillows.

"Tomorrow."

They set out at ten o'clock.

Therese could scarcely breathe as, for the first time in her life, she stepped into the outside world. Was this it, this mean little twisting alley, these mean little huddled shacks? She held fast to her mother's hand.

Rebecca had washed and done her hair. She had found an old dark dress and a cap in a pile of Solomon's rubbish and a large woebegone hat with a black plume. It served to hide her face. She moved slowly like an old woman, swaying from side to side. It was so long since she had been out in the open air.

The shapeless hulk and the girl with the brilliant hair, in her gaudy theatrical costume, made their way through the ghetto. Therese walked awkwardly because the toes of her satin slippers were stuffed with paper. She was stifling between terror and excitement.

In a dream she passed through the gates of the Muranov into the world.

Everything overwhelmed her by its size and variety. So many houses! So many people! Such a dizzying sense of movement and activity. Children running in and out of the crowds, shouting and chasing each other. Dogs chasing the children, barking. Such a hubbub! Such a crush! A man sharpening knives at a droning wheel that sent out showers of sparks. A young woman with a big flat hat with a fringe of multicolored candles. Stalls of bright fruit and vegetables. Stalls with buckets of flowers. Stalls with hundreds of things she had never seen before. And the trees! The windows! And in every window faces and pots of flowers, cats sleeping, pigeons flying, a rumble of hooves and a crying of voices. This tidal wave of humanity with its hats and bonnets and boots and shoes and embroidered waistcoats and flannel shirts, so many shapes and voices, all hurrying and pushing, laughing and chattering! There was an infinite, unbelievable, staggering amount to see. Suddenly she drew back and her mother was forced to stop. A ruddy-faced rogue with a red kerchief around his neck was churning out music from a box while a sad little creature with frightened eyes beat miniature cymbals tied to its wrists.

"Oh look! Oh look!"

"It's nothing. A monkey."

"Is it real? Is it alive?"

They turned a corner and there, marvel of marvels, was the river. It was spanned by bridges of stone and bridges of wood. Barges idled by on the greenish water laden with wood and oxen and bales of merchandise. Here the houses were even taller. There were trees so tall you couldn't see the tops. And beyond the wide curve of the river towers and turrets, domes of immense buildings, colonnades and flights of steps. The grandeur and power and solemnity took her breath away.

She clung to her mother's hand.

They reached a stone bridge. A rush of birds startled her as they wheeled past and circled up and up into the sky. This was where the sparrows flew when they sped away from the almond tree. This was the whole sky.

"Where are we?" she asked in awe.

"In Warsaw."

"Where is that?"

"In Poland."

"Is this the biggest place on earth?"

"Some say there are bigger."

It was impossible. This was all there could ever be.

"Where are we going?"

"To the Ujazdov."

They walked slowly. Rebecca was so unused to movement that every bone in her body ached. There were benches beside the river. She sank onto one with relief, struggling to catch her breath.

"Don't sit down. You'll soil the dress."

Therese was staring at the houses across the street. They were four stories high with tall, shining windows and tall, polished doors with golden doorknobs.

"Who lives in such houses?"

"Nobles."

"Who are they?"

"Rich people."

"But who *are* they?"

Her mother sighed. "Who knows? They have always been there."

She gathered herself together. After a long slow trudge they came to a broad avenue bordered by palaces so vast they seemed like the citadels of giants. Some were set back behind iron gates and walls, surrounded by parks and gardens with many trees.

"Do nobles live here too?"

"The great ones."

One of these palaces was painted yellow with gold around the windows and classic busts in niches. It stretched as far as the eye could see, splendid and unapproachable. Rebecca drew Therese to the wall near the great double doors surmounted by a coat of arms under a crown.

"You're to do exactly what I tell you. When a certain great gentleman comes out you are to go up to him and say, "I am Therese Lachmann. You understand? Repeat it."

"I am Therese Lachmann."

"Just that. Nothing more."

"Who is this great gentleman? Is he a noble?"

"Yes, the finest."

"Why do I have to say that?"

"Because I tell you to. Now wait."

They waited a long time.

Something about this immense painted palace with its rows and rows of windows seemed in some unaccountable fashion familiar to the girl. She felt in some way she could not explain that she belonged there, to this wide avenue, to all this graciousness and grandeur and that all her life she had been a hostage in the dark squalid burrow of the Muranov like the monkey that was forced to beat its cymbals because they were tied to its wrists. One day, she thought, I shall live in a house like this and look out of such windows at the world.

One day!

Two black horses drawing a carriage, shining like black glass, were prancing down the avenue. They slowed up as they approached the palace. Rebecca gripped her arm.

"Now! Stand by the carriage. What do you say?"

"I am Therese Lachmann."

The girl hesitated. She was frightened. Her mother gave her a push. She went uncertainly forward and stood in the middle of the pavement. Two footmen sprang from the box. One went to the great doors and ceremoniously rapped three times. The other signaled to the girl in her outlandish costume. "Shoo! Shoo! Get away! Out of the way there!"

He went to the carriage door.

"I am Therese Lachmann," the girl said timidly to the footman's back.

He glanced angrily over his shoulder and signaled again that she remove herself from his master's right of way. A man in a sky blue coat and impeccable gray trousers stepped out of the carriage. He was magnificent. He could not avoid seeing the girl. She was so conspicuous, so absurdly dressed, so beautiful.

He approached. Yellowish-green eyes looked into yellowish-green eyes. A handsome, classic head inclined toward the perfect classic features of the girl.

"I am Therese Lachmann."

The great man stared. His expression softened with recognition. He glanced down the street at the shabby woman in the black hat standing against the wall.

"So you are Therese Lachmann."

"Are you a noble?" the girl inquired, impressed by his beauty and by something exalted about him.

He was gazing deep into her eyes in which he saw his own. Everything about this girl, at once so timid and so imperious, reminded him of himself, except for the burnished hair. That recalled an incident in his youth he seldom, if ever, thought of.

She was remarkable, perfectly proportioned, with coloring

that would have inspired Bronzino. Far more beautiful than his other pallidly civilized children. This girl had fire.

He pulled off one of his gloves. He was wearing a ruby ring carved with an odd device. He handed the ring to the dazzling, enigmatic fruit of his lost youth.

"If you ever need me bring me this ring. I will always see you."

He touched her hair, glanced again at the desolate woman by the wall, and went through the high doorway into the palace.

Therese stood there in amazement. The doors closed. The footmen glared. "Be off!" She ran back to her mother who was leaning against the wall, weeping.

"He gave me this."

Her mother wiped her streaming eyes with the edge of her cloak.

"What did he say?"

"That I was to bring him this whenever I needed him."

The mother looked at the ring, carved with an S under a crown. She was crushed by a grief as annihilating as death, but worse; it was death in what remained of life.

Suddenly rage and frustration seized the girl. "I don't like that man! I don't like being in Poland!"

The mother pressed the ring into her hand.

"Remember; he always keeps his word."

All that night Therese lay in her cupboard staring at the darkness. Something tremendous had happened. It was too tremendous to talk over with the dolls. It belonged to another reality altogether. She stared and stared at the ring, turning it over in her hand. It was the first thing she had ever owned.

Who was the man in the blue coat? Why had he stared so strangely into her eyes? "I am Therese Lachmann," she said to herself over and over. It was her name, it was her password, but it did not belong to her like the ring.

She was filled with a passionate curiosity to find out more. She wanted to know everything, to see all Poland, all the world. It was fearful and vast and bewildering, but it was marvelous. She knew that she was not meant to stay up in this ruinous old house with nothing but the dolls and the almond tree. "I am Therese Lachmann." She belonged somewhere, in some place of her own, out there.

She thought of her plan to climb over the palisade. She could put the stool against the pilings and climb over. But then it struck her that, once outside, she would not be able to get back. She must think of some way of getting out and getting in, until she had seen enough, until she had found the place, out there, where she belonged.

For days she plotted and schemed. She knew that she could not get out of the house by the street door. Solomon carried the keys on a leather strap under his kaftan. It was useless to ask her mother to help her. Her mother had not stirred from her bed since their expedition. She retreated into a murk of dreams, shifting images of despair.

In one of the storehouses under a pile of rugs was a tin trunk tied 'round and 'round with rope. She had come across it long ago. If she could steal the rope she could make knots in it to hold on to. She would loop the rope over the point of one of the pilings, let herself down and draw herself up again. And then she would hide the rope.

The leaves of the almond tree were turning yellow. She had to complete her plan before the leaves fell and the rains started. It would be more difficult then because everything turned to mud.

She was never certain what Solomon was up to. He shuffled from room to room, cogitating and computing, appraising and estimating just how much he might have tied up in all those boxes and bundles, in all that brass and silver, in all those rugs and pictures and trunks and clothes and furs. He shuffled from room to room, the old miser, in his dirty kaftan, fingering his corkscrew curls.

Her chance came unexpectedly. Solomon went out. He put on his broad-brimmed hat and unlocked and relocked the doors. She heard him go out into the street.

He had hardly ever done that before.

She darted down to the storeroom and dragged the rugs and the mirrors and the boxes off the trunk. Clouds of dust rose around her. There was a scurrying of mice and spiders. She brushed away the webs that stuck to her hand. The trunk was heavy. It was difficult to untie the rope. She tugged at the knots, but they were old. They had petrified with the years. In an inlaid chest she found a bundle of blackened knives. She sawed and sawed at the rope, but it was strong and the knives were rusted.

She dragged the rugs back and the mirrors and the bundles. She was half choked with dust. She threw the useless knives back in the chest and climbed into her cupboard. She crouched there and told the dolls everything.

It was Bubilala who gave her the idea.

She crept into her mother's room. The light was already fading. The room was rank with the smell of the sleeping woman. She tiptoed to the cabinet with the little drawers and found the scissors. Softly, softly, she opened the trunk at the foot of the bed and softly, softly, with no more than the rustle of a mouse, drew out one of the fine linen sheets.

Back in her cupboard she cut the sheet into strips. The dolls were listening to warn her when Solomon returned. They heard the unlocking and relocking of the doors.

After a while he called her.

She hid the sheet and the scissors under the rugs and went down to the back room. He was sitting by the stove eating his dinner. He ate with his fingers, with a slobbering, slithering sound, making little mounds of kasha and sliding them into his mouth. Therese helped herself, took a handful of dried fruit, and sat down in a corner on a pile of clothes.

She had known Solomon all her life but she had never seen him before. In comparison to the sleek, magnificent man in the blue coat and the spotless trousers, he was old and hideous.

He finished his plate, licked his fingers, and wiped them on his kaftan. He watched the girl as she ate.

She was beautiful indeed, more beautiful than her mother. But what was beauty? A curse. It had brought shame into his house. She was like a lamp in her corner, like the gleam of the candlesticks and the church vestments the goyim sold him. Jezebel and Potiphar's wife and the women of Gomorrah. Her beauty was sinful. It would lead into temptation. She would sell her beauty for gold like her mother. Gold should be hidden and such beauty should be concealed. Women were the corruption devised by the Lord to lead men from the path of righteousness.

He wheezed softly and fingered his ringlets.

"So—you saw him."

The girl looked up.

"Who you went to see."

She nodded.

"And?"

She said with a flash of defiance, "He gave me a ring."

At once he was interested.

"What sort of ring?"

"A ring with a red stone."

"Let me see this ring."

She finished her plate and put the dried fruit in her pocket.

"Let me see it, Therese." His voice shifted to the whining plaint that accompained his business transactions. "I would like to see this ring."

The girl got up and went to the door. Her eyes were hard and yellow as a cat's.

"No. It's mine."

She darted upstairs and told the dolls.

The dolls consulted with each other. Again it was Bubilala who gave the best advice. Therese ripped off a swatch from her tattered dress, wrapped up the ring and hid it in a crevice of the wall.

The old man brooded beside the stove.

The daughter of a whore. She'd become a whore. Mother and daughter had brought shame into his house.

Her first attempt to escape was a failure. She was defeated by the gates of the Muranov.

She had waited till dark, eased back the bolts of the yard door and slipped out. The almond tree was shedding its leaves. She whispered, "Goodbye. Goodbye."

She climbed on the stool and knotted the sheet 'round the

spike of one of the pilings. It was easier than she thought to climb up. She was so thin she could straddle the palisade between the spikes. She dropped her slippers into the alley, pulled up the sheet and swung it over. In climbing down, she caught the skirt of the blue dress on the spike and ripped it. She slid to the ground.

There was a long tear in the skirt and the spike had grazed the inside of her thigh. She was too excited to care if she was bleeding. She retrieved the slippers and ran barefoot.

She remembered exactly the route her mother had taken.

She ran through the foetid alleys. The squalid little houses watched her through squinting eyes.

Suddenly she was faced by a wall. There was no door into Poland. The gate through which they had passed was barred.

She was shocked and incredulous.

She went up to the gate and examined it. It was shut from the other side.

She stood there in the darkness before the wall.

She was *inside*.

Outside were the streets, the crowds and the tall buildings. Outside was the river and the avenue with the yellow palace. Even the sad little monkey with the cymbals was better off than she.

Why was she forced to remain inside?

She brooded for days in her cupboard. The dolls had no explanation. Even Bubilala, queen of the goyim, could tell her nothing.

She and Solomon watched each other while they ate.

At last she asked, "Is the door into Poland always open?"

"Into Poland?"

"The door we went through that day."

Solomon molded a little ball of kasha and slid it into his mouth. "I'll tell you about the door if you'll show me the ring."

She debated. It was a trap, but she had to find out about the door.

She extracted the ring from its hiding place and brought it down to the back room.

She unwrapped the ring and handed it to him, standing close so that she could snatch it back.

He examined the ring and his eyes grew a little keener and brighter.

"Ech! A fine ring. A very fine ring. A ruby."

"What's a ruby?"

"A fine carved ruby." He peered at the ring until his nose was almost touching it.

"You see what this is?" He pointed to what was carved on the ring. "A crown."

"What's a crown?"

"A circle of gold and gems that kings wear on their heads. And that—you know what that is?" He pointed to a serpentine sign under the crown. "It's the letter S."

"What is S?"

"The sign of a king's name."

"He's a noble."

"Now. Once, long ago, they were kings."

His crafty fingers fondled the ring.

She grabbed it and stepped back.

"Now tell me about the door."

He hummed and grimaced. "Why do you want to know?"

"You said—" she accused, "if I showed you the ring."

The old man shrugged. "It shuts at nightfall and opens at daybreak. No one from the Muranov is allowed outside at night."

"Why are we kept inside?"

"We are the Chosen. The goyim do not forget."

The rains had started. She was desperate.

All next morning Solomon was rummaging in the store-rooms, unpacking old boxes, peering into corners, rubbing up blackened objects with his sleeve. He shook out fur coats so moth-eaten that they fell apart like exhumed flesh. He un-wrapped church vestments with gold and silver thread, sewn with seed pearls and semiprecious stones. The rats had nibbled them for so long they were no more than glinting filigree.

He was thinking about the ring. That ring was worth more

than all this rubbish, more than anything he possessed except for the box under the stove. No one but he knew what was in that box. That was why he always sat by the stove; to guard his secret.

The thought of what was inside that box warmed him. Rebecca's topazes were nothing, even the ruby ring was nothing beside that treasure under the stove, under his heart.

Still the ring was rare. A good color. A Ball of Fire ruby from Ceylon.

What deal could he make with the girl about the ring? He rubbed his chin and shuffled into the back room and sat brooding over the stove. The girl had hidden the ring somewhere. It gnawed at his brain that she should have something so valuable. Better that she didn't know how valuable it was.

Solomon had never made a will. He was superstitious. People who made wills died. He was no longer sure how old he was. Time stretched back into a dim wasteland. He could make a will leaving her everything but the box under the stove. That would be buried with him. He would take that treasure with him to Paradise. But the rest he could leave Therese in return for the ring.

As dull and dark and monotonous as his life was he dreamed of Paradise as a young girl dreams of love. He had no doubt that he would go there. Hadn't he earned it? Hadn't he stored it away year after year in the boxes and bundles and trunks and piles of merchandise?

He would tell Therese that he wanted the ring to keep till she was old enough to wear it. He would take her with him to the cohen to draw up the will; that would impress her. He wanted to own and fondle the ring, to turn it over and over behind locked doors in the dead of night. It would gleam in the lamplight like the contents of the box under the stove glowed and shimmered and shot forth sparks of iridescent fire. That had been his one great stroke of fortune, to have been given that box to hide. Years had passed. The thieves had never come back to reclaim it. Dead, long ago. That was his miraculous good luck. Dead. No one had ever known.

To own. Not to sell. He hated to part with anything. *To know it was all there!*

With the slippers clutched in her hand and her other hand holding the ring, wrapped in a scrap of rag, tied with a string around her neck, Therese ran through the maze of alleys, swift and graceful as a deer.

A few people noticed the wild girl in her strange blue dress, with her red hair streaming; men in broad flat hats and kaftans, shuffling with downcast eyes, handsome dark-eyed women who walked like queens, with bundles on their heads.

There was the gate.

Open!

Beyond lay Poland.

Her heart soared as she darted through.

She was fascinated and absorbed anew by the kaleidoscope of the city. The crowds, the buildings, the stalls of fruit and flowers, the carts, dogs, trees and people. The infinite variety of bustling activity filled her with wonder and excitement. There was the wide river with its gray-green water carrying scraps of sky under the bridges and the trees yellow and gold shedding their leaves through the moist warm air. Her bare feet made a rustling laughing sound as she sped through the fallen leaves. She was running for joy across the world.

She came to the wide avenue with the stone fortresses in their parks and gardens. Carriages with prancing horses and footmen perched behind went bowling by.

There was the yellow palace. It was the same color as the trees. The leaves fell like flakes from the facade. Over the double doors the eagles guarded their golden crown.

She paused by the wall to catch her breath.

She loved the world far more than she had ever loved the dolls and the almond tree.

She waited there as her mother had waited. She was part of the palace. It belonged to her. She was certain that the carriage with the two black horses would come and the flunkies would jump down and the magnificent noble in the blue coat would get out and stare into her eyes and she would show him the ring and say, "I am Therese Lachmann."

She waited a long time. The yellow palace was closed and silent. She ventured from the wall and stared at the great door.

The light was fading.

The trees cast shadows across the street. There were fewer and fewer carriages.

She stood there holding the slippers and pressing the ring against her heart. She stared up at the rows of windows.

Evening.

The air was filled with the twittering of birds. They were settling in the trees, exchanging the day's gossip. The sky turned to violet and rose and then to peacock green.

A chill of disappointment blew down the avenue.

He was not coming. Something had gone wrong.

She walked sadly away, deceived.

She sat for a long time on the bench by the river where her mother had rested. For the first time in her life she was aware of a great sadness, of a great loneliness both in her and in the world. It was so vast and strange, threatening and indifferent. Its strangeness and sadness wrung her heart.

She had nothing and no one but the ring.

She remembered the door to the Muranov that shut at sundown. She was outside now. It was worse in a way than being inside because it was so vast, as vast as the darkening sky.

She ran across the river into the city.

Here a new wonder seized her. All the houses were boldly lighted. Crowds of people were strolling by. There were so many windows filled with wonderful things, pyramids of fruit, rings and necklaces and brooches, cakes and pies and sweetmeats. Flowers of such beauty and variety! Pressing her face against one window she could see people sitting at little tables sipping colored drinks. Music drifted into the street. She had never heard such heavenly sounds in the silent warren of the Muranov. They set her heart swaying and her blood tingling. They were like all the dreams she had shared with Bubilala brought miraculously to life.

People glanced at the strange girl in the torn brocade dress with the brilliant hair; peering into the restaurants and shops and taverns. A young whore probably. Scarcely more than a child. A whore or a thief or a gypsy. A shame. It was shameful really to be sent out on the streets at such an early age.

She was intoxicated by the beauty of the city. She had forgotten how long she had been wandering, forgotten that it was night and that the gate to the Muranov had long since been shut.

The concert, as usual, had been a great success.

Henri Herz was used to applause. Applause was a natural accessory to fame. The public applauded him everywhere. It was always the same public, in London or Paris, St. Petersburg or Rome. This mass of clapping and cheering people. He bowed as the waves of applause washed over him. They were acclaiming him as an artist and as a celebrity, Henri Herz with the classic profile, with the pale gold hair, now discreetly touched up since he had passed forty, the slim elegant figure, cautiously corseted to preserve the illusion of youth and the famous hands, those hands that had been reproduced in plaster for adoring ladies. It no longer mattered whether he played the Field "Nocturnes" like a lovesick school girl. The ladies cooed and wept at the sight of the white hands skimming over the keyboard and the men kept their own clumsier paws in readiness to applaud. They applauded without even listening; for that privilege they had paid their money.

The idol smiled, raised his arms to the gallery and blew a few charming kisses, mouthed his "thank yous" to the well-dressed patrons in the orchestra who thought they loved music. He had given them just what they wanted, sugar plums for the women, bravado for the men.

Actually he had played well that night, except for a few slips in the *Etudes Symphoniques*. They needed a good deal more practice. Perhaps he would drop them from the repertoire. Stick to the Nocturnes and old war horses like the Mephisto Waltz.

Thank God this tour was almost over! It would be a relief to be back in Paris.

He walked smoothly off stage. The applause continued, eddying, swelling, then subsiding. They wanted another encore.

No more tonight.

Prelati was waiting in the dressing room with his cloak and hat.

"Three notes were left with the flowers."

"Let's escape before the stampede."

They made a quick exit. But the first batch of devotees were already crowding in through the stage door. He smiled, thanked them, excused himself and pushed. Always the same crush, the same silly phrases. "Too kind. A pleasure to play in Warsaw. The most musical audience in Europe. Thank you so much. A previous engagement. Perhaps next time."

They had to fight their way into the street.

"Where the devil is the cab?"

"Over there. I'll get it."

"Hurry."

He was left to the pack of adoring young ladies, pale young composers with their latest compositions, charitable matrons who wanted him to appear at benefits, cadgers, pickpockets, romantics and failures who sought a reflected glory from the famous. He edged his way to the curb.

He noticed the girl because of her astonishing hair. She was staring at him as though he had fallen off the moon. What on earth was she, decked out in a sort of masquerade dress, and holding a pair of mud-stained slippers?

A little tart! Delicious! She couldn't be more than twelve or thirteen. He could do with an evening's amusement, something stimulating and unusual. He was weary of mature women who wanted to offer him their hearts. A distinctly odd little creature, but captivating. That hair!

He heard Prelati's shout as he ran up alongside the cab.

"That girl with the red hair," he said quickly. "See if you can get hold of her."

He climbed into the cab. The girl had been jostled by the crowd almost up to the window. A perfect little face like a Greek intaglio.

What did it matter what anyone thought of his morals in this godforsaken city? He'd be gone in two days. He smiled at the girl and, from the shadowed interior of the cab, beckoned. She looked completely lost and bewildered. Perhaps she wasn't a whore. Well, it would be a pleasure to show her how to become one.

Prelati had reached her and was trying to catch her attention. She stared at him, frightened, uncomprehending. Prelati had taken her arm and was urging her toward the cab. She hung back, wrenched away her arm and, pushing her way through the crowd, fled down the street.

Prelati got into the cab.

"I couldn't make her understand. It's the language."

The crowd was pressing up to the windows. Always the same silly, gawking, semihysterical faces!

The public! In the end one was left with that. The anonymous lover who appeared and reappeared wherever one went. Just as well! He was tired. A light supper and bed—alone.

In the final count artists and performers were always alone. The great orgasm occurred in the concert hall.

The cab started and the crowd fell away like pebbles washed back into the sea.

At the corner of the street he saw the girl. She was hesitating at the curb, poised like a bird for flight.

The pianist stopped the cab and got out.

"I'll have a shot. Wait here."

He approached. She stared with startled eyes of the strangest color he had ever seen.

"*N'ayez pas peur, mademoiselle,*" he said in well-oiled tones. "*Vous avez l'air un peu perdu!*"

She had understood not a word.

"*Kan ihnen helfen, Fraulein?*" he tried again. "*Sind sie verlöhren?*"

She shivered and glanced 'round for the quickest means of escape.

He signaled to his mouth. Was she hungry? This she understood. She hadn't eaten all day.

He smiled, trying to reassure her that he had no evil intentions.

"Would you like some supper?" he asked in French. "I'm sorry I don't speak Polish."

She looked from him to the cab. She was indeed very hungry and very tired. The noble seemed kind. He reminded her of the magnificent prince who lived in the yellow palace.

"I am Therese Lachmann," she said timidly.

"Come along, then. You look as though you could do with some supper."

Prelati's face was a mask of discretion. His master invariably got his way with women. This time Prelati thought he was going a bit far. This girl was scarcely more than a child.

Therese pressed herself into the corner of the cab, clasping the slippers to her breast. She was at once fearful and excited. To be actually riding in a noble's carriage!

At last they arrived at the house where the pianist had taken rooms. He preferred to rent an apartment on tour. People pestered him if he stayed at a hotel. In his peripatetic life he had no time to establish lasting relations with women and perhaps did not want to. Whatever was romantic in his nature was expressed in his playing. His passing amours were a relaxation; a salutory relief for the nerves.

The doorkeeper, roused from his slumber, let them in. The girl stared about as though entering a cathedral. Herz led her upstairs.

In the pleasant salon a fire was burning. A table had been laid for supper. Generally, after a concert, Herz ate alone. Sometimes, if he wanted company, Prelati shared his meal. Unless there was a lady, in which case the tactful Provençal took his repast in his room.

The girl hung back on the threshold of the darkened room while Prelati was lighting the candles. But then curiosity got the better of caution. She ventured, wide-eyed, inside.

She was thunderstruck by the piano. She could not imagine the purpose of this strange piece of furniture. There was a gilt mirror over the fireplace with sconces in which candles flickered, big chairs covered in damask and a painted cabinet like the one in her mother's room. She investigated the room, oblivious to the amused gaze of her host, like a cat cautiously making sure of an unfamiliar environment.

Prelati drew the cork from the champagne with a pop that made the girl start and look 'round. He removed the covers from the dishes and proceeded to mix the salad.

"Will you join me, mademoiselle?" Herz motioned to the table. He nodded to Prelati. "Thank you. I'll ring for you in the morning."

The future course of the evening was understood.

Herz carved the chicken. "Sit down, mademoiselle."

She perched uncertainly. Some instinct warned her that she was not suitably attired for the occasion. She maneuvered her slippers onto the floor and slid her feet inside them.

She had never seen such food as he offered her and did not know what to make of it. She poked at the chicken breast, tore off a sliver, sniffed it, and tasted. Delicious! She ate rapidly, forgetting about the noble, picked up pieces of tomato, licked off the dressing and adventurously popped them into her mouth. He watched her, amused and mystified. What sort of creature was this who looked like a princess and had the manners of a street urchin?

She was baffled by the asparagus and waited till he had started his before venturing to deal with it. It proved to be a delightful game, this dangling of the limp green spears into her mouth.

He offered her a glass of champagne. She took a sip and wriggled her nose like a rabbit.

The strawberries and whipped cream elated her with their beauty. She selected a strawberry, turned it about and examined it thoroughly, nibbled and laughed. She had soon finished her plate and was licking the cream from her fingers like a cat.

Herz' intention of rapid seduction had been somewhat deflected by the novel experience of dining with an exquisite wild animal who had somehow strayed from the forest primeval. It was like dining with a bear cub or feeding tidbits to a rare Brazilian parakeet. She was quite merry now, giggling and looking about to see what fresh wonder might be in store. She sipped the champagne, found that she liked it, and swallowed the rest at a gulp. She had kicked off her slippers and was swinging her legs under the table. She had never felt so perfectly happy before.

But there was the piano, that extraordinary object that needed investigation. She hopped off her chair and examined the keyboard, touched one note, and was startled when it emitted a sound. She looked at him for an explanation.

"What is it for?" She struck another note and another and then brought her fist down—bang! What a wonderful toy!

He came over, sat beside her and played *Für Elise*.

As the simple melody unfolded she became perfectly still. She listened as raptly as the young Joan of Arc must have listened to the voices of her saints in the fields of Domrémy. Her innocence and purity of heart shone like an aura.

He felt it imperative to find out who and what this wild untouched creature was, went out onto the landing and called down to the doorkeeper who had returned to his slumbers in a porter's chair.

Groaning and grumbling, the old man trudged upstairs.

"This girl and I can't exchange a single word. I'd be grateful if you'd translate. Ask her where she comes from and why she is out so late."

The doorkeeper spoke to Therese in Polish which she understood none too well. She says that she cannot go home because the gate is closed."

"What gate?"

"I think she comes from the Muranov, sir. That's the Jewish quarter."

"Ask her if she often goes out to dinner with strange men."

She seemed baffled by this question and shook her head.

"She says she has never been in the city before. She calls it Poland."

"Does she have a family?"

Therese nodded and explained. "Her mother and someone called Solomon. Her name is Therese Lachmann. Jewish girls her age seldom leave the Muranov."

"Ask her how old she is."

Therese shrugged. She had no idea. She felt from the tone of the doorkeeper's voice and Herz' expression that she had done something wrong and was about to be punished for it. Her gaiety faded and her former anxiety returned.

"You take my advice, sir, you'll put her out of the house. The Jews are all thieves like the gypsies. She was sent out to steal, I fancy."

The pianist was torn between the girl's unusual beauty and her disturbing innocence.

He said to the doorkeeper. "You're probably right. I'll send her away."

He took a silver florin from his purse and gave it to Therese who took it doubtfully. She felt that she had displeased him in some way and wanted to make amends.

He said kindly, but firmly, "Put on your shoes."

She stood there abashed, wanting him to forgive her. He retrieved the slippers from under the table and handed them to her. Oh, was that it? He was annoyed because she was barefoot. She put on the slippers obligingly and smiled. Was it all right then? He found her, against his will, profoundly affecting. It was not merely her exceptional coloring, her white skin, astounding hair and those equivocal eyes that seemed to change color with every passing mood. She presented problems of conscience that were not worth confronting for the sake of a night's pleasure.

He led her onto the landing and called down to the doorkeeper, "Let her out, will you? She's leaving."

Therese knew that she had been dismissed. She had somehow spoiled this fairy tale. The noble had been kind, but had found her wanting.

Henri Herz felt a pang of remorse as he watched her go with bowed head, a disappointed child, downstairs.

She was waiting outside the Muranov gate when it opened.

She had slept in a doorway for a while and then on a bench under some trees. She was chilled and stiff and disgruntled. Her great adventure into the outside world had proved a disappointment. She wanted to hide in the cupboard and talk it all over with the dolls.

She couldn't bear to think of the noble who had started out by being so kind and then unaccountably turned against her. He had found her ugly and clumsy and ignorant. She hadn't known how to eat properly and she hadn't understood about the piano.

Perhaps Bubilala would explain. She was queen of the goyim and must have known many nobles. She had thought the pianist almost as beautiful as the great prince who lived in the yellow palace.

She hurried through the twisted alleys where no one was yet about except for the mangy cats. The stunted old houses seemed more derelict than ever. She was aware of the meanness and ugliness and squalor of *inside* in a way that she had not been before. She had committed some unknown sin which the noble had discovered last night. The old man from downstairs must have told him. It was because of this sin that she was condemned to live in the Muranov.

She was crying when she reached the hovel with the tilting roof and the two little squinting windows. The knotted sheet was still hanging from the palisade where she had left it. It occurred to her that it looked conspicuous, so white and strange, among the shadows.

She threw the slippers over the palisade and hauled herself up. The yard was no more than a patch of dirt and the almond tree a poor little stunted thing with only a few branches. The great sky of Poland had shrunk to a scrap like the patches of old clothes from which she made the dolls.

As she climbed down onto the stool she saw that something was different. The side door into the house was wide open. Such a thing had never happened before. Had Solomon discovered her absence and left it open for her? She had expected to rouse him by knocking and to tell him that she had slept in the yard because she needed fresh air.

The instant she entered the house she knew that something terrible had happened.

The storeroom had been hit by a hurricane. Everything had

been overturned and torn open and flung aside. The rugs and pictures, silver and brass objects, a tempest of old furs and clothes. A silence heavier and deeper than she had ever known hung like a pall over the house.

The door to the back room was open. She looked in. Here, too, everything was in wild disorder.

Solomon was lying in an ooze of blood stretched out by the stove as though in a last frenzied moment he had flung himself forward to protect it.

His head had been battered in.

She stood paralyzed, without breath, and then dashed upstairs. She burst into her mother's room.

It had been wrecked by the same storm. All the little drawers of the cabinet had been hurled about as though by demons. The precious contents of the trunk littered the floor.

Rebecca was lying across the bed with a fat gray rat crouched on her shoulder lapping her blood. Her head was half severed from her body.

Therese fell back, stumbled downstairs, out of the horrible, congealing silence, into the yard.

She managed to climb over the palisade. She ran, seeing nothing, blind with horror.

She ran through the gate of the Muranov into the outside world.

Henri Herz liked to rehearse in an empty theater.

The void, the calm immensity of row upon row, tier upon tier, of unoccupied seats, gave him a sense of sublime freedom. Not only could he judge the volume of sound that certain pieces required which he never could quite estimate in a room, even in his Paris studio, but also an empty theater was like a temple. In this great cathedral hush he could play as he wanted, as he felt, as in his youth he had dreamed of playing before he had been trapped and subjugated by the demands of a career.

He was going over the difficult passages of the *Etudes Symphoniques*. Now that he was alone he could manage them easily. The glory of the music flowed through his fingers. He was never able to play like this in public, with such perfect balance and freedom. A career spoiled the joy of accomplishment. Vanity intervened and money and fame. If he could just rent an empty theater and play for himself when the mood was on him, without applause, without trying to cater to all those tedious, clamoring people, all the years of hard work, of obscurity and disappointment, would have been worthwhile.

He switched to *Carnaval*. How lovely, pure and lyrical! Tenderness, sincerity and pathos. Schumann had composed these little pieces for Clara Weick. They were the love letters he had been too clumsy to write. Wonderful to be in love with another pianist, to communicate love like this without the hampering banality of words.

He had never found a great love like Schumann. Perhaps it wasn't in his nature to love so deeply. When he could play like this, fully and calmly, he did not regret it. Love turned into domesticity, quarrels over money and infidelity. He'd seen it too often, the nagging boredom that took over when romance had cooled. Love only lasted in music. As long as there was a pianist left to play *Carnaval*, love was secure.

He thought of the strange girl of the previous night. What an absurd experience! Certainly a departure from the usual encounters on tour, if only that it had turned him into a moralist. To think that he who had had dozens of women, wives and virgins, taken casually and discarded without remorse, should have suddenly been seized with scruples. A mystery, that girl, with her perfection of form and feature, a lily that had somehow bloomed on a dungheap. He had been unkind, he supposed. He had wounded her, but he was glad to have avoided the alternative.

Odd! What had it been about her? A shining innocence, a strange little distinction, some unawakened force of character that had flashed for an instant from those astonishing eyes. He thought of her standing by the piano while he played *Für Elise*. She had been transfigured, in a trance of wonder. She would be wasted probably. Fate had played her a mean trick by placing her in circumstances where rarity was a disadvantage. She would be ground under by poverty, lack of opportunity, married off to a boor and shoveled away with the rest of the human refuse of a city.

He heard a commotion in the wings, shouts and protests and a scuffle. Some blasted enthusiast forcing his way in with yet another impossible composition!

Suddenly she was there, distraught, wild-eyed, with her brilliant hair flowing about her shoulders.

The stage doorman had run after her and grabbed her. She struggled like a wild animal and screamed, "Help me! Help me!"

Herz jumped up. "Stop that! Let her alone!"

The girl ran to him and half collapsed against him. She was shuddering and weeping, clinging to him as though he were the last refuge on earth.

He said sharply, "What is it? Stop this! What are you doing here?"

"She pushed past me, sir," the doorman put in. "I tried to stop her. I thought she might do you harm."

The girl broke into a paroxysm of weeping. Her body was convulsed by something more terrible than tears.

Herz shook her. "Stop that. Ask her what is the matter and why she has come here?"

The doorman spoke to her roughly as though she had been caught in the act of stealing.

The girl blurted out a few incoherent words.

"She says they're dead and that it's all her fault."

"Who? Who is dead?"

He held her sternly at arms' length. Her head fell back, revealing the lovely curve of her throat.

"Who is dead?" he demanded. "Who?"

She was crying and mumbling, her face half hidden by a cascade of shining hair.

"Her mother, she says," the doorman translated. "And the old one. Something to do with a sheet she left on the wall."

"Get my valet. He's in the dressingroom."

The doorman hurried off.

Herz led the girl to the piano stool and sat down. He drew her to him. She was sobbing more quietly now.

"Stop crying," he ordered curtly.

Her misery was so intense, so animal, that he could feel it inside his own body.

Prelati appeared. The moment he saw the girl in his master's arms, he feared the worst. These women! There was no end to the scenes they created. Even a girl that age—!

"Prelati, take this girl back to the apartment. She says her mother has been killed. When she's calmer we'll get the police or whatever passes for the police in Warsaw."

Prelati had no desire to be involved in another of his master's escapades. He had grown weary of lying to hysterical women or outraged husbands or mothers who threatened to have him horsewhipped. Prelati was a respectable bourgeois. And now this street urchin! He'd get himself killed one day.

"Go along," Herz said to Therese, handing her over to his reluctant valet.

"What am I to do with her?"

"Let her rest. Give her something to eat. I'll be along later."

Prelati took the girl's arm. She looked pleadingly at Herz like an animal about to be led to the slaughterhouse. Something in his expression partially reassured her.

"Go along with him. He won't hurt you."

Her frenzy had drained away. She looked so pathetic and desolate that his heart went out to her.

She allowed herself to be led away.

Herz shook his head. Really, the results of heeding one's conscience were more compromising than if one followed one's instincts! Everything about that girl spelled trouble. Her beauty, her hysterics, and some fatality about her that would attract disaster, warned him not to become involved. Why, in heaven's name, had she turned to him?

Someone had killed her mother and some old man and she held herself to blame. It was tragic, of course, but there was no reason for him to be concerned. He would give her some money and turn her over to the police. She must have relatives who would know what to do for her.

He tried to compose himself and concentrate on what he'd been playing. What *had* he been playing? *Carnaval*. But he knew that by heart. He knew all his repertoire by heart. He would drop the *Etudes Symphoniques* from the next concert.

This preposterous incident had upset him. He needed exercise. He hadn't been out for a week. What a grind, this perpetual performing and rehearsing! If one tried to have a little amusement one landed in the midst of an incomprehensible drama. Damn that girl with her marvelous burnished hair!

He went to his dressing room, collected his hat and cloak, and went out into the street.

The doorkeeper was standing outside watching the cab in which Prelati and the girl were driving away.

"You're making a big mistake, sir. Take my word; that girl is some sort of criminal."

"You may be right." Herz tipped him and walked away.

It was a soft autumn day with rain in the air. Warsaw was an interesting, even a beautiful city. Fine medieval churches, handsome palaces. The Ujazdov Avenue had real elegance, that particular refinement that alone among Slavic people the Poles achieved. Unlike Russia with that unwieldy mélange of Byzantine splendor and painted Italian rococo. Warsaw was softer, more intimate, more French. But no city in the world could compare with Paris. Paris was civilization. London, Madrid, Vienna had their points. But Paris was the ultimate of cities. Even with all the unrest of the last years, the revolution of '48, strikes and Socialism, it always recovered, always reflowered. Bloodshed and barricades were forgotten when the chestnuts bloomed. It was true pleasure to walk into the Câfé Anglais and see the *grandes cocottes* in their resplendent *tenues* ablaze with jewels, flaunting their latest conquests. Paris of the English milords and the Russian Grand Dukes. Paris of the Tuileries in flower and Notre Dame in the glow of sunset. Just to breathe that unique air!

He couldn't wait to wake up in his own room at the Pavillon, look out of his window at his own garden. The September roses would be in bloom.

He'd been offered a long tour of the United States. The very thought of it filled him with gloom. Of course, there was a fortune to be made there. But oh! the journeys, the raucous people, the grim hotels!

Perhaps he was getting old. Forty-two! He'd been at it twenty-five years. Perhaps he would turn down that offer and spend a whole year in Paris, giving an occasional concert to keep his name before the public. The damned demanding public that paid and paid.

A few light drops of rain were falling. A shower was coming on. He hailed a cab and drove back to the apartment. That girl would be there. He had an uneasy instinct that fate was preparing a trap for him unless he was deft enough to avoid it.

Prelati let him in. He was obviously annoyed by the whole thing. Prelati was so smug and prudish. He'd had the same mistress for fifteen years, an amiable matron who ran a pastry shop. They made love in a cloud of confectioner's sugar.

"How is she?"

"I offered her food, but she refused. She's asleep in there."

Herz handed over his hat and cloak.

"What are you going to do with her, sir?"

"Go and ask the doorkeeper to fetch the police. At least they'll be able to understand her."

Prelati was not convinced. The day had not yet dawned when his master would let a redheaded virgin slip through his fingers.

She was lying on the sofa asleep.

The firelight dappled her skin with rosy tints. That wave of resplendent hair fell across her forehead and over the cushions. Every line of her body was subtly harmonious.

He was touched by an awe inspired by certain rare works of art.

Part Two

The Pavillon
d'Armide

*T*HE PAVILLON D'ARMIDE was one of those charming oversights which occur in ancient cities. When builders and profiteers carve out new thoroughfares through pleasant old jumbled quarters, knocking down buildings right and left like testy children with sandcastles, sometimes old corners are left behind, not because of their charm, but because the plans of those energetic marauders have somehow or other overlooked them. They remain untouched, like a sensible people who survive revolutions just by keeping out of sight. A good many ambitious iconoclasts had crashed back and forth through the Marais in two hundred years. In the time of Richelieu and Louis XIII this quarter had housed the cream of the old aristocracy. Now their splendid *hôtels* were occupied by artisans, makers of gold braid and corsets, restorers of furniture, importers of silks and spices. Some builder in an ill-considered burst of enthusiasm had razed half a street and then decided that he was in the wrong neighborhood. He had quickly erected a row of nondescript houses with shops on the ground floor, and had then no doubt offered his services to Baron Haussman who had more ambitious plans for remodeling Paris. The Marais became the most charming slum in the world.

The Pavillon was all that remained of the mansion built by the favorite composer of the *Roi Soleil*, Lully, after whose opera *Armide* it was named. The mansion itself had gone, to be replaced by the sullen houses and dingy shops and a restaurant, Le Provençal, haunt of the culinary cognoscenti. Behind, reached through an iron gate and a little alley, was this enviable retreat.

It consisted of a high-ceilinged sexagonal room of perfect proportions in which Lully had rehearsed his singers and given his musical evenings. It had five long French windows opening onto a garden, enclosed by a high wall. It was a room that by some happy accident had perfect accoustics. Behind it was a foyer and a dining room and "the usual offices."

Henri Herz had been searching Paris for somewhere to live that provided space and solitude. He had stumbled on the Pavillon which had not been occupied since the Revolution. It stood desolate and decaying in a sea of weeds. He had fallen in love with it on sight. The music room still contained by a miracle the original hoiseries, a pink marble mantelpiece, and a painted ceiling, invisible under fifty years of cobwebs, which, when cleaned, revealed Euterpe, the muse of music, floating across the heavens with a lyre, her scanty garments upheld by dimpled cherubs. In prerevolutionary times the Pavillon had perhaps been home to some cocotte whose pretty head had been chopped off by the champions of liberty, equality and fraternity. It retained a wistful feminine charm.

Henri had restored it lovingly and added, above the dining room and the "usual offices," two bedrooms and a bath and, at the side, pleasant quarters for a manservant.

Henri had always enjoyed gardens. He became a jardino-maniac. He cleared the weeds, unearthed the ancient paths, replaced the choked privet hedges, saved the four great chestnuts and planted a profusion of lilacs, pinks, roses and other flowers with old-fashioned names. The garden was surprisingly large to have survived in the middle of a crowded city. Behind an entanglement of briars and creepers he uncovered a fountain with a figure of Hebe offering her votive cup, her breasts and thighs delicately mottled with saffron moss. He had the basin cleared and filled with Japanese fish that rushed in a swirl of gold and scarlet for their morning feed.

This enchanted spot never failed to restore his peace of heart after tours and concerts. He, too, gave evenings of music. In the summer the guests disposed themselves about the garden, while the pianist played or accompanied a singer or a string quartet. It would seem, as the limpid sounds floated from the candlelit room into the darkness, where moths flitted like sylvan ghosts, as though the present had dissolved and another age of grace and "sensible soft melancholy" had returned. Afterward, supper, sent in from the Provençal, would be served under the trees.

Henri Herz loved his home. Therese came to adore it.

The advent of Therese into his bachelor existence was a revelation. It transformed the structure of his days and revealed a range of entirely new experience. It was as though unimagined octaves had been added to his piano. He often wondered how this reversal of his entire mode of life, his outlook, pursuits and pleasures, had come about. There was no logical explanation; Therese was a gift of fate.

On his journey from Warsaw to St. Petersburg Herz had been haunted by the girl's terror at being handed over to the police. She had clung to him, pleading incoherently. He had difficulty in tearing himself away. During the interminable stages across the wastelands of western Russia the memory of that exquisite waif, clutching her tattered slippers, had returned accusingly. It caused him to ask himself, after a lifetime of self-interest and self-indulgence, what sort of a man he had become. It was hardly to be wondered that of late he had felt a growing indifference to his career. His parents were long since dead, his sisters both safely married. What was the purpose of pursuing fame which he already had and money which he no longer needed? He had fallen short of becoming a great pianist in the caliber of Moscheles and Liszt. Success had robbed him of incentive. What he had done for that girl in her desperate plight he now saw in the light of his general lack of commitment. He had settled for undemanding attachments which he could break off when they bored him, for a reasonably pleasant and selfish life. He had condescended to pity Therese Lachmann and had abandoned her to the police after leaving some money for her which, in all probability, she had never received. An easy way out indeed! This incident typified what he now recognized as the moral stagnation of middle age, an indolence, perhaps an impotence, of heart. But then, he argued, what else could he have done?

"Nothing," Prelati assured him. "She was a total stranger and not your concern."

"All the same, one should occasionally bestir oneself for a fellow human being in distress."

"You did what you could," Prelati said flatly.

He had his usual success in St. Petersburg. He received the usual accolades in the press. He had begun to feel that the words "charming and sensitive" would be his only obituary.

At the Youssopof palace where he was entertained with that barbaric extravagance that typified aristocratic Russia, he found himself sickened by so much display, by the endless succession of brilliantly lighted rooms, crowded with opulently dressed women and arrogantly self-assured men. This was his reward for being "sensitive" and "charming," gushing compliments from people he didn't care about and platefuls of indigestible food. He thought of Therese examining a strawberry with wonder as flunkies in gold and yellow liveries offered him golden trays laden with golden bowls of caviar and sturgeon.

Prelati, who could read his master like a book, knew what he was brooding about and prayed that it would not be necessary on the way back to spend more than one night in Warsaw.

In Warsaw Henri, like a guilty schoolboy, escaped from the surveillance of his manservant on the excuse that he needed exercise. He went straight to the police station and demanded to see the officer in charge who was by no means delighted to see him, having pocketed the hundred zlotys that Henri had left for Therese on his earlier visit.

He pretended at first to have forgotten the case but, after rummaging through a pile of documents, managed to recall that the murders in the Muranov had indeed been committed. The criminals had not been apprehended. He elicited the information that the old man, Solomon Lachmann, had been a receiver of stolen goods and that the contents of his place of business had been sequestered. He thought it doubtful that the girl stood to inherit anything. Nothing was known about the Lachmanns and even the girl's relationship with the deceased had not been established. There were no records or birth certificates. The Muranov had long been a refuge for underworld characters who hid from the law in that warren of squalor and anonymity.

And the girl? Where was she?

The Inspector rummaged through more documents. As far as he knew she had been removed to an orphanage. And where was the orphanage? The Inspector wasn't sure. It was really a matter outside his jurisdiction. Under whose jurisdiction was it then? Well, there were other authorities who dealt with such matters. He rose to terminate the interview. *Which* authorities? That depended on the circumstances. He bowed his visitor to the door.

Henri took out his wallet and from it extracted two notes. He held them sufficiently close to the Inspector's face to cause a distinct twitch of official nostrils.

The Inspector wavered and sighed. He reexamined the documents and reluctantly disgorged an address.

It was a sad gray building run by an order of sad gray nuns. The Mother Superior, grave as a cenotaph, declined to allow Monsieur Herz to see one of her orphans without some proof of family relationship. She was, she reminded him, not only responsible for her charges' physical well-being, but for their spiritual salvation. As Monsieur Herz agreed that Therese Lachmann's salvation was of the utmost importance, he happened to glance through the window and saw a sad gray shoal of orphans in sad gray uniforms perambulating two by two 'round a courtyard under the supervision of a nun who was reading aloud from some elevating religious tract. He recognized Therese at once by her hair.

Disregarding the protests of the Mother Superior, he raced downstairs, burst through a door into the courtyard and yelled, "Therese!"

Her face lit up when she saw him. She broke ranks and rushed into his arms.

"Quick! Out of here!"

Nuns appeared from everywhere like outraged seagulls. Henri recalled afterward actually striking one as he pushed Therese through the front door.

"Run!"

Pursued by high-pitched commands, cries of horror and invocations to the Blessed Virgin, Henri and Therese raced down the street. At the corner he threw her into a cab. She collapsed on his shoulder.

Prelati's face fell when they entered the hotel suite. He did not underestimate the fatality of this event.

All the way to Berlin Therese uttered no word. It would have made little difference if she had since neither could understand her. She huddled in the traveling coat Henri had bought her, clutching his hand. She was too frightened to let go. When he got out at inns where they stopped for a change of horses, she pressed her white face to the window, trembling with apprehension that he might not return. At Berlin she was reluctant to leave him even to go to bed. He left her door open and slept on the sitting room sofa. She was terrified of the train and sat bolt upright, hardly daring to breathe. Henri's hand was the only thing in the world she could count on.

Paris bewildered her by its size, by the throngs of people, by the dazzling diversity of the boulevards. Only when at last they reached the gate of the Pavillon and he led her into the garden did the tension of that nightmare journey subside. She exhaled it all in a single breath of relief.

Prelati had realized that it was useless to reason with his master in his present euphoric mood. It was the madness that occasionally seizes middle-aged men who will throw up marriage, children, business, social position, to run off for a last adventure with some girl they hardly know.

By stretching his sense of propriety to the utmost, Prelati might have accepted it on the grounds of passion. He was sufficiently Latin to admit that passion was a sort of divine lunacy capable of disorienting the most rational of men. But what Henri Herz, the confirmed bachelor and hedonist, proposed, as it was gradually revealed, was beyond the farthest reaches of emotional aberration. He proposed, he explained with the light of heaven shining in his eyes, to adopt Therese. He was determined to adopt her legally as his daughter.

Prelati stared at him, aghast.

"I can't exist any longer solely for myself," Henri declared. 'Without someone to live for my life is meaningless. I need the responsibility of another human being, someone to work for and plan for, someone whose happiness is in my care. Do you realize that I've never done anything, ever, for *anyone*? I've been slowly decaying inside—yes, from egotism; that's what living alone becomes; dry rot. I've become like the Pavillon when I first saw it, uninhabited, full of cobwebs. Therese will restore me as I restored this place."

"If you want to have children why don't you marry and have your own?"

Prelati was a hopeless bourgeois incapable of grasping the miracle that had occurred.

A miracle in many ways it was.

Having seized upon the notion of resurrection, Henri had cast himself in the redemptive role of parent. Therese, in her role as the redeemed, exceeded his expectations.

As the terrors of her last days in Warsaw faded, she bloomed in that secret garden. She explored every corner of it, was familiar with every bush and flower. From his bedroom window in the mornings Henri would watch her as she ran down the path in her white nightdress to feed the goldfish with the early sunlight gleaming in her hair.

He bought her dresses and shoes, stockings and little hats that did not become her and a host of other accessories. "For my daughter," he would explain to surprised salesgirls as he selected ribboned bodices and petticoats edged with lace. Therese wore them obligingly, but it was not this snowstorm of gifts that gave her the confidence to risk a tentative happiness. For the first time in her life she was loved and cared for. She was surrounded by beauty and she was free.

For over a month they were not able to exchange a word. They conversed by smiles and gestures. Henri engaged Mademoiselle Ernestine Dufour, a retired teacher from a Young Ladies' Academy, to instruct Therese in French, reading and penmanship. Henri's instinct that Therese was exceptional proved to be accurate.

She learned French in six weeks and spoke it fluently without an accent. She could read and she could write in a firm and upright hand. Mademoiselle Dufour agreed that she showed remarkable application. She applied herself not because she was enthralled by her textbooks with their stilted phrases, but to please "Henri," to express the gratitude that overflowed from her heart.

Encouraged by these successes, Henri hired an Englishman, Horace Willing, to teach his daughter-to-be the rudiments of mathematics, English and history. Mr. Willing had been tutor in a number of French families and was used to dawdling schoolboys, counting the moments till they were released for games and birdsnesting. Therese proved the exception. She listened, applied herself, and learned.

"Remarkable," he conceded. "She has exceptional intelligence. It's quite unusual to find any woman able to grasp the principles of mathematics so quickly. She has learned in a few weeks what it takes most boys her age a year. One might almost say that she has a mathematical brain."

Henri's delight knew no bounds when Therese recited a list of the kings of England without, as far as he knew, a single mistake. She was able to multiply 300476.3 by 472139.7 in exactly three and a half minutes. It took him twenty minutes to check that her answer was correct.

"Il fait très beau aujourd'hui, n'est ce pas?" she said in her schoolbook French. *"Voulez-vous promener dans le jardin avec moi?"*

He was enchanted to *promener dans le jardin*.

He installed a dovecote near the fountain because he imagined how exquisite Therese would look with white birds perched on her arms and shoulders, eating crumbs from between her teeth.

Therese trained the birds in a week. She did indeed look exquisite as the doves fluttered onto her arms and shoulders and ate crumbs from between her teeth.

Oh, how right, how perfectly right he had been! "You see, Prelati, one should always follow one's instincts. They spring from the subconscious soul which knows more of truth than our conscious minds."

Even Prelati had to admit that Therese had transformed the Pavillon; although, watching his master's face light up when she ran in from the garden with a handful of freshly picked flowers, and a kiss for her dearest "Henni," he wondered for how long Henri's infatuation could remain paternal.

She was beautiful. She was rare. She was disturbing. There was something about her that neither Prelati, Mademoiselle, nor Mr. Willing could put their fingers on. Admirable as they agreed she was, they could not quite bring themselves to like her.

Mademoiselle, a realistic Frenchwoman, assumed that this startling prodigy's relationship with Monsieur Herz was more than that of a patron for his protégé. That designation covered a multitude of sins. What Monsieur Herz precisely felt for her pupil and what her pupil precisely felt for him was, after all, outside her jurisdiction. Therese was not subject to the strict moral precepts of the Academy. But Mademoiselle, putting questions of morality aside, was vaguely troubled that, in spite of Therese's diligence and good manners, she could not find in herself the natural affection she had often felt for less talented and amiable pupils with whom she prided herself she had remained friends in later life. It was some lingering, unacknowledged awareness that Therese was superior, not by intention, not by the least conceit. She was outwardly simple and accommodating, but in herself, in her innate, though unformed, character. It was a little like teaching a girl who was destined to become a queen.

"She grasps without difficulty whatever one explains," Mr. Willing said, trying to clarify his own equivocal reactions, "but I have the impression that she understands none of it. She learns, but does not understand, almost as though it is not worth her while to do so."

"Mathematics are not like art or philosophy," Henry objected, taking umbrage at the slightest disparagement of Therese's general perfection. "One either learns to add and subtract or one doesn't. It's hardly a matter of enthusiasm."

"Yes, quite so. All the same, what she learns seems to have no significance for her. I can't quite explain. Perhaps she learns too fast."

"You can hardly expect a girl of her age to go into ecstasies over vulgar fractions," Henri tartly replied. "You should be gratified that she's made such progress."

"Oh, I am. Indeed yes." Mr. Willing could not pinpoint his reservations. "How old exactly is she?"

"Oh, fifteen." The truth was he didn't know.

He had several times taxed Therese on this subject but with only negative results.

"You must know how old you are!" he had insisted.

Therese dutifully considered, but shook her head. "There was no time in there. I knew from the almond tree and from the snow that the year was changing. But how many times I saw them change—perhaps ten, perhaps fifteen."

Her face clouded. She turned away. She did not like to be reminded of the Muranov. That was a dark dream from which she had still not fully woken.

There was a good deal of conjecture among Henri's circle of friends as to what was going on at the Pavillon. He had dropped out of sight since his return from Russia. It was assumed that he was involved in some new and absorbing affair.

In this euphoric interlude in which he heeded his instincts or, as Prelati preferred to think, indulged his fantasies, Henri conceived the notion of dressing Therese in a green and white livery and having her ride postilion behind his carriage when he went for the afternoon *promenade* in the Bois. She sat very stiff and still with her hair pulled up in a chignon under a smart little billicock hat, determined as in everything to acquit herself perfectly in order to please "Henni."

A good many fashionable eyebrows were raised at the sight of Henri Herz' suspiciously good-looking young coachman.

"I never guessed," one lady who had been intimate with Henri for a season remarked, "that our favorite pianist was a student of ancient Greece."

"One can hardly blame him," her companion laughed. *"Ce petit monsieur est adorable."*

Casimir Fabre-Marquet, Henri's lawyer and business manager, who concealed an insatiable greed for money under an elaborately suave and worldly manner, shrugged expressively and said, "Why not? There comes a time in every man's life when he tires of women."

As they rode through the Bois, *"Tout Paris"* noted the dazzling coachman who sat so straight and so still and never batted an eyelid when Henri drew up to greet his old and, as they complained, neglected friends.

Therese did not quite understand the purpose of this joke. When they returned to the Pavillon she asked, "Did they really think I was a boy?"

"You carried it off to perfection."

She looked at him solemnly. "Are you ashamed of me, Henni?"

He was appalled. This masquerade had been an unforgivable lapse into his cynical, self-indulgent way of life. He had offended her; she had been humiliated. He was contrite.

Next day he took her out seated beside him in the carriage in a flowing white dress and a white straw hat with pale green ribbons. She looked equally appealing holding a tiny parasol with a fringe of green and white tassels which she didn't quite know what to do with.

"Tout Paris" noted the metamorphosis. Fabre-Marquet said in an aside, "She's charming, of course, but I hoped you had more panache."

Everyone wanted to know where Henri had discovered this grave and patrician girl.

After the first few months they went everywhere together, Therese always decked out in the girlish, summery frocks that Henri selected and that were not her style. She sat in the right-hand stage box at his concerts so that he could look up from time to time and meet her yellow-green eyes. At the musical evenings which he revived that summer he introduced Therese as his adopted daughter. No one could understand why he found it necessary to play this charade.

Casimir Fabre-Marquet had tried to reason with his client when Henri had asked him to draw up the necessary papers that would legalize this relationship. "Why raise the impediment of adoption? Marry her, if you must."

"You don't understand, Casimir. This is something entirely different. I am her guardian, her friend and mentor. I am devoted to her. I want to give her the best I can. There's no question of marriage. Besides, she's only fifteen."

"Wait two years. Seventeen's the legal age of consent."

Like most of Henri's friends, Casimir discovered that Henri became very testy and obstinate and, what was worse, indulged in flights of lofty rhetoric when his intentions regarding Therese were questioned. He insisted that this was the one pure and elevated emotion of his life. He would never degrade it by placing Therese in a false position. She must be free to make her own decisions later, unencumbered by any sense of gratitude or obligation. Meanwhile he intended to bring her up, educate her, develop her potentialities which were considerable. It was a mission he found deeply rewarding. He regarded it, without wishing to sound pretentious, as—well, his sacred duty.

It was not that his friends were more cynical than most or that they denied the possibility that the Henri they knew so well could be capable of such selfless idealism. They could only observe what was obvious. As Casimir Fabre-Marquet put it, "He's besotted. It was one thing for Circe to turn her lovers into swine; that was to be expected. But Therese is really unpardonable; she's transformed Henri into a parent."

His kinder friends thought that after a lifetime of philandering, Henri had simply failed to recognize love. He had been inoculated by casual romances, and was unable to diagnose the symptoms of the divine complaint.

Therese was aware of the equivocal impression she created. It made her uncomfortable. Was she doing something wrong? She made special efforts to be polite, not to thrust herself forward, only to speak when spoken to. But she felt that in whatever way she behaved she did not achieve the desired effect.

Mademoiselle remained reserved. Therese tried to win her

over with little bouquets of carefully chosen flowers. Mademoiselle accepted them but did not respond. Mr. Willing, she knew, positively disapproved of her doing her sums so quickly. She couldn't help it if her mind jumped ahead of its own accord like a grasshopper. She debated whether to give him wrong answers in order to placate him, but this seemed dishonest. She pretended to ponder and calculate long after she knew the correct solutions.

The musical evenings presented a special problem. She wanted to do Henni justice, to give him pleasure, to make him proud. She was studiously modest to the point of being self-effacing. The trouble was that she could not efface herself and her efforts to do so appeared to others as haughtiness and disdain. Wherever she sat the guests were aware of her. When she tried to conceal herself behind a lilac bush or a tree they thought she was deliberately avoiding them. She knew that they were watching her, putting their heads together and laughing. It must be because they found her unacceptable or intrusive or absurd.

Casimir Fabre-Marquet was more direct in his attempts to disparage her. For some reason that she could not fathom, Henri's friends found it amusing when she spoke the truth. She thought that she was supposed to speak the truth, as she was supposed to give the correct answers to Mr. Willing's sums.

"Now, Mademoiselle Therese," Casimir would begin in his pontifical manner. "It's very instructive for jaded souls like us to hear a perfectly fresh and honest opinion. Out of the mouths of babes et cetera et cetera."

A little amused silence would fall at the table if, on a rainy evening, they happened to be dining indoors. It was the moment before a conjurer produces a rabbit from a hat or a dog jumps through a hoop.

"What is your honest opinion of Paul Alexis? Will you enlighten us?"

Therese would look down at her hands and try to collect her thoughts.

"I think he is not very clever but tries very hard to seem

so. Also he is frightened of growing old because he wears a wig."

There would be a ripple of laughter. Therese would look at Henri, her eyes wide with alarm. Had she said something wrong?

"Bravo," Henri would reassure her. "You are perfectly correct."

"And what, peradventure, is your impression of Louise de Lormes, if we may presume to ask, Miss Oracle?"

Therese would endeavor to reply as truthfully as she could.

"She pretends to be warm but is actually quite cold. She wants everyone to love her but she doesn't love anyone, even herself."

There would be a gasp of disbelief at this quite accurate appraisal. Really, this girl was impossible! Did she think she could attract attention by being impertinent?

"And what, Therese," one woman maliciously inquired, "do you think of Henri Herz?"

Henri protested, "You shouldn't make fun of Therese because she happens to be sincere."

"No no, Henri, fair's fair. After all, she knows you better than anyone."

Therese was looking down the table. Her face was illuminated in a way that was unmistakable to these people who were so experienced in love but so seldom experienced it.

"Henri tells me that I must believe in God and say my prayers. He doesn't know when I do that I pray to him."

She had embarrassed everyone. Only Henri felt his heart lift with a proud and tender joy.

The women glanced from Therese to Henri and recognized the current that passed between them. What, then, was this nonsense of pretending she was his daughter?

It was not that this strange girl wasn't beautiful. Her appearance was striking. One couldn't say that she was deliberately impolite, even if she wasn't amusing. It was that in some undefinable way she did not fit in. She threw a certain malaise into these otherwise agreeable gatherings. The circle wished that Henri would keep his unorthodox paragon to himself.

"The fact is," Casimir summed up, "she's devoid of charm. After all, beauty is not what men look for in women. Who wants to make love to the Venus de Milo or the Virgin Mary?"

"Evidently Henri does, but shrinks from committing sacrilege."

"He's suffering from impotence caused by an excess of divine worship."

Therese observed.

She often wished that she need not observe, that she need not be forced to note in the faces and conversation of Henri's friends what she found so disturbing. She did not presume to judge them, they were part of Henri's life, but she was unable to overlook their shallowness, their pretensions, all their deft prevarications and dissembling. She came to see that they were playing a game and that this game, at once trivial and complex, was considered essential. Their smiling evasions and urbane dishonesties, their malice sugared with wit, were like tinsel balls they patted back and forth with untiring ease.

It put her at a disadvantage because she was never quite sure what anyone meant. It made her feel clumsy and inept, as though they were conversing in a language she thought she had learned, but that she found she did not comprehend.

"Society is based on the principle of not saying what you think," Henri tried to explain, "but saying it as agreeably as possible. If everyone spoke the truth society would revert to a jungle and no one would have any friends."

"They only speak the truth when they have something unpleasant to say."

"Don't let them upset you, my dear. Remain as honest and open as you are."

But what was the point of honesty, Therese wondered, if it caused people to dislike you? She knew that Henri's friends did not like her and this distressed her. It was a reflection on her efforts to be perfect in Henri's eyes.

It did not take this star-crossed pair long to discover that they were happier alone.

Henri had never been able to tolerate anyone near him when

he was practicing. Now he insisted that Therese remain in the music room when he was working on a new recital.

She had the gift of stillness and would sit motionless while he went over and over certain passages in search of the right approach.

"Which way did you like best?"

"The second, Henni."

"Why?"

"You felt it the most."

"How could you tell?"

"I was watching your face."

He played and she listened. He was playing better than he had in a long time. Since Therese had entered his life he found that his taste in music was changing. He had taken an aversion to the show pieces he used to dash off with such *éclat*. The *"Mephisto Waltz"* seemed no more than a tawdry firework display. He turned back to Mozart, the quintessence of discipline and grace. Scarlatti and Couperin were exhumed and reexamined. It seemed appropriate to study these composers, so scintillating and yet so pure, when Therese was listening.

She was patient. Unlike artist's models who complain after holding a pose too long, she remained attentive and relaxed for hours. She was never happier than when Henri was producing these rippling cascades of notes that always came together with a precision far sweeter and more satisfying than the solutions to Mr. Willing's sums.

On fine days they would go driving. She came to know various ways out of Paris; to St. Germain where they would leave the carriage by the park and stroll the length of the Grande Terasse, that stateliest of promenades where a walk becomes a pavane. Often they would barely exchange a word. Their silences had a language of their own. Or St. Cloud where the Emperor held court. One day a carriage with outriders swept past. Therese caught a glimpse of a beautiful woman seated in a cloud of blue crinolines.

"Who was that?"

"The Empress Eugenie."

In her enchanted cage, Therese knew not much more of the outside world than she had in the Muranov.

They would return from these expeditions laden with flowers and baskets of vegetables and fruit.

Prelati would serve them dinner under the trees.

In every Garden of Eden, along with the other amenities, is a serpent. The serpent in Henri's garden was his need for sex.

He had been used to regular sensual exercise. His conquests were not entirely from vanity. He was a connoisseur of physical pleasure and needed both to give and to receive satisfaction, the more complete in his case if he was not too deeply involved. He approached sex with the expertise of a master chef who is concerned not merely with the nourishment provided, but with subtleties of flavor, harmonies of color, and the style of presentation.

Henri had always been attractive to women. He appreciated them, not merely for their physical attributes but also for their temperament and charm and the artistry of their indiscretions. If women came to regret their failure to capture his deeper loyalty, they seldom harbored resentment when he deserted them—he was especially deft at disengagement—and, more often than not, remained his friends.

"Henri's not made for grand passions," one of his ex-mistresses reflected. "He skates over the surface of love as he does over music. *C'est plutôt Chopin que Beethoven.*" Because of a certain innate detachment—what one lady described as his clinical approach—"He gave me a thorough examination and pronounced me a fit subject for treatment"—he was remembered as an expert but illusive lover. He enjoyed sex for the sake of sex without the French weakness for sentiment or regret.

But he had adopted a goddess. He was the high priest of a cult. He was determined that nothing earthy, vulgar or sordid should intrude on the temple in which he had enthroned Therese. No father had ever safeguarded the virtue of his daughter with more fierce, but tender care, than this converted hedonist.

His friends had judged the situation correctly as far as worldly people are able to judge conditions of the soul. By enriching his life with the joys and responsibilities of parenthood, Therese had polarized her protector. She inspired the best in him; the alternative was the worst.

He had tried at first to revive certain *amitiés* with women who were willing to gratify his desires without making demands. They were mostly married with complacent husbands who were conducting affairs of their own and were ready to accept Henri because he was unlikely to disturb the sanctity of the coocoo's nest. Or widows who were unencumbered, but amorous. Or young actresses who enjoyed attention from a celebrity and had no compunction in allowing him to augment their modest salaries.

But he found that these embarkations no longer justified the voyage.

One was expected to observe the amenities.

First, dinner in a suitable restaurant where a lady could go through the motions of not being seen at a good table. There would be two hours of gossip about acquaintances past and present, reflections on life, on art, on politics, deceptions in the form of compliments, deceptions in the form of promises, delivered in an intimate and endearing tone that was intended to persuade the victim that she was being wooed for her charm and intelligence and not merely as a target for sexual release.

Already wearied by these preliminaries, Henri would be called on to endure, if the lady had pretensions to culture—and who didn't—a concert or a play during which he would be irritated by flaws in the performance or drowned in a mudbath of dialogue. After which, at long last, the *dégagé* invitation to stop by for a nightcap—"If you're not too tired and have nothing better to do." Upon arrival at the lady's establishment, *more* conversation, *more* wine, tentative advances tentatively rebuffed, all sorts of elegant evasions and romantic innuendos, and a positive assurance that she seldom, if ever, went in for this kind of thing and was only tempted for old time's sake and because of the sincere penchant she had always harbored for Henri who, if the truth *must* be told, had not behaved very well, had *not* considered her feelings in breaking off so abruptly an attachment on which—yes, she had to admit—she had counted. There would be a few charming tears shed for what might have been and sighs as she struggled—and what a sincere struggle!—to find it in herself to forgive.

By the time the lady had dimmed the lamps, attended to numerous domestic duties and taken half an hour to disrobe, comb her hair, repair her makeup, perfume her navel and armpits, select a becoming nightdress and arrange herself in bed in a Pompadour posture, Henri's hopes of a good sexual romp had dwindled to that irritation one feels after waiting three hours in a railroad station for a train delayed by repairs on the line.

When he thought of Therese's directness, her simplicity, her complete lack of subterfuge, he positively resented the silly temporizing creature who, having wasted a whole evening, was now ready to be serviced like a cow in the mating season.

He found that he could no longer tolerate "civilized" women as bed companions and took to visiting Lucine's on the Rue des Moulins where one was required to do no more than buy champagne for the house, say, "I'll take that one," go upstairs and pump it out of one's system.

Lucine's was a brothel established during the Revolution, where national heroes, exhausted by oratory, could replenish their ardor in the arms of a plump whore. It had survived the Empire of Napoleon, the reigns of Louis the Eighteenth, Louis Philippe and Charles the Tenth. It had not closed during the tumults of '48 when all good patriots were manning the barricades. All good patriots found more immediate rewards in copulation than in the benefits of social change.

Madame Lucine, who had grown up in the establishment and had, by dint of hard pelvic work and diplomacy, become the proprietress, was an impressive old monster of unknown years, painted up like a hobbyhorse, with a crimson wig and enough false jewelry displayed on her portly bust to light up a boulevard. She had a relaxed view of humanity and invested her profits in an undertaking business and in a discreetly out-of-the-way "home" where impetuous ladies could be relieved of unwanted offspring. She felt that she thus catered to the basic needs of society and considered herself an asset to the moral stability of France. She was a conservative and attended Mass every Sunday as a mark of respect to an institution akin to her own. She took a tolerant view of politics which she considered incidental to the main objectives of life: solvency, sexual gratification and decent burial.

Lucine's had the lugubrious atmosphere of a slaughterhouse. It was a place of business invested with all the more or less depressing accoutrements of its trade. The doorways were shrouded with heavy velvets, the floors palled with heavy carpets. On gilt tables of repulsive ornateness, vases, supported by unclad nymphs, displayed bouquets of red paper roses. On uncomfortable carved sofas and uncomfortable carved chairs, the denizens of this lupinar lolled like fish beached by a squall at sea. Madame Lucine endeavored to accommodate every taste. There were tubercular wraiths from the Baltic, stalwart caryatids from the South, an Indo-Chinese in a sarong, an Algerian clanking with bracelets, a baleful Negress from Martinique who told fortunes in coffee grounds and a middle-aged bargeman with dyed moustaches who had once been Madame Lucine's lover and occasionally obliged gentlemen who wished to enlarge the sphere of their activities by a game of l'amour à trois.

Lucine's was dreary because it was respectable and because its employers derived no more pleasure or disgust from their profession than their sisters—were they more fortunate?—who sewed shirts for wholesale manufacturers or scrubbed floors and emptied chamber pots for the bourgeoisie.

Henri was always welcome at the Rue des Moulins. He liked "the girls" who at least had no pretensions, brought them boxes of sweets and pastries from Sophie's pâtisserie, and played the piano for them. In his company "the girls" threw off their despondency and, with modest laughter, danced together in their white shifts and sang popular songs, grouped around him at the piano. With a gentleman they thought "*gentil*" they were demure and as correct as young ladies lately out of a convent. One would hardly have thought, as they nibbled their Baisers Sucrés and sipped their champagne that they surrendered their bodies nine or ten times a day to clients of whom they thought no more than shop girls who sell gloves or hand-kerchiefs in a store.

Madame Lucine would occasionally join these impromptu parties. She respected Monsieur Henri as a gentleman and an artist and would consent to partake of Sophie's delectable creations, seated majestically in a high-backed chair designed for a cardinal.

She had no objection to "the girls'" enjoying themselves. It encouraged them in their work and it pleased her to exchange with this well-informed habitué reflections on important events of the day. When in an expansive mood, she would oblige in a hoarse contralto with airs of bygone decades before she had risen in the world. Henri detected in her voice a certain nostalgia and wondered if she regretted her life which had deprived her of the joys of motherhood. As it happened Madame Lucine had three children of whose fathers she was uncertain. Her son was an army sergeant stationed at Nancy, her elder daughter had married a Gascon who ran a prosperous ostlery and her younger daughter was suitably kept by the chief of police at Orléans. She had given her son a good education and had settled sizable dowries on her daughters. She never saw her children, but it gratified her to feel that she had done what was right and proper.

But it was not for these lackluster festivities that Henri visited the Rue des Moulins. It was on account of Ottoline, known in the household as The Crab.

Ottoline came from nowhere and resembled no one. She was squat and pulpy with bowed legs, hunched shoulders and a slatternly gash of a mouth. If she could be said to have any features it was her dark and impenetrably murky eyes from which no light ever shone. Ottoline was a mollusk on the hull of society and existed below the water line.

Madame Lucine had rightly judged that this subhuman creature would appeal to men who did not wish to be reminded of their wives or daughters and wanted copulation without stirrings of sentiment or conscience. Ottoline was a sexual mechanism one step removed from those rubber substitutes favored by the Japanese. She appealed to Henri because of all living creatures she bore the least resemblance to Therese whose image, when he was purging himself of excess sexual energy, never came to mind.

Ottoline seldom spoke and only occasionally grunted. Once when he was washing himself after mortal combat in her drab little cubicle that contained a bed, a bedtable with a chamber pot, a dresser and a chair, he noticed on the wall a watercolor of a country churchyard.

"What's that?" he inquired.

"The graveyard in my village," she answered glumly.

"Is that what you think about?"

"I think about the next client, what else?"

Ottoline's existence was a cortege of genitalia. She had only one attribute; no one had ever pitied her.

Henri would walk from the Rue des Moulins to the Turkish Baths on the Rue 24 Septembre, an event in French history of which he was ignorant. He would sweat in the steamroom for half an hour and enjoy a massage from a morose Moroccan who kneaded his tired limbs like dough. After an invigorating plunge in the pool and three cups of China tea he would emerge refreshed into the half light of dawn.

Often he would walk back through the deserted streets to the Marais and, as he lifted the latch of the Pavillon gate, his heart would fill with a secret joy. There was the garden asleep in the opaque shadows of early morning. He would look up at Therese's window and think of her dreaming perhaps of their walks in the country, of her doves or his music. The very thought of Therese was absolution.

As he enjoyed a peaceful cigarette under the trees, among the perfumes of awakening flowers and the soft chirruping of sparrows, he would thank God for allowing him to know the blessedness of parenthood, more personal and more rewarding for being unencumbered by the tedium of married life.

Prelati discussed it with Sophie in her cozy bedroom over the pastry shop. They had made love as usual and, as usual, were lying on the bed in that domestic nudity that no longer surprised them, with a plate of Baisers Sucrés between them.

These delicious confections caused them to emit little puffs of pastry crumbs and powdered sugar as they talked and left them with white moustaches.

"For me," Sophie declared, "it's beautiful. That Monsieur Henri should feel such sensitive devotion to a young girl he rescued from Heaven knows what shows to my mind a true loftiness of soul. He is to be admired and Mademoiselle Therese is very fortunate."

"Oh, I don't deny that he's done everything he could for her except the one thing they both want—which would make sense of the whole affair."

"The human soul *aspires*," Sophie, who considered herself a philosopher, reminded him. "You mustn't deny Monsieur Henri the right to aspire to sentiments too pure to be expressed in the usual way. After all, he's an artist. His love for Therese is an artistic creation. That's how I see it."

"Self-delusion, my dear Sophie. Are we any less noble because we don't, as you say, aspire? Do you aspire?"

"I have my dreams, of course," Sophie admitted. "Because I make excellent pastries doesn't mean I don't dream of wedding cakes, three tiers high, decorated with angels and pink roses, and crowned with a carillon of bells."

"Pouff!" Prelati protested, depositing a small cloud of crumbs and sugar on Sophie's charming bosom. "What you don't see is that he's out of his depth. Aspiration may be all right for Joan of Arc or—or Michelangelo or even Napoleon the Third who made himself Emperor. Monsieur Henri is not that kind of man."

"You know him too well to believe in him. I've heard him play. He gets carried away by beautiful music; he's lifted out of himself. That's what she is to him, beautiful music. And that's understandable. She's exceptional."

"In what way?"

"Oh, she comes to the shop sometimes. I've had the chance to observe her. And I'm not speaking of beauty because for many people she's too classical—like a statue. She's not the kind of girl most men will get themselves in an awkward condition just by looking at. She'll be loved, even worshiped, but only by superior men. It's some kind of quality she has."

"Balls, Sophie. She's eighteen if a day. She's got breasts as full as yours and a fine strong figure. She wants what all girls want at that age. Why go on with this game of canonization? He's not the Pope."

"Maybe he'll marry her when the time comes. It takes courage to climb Mont Blanc. When he does I'll make them the most beautiful wedding cake ever dreamed of." She lay back and stretched her arms. "I can't help being a romantic. What's life without romance, you dry old materialist?"

Antoine Prelati was right. Therese had become a woman.

It was not merely the physical changes which had occurred and which at first had frightened her. Mademoiselle had tactfully explained their cause. It was that living eagerly from day to day, satisfied with what each might bring, she was now aware of waiting for something. She was conscious of a tremulous expectation that filled her with uncertainty and longing.

Everyone noted, when she appeared with Henri in public, that she was no longer a dazzling and enigmatic child. She had grown and filled out and carried herself with aloof distinction. She no longer looked at Henri with the same innocent adoration, but with a more critical and proprietary air. She was aware of women as possible rivals and of men, especially Fabre-Marquet, as potential threats to her position at the center of Henri's life. Stranger, even to herself, were her moods of impatience if he was late, if he did not ask her opinion, if he failed to notice how she was dressed. She would exhibit signs of petulance of which she was ashamed but could not control. She would shrug and turn away and run to the dovecote and feed the doves which she had fed half an hour before. Then, overcome by remorse, she would run back and hide her face against Henri's shoulder. Like a husband who at last discovers that his wife is unfaithful long after his friends have been aware of it, Henri was forced to face what he did not want to face—that the halcyon days of innocence were over and that it was no longer a child he soothed, but a woman whose ripening breasts he felt against his body and whose strong back he clasped as he drew her to him.

She cried for no reason and then laughed and then sank into melancholy abstraction. When he asked her the reason, she would blush with confusion, vanish into the house and reappear a few moments later in another dress with flowers in her hair.

He was confronted by an approaching tidal wave which, by strength of will and imagination he had hitherto held back, but which now threatened to engulf them both.

He found her one day dreaming by the pool into which she was abstractedly throwing dried eggs for the fish.

"Therese," he ventured, "I think it is time that we had a talk."

She looked up. Her astonishing eyes reflected the green ripples of the water and the yellow of autumn leaves.

"I know," he began, sitting beside her, "that you're not sure how old you are, but let us assume that you are seventeen. Have you thought at all about what you would like to do in the future?"

For once her frankness disconcerted him. "To be with you."

"Yes, my dear child, I appreciate that. Of course it's been idyllic living here, but I'm speaking of your future—if you have given any serious thought—"

He saw with a sudden sinking of heart that there had been no need for her to give the future any serious thought or, indeed, any thought at all.

She shook her head as though baffled.

"What other future could there be?"

He nodded. He tried to feel paternal. He tried to invoke the forbearance of a father.

"Well, say that you're seventeen—even eighteen—you know that I'm forty-four."

"Are you, Henni?"

"What I'm trying to say, Therese, is that at forty-four one does not have so much time ahead as at seventeen. People— men often—well, things happen, my dear, to men of my age. When one reaches forty-four—"

"What things, Henni?"

He took a deep breath to steady himself. "At forty-four one's life expectancy is considerably diminished."

Her look of dismay was almost comical.

"But you're not ill, are you, Henni?"

"No, I'm not ill. Not in the least. I'm merely pointing out that you should consider what, in the event that something *should* happen to me, what you would do—so that I can make some provision, so that I could arrange matters."

Her eyes filled with tears. She jumped up and said sharply, "Don't talk like that. Don't even mention such things."

He got up and took her arm, but she wrenched it away.

"Why do you talk about your life expectancy—? I could fall into this pond and drown. Anything can happen however old you are."

She burst into tears.

He took her in his arms and murmured over her bright, bowed head, "Don't be silly, Therese. I'm just thinking of you. One has to think of the future sometimes."

She raised her head. Her brilliant eyes struck him like arrows. "If anything happens to you I shall die." She thrust him away and said with passionate finality, "I shall die. *Like that!* You see?"

The tidal wave rolled over him, sweeping away his resolutions, his fantasies, his happiness—and his independence.

The Pavillon was abruptly no longer the Garden of Eden. It was an arena of unanswered questions, of irrational contradictions, of tender enmities.

Therese sighed profoundly when she listened to him practicing for his forthcoming recital. She sighed three times and twice shifted her position on the sofa.

"If you're restless," Henri suggested, "go into the garden."

"It's raining," she pointed out.

"Then go upstairs."

"I'm not restless. I sighed, that's all."

He couldn't concentrate.

"Haven't you a book to read?" he asked as he started again

on the second movement of a Mozart sonata. "Or some geometry to do for Mr. Willing?"

She pouted. "Geometry!"

"Then sit still."

She remained frozen in an awkward position which he couldn't help noticing.

He practiced for half an hour and then announced, "I'm going out."

"Can I come with you?"

"No, I have to talk over some business with Fabre-Marquet."

"I hate Fabre-Marquet," she blurted out. "You shouldn't trust him."

"Why?"

"Because he's dishonest and he will cheat you."

"He's looked after my business affairs for years."

"He'll cheat you'in the end. You'll see."

He was genuinely taken aback. She was sitting curled up like a cat about to spring.

"I don't know why you should say such a thing. He's a very old friend."

She looked at him with positive contempt.

"You don't see what he is." She added glumly, "You don't see what anyone is." She was fingering the fringe of a cushion, giving it little tugs.

"What is the matter with you, Therese?"

He knew quite well what the matter was. Their position in regard to each other had changed. The young woman on the sofa was an unknown quantity with all sorts of feminine crosscurrents of malice, willfulness, possessiveness and a new capacity for pain and for inflicting pain, both from self-protection and from love.

It all reverted to the question of love. Even the joy they had known and which had seemed unassailable was not immune.

He loved her; that was the problem. And what compounded the problem; she loved him.

He walked a long way in the light rain.

For a bachelor of forty-four to contemplate marriage requires a reversal of his whole concept of life. As there are men who are not joiners of clubs, who do not contribute to organized charities, who are not respecters of institutions, so there are men not disposed toward marriage which they regard as a threat to free enterprise. It was not that Henri loved Therese any less. He was now forced to consider her, not as his inspiration, as a source of spontaneous delight, as a constant reaffirmation of his good opinion of himself, but as an obligation like military service. She was no longer the darling extravagance of his heart, but that most problematic of all intruders, a wife.

It would have been easier to make this transition had Therese been his mistress. Prelati and Sophie were a married couple in everything but name. A certificate of marriage would have meant little more to them than the inconvenience of a change of address. They would know what to expect and, what was more important, what not to expect. But to dethrone a virgin goddess at whose shrine he had happily worshiped, at whose feet he had laid his ideals, his illusions, a whole mythology dear to him, came uncomfortably close to desecration, to capitulation, to a loss of faith.

But as he walked those familiar streets he thought that all such reservations were, after all, selfishness, his old reluctance to make commitments, a prolonged adolescence disguised as an artist's need for independence. He had never faced up to human obligations on the grounds that as an artist he was exempt by virtue of his higher calling, as a man with a heart murmur is not required to risk his life for his country. To give up his freedom, or at least an aspect of it, was not much, in the final count, in exchange for Therese's unquestioning devotion.

To live with her as his mistress would place her, at whatever extreme remove, in the same category as Ottoline, a thought which totally repelled him.

It was marriage or nothing.

He had baited his own trap.

It was spiritual incest.

It would be a great adventure at an age when he had thought himself past adventure.

It would solve everything, for better or worse.

It would solve nothing. It was simply something one had to do.

He went into a jeweler's on the Rue de Rivoli and, after examining a number of pieces, selected a large emerald-cut peridot, surrounded by foliage of small peridots made into a pendant.

It was the color of her eyes.

He was conscious on the way home that this was the last walk he would ever take as a free man.

She was curled in a chair studying her geometry. His heart overflowed with tenderness.

She looked at the pendant without expression.

"What is it for, Henni?"

He jumped from a high cliff into the sea.

"Will you marry me, Therese?"

The great subsidence of relief into which the Pavillon sank was disrupted by a note delivered one fine autumn day when they were sitting in the garden after lunch.

"Do you want to be married in Paris with a big reception and all the usual fanfare?"

"Whatever you say, Henni."

"I thought it would be nicer to have a simple ceremony in the country with just Prelati and Sophie for witnesses."

"Yes, I would like that. Could we drive in the carriage as we do when we're going on an expedition?"

He leaned over and kissed her.

"Whatever will please you most, my dear."

After all, it was very simple once one had taken the plunge. She expected no more than she was used to. Everything would go on as it had. He was surprised that he had thought it such a momentous step.

Prelati had been immensely gratified by the announcement. For him, too, a period of prolonged uncertainty was over. He went about his duties wreathed in smiles and made love to Sophie with unusual vigor both before and after imparting the good news. She was equally elated and immediately started planning the wedding cake, considering and rejecting a number of grandiose designs like Michelangelo contemplating the decoration of the Sistine Chapel.

"Why don't you let Sophie make an honest man of you at last?" Henri had inquired. "Then we could have a double wedding."

Prelati was shocked by the suggestion. He and Sophie had long since passed the point where marriage would add anything to their relationship.

"It would be awkward. She lives over the pastry shop and I live here."

Henri regarded Prelati with the condescension that a man who has volunteered for Active Service feels for a friend who has chosen to remain in civilian life.

The note which Prelati brought out to him was, surprisingly, from Madame Lucine.

> *My dear Monsieur Henri,*
>   *It has taken me some time to find your address.*
>   *Would you be kind enough to call here at your earliest convenience on a matter that concerns you closely?*
>   *I beg you not to delay.*
>   *With my distinguished salutations,*
>
>   *Lucine Gallatin.*

It had never occured to him that Lucine had another name.

He read the note again. "A matter that concerns you closely—?"

An odd shiver of apprehension passed through him. What could that old monster have to discuss with him?

The peace of that garden, the familiar harmony of shadow and sunlight, the presence of Therese in a white dress with her shining copper hair and the great peridot gleaming at her breast, so pure, so safe, so entirely and personally *his*, shifted like a landscape in an earthquake tremor.

He stood up. What could there possibly be about the Rue des Moulins that could concern him closely?

He bent over and kissed Therese.

"I have to go out, my dear. I shan't be long."

"Not bad news, Henni?"

"No. Almery wants to discuss an offer for a tour of the United States."

"The United States? Will you go?"

"Quite unlikely. I don't want to leave here—especially now."

She was white against the green of the garden like a Canova marble. Her eyes reflected the shifting lights and shadows of the trees.

He took a cab to the Rue des Moulins. The ex-bargeman let him in.

"She's in the back room."

The old brothel by daylight was horrible with fifty years of postcoital depression.

The bargeman, who had the shoulders and buttocks of a prizefighter, led the way through dark portières into a dining room, at one end of which was a stage on which, on gala occasions, erotic performances were given. Everything about the place disgusted him. He was disgusted with himself for ever having gone there.

Madame was in her private sitting room having a tizane under an oil painting of a nun being sodomized by an ape.

She looked like an aged male impersonator. Instead of the mandatory red wig, her head was enveloped in a turban the color of dried blood, skewered by a pin at the end of which a clot of yellow glass glinted like the eye of a serpent.

"I am glad you have come," she said graciously, extending her hand like a duchess. "Will you join me in a tizane?"

"No. Thank you."

"A glass of Madeira?"

"No."

"Pray be seated, Monsieur Henri."

She was Nemesis with the filth of ages in her marrow.

The ex-bargeman reclined on a sofa, exhibiting thighs like sides of beef, and immersed himself in a newspaper.

A sinister and airless silence hung over the room.

Henri knew without doubt that the news the old harridan

had to impart could only be the worst. She exuded the grandeur of disaster.

"I asked you to come here because you are a friend of the house, for whom I have, if I may say so, a personal regard," Madame Lucine intoned like a priest pronouncing the office for the dead. "The girls are all very fond of you. You have shown them unusual consideration. Believe me, Monsieur Henri." She leaned forward, revealing a cleavage as murky as a crevice in a sepulcher, "I do not wish to alarm you. That is far from my intention. I wanted merely to give you—at the best—a warning which hopefully will prove to be superfluous." She added something so offensive that he was staggered by her effrontery as though he had witnessed an act of sacrilege. "We are all in the hands of God."

"Will you please come to the point?" Henri said nervously, possessed by the desire to escape. "I have an appointment shortly."

"Of course, dear friend," she murmured with a dreadful purr. "You know that I have always made it a point, as a matter of principle, to see that my girls are in good health. It is an obligation which I owe my clientele. Occasionally, alas, very occasionally, an accident occurs."

Henri felt a cold nausea rising up his spine.

"It seems that Ottoline did not take the precaution, on which I have always insisted, of visiting the doctor as regularly as she should."

"Ottoline?" Everything swam before him.

"I cannot forgive her and I have banished her from my premises," Madame said grandly like an Inquisitor condemning a heretic to eternal perdition. "She is, I'm afraid I discovered—tainted—"

"Infected, you mean? With what?"

The word fell between them like a hissing reptile and writhed toward him across the carpet.

A white curtain fell before his eyes.

"Naturally that does not mean that you—" Madame made a conciliatory gesture. "I thought it my duty to warn you, so that you can take precautions."

"Precautions?"

"You should visit a doctor—to assure yourself—"

Henri jumped up. "You old hag!" he shouted, "I'm going to be married!"

The bargeman stirred on the sofa. "Don't take that tone. She's doing you a favor."

"A favor? You call this a favor? Why the hell didn't you know before?"

"It was not my fault that you preferred her to the others."

"Oh God! I'm going to be married!"

"You should have thought of that," the bargeman sourly reminded him. "Don't you address Madame in that way."

Henri looked wildly 'round. He would gladly have killed them both.

"Are you sure? *Are you sure?*"

Madame Lucine rose. For a moment she felt a stirring of sympathy for this distraught human being.

"Don't upset yourself. It's only a warning—"

"What use is a warning?" Henri cried. All the life went out of him. "Now!"

Madame came toward him. She actually extended her arms with a ghastly solicitude and said reasonably, "Don't, my dear boy—don't upset yourself. It may mean nothing—"

He gave her a frenzied glance and rushed out of the room, out of that infected charnel house, down flights of stairs, into the street.

The daylight blinded him. He walked at top speed. He didn't dare to stop. This reality, beyond everyday reality, would have felled him. He ran to the corner of the street.

Suddenly he thought, "It's nothing. It means nothing. A stupid scare. I've slept with dozens of whores." He thought of the picture of a graveyard on the wall of Ottoline's room. Why hadn't he realized the omen? He felt that his body was already swarming with spirochetes. Cankers were breaking out all over him. It was inevitable, after those monstrous couplings, that paresis would strike his brain.

He rushed to Dr. Cottard's and was driven mad by being

forced to wait in the anteroom under the disapproving gaze of several black-garbed women suffering from liver complaints.

Dr. Cottard was annoyingly noncommittal. His impersonal professionalism, far from reassuring Henri, seemed inhuman.

"There's no sign of infection. If any external manifestations occur come to me at once. We'll start the mercury treatments."

"What chance do I have? I'm supposed to be getting married."

"I should not advise that for the time being."

"But if I have the treatments—"

"There's a good chance of immunization."

Such clinical terms appalled him. "How long—how long would it be?"

"That depends on how you respond. I should say it's out of the question to contemplate marriage under a year."

"A year!" Henri echoed in despair. It was a life sentence!

"I'll give you a mild sedative. It's important that you don't allow yourself to get into states of excitement or depression. Try to stay calm. Continue your normal life and don't allow your imagination to run away with you."

Stay calm! A normal life! With this sword of Damocles hanging over him it would be a miracle if he didn't go raving mad.

Dr. Cottard handed him a prescription.

He saw that Henri Herz was on the point of collapse and patted his shoulder.

"Come, you are not the first man to find himself in this situation. It's a calculated risk that anyone runs who visits such places."

He found himself in the open air, an outcast in a city of sane, healthy people who had never copulated with Ottoline.

It was the most terrible time of his life, but also the most wonderful. In the following weeks he discovered the true meaning of love.

He had confided in Prelati and Prelati had wisely suggested that Therese should only be told that he had developed an infection of the blood which was not altogether far from the truth. As, in due and dreadful course, the outer manifestations occurred and the treatments began, he was sustained not by the faithful Prelati nor by Dr. Cottard, but by Therese. She exhibited a calm and strength, a watchful restraint and tenderness far beyond her years. Everything in her being fused in the single desire to help and succor and encourage him.

She was his mother, his nurse, his companion in distress. Whatever his feelings for her had been, whatever excesses of fantasy he had indulged in of which she had been both the inspiration and the victim, he came to know her as a woman capable of selfless patience and devotion. Although she did not know the precise nature of his disease—and would not have understood it if she had—she knew that it was serious, that he was devoured by anxiety, that he suffered horribly. She was the willing scapegoat of his depressions and guilts and offered him the unstinting support of her courage and confidence. Even Prelati who, as usual, discussed the whole situation with Sophie, admitted, "I have to hand it to her; she had more plain guts and self-control than a woman twice her age, more than most women of any age. Whatever doubts I may have had about Mademoiselle Therese I withdraw them—unconditionally."

"I told you," Sophie reminded him. "She's exceptional."

"Naturally," Prelati sighed, "he doesn't help matters. He's an artist; he dramatizes. You'd think he was the first man in history to catch this disease. What a fool! There were plenty of women he could have had a safe roll in the hay with."

"Poor girl! On the eve of her marriage!"

"I can tell you one thing; she'll stand by him, whatever happens."

Without intruding on Prelati's duties, Therese took over the running of the Pavillon. She supervised the routine of Henri's life, smoothing away the smallest irritations. She served his meals in the garden when the weather permitted, and when the autumn drained into winter, by the fireside in the music room. She came to know every one of his moods, when he needed to be alone, when he needed her with him. Her natural gifts

for silence and composure were blessings that eased him far
more that Dr. Cottard's sedatives.

As long as she was with him he clung to hope. When she
went out on some errand he was restless and fearful till she
returned. She made the unbearable bearable in every respect
except for his constant fear that, in some unforeseen fashion,
he might infect her.

In the midst of this daily ordeal there were gleams of a joy
deeper than any he had experienced before, even in music. He
realized that, in his superficial way, he had never understood
the essential nature of love. It was as if a contralto octave had
been added to his life and instead of the swift scintillating notes
of the piano Therese accompanied his days with the deep warm
notes of a cello.

She could be firm.

He announced in a fit of gloom that he intended to cancel
his forthcoming recital.

"I can't go through with it. I can't concentrate. I am not
going to appear in public until I'm completely well."

She waited till this outburst was over and said calmly, "I
don't think you should do that, Henni. You must give the
concert. Antoine and I are here to see you through."

"I can't practice. My mind isn't on it. I don't want to go
out there and make a spectacle of myself."

"You'll give a beautiful concert. You can give it for me,
just like you do at home."

She sat with him while he practiced. She willed strength
into his hands, control into his mind. On the night of the concert
he was a nervous wreck, certain of disaster. She massaged his
hands with warm oil, washed them in milk of almonds, fixed
the diamond studs in his shirt, brought his cloak, his top hat,
his gloves and rode beside him in the carriage, holding his
hand.

At the last moment he thought that he couldn't go through
with it. The subdued hubbub in the hall terrified him. In a fog
of horror he found himself walking on stage. The applause was
like the roar of a mob exulting over a fallen gladiator.

And then he saw Therese in the right-hand box where she

always sat with Sophie a little behind her. Therese in one of the flowing white dresses he had chosen for her, with his jewel at her breast, serene, almost severe. He felt a sudden exaltation as though the hand of God had touched him.

For her. He would do it for her.

She raised her hand in a simple gesture of recognition as though she had never for a moment doubted that he would play superbly.

He knew, half way through the first part of the program, that it was one of the best, if not *the* best, performances of his career.

Sophie said afterward to Prelati, "It was uncanny. She mesmerized him. I could feel it. She was casting a spell. Everything in her was concentrated on him, willing him to succeed. She never moved. She was hardly breathing. She—well, I don't know—if it's just that she loves him then I never saw love like that."

He played with a passion that the Parisian public did not expect from Henri Herz. There was a luminous purity to the Mozart, the power of a great master in the *Etudes Symphoniques*.

"Just when it was over," Sophie reported, "just as the storm broke, she gave a little sigh as though everything went out of her."

The ovation continued for twenty minutes.

They rode back together as they had come, hand in hand, in silence. He had refused all invitations, cut short the clamor of the crowd. He wanted to be alone with Therese at the Pavillon where they belonged.

It was a new dimension, this sense of belonging. Nothing else in the world compared with it. He longed to take her in his arms, to be physically one as they were one in spirit, but his disease like the third party of a triangle stood between them.

When they came into the music room he thought that he had never seen it before, never realized how beautiful it was, dappled with the soft gleams and shadows of the fire. She had taught him to see, she had opened his heart, this girl of eighteen who was ageless, a woman of all time.

"You've been so patient. I promise you that everything will be as we want it—in just a little time, as soon as I'm well again. I love you so much, Therese."

She gave a soft little laugh, came to him and gave him a playful push on the shoulder.

"You are silly, Henni, pretending you wouldn't give a good concert."

As he held her close she thought that although there was so much about the world that baffled her, so much about the behavior and motives of people that seemed dishonest, there was a small area at the center of her mind where she could see quite clearly. During the last weeks she had become much older than Henri.

Her father had become her child.

The final phase of their relationship occurred abruptly.

As a result of his last recital and the reviews that raised him to that Olympus of great artists reigned over by Franz Liszt, he received an offer of a three month tour of the United States. The terms were more than generous. He stood to make, over and above his living and traveling expenses which were to be paid for by the impresario, Mr. Edwards, the sum of fifty thousand dollars. Dr. Cottard informed him that he was responding well to the treatments, that a sea voyage would be beneficial and that the bi-weekly applications of mercury could be continued in America. He decided suddenly. He felt a compulsive need to get away from Paris, from the events of the past months, even, against his heart, from Therese. He needed to regain a normal outlook, to breathe again, to escape from the torments of self-disgust and self-recrimination.

He talked it over with Prelati who agreed to come with him. Prelati talked it over with Sophie who agreed to take Therese to live with her over the pastry shop. Mademoiselle and Mr. Willing would continue with their lessons at the Pavillon and Casimir Fabre-Marquet would see that Therese was supplied with spending money and would settle up all the bills. Henri was pleased with the efficiency with which he made all these arrangements that seemed to cover every contingency.

The only opposition he encountered was from Therese.

She froze into a silence that rebuffed his explanations. She refused to acknowledge his good intentions. He found himself confronting a stone wall.

She said frigidly, "I won't stay here alone."

"You won't be alone. You must please try to be reasonable. I don't want you to interrupt your education."

"I am educated. I know more than Mademoiselle and Mr. Willing."

"I want you to improve your English and to learn Italian."

"I know English. I know geometry. I can study Italian when we come back."

"Therese, it would be very unwise for you to come with me. Apart from being expensive, America is a semibarbaric country. Traveling is difficult, the hotels are awful, and the cities are full of criminals."

"If you're in danger, I want to be in danger."

"I need you to stay here and look after the Pavillon. This is our home."

"Prelati can stay. There's nothing he does for you that I can't do. Besides, there's no reason for you to go to America at all. If it's so awful you can go on another European tour and then I can come with you."

"I can make enough money out of this tour to keep us for a long time. We can buy a little place in the country such as we've talked of."

"We can do without a place in the country." The force of her obstinacy rocked his illusions that marriage with Therese would be an idyll of peaceful compliance. "I don't want you to go to America. I have a bad feeling about it," she said.

He sighed, but he was disturbed. "I've signed the contract."

"Tell them you're ill, that your doctor's against it. Tell them that I'm against it."

"Why, precisely? Why?"

"You've said often enough that I'm right about things. You should not go to America now. Later on perhaps. Not now."

"You're being unreasonable. It's a very lucrative offer. It will enable me not to work so hard for a long time."

She faced him with the opposition of a mature woman combined with the petulance of a child.

"If you go on this journey I—I won't marry you."

She stalked out of the room.

The silent thunder that falls between the delivery of an ultimatum and a declaration of war descended on the Pavillon.

Therese locked herself in her room. She refused to respond to Henri's pleas, his commands, his angry poundings on the door. She answered not a word to Prelati's requests that at least she have something to eat.

All the next day while Henri was dejectedly packing his scores, while Prelati was helping him to select his clothes, they were aware of Therese barricaded in her room, like a time bomb ticking away to the instant of detonation.

By evening Henri could stand it no longer.

"Therese, stop this nonsense. Open the door."

Silence.

"Open the door! Will you do as I tell you?" A frantic rattling of the doorknob elicited no response.

"You're behaving like a child. You have made me very angry. You know I'm not well, that I'm not supposed to get upset. I have enough on my mind without this absurd behavior."

He was startled by her voice from directly behind the door.

"Go away. I don't want to talk to you."

"Will you at least have something to eat?"

"I have eaten. I ate in the middle of the night."

So, she had cheated!

"I want to talk to you, Therese."

Silence.

"If you don't open the door I shall break it down."

He landed a kick on the lower panel that almost dislocated his ankle.

"Open this goddamned door!"

She was implacable.

"This is the end, you hear? I will not put up with this hysterical selfishness." He broke off in despair. She hadn't been hysterical or selfish. She simply didn't want him to go without her.

He tried a last appeal.

"Therese, I love you. I know that you love me. We'll be married as soon as I get back. You've helped me so much. Please, help me now. You know that I need you."

He had humiliated himself. He had groveled. She had not conceded an inch.

Silence.

He went downstairs. Dr. Cottard had forbidden him to touch alcohol while he was having the treatments. He downed a neat glass of brandy and then, having drunk half of a second, fell into a morose slumber by the dying fire.

He woke to find her kneeling beside him with her head on his knee. The wave of her lovely hair like distilled flame flowed across his lap.

He stroked her head. "We mustn't fight. Do you think that I want to leave you?"

He felt her tears on his hand.

The fire died to a few embers. In the darkness of reconciliation they both slept.

Just before his departure an Indian summer bloomed in the arms of winter.

Therese was quiet with fatalistic acceptance. She offered no suggestions and made no comments.

They were both aware of defeat.

On the last morning when the trunks were ready in the hall, Henri asked: "Shall we go to the country?"

They drove in silence along the familiar route to St. Germain. Once out of Paris Henri turned down a road that ambled beside the loops of the river and stopped at a workman's bistro, almost deserted at this time of year. It was a rendezvous for Sunday fishermen and lovers.

They ate a simple luncheon. The river was streaked with the yellow reflections of almost denuded willows.

He held her hand across the table.

She looked more beautiful than he had ever seen her. Sadness softened the clear-cut features and deepened the color of her eyes.

He wanted to formulate all that she had come to mean to him. The months of conflicting emotions and foolish fantasies, self-deception and discovery, moments dredged up from his inmost being, had merged and melted into one pure grain of gold, this knowledge of love, at once so simple and so encompassing. He knew how many mistakes he had made. He had been like a traveler threading his way through uncharted territory. She had known much sooner, with that clarity of instinct that was not misled by halftones, but saw only essential color.

"What would have happened if I hadn't seen you that night outside the theater in Warsaw?"

"We would have met in some other way."

"You think it was destiny?"

"I don't know what that means, Henni."

"It means that you're a fatalist, Therese."

There was no use in telling him how full of foreboding she was and that she knew these moments were not a prelude to the brief parting he intended.

They walked hand in hand beside the river in the soft damp air that flowed through the willows. Birds were flying south in their wise formations.

She said suddenly, "It isn't because you rescued me, because you've given me so much, even because of your music. Everything I am is because of you." She stopped and made a last appeal. "Don't go, Henni. Please don't go. Surely it doesn't matter so much about the money."

For a moment he was tempted. It would be a relief to cancel the American tour. And it wasn't the money; she was right. Whatever happened, Therese would be well provided for.

But then he thought that he must go. He needed to escape from the burden of so much feeling, from the strain of daily concealing from Therese the nature of his disease, from this all-consuming love.

"The bookings are all made. Besides, it's for the future. To be able, now and then, to earn so much—" He put his arm around her waist as they resumed their walk. "Think of Italy next spring. There'll be so much to see and experience together.

That's what I shall be thinking of all the time I'm pounding away for the aborigines."

She said nothing on the way back or during the rest of the evening. He longed to spend the last night with her, to hold her close against his heart, but as usual he had to content himself with a fatherly kiss on the forehead.

Neither of them slept.

In stricken silence they drank their morning coffee and heard, with sinking heart, Prelati and the driver dragging the trunks out to the cab.

He looked 'round the familiar room. He was saying goodbye to everything that had been best and happiest in his life.

She followed him outside. He embraced her. She barely responded. He got in. She kissed Prelati goodbye.

As the cab started, Henri jumped out and took her in his arms.

"It won't be long, my darling. A few short weeks."

He laid his hand on her white cheek. Her eyes were blank with an agony that effaced all feeling.

"Soon, Therese."

He got back into the cab, tears streaming down his cheeks.

She stood by the gate in the chill gray morning watching the cab as it trundled down the street. It turned the corner and was lost from view.

She knew in her soul that she would never see him again.

Three weeks later Casimir Fabre-Marquet, somberly garbed in black, but with an acquisitive gleam in his eye, called at the Pavillon.

Therese was in the garden feeding the doves. She stood very still watching him approach as though she already knew what he had come to tell her.

He informed her with an unctuous display of grief that Henri Herz and Antoine Prelati had never reached New York. Theisteamship, the Jeanne d'Arc, the newest and most luxurious built in France, had gone down in a storm at sea.

She received the news like a graven image, without a word or tear.

She had shed all her tears and what was there left to say?

Part Three

---

22 Chaussée d'Iena

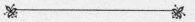

*I*T WAS A parvenu empire presided over by a parvenu emperor whose right to call himself the nephew of Napoleon was open to debate.

His brother, the great Duc de Morny, was frankly illegitimate. His mother, Hortense de Beauharnais, Josephine's lovely and wayward daughter, had beguiled herself with various admirers. Over the Emperor's birth hung the shadow of a certain Dutch admiral.

There was something ambiguous about his appearance which supported these rumors. He had the nose of a conspirator, with a whiff of gunpowder in the nostrils, profoundly indolent eyes, the dyed black hair of a provincial actor and immense waxed moustaches stuck to his face like advertisements on a billboard. They added to his unimpressive exterior a certain dubious authority. He was phlegmatic, fatalistic, a speculator in power, a manipulator of circumstance. It seemed implausible that this halfhearted adventurer, after a lifetime of failures, mismanaged coups d'état and years of imprisonment, had had the initiative to get himself elected President of the Republic and, later, to declare himself Emperor of France.

The empire that burgeoned under his aegis was, like himself, an immensely prosperous charade, a gilded hippodrome where speculators, contractors, charlatans and whores wallowed in a flood of new wealth. Everyone gambled. Modest businessmen became millionaires overnight and millionaires, with equal rapidity, went bankrupt. Manufacturers of rubber goods or kitchenware bought titles and moved into the mansions of the old aristocracy who retreated to the chilly stronghold of the Faubourg St. Germain and tried to ignore these upstarts whose money could buy them anything but the right to intrude on polite society. These ambitious vulgarians cared not a damn for polite society. They set about creating a society of their own, less exclusive but more entertaining. Their only standards were profit and pleasure. If the Faubourg acknowledged the Second Empire at all it was only when the scion of some ancient house had the lack of good taste to marry for money. Such faux pas occurred with disturbing frequency. As the Duchesse de Faucigny-Licinge remarked when her nephew espoused the daughter of a cloth manufacturer who had made a fortune supplying uniforms to the army, "One has occasionally to manure one's fields."

The pastures of Paris were plentifully manured with newly minted and newly plundered gold. It was the greatest boom the city had ever known. What made it so scandalous to the Faubourg was that those who benefited most did not do so by right of birth or inheritance, but because of a knack for shrewd and shady transactions from which anyone of good breeding shrank as from the plague.

The Court at the hub of this harlequinade was extravagant, ostentatious and dull. Mademoiselle Montijo—as the Empress was referred to by dowagers of the *ancien régime*—was little more than a clothes horse. Her gowns, designed by the Englishman Worth, grew vaster and vaster until she wafted across the floors of the Tuileries like a flagship in full sail. She was beautiful, featherbrained and vindictive. The redeeming features of the Emperor who was not quite an Emperor were his unfailing good manners, his loyalty to those who had stood by him in the past, his devotion to his son, and his singular tolerance of the refractory elements that seethed beneath the surface of the gilded Sodom and Gomorrah over which he reigned. He actually sympathized with the working man.

Among the phenomena of this age of flamboyant optimism was a new class of demimondaines known as the Grandes Horizontales because their successes were seldom achieved in an upright position. Unlike their predecessors who had remained for the most part discreetly withdrawn from society unless they were the acknowledged mistresses of kings, these later votresses of Venus displayed themselves everywhere with the greatest éclat and were acclaimed as popular idols and arbiters of fashion with whom it was considered a distinction to be seen. They lived in elaborate apartments, drove dazzling *équipages*, swirled into restaurants, bedizened with jewels, on the arm of their latest protector, and presided over salons where the literary and theatrical great mingled with politicians and financiers and the less austere members of the aristocracy. It was the time when the Russian grand dukes, those Genghis Khans of limitless wealth, first conquered Paris and soon eclipsed in extravagance their English counterparts.

Alice Ozy, whose thighs were as well supported as the Banque de France, climbed rapidly through the Romanoff family tree and made herself several fortunes. Leonide Leblanc who had charmed any number of rare birds from the topmost financial branches consented to spend one night with "a Tartar Chief" for eighty thousand francs. After this ordeal she remained in bed for three days. "I think I shall stick to French lovers," she declared weakly. "No wonder the Russians defeated Napoleon."

These much publicized odalisques whose photographs, in various states of undress, were exhibited all over Paris, were the queens of a society that adhered to no other morality than success.

Among the waterlilies that floated to the surface of these glittering but treacherous waters was Therese Lachmann.

It came about in this way.

After allowing her a few days to assimilate the news of Henri's untimely death, Casimir Fabre-Marquet had called again to inform her, with the greatest tact and solicitude, of equally painful tidings; namely that Henri had died insolvent. Worse, he had mountainous debts. Worse, such money as remained, carefully withheld and nurtured against just such an emergency by his business manager, was already claimed by his creditors. Worst of all, the dear Pavillon would have to be sold to satisfy the demands of the moneylenders. It was, Casimir assured her, the most painful duty of his career.

Therese knew he was lying. She was too stunned by grief to protest. And even had she done so, to whom could she have turned for help and redress? She hadn't a friend in the world but Sophie, equally prostrated by loss. She listened without interest to Casimir's involved explanations of how for years he had juggled Henri's earnings in order to enable him to live in his easy, profligate way. How often had he begged Henri to economize! Like all artists Henri had absolutely no head for finance. As long as he could go on giving concerts, Casimir had managed to keep the bubble afloat, robbing Peter to pay Paul. Alack, the bubble had burst. Even with the receipts from the American tour it would have been years and years—

"I would like to see the will," Therese interrupted him.

"Will?" Casimir's stupefaction was equal to that of a baby presented with its first rattle.

"Henri made a will before he left for America."

"My dear child, there was no will. He may have intended. But even had he made a will the facts of his financial condition are incontrovertible. Perhaps," he suggested with an implied challenge, "You'd care to go over his accounts?"

Therese only wanted one thing; to see the last of this Judas she had always detested.

But Judas was not one to shirk his responsibilities. She must not despair—Judas actually pressed her hand—he had her interests at heart. What she needed in this tragic emergency was a woman friend, someone knowledgeable in the ways of the world, someone to guide and advise her. "A mother, in fact, dear child."

The lady designated by Casimir to assume this compassionate office was a Comtesse Henriette Vibert, a plump, energetic little personage, primped out with ribbons and laces and feathered hats. She lived near the Opera in a small apartment which by lamplight, cluttered as it was with mementos of better days, seemed quite a charming, and even seductive, retreat. The harsher light of day revealed its tawdryness.

The Comtesse was all sweetness and sympathy. She deplored the cruel fate that had plunged this lovely young innocent into such grief and penury. She asked a great many pertinent and, to Therese, impertinent questions, about her prospective protégé's experience with men. Therese looked at her blankly. Experience?

"Well, dear child, when you first met Monsieur Herz—let me put it this way—had there been others?"

"I never knew anyone before Henri."

"Ah, you say 'knew.' I understand that you lived for some time under Monsieur Herz' care. You lived, did you not, on terms of some intimacy?"

"We were going to be married."

"Precisely; that's understood. But during that time did you—were you—intimately connected?"

The Comtesse found it hard to believe that Therese's bewildered gaze could be quite as guileless as it seemed.

"I knew him as well as it's possible to know anyone."

The Comtesse finally lost patience with this temporizing. She said briskly, "What I am trying to get at, my dear, is simply: Are you a virgin?"

The bewildered gaze remained bewildered.

"Don't you *know*? But it's inconceivable! Stand up, my dear. Be so good as to raise your skirts."

A brief examination which shocked Therese profoundly confirmed the astonishing fact that this beautiful and unworldly creature was as unblemished as she appeared.

This discovery added a new dimension to the Comtesse's notions of motherhood. She had stumbled upon a prize potentially far more valuable than Casimir Fabre-Marquet had indicated.

She considered Therese from every angle. She was certainly not the usual commodity to dispose of to any prosperous business man in need of a mistress. She had her own little air of proud distinction. Her coloring was astonishing. Her figure was exquisite, her voice low and cultivated. All in all, the Comtesse shrewdly estimated, Therese Lachmann, despite her unfortunately plebeian name—was certainly worth an investment.

She explained; Therese listened. She advised; Therese pondered. What was essential for someone in her position, of her age, of her lack of practical experience, was a protector. But the right protector, someone who would appreciate her qualities, someone of taste and discrimination, above all, someone *rich*.

The Comtesse planned her campaign. She was an experienced strategist.

She consulted lexicons and atlases. She weighed Christian names against patronymics, patronymics against towns, districts, countries. She wanted something original and stately, a name with a touch of mystery, of the exotic, a name that was not to be trifled with, a name—well, a name that would inspire a man of distinction to visit the jeweler's.

She burst into Therese's room at two in the morning. Therese was listlessly reading. She read, as men walk in moods of despair, to stop herself thinking.

"How do you see yourself as Thaïs de Teschen?"

Therese evinced no reaction to this misnomer.

"Thaïs de Teschen. It has a certain power, a certain nobility. Madame la Duchesse de Tallyrand, née Thaïs de Teschen. Forget about Therese Lachmann which is altogether impossible. You will be Thaïs de Teschen from now on."

Therese took little interest in these preparations to launch her on a horizontal career though, to do her justice, the Comtesse did not put beyond the bounds of possibility a more permanent establishment with a man sufficiently infatuated. Better to have no family than one that needed to be explained away. Therese felt herself propelled by forces beyond her control. Her real life had ended when she left the Pavillon. What was happening to her seemed like a blurred and disagreeable charade.

She protested mildly at the billowing white ball gown for which the Comtesse insisted that she be fitted.

"I really don't care for white." In fact she detested it because it reminded her of the white dresses that Henri had bought for her.

"And what colors do you prefer, Mademoiselle?" the Comtesse tartly inquired.

"Lilac or gray or gray-green."

"Lilac or *gray*? Ridiculous! Middle-aged colors. Entirely unsuitable. Thaïs de Teschen will wear white, the color of purity, the color of joy."

Even so, washed out by this avalanche of snow-white silk with skirts as wide and unmanageable as the Empress', a parure of paste diamonds and an ermine stole (rented by the week), Therese still managed to look remarkable.

The Comtesse was satisfied with her creation. She wrote two business letters, one to a certain milord, the most celebrated and the richest rake in Paris, and the other to Therese Lachmann in which the latter bound herself over for a period of five years to Henriette Vibert with the understanding that she would indemnify the above-mentioned with forty per cent of all monies received for services rendered.

The services were not specified. Therese shrugged and signed.

The Comtesse's calculations were correct in every respect except one. The flaw in that enterprise was Therese.

Accompanied by her mentor who had decked herself out in royal blue billows with a harlequinade of ribbons and laces, bangles, beads and brooches, Thaïs de Teschen was presented to the slave market of Paris from a box at the Opéra Comique, well chosen so that her charms could be scrutinized by the gentlemen promenading in the orchestra.

The golden salmon rose to the bait. Lord Stanley introduced himself in the interval and asked if he might take the Comtesse's niece to supper.

"I'm afraid," the Comtesse demurred with a telling simper, "that my niece is quite unused to society. She has only just arrived in Paris, having spent her life in a convent since the unfortunate death of her parents."

"I shall be happy to be the first to give her a glimpse of the great world," Lord Stanley said in execrable French.

"What do you say, dear child, to this kind invitation?"

Therese had nothing to say. Lord Stanley was large, imposing, about forty, with a yellow wig and a yellow waistcoat, small bloodshot eyes and a drooping mouth. Therese regarded him with distaste.

"She's so shy and demure," the Comtesse hastened to explain. "She has the most tender soul. But, I'm sure, since it's you, milord, that I can have every confidence. You will return her to me, won't you, on the very stroke of midnight?"

They dined at the Café Anglais where Therese's appearance caused many heads to turn. She was a new entry into the boudoir sweepstakes and it was greatly to her credit that she had started at the top. Lord Stanley was famous for his conquests, several of whom were now established courtesans of the first rank.

She found it difficult in her present state of numbed desolation to concentrate on what this gross and overbearing man was saying. Lord Stanley was used to limitless respect. He was bestowing an honor on this novice by condescending to deflower her.

They went from the Café Anglais to Lord Stanley's apartment.

Having failed to maintain a pretense of conversation, Stanley proceeded to business. He tossed off a glass of brandy and started to slip Therese's gown from her shoulders. She stepped back and quickly replaced the folds of silk that covered her breasts.

"Surely you're not going to deprive me of the usual amenities?" Stanley said as though reprimanding a servant for failing to open a door.

"That depends on what you consider the amenities," Therese replied in a tone that Stanley thought highly impertinent.

"I'm afraid I don't understand your game, Mademoiselle— Mademoiselle-whatever-your-real-name-is."

"I am Therese Lachmann," she informed him, picking up her rented stole and making firmly for the door.

"You did *what*?" the Comtesse exclaimed when Therese returned two hours before she was expected.

"I don't see why because he takes me to dinner he has the right to undress me," Therese stated. "I found him disagreeable and uninteresting."

The Comtesse gasped.

"May I point out that Lord Stanley is a millionaire many

times over. You have offended a man who, if you played your cards right, could quite easily make you rich."

"He may be a millionaire, but he's vulgar and he speaks bad French."

The Comtesse was not going to tolerate such arrogance from a girl in whom she had invested both strategy and money. "I think it is time that you and I had a serious talk, my girl."

Lord Stanley had been at first affronted by this rebuff. On consideration he was surprised by Therese's daring. He was not used to rejection and believed that his wealth and amatory prowess made him irresistible to women. But it was certainly a novelty that an inexperienced girl from nowhere should presume to snub him. He decided to teach her a lesson.

An immense basket of flowers was delivered the following morning with a note asking if Mademoiselle—(he couldn't remember either of her names) would care to come for an afternoon drive in the park. He would send his carriage at three.

The Comtesse was overjoyed. It was a reprieve. She delivered a tirade on the absolute necessity of cashing in on such an opportunity. Therese had no desire to go driving with Lord Stanley, but the Comtesse bustled and coerced her into one of Henri's white dresses and one of Henri's wide-brimmed straw hats with a pale green ribbon. Therese felt it was desecration. The Comtesse positively pushed her into the arms of Lord Stanley's coachman who came to announce that the carriage was downstairs.

Both the carriage and its owner were waiting.

"So you decided to forgive me," Stanley remarked with sarcasm.

"I decided to go for a drive."

Lord Stanley was forced to consider that perhaps this young woman's cold and challenging manner did not merely stem from impertinence. She actually appeared to consider herself his equal and expected the sort of consideration that he would have been called upon to show a woman of his own class. It was really incredible. And what surpassed the incredible was that, entirely against his will, he began to feel a certain respect for her. He was mystified as to how this creature with her natural air of breeding could possibly have fallen into the clutches of a notorious procuress like the so-called Comtesse de Vibert. On further acquaintance, Mademoiselle—whatever her name was—did not seem to be the usual ambitious young woman. She conducted herself like a product of the Faubourg who had spent her life in the company of dowagers of the *ancien régime*. Stanley was puzzled but intrigued.

They drove and conversed. Stanley put himself out to be agreeable. Whatever his current mode of life, he had considerable knowledge of the world. He had traveled widely and, in his younger, more conservative days, had moved in the highest social circles. Being with Therese made him regret that he had given up a life to which his rank and fortune entitled him for his present profligate existence with wastrels, rakes and renegades and women of the demimonde. He had wasted his patrimony on dissipation. Therese made him remember himself as he had been; he was not altogether grateful.

Virtue is a dangerous temptation to the unvirtuous. Stanley escorted Therese to her door, kissed her hand and invited her to the opera—which he detested.

They established an uneasy truce. Therese was prepared to admit that Stanley had a civilized side. Stanley was not prepared to admit that he was becoming involved with a young woman too self-possessed or too cold to play the coquette. After a few outings he was no longer sure that he wanted to seduce her. He was not sure that, unless he did so, he should go on seeing her. The alarming thought that he might end up by marrying her crossed his mind. Oddly enough she would have fitted in very well to his mother's circle.

Her distinction and detachment constituted a threat to his right to destroy himself in his own way. She was one of those damnable women capable of making an honest man of him.

"Look here, Therese," he said at last as they were driving back from the races at Longchamps. "I don't know about your association with the Vibert woman, but presumably you know by this time, if you didn't in the beginning, what her profession is."

Therese tilted her head slightly so that her face was shadowed by the wide brim of her hat. "Yes. I know."

"I'm quite ready to do what's customary on your behalf, perhaps more. But I really don't know where I stand. I originally had the intention of forcing the issue in the usual way. If it means anything, I am no longer inclined to do so."

"Thank you."

"I realize that you are not what I thought, but I simply don't understand what your intentions are."

After a silence Therese answered with difficulty, "I have no intentions. I lost everything I understood."

"Then I suggest that, for the time being, you trust me. I am not a saint, as you have doubtless surmised, but I am not altogether a monster. We must adapt ourselves to the world as it is."

More to protect his independence than from desire, he took her virginity that afternoon. She was sickened by an act that seemed to her a violation of every last shred of human dignity. She felt degraded and crept from the blood-stained bed like a wounded animal.

"It's only the first time that's like that," he assured her. "You happen to be rather small and I'm rather large. It won't be so painful in the future."

In the future! She couldn't conceive of ever submitting to such a loathsome procedure again. It was worse than an operation in a surgeon's office. It was the worst thing that had happened to her since Henri's death.

Far from reinstating Lord Stanley in his own esteem as a Man of Pleasure, possessing Therese aroused in him unwelcome feelings of guilt and of compassion.

The Comtesse saw at once what had happened. Therese gave her a look of loathing, went to her room and locked the door.

That evening Stanley went to a rout at Alice Ozy's. Usually he enjoyed himself in such company. For some reason he was less than amused by this familiar gathering of rowdy, gossiping hedonists. He gazed at the perfumed bosoms swelling from billowing gowns, the dazzling eyes enlarged with belladonna, the painted lips excreting profanities, and thought of Therese's stark white face as she had left his apartment.

He thought, as he seldom did, of his mother, beautiful, gracious and impeccable. He had repaid her devotion with shame and disappointment. He thought of his charming, worthy sisters and their merry, rosy-cheeked children. He realized, with a sort of horror, what a discreditable spectacle he had made of his life.

He appeared at the Comtesse's the following morning. She was totally unprepared for the volley of high moral indignation hurled at her by this notorious rake, and vainly protested that she had taken Therese under her wing out of Christian charity. Stanley demanded to see the contract she had doubtless forced this innocent to sign. A contract? Unthinkable! "I have acted from the highest, the most generous motives."

"I know the procedure, you old hag. Give me that contract, or, by God, I'll go straight to the police."

Amid tears and protests and imprecations, she produced the contract. With a fine show of contempt Stanley tore it up and threw the pieces into the fire.

"Let me make this plain; if you as much as speak to Therese on the street, on any pretext whatsoever, I'll have you behind bars and, rest assured, there you will remain."

The Comtesse collapsed on the sofa. The unthinkable, the unspeakable, the unprecedented had happened. Lord Stanley was in love.

The avenging angel who had, for the moment, taken possession of the reprobate knocked on Therese's door.

"Pack your things. I'm taking you out of here."

She obeyed meekly. She was too bewildered to know what was happening to her.

He drove her to a charming apartment on the Ile de la Cité which he had rented that morning. Its windows looked out over the river.

"You're to stay here. Everything has been paid for. I've engaged a maid. She'll be here tomorrow."

Therese looked 'round the pleasant little sitting room, furnished with pieces of the Régence, its walls and chairs covered in pink Toile de Jouy. She looked at her seducer who had abruptly become her benefactor.

"Why—?"

"I ask you to show a little patience," Stanley advised her sternly. "Give yourself the chance to get used to me."

She looked exquisite, he thought, in her bewilderment and distress. He felt purified as though by a spiritual purge.

"I know. I know," he said impatiently. "You're inexperienced. You don't understand how things work. I'll see you some time tomorrow."

He left her abruptly without even shaking her hand.

Their romance lasted a month. It was not successful. Stanley grew tired of restraining his natural appetites, of being on his best behavior. His worse and more familiar self struggled to escape the bondage of good intentions. Therese's idea of a pleasant evening was to sit through Racine's interminable tragedies at the Comédie Française. He yawned his way through "Phèdre" and through "Athali." After an act of "Andromache" he left her and repaired to a neighboring bar. His high regard for Therese depressed him.

She, in turn, tired of trying to accommodate him, of pretending that she no longer found his embraces distasteful. She tried to be gay and tender; high spirits reminded her of Henri. They went riding in the country. At St. Germain on the Grande Térrasse she broke into a flood of tears.

He knew it was useless. She was not cut out to be his mistress. He had traveled a certain path too long to be capable of reformation.

The truth was that they bored each other.

She was alone a good deal and took to wandering the quaies, picking up at the stalls old books that she read by her window. She spent hours staring at the water, watching the slow barges and the men bemused over their fishing rods.

One day a carrot-haired, tomato-cheeked Englishman called. He introduced himself as Sir Henry Wyandote, a close friend of Stanley's.

"Ay-cou-tay, Mady-moy-zelle," he said in music-hall English, "I'm afraid the old boy's been called to England. Family business and so on. He asked me to stop by and see you were all right, take you out if you like, so you don't feel neglected. And, by the way, he told me to give you this."

He handed her an envelope stuffed with bank notes. It was Stanley's way of saying goodbye.

Wyandote was a jollier, less intelligent version of Stanley. He lived in Paris, having been cashiered from his regiment for seducing the Colonel's lady. He had two interests; horses and women. He spent his life in the saddle.

He couldn't make head or tale of Therese, though he had to admit she had a stylish seat on a horse. He found her gravity chilling.

Their relationship lasted two weeks. "The fact was," Wyandote confessed to Stanley afterward, "she was a bit of a drag. Not a giggle in her. The sort of girl, dontcha know, the Prince Consort would approve of."

He was not very generous, but Therese continued her afternoon rides; she enjoyed the exercise. She rode alone because she knew no one. It was assumed by numerous gentlemen who observed her that she was out looking for assignations.

It was not merely that she was alone; she was alone in a world in which she could find no place. She realized dimly that she must try to make something of herself. She did not know how to set about it. She had not been trained to do anything and when she went into shops or stores that employed women the manager always approached her, mistaking her for a lady of quality who had come to make an expensive purchase. She felt that she was capable of something more than selling gloves or embroidering underwear. She knew that she must look to the future. But the future had died with Henri. There was only a succession of todays in which she drifted, vaguely ashamed of her weakness and indolence and lack of enterprise.

Men propositioned her. She despised them for their vanity and their shabby, schoolboy desires. She despised herself because they considered her in the only light she supposed she merited.

The landlord called to inquire if she intended to keep on the apartment. She paid the rent by the month. The money Stanley had given her was almost gone. She had dismissed the maid.

The iron of acceptance entered her soul. She had to overcome her aversion to sex in order to pay for her solitude.

The Viscomte de Persigny, "Par Tout Par Tout" to his friends, had seen this arctic beauty riding in the Bois. He had several times raised his hat and received not so much as a glance. He determined to possess her.

He rode up to her one day and performed his mating dance, as elaborate as a ritual at the court of China, punctuated by subtle smiles and suggestive simpers.

Her gaze remained as steady and unresponsive as that of a statue. She cut him short by inquiring, "Do you wish to sleep with me? It will cost you fifty thousand francs."

He was shocked, not so much by her bluntness, but rather by the price, equal to that of any established courtesan in Paris.

He paid the fifty thousand.

"A total waste of money," he told his friend, Armand de Gramont-Caderousse next day. "She lay there like a block of marble. I was pounding away like a steam engine—not a muscle moved. Not the twitch of a little finger."

Gramont-Caderousse, the self-appointed leader of the *jeunesse dorée*, was highly amused. Poor old Persigny was losing his grip! Evidently this amazon required a more vigorous approach.

He encountered Therese riding as usual in the Bois. Without raising his hat and with that insolence that he deemed a mark of distinction, he asked, "I understand you charge fifty thousand for a few hours entertainment. Do you happen to have any free time?"

She considered this question and, as though making an appointment with a hairdresser, replied, "Tuesday at ten." She gave her address and rode away.

Gramont-Caderousse was not any more successful. He broke off in the midst of his endeavors. "What's the matter with you? You're like ice. Do you spend your days at the morgue?"

"I'm not to blame if you fail to rouse me," Therese replied

with quiet contempt. "But then, how could you? You must have the smallest organ in Paris."

Gramont-Caderousse went white with rage. If she had been a man he would have killed her. He flung a few insults about, dressed in a flash, and rushed from the apartment, slamming as many doors as possible.

"She's a lesbian," he told Persigny. "It's the only explanation."

He took care to spread the word among the dandies who took their afternoon promenade in the Bois that this frigid Cyprian was only interested in women.

The rumor gathered some weight when she became a friend of Leonide Leblanc. Why else would this celebrated seductress take an interest in a potential rival?

Leonide, truth to tell, had other fish to fry.

She noticed Therese one night at the Café Anglais, dressed in a smoke gray gown that set off her copper-gold hair and her indolent yellow-green eyes. She wore no jewelry but a single ruby ring. "My God, if I had that girl's looks and coloring it wouldn't be that insipid Montijo who'd be reigning at St. Cloud! She has everything but the one thing to make it all work; she has no charm."

She saw her on other occasions and finally invited her to tea.

Leonide was a popular actress as well as being a courtesan. After riding the Parisian roundabout for ten years she could spot an unusual personality with a potential for success, as she could judge a man's virility by the shape of his hands.

What she lacked in beauty Leonide made up in vitality and a generous capacity for life. She had an alluring figure, a mass of chestnut hair and fine dark eyes that darted ironic glances at a world she had conquered by wit and willpower, a good sense of timing, and a well-controlled temper, only unleashed when she was threatened by not getting her own way. If she had suffered a few hard blows from Fate, she had dealt an equal number in return. She and Fate had reached an understanding. The public adored her, and her lovers, too numerous to mention—"I never had a good head for figures"—retained a warm affection for her after they had quit her embraces and she had relinquished her hold on their bank accounts.

She saw at once that this new entrant into the Paris sweepstakes would never make a career in the demimonde. She lacked the talent for dissimulation and her classic beauty did not offer the promise of tender debaucheries. She was distinguished in an undefinable way, and intelligent. She answered Leonide's questions with a candor that was disarming, and recounted the whole story of Henri Herz and of Casimir Fabre-Marquet's duplicity.

"It doesn't surprise me," Leonide remarked. "I shit on all lawyers from a very high altitude. Am I right in assuming that you are not very happy with the life you are leading at present?"

"It's chiefly because I'm afraid I'm not very good at it."

"I understand; you can't help thinking of *him*. We've all been through it. Love is a marvelous agony, but when things go wrong one has to get on without it. One can't always stop to consider which man that little appendage belongs to."

She was reclining on the sofa in her pretty, haphazard drawing room, cluttered with souvenirs of romances and props from plays in which she had scored successes.

"Have you thought of an alternative?"

"I know that I have to do something," Therese admitted. "But I know nothing except what Henri taught me about music and what I have read. I see now that it's very difficult for a woman alone to make her way without a family or connections."

"Yes, it's difficult, but not impossible. I had no education at all. My father kept a workman's café and my mother was a farm girl. I ran away with an army captain when I was eighteen because I wanted to get to Paris and make something of myself. I had only one advantage; I came from Angers where every peasant speaks perfect French."

"It's different for you, Madame," Therese said with ingenuous sincerity. "You have such a wonderful personality, a magic that's quite your own."

"I'm an actress, my dear, both on and off stage. It is not

so much what one has that counts, but how one learns to use it. You have a great deal to offer, but it's not of the usual kind."

She invited Therese to a few parties and noted that while experienced womanizers admired her, they did not court her. She had more success with writers and politicians. The latter were impressed by her capacity for remaining silent while they expounded their pet opinions on world affairs. They pronounced her very intelligent. Men, Leonide decided, preferred to talk to Therese rather than sleep with her. It would be difficult to put such an attribute to good use.

She included Therese in a small supper for the Duc d'Aumale, her current "Protector." The duke was a great Conti prince, a connoisseur of the arts, who lived in splendor at Chantilly. He was the epitome of the eighteenth century grand seigneur who, to keep up with the times, went to uncommon lengths to appear democratic. He gave Sunday luncheons to which he invited all the wrong people; duchesses found themselves seated next to professors of chemistry and literary celebrities next to dimwitted dowagers. The result was that no one enjoyed himself.

The duke took a liking to Leonide's discovery. He thought her distinguished and invited her to Chantilly where he conducted her on a "tour of the premises." For once Therese's unfortunate honesty was not out of order. She complimented the duke on his collections and showed such attentive interest in all he said that he deemed her remarkably cultivated.

Emboldened by this success Leonide set her sights even higher. It was a challenge to launch this enigmatic beauty who might prove of use to her later on.

She asked Therese to stop by one night after the theater and greeted her warmly—like an old friend—in cascades of violet silk. Therese admired her profoundly and never ceased to marvel at the ease with which this Pompadour of the boulevards cut through social distinctions by the simple expedient of being what she was; the Eternal Feminine.

A presence entered the room.

Darkly impressive, with a steely urbanity, Alphonse de

Morny veiled with an air of nonchalant power a mind as merciless as a guillotine.

He was the second most powerful man in France. His half brother, Napoleon III, had made him a duke in return for De Morny's having made him an emperor. They were strikingly similar in appearance, but where the Emperor had somnolent eyes that gave him a certain charm, de Morny's eyes were black, piercing and aggressive. He was an adventurer turned diplomat, a gambler who had not only broken the bank but now owned it.

He instantly appraised Therese Lachmann as a young woman who, despite her remarkable looks, he would have no desire to seduce. After half an hour in her company he was forced to admit that there was something unusual about her. It was hard to say just what. There was strength behind her composure, intelligence behind her restraint. She said little, but her occasional remarks were succinct and pointed and expressed in a low, well modulated voice. Unlike Leonide who was unmistakably a woman of the people, Therese Lachmann belonged in the circles in which he and his brother moved. It was a pity, he thought, that she was not the daughter of a reigning prince; he might have arranged a useful dynastic match.

As they sat over coffee, their eyes—the eyes of the illegitimate offspring of Polish kings and the eyes of the illegitimate offspring of a dynasty of usurpers—met in a look of appraisal and recognition.

A number of Henri's friends, the erstwhile frequenters of the Pavillon, encountered Therese on her afternoon rides in the Bois. She greeted them distantly and appeared to have no desire to renew their acquaintance. As they had never much cared for her, they did not pursue the matter. After her brief liaison with Stanley they assumed that she had adopted the only profession open to a young woman with looks, but without backing or background.

Casimir Fabre-Marquet summed it up. "After all, it was to be expected. She was a tramp from the Warsaw ghetto. Perhaps if poor Henri had left her some money she might have followed a different course. But there was nothing, not a penny. I was forced to buy the Pavillon to settle the remainder of his debts."

Casimir had repeated his version of Henri's post-mortem bankruptcy so many times, with so many variations, that even his closest friends no longer believed him.

He bumped into Therese one day on the Boulevard Sevastopol as he was leaving the Marais. She was on her way with an armful of flowers to one of her infrequent visits with Sophie.

"My dear Therese," he greeted her with his crocodile smile. "I am delighted to find you so prosperous."

"We make our money in much the same way, Casimir. I cheat my lovers and you cheat your friends."

"That monster!" Sophie exclaimed when they were settled by the fire in the little bedroom over the pastry shop. "It makes me boil when I think of it. He stole everything—Antoine's annuity, my little legacy, and you worst of all. Don't tell me Monsieur Henri didn't leave any money. He'd been giving concerts for twenty-five years and he wasn't extravagant. He wanted you to have everything *and* the Pavillon to live in. Oh, it's wicked—wicked!"

"I'll have my revenge one day."

"He had the effrontery to come in here with that trollop he's living with. Bold as brass, he ordered a box of Baisers Sucrés and some Mille Feuilles. I looked him straight in the eye. 'Monsieur Marquet,' I said, 'this is a respectable shop. I do not do business with criminals.' I said that. He went crimson and started to shout and grimace and wave his arms like a ham actor. His tart let out a shriek like a parrot. 'Out!' I said. 'And don't dare show your face here again.'"

Therese was not concerned with Fabre-Marquet at that moment. Of far greater significance were her two further meetings with Alphonse de Morny, one at Leonide's, when he had scrutinized her like an etymologist about to dissect a rare butterfly, and the other at a mysterious villa he kept on the outskirts of Paris.

A carriage had called for her late one night. She had feared that it was, after all, the same old story, but it turned out to be otherwise.

He had received her seated at an ebony desk in a large hushed room with windows opening onto a park, arrayed in a padded wine-colored dressing robe that gave him a certain reptilian allure. He was immensely dangerous, but she had steeled herself not to show that she was afraid of him.

A cold supper was waiting. De Morny spread his pâté on thin slices of toast as though savoring state secrets. He questioned her like a chief of police about her family, her upbringing, her reason for coming to Paris, the people she had met, the number and names of her lovers.

She answered him with the directness that Henri's friends had found so disconcerting but which de Morny seemed to appreciate. She held nothing back.

"Do you think the Duc d'Aumale has political ambitions?" he asked abruptly.

"No. He is much too amiable. If he were offered the crown of France he'd put it in a glass case and show it off to the people he asks to lunch on Sundays."

She was unable to gauge his reactions. Did he find her gauche, stupid, impertinent? She tried to retain her composure.

He asked her to walk up and down the room, to lean on the mantelpiece, to refill his glass. He seemed, like an impresario, to be considering her suitability for some unspecified role.

"You are very mysterious, Monsieur. I have the impression that you are thinking of selling me into slavery and are debating how much you should ask."

"To the contrary; I am debating whether I should rescue you from slavery. It would depend largely on your capacity for discretion."

He rose; he was omnipotent.

"I will tell you one thing; you will never succeed at any ordinary occupation."

"What other occupations are there?"

By the time he returned to his desk, he had apparently made up his mind.

"I will take care of your financial needs for three months. During that time I will ask you not to go riding in the afternoons where you might meet people you know or to frequent places where you might be recognized. In fact I want you to disappear. If what I have in mind comes to pass I will let you know. Meanwhile I should be grateful if you do not mention this meeting to anyone except your friend Leonide."

He rang a small bell. The interview was over.

"But why," she had asked Leonide, "should the Duc de Morny take an interest in me? If it were you, I could understand."

"Oh, de Morny has done me a few favors and I have done him a few. Be patient, Therese. If anyone can open the door to a new life, it is he."

"But why? I'm no one."

"That is evidently not his opinion. He has an absolute instinct about anyone who can be useful to him. Do what he tells you and wait and see."

She heard nothing further. She might have concluded that he had forgotten about her, but her rent had been duly paid and she had received an envelope containing some money "for current expenses." There were no further invitations from Leonide.

Sophie tactfully refrained from referring to the mode of life she assumed that Therese was leading. She had hoped that one of her admirers would recognize her qualities and set her up on a permanent basis or even marry her, but with each visit she detected a hardening, a disdain, that she knew was not conducive to lasting attachments. A man was not likely to support a woman who despised him. That was the problem; Therese was superior and men were mostly inferior and did not care to be reminded of it. Antoine had been right. Antoine had always been right. Sophie regretted him more and more.

"You know," she confessed, "I've been thinking of making a change. I've had this shop twenty years and I've saved some money. I've a fancy to go to the Midi. I like the sun and the people are pleasant. I can always earn a living because I'm a good pâtissière. If the idea appeals to you, you'd be welcome to come along. At your age you never know what might happen. You might find a husband with a good business and a nice farmhouse with olive trees."

"Thank you, dear Sophie. It sounds wonderful. We'll see."

They both knew it would not come to pass. Truth to tell, despite their affection for each other, their meetings were saddening. They could not help being reminded of the men they had cruelly lost.

They went down to the shop where Sophie filled a box with her charming confections.

"They're nice to nibble on with a cup of coffee." As she arranged, with her natural artistry, the Baisers Sucrés, the Doucets de Lyons, some éclairs and Mille Feuilles, she admitted, "My pastry is not what it was. It lacks élan. But then I don't have the inspiration I had." She thought of Antoine nibbling crumbs from her breast and sighed.

At the door they kissed and embraced.

"You know, my dear, as long as I have a roof over my head—"

Therese kissed her friend again. Such simple kindness was rare in the world as she was beginning to understand it.

Sophie watched her as she walked away with her strong, proud stride. What was it Monsieur Henri had called her? A young Diana. It pained her to think that such an exceptional creature should have been victimized by a scurrilous schemer like Casimir Fabre-Marquet.

Among the young men about town who were savoring the diverse pleasures of the City of Light was a young Portuguese, the Marquis Manoel de Païva. He came from old but impoverished stock and, through family connections, had been appointed third secretary at the Portuguese Embassy, a post which gave him plenty of time for diversion and just enough money to spend too much.

He was a pleasant enough gadabout, not so different from many others, except that he was possessed by a single passion. Manoel no longer thought of his diplomatic career, of his family or friends. He was a Faustus who had sold his soul to the Demon of Baccarat.

He gambled incessantly for stakes far beyond his means. As he plunged deeper and deeper into debt he took greater and greater risks. An occasional spurt of good luck rekindled his enthusiasm to make back all he had lost; and when he almost succeeded, his imagination soared to dizzying prospects of winning a fortune, after which he swore by all that was holy, by his mother's sacred memory, he would stop.

As with all compulsive gambling, losses and gains were incidental to the electrifying moment when he and his fate were joined on the flick of a card. Time stops. Identity vanishes. God and Creation are wiped from space. The hand turns. The card falls. Reality crashes onto a green baize cloth.

In between the hours of oblivion at the card table, he suffered agonies of remorse. There were days at a time when he never appeared at the Embassy and, when he tried to discharge his duties, he could think of nothing but sequences of cards. His life rocketed between red and black.

He was summoned before the Ambassador, a distant cousin of his father's, and reprimanded for dereliction of duty. Chastened, he struggled for a week against the terrible but divine temptation, nagged by the conviction that he was wasting an opportunity to make millions. He felt in his bones that luck was with him and that he was denying the obvious promptings of destiny.

He borrowed a large sum and hurried back to the gaming club near the Palais Royal.

Like Alexander the Great, possessed by a power that would enable him to conquer the world, Manoel lost everything in a single game.

He was wiped out.

He left the club with nothing but the icy knowledge that at last he was free from the tyranny of hope. He had no conceivable means of paying his mountainous debts.

He wandered about the streets wondering what alternative to blowing his brains out remained. To ask his father to pay his debts, which the old man as a point of honor would try to do, would reduce his family to penury and deprive his sisters of their modest dowries. He had sold or pawned everything he possessed. The full horror of his position stalked him like a phantom. He walked aimlessly about the streets cursing his madness in succumbing to a vice which had robbed him of everything and given him nothing but a few hours of futile excitement. Unlike a man who has ruined himself for a woman, he did not even have the consolation of happy memories.

He was young. He had no inclination to die. He was tormented by thoughts of the happy and prosperous life he might have had if he had capitalized on his opportunities and applied himself to his profession. The Ambassador had shown him kindness and encouraged him. He had been introduced into circles where he might have made an advantageous marriage. The bright vistas that could have opened before him were now inexorably shut behind bars of iron.

He found himself walking beside the river. Was this the simplest solution? To open his lungs to that rush of polluted water and allow himself to be dragged down and carried away with the rest of the refuse of the city? The trouble was that he was an expert swimmer. To poison himself in his lodgings would cause a scandal and death by poison was painful. Blow his brains out? He had pawned his pistols.

Perhaps his guardian angel, who had been unavailingly wringing its hands for the past few months, guided his steps to Leonide Leblanc's. He had been taken to one of her parties and had struck up an acquaintance with this charming and worldly woman. Manoel de Païva was of no personal interest to Leonide. He was neither rich nor prominent enough. But she occasionally invited him when she needed an extra man. He was titled, well-mannered and attached to an embassy.

Manoel never knew what prompted him to ring her doorbell on that particular night except that, in a vague way, she represented life, achievement, success, everything that he had thrown away on the turn of a few cards.

She was having a party and welcomed him with her usual warmth. Her drawing room was filled with clever, seductive women and ambitious, affluent men. Later, as the gathering thinned, Leonide found him in the dining room staring gloomily into an empty champagne glass. It was the symbol of his wasted life.

"What is the matter, Manoel? You look downhearted."

He nodded somberly.

"I was wondering how one makes a tactful exit when one has reached the end."

She refilled his glass and sat down beside him.

"My dear boy, if you knew how many times I have reached the end! Only it never is quite the end. There is always a way out."

"Not for me. This time the curtain has fallen."

"The curtain comes down on one play and goes up on another. What has happened?"

He told her. She asked in her practical way, "How much do you owe?"

He named a sum.

"It's a lot, but not monumental."

"It is, if one hasn't a penny."

She contemplated him for a moment.

"Would you consider a proposition?"

"What proposition?"

"You have one asset which you did not lose at baccarat. Your title."

"What of it?"

"Would you be prepared to part with it—under the right terms?"

"How could I—unless I married?"

"Precisely."

"Who would marry me in the condition I'm in?"

Leonide stood up abruptly. "Don't blow your brains out tonight. I might—I just might—be able to arrange something."

"You think some old frump with a fortune would pay my debts just to become a marquise?"

"Not necessarily an old frump."

"It's a disgusting idea. I may be bankrupt but I have some pride."

"The poor have no pride, my dear, and the dead have less. Come and see me tomorrow at two o'clock."

"It's not worth it, Leonide. I have made a mess of my life; I must pay the price."

"Spare me the mock heroics. You've got into a scrape, let

me see if I can get you out of it." He started to protest, but she silenced him by offering him her hand. "Tomorrow. At two o'clock."

With a rush and rustle of silk she rejoined her guests.

When, the next afternoon, he was shown into Leonide's drawing room he was taken aback to find her alone with a young woman of remarkable beauty. She was more than beautiful, she was patrician.

"This is a friend of mine," he heard Leonide say, "who might be interested in the proposal I made last night."

Manoel was so nonplussed he could only say, "You can't be serious. Mademoiselle would have no difficulty in marrying anyone she chose."

"It isn't a question of marriage. It's a business transaction, as I thought I explained."

The object of the transaction was not even looking at him. She was staring, abashed, at the carpet. Perhaps because the last twenty-four hours had heightened his awareness of pain, he saw in her face a profound sadness. It was the same bleak isolation he had experienced the previous night during his wanderings about the city.

"I wouldn't consider it," he said. "Mademoiselle is young and beautiful. I'm sure she has other dreams than simply to marry for a title."

The young woman looked up. Her extraordinary eyes confirmed his impression that she found this meeting acutely embarrassing.

"Thank you," she said. "I understand that you're in trouble; I am, too, in another way."

It flashed through his mind that she was pregnant and was looking for a man to give her child a name.

"The terms of the agreement," Leonide said in a businesslike way, "would be that, in return for a settlement of your debts, you would marry this young lady—in a civil ceremony—so that if, at some future date, either of you want a divorce it would not be hard to obtain. You would return to Portugal. Your fare would be paid to Lisbon with a sum sufficient to tide you over until you're on your feet again. You and your wife would not see each other again."

The baldness of these details appalled him. He looked at his prospective bride for confirmation. She looked away.

"And you—you would agree to this?"

She nodded slowly.

"Why? I don't understand. I simply do not understand how anyone with your looks, with your obvious qualities—"

The young woman sighed and stood up. She faced him as though they were two people who found each other in the same prison awaiting trial for a similar offense.

"Do my motives matter? This isn't the kind of situation we would either of us have chosen."

"I'm forced to ask you; are you with child? Is that the reason for this incredible offer?"

"It has nothing to do with that."

Manoel laughed. He was surprised to hear himself laugh after the events of the last twelve hours.

"Then I consider it absurd. I thought you'd be a middle-aged widow with a fortune inherited from a chocolate manufacturer who wanted to break into society."

Leonide was getting impatient. "Look, Manoel, do you want to get out of the mess you're in or don't you? I'll leave you to decide."

She swept out of the room.

Manoel went to the unwilling victim about to be sacrificed on Heaven knows what profane altar and took her hand. "But why? Why should you think of this?"

She withdrew her hand. "It isn't my wish. It's to do with other people. You don't need to consider me. Certain things have happened to me and I would prefer other things to happen."

"It sounds like a real conspiracy. Who's behind it? Leonide?"

"It doesn't matter. I'm sorry," she added in a low voice, "that you should find yourself in this position."

His sympathy for this girl, enmeshed in some intrigue of which she evidently had misgivings, relieved his conscience to some degree. Nonetheless, for form's sake, he felt impelled to ask, "Is it something dishonorable? You understand that I can't lend my name—"

"You mean am I going to defraud someone—?" she replied unhappily. "No. Nothing quite in that way." She thought for a moment and then admitted, "They think if I were established—"

"But what do they want of you?"

"Oh—to act as a hostess—to listen. They move in very high circles."

It was useless to try and explain what she herself did not fully understand. She turned with a flash of those unique and disturbing eyes. "It's yourself you must think of. What else can you do?"

They were indeed in the same prison with only this nefarious means of purchasing a reprieve. It occurred to him that under different circumstances he would have jumped at the chance to marry this lost and distinguished girl who would have fitted perfectly into the feudal formalities of Portuguese life.

"Well—if it will help you—"

"Don't do it on my account. I am only a means to an end."

She moved away and stood with her back to him, uncertain and ashamed.

"If you agree—will you come here tomorrow—at eleven? It can all be done here. I will have the money."

He stared at her back as if it were an inscription in hieroglyphs on the wall of an Eygptian tomb.

"I don't even know your name."

She said in the same low, troubled tone, "I am Therese Lachmann."

He appeared for this strangest of ceremonies to find Leonide dressed for once rather severely and Therese Lachmann, the catspaw of schemes in high places, sitting on a sofa with downcast eyes. She was wearing a plain gray dress, with only a ruby ring for adornment and her wonderful iridescent hair pulled back from her forehead. She was deathly pale.

In another part of the room two musty nonentities, minions

of officialdom, were conversing in a secretive fashion over a ledger, open between them like the Book of Judgment.

Manoel felt profoundly depressed by this parody of an event intended to inspire the greatest joy and the highest ideals. There was no question of loving and cherishing in sickness and in health, or vows of eternal fidelity. It was like drawing up the terms for a loan from a moneylender

Leonide pulled herself together. "Well, let's get on with it." She called out in a harsh voice that betrayed her humble origins, "Toinette! We're ready."

Her maid bustled in. She had been mending a torn petticoat and had a small pincushion on a velvet band around her neck from which dangled a long pink thread. For some reason Manoel's attention became riveted to this incongruous object.

Therese and he stood side by side like condemned prisoners while one of the dingy officials hurried through the formalities. He had peculiar eyebrows, Manoel noted, like the bristles of an English terrier. He had had such a dog as a boy, named Wellington. Who would have thought that twenty years later he would be marrying a stranger in order to pay his debts?

"The ring," the official said with a testy snap of his fingers.

Manoel had given no thought to a ring. Leonide exclaimed, "Wait a minute." She swooped down the room and extracted a gold ring from a box in which she kept throat pastilles.

The ring was laid on the page of the textbook from which the official had been reading. Manoel was conscious of having nodded and said yes several times, and was aware that the girl at his side had done likewise.

"The ring," the official repeated, vexed that Manoel should betray such ignorance of procedure.

Manoel picked up the ring and slid it onto Therese's finger. She had very fine hands, stronger and more capable than were usual in a woman.

The official shut the book with a snap and said briskly, "Sign the register."

Manoel signed his name. Was this his name? Did all these patronymics belong to him? Manoel Jorge Enrigo Castelmare de Montefacenza Obrador de Païva; it seemed an interminable imposture.

He handed the pen to his bride. She wrote quickly, "Therese Lachmann."

Leonide signed in a florid hand that sprawled over the place alotted to the second witness and added with a flourish: Actress. Her maid hesitated, uncertain as to where she could squeeze herself onto the page, and finally scrawled at the acute angle with which people sometimes sign photographs, "Antoinette Dax." She looked nervously up at the official. "How do I describe myself?"

"What do you do?" he demanded as though addressing the inmate of an asylum.

"I am Madame's maid."

"Write 'domestic'."

The poor woman was in a quandary. She didn't know how to spell such a difficult word.

"D-o-m-e-s-t-i-c," the official rapped out.

This feat of orthography completed, the official laid hands on the ledger and, sitting down, proceeded to fill out two copies of the marriage certificate while the bridal pair hovered in a limbo of anticlimax.

There was more signing. Manoel shortened his name to de Païva; Antoinette misspelled "domestic." Pieces of paper were exchanged and the official brought matters to an abrupt finish.

"Twenty-five francs."

Manoel hadn't a cent in his pocket. He looked 'round as mortified as though his trousers had fallen off at a court ball. Again Leonide came to the rescue, fished some notes from her bag, paid the fee and gave each of the registrars ten francs.

They accepted this gratuity as their due, folded up their equipment and departed.

It was done.

They were married without being in the slightest degree man and wife.

Manoel, in his general state of shock, had forgotten about the money, the reason for this appalling counterfeit of a wedding. The new Marquise came to life sufficiently to take a large Manila envelope from behind a cushion, and handed it to him.

"Perhaps you had better count it. I think it's the right amount."

He nodded numbly. The envelope was too big to go inside any of his pockets. He felt blindly about for some place to secret it and at last concluded that there was no alternative; he would have to carry it.

Leonide said, "Well, that's accomplished. I suppose we might as well have a glass of champagne."

A bottle had been on ice on a corner table.

"Will you open it, Manoel?"

Like a sleepwalker he struggled with the cork which suddenly shot through his fingers. A foaming flood inundated his legs. It was the final mortification. He looked and felt as though he had burst his bladder.

He was on the point of tears as they filled the glasses.

"There's a towel in the bathroom," Leonide said. "For once I can't think of an appropriate toast. Oh, to the end of what's over and the beginning of what's to come. That's as good as anything."

She gulped down the champagne and announced, "I must go. I'm late for rehearsal."

Manoel felt a sudden distaste for this woman whose worldliness had become so brazen. It was far from the first sordid transaction over which she had presided.

The new Marquise was standing uncertainly in the middle of the room, waiting for him to go so that it could all be over and done with.

For some reason, dazed, damp and dishonored as he was, he felt sorry for her.

"Well, I suppose—" he began lamely.

"Don't forget this." She handed him the envelope for the second time.

He wanted to say something to alleviate their mutual discomfiture, but there was nothing appropriate. She followed him politely into the hall.

At the door he came to the surface sufficiently to say, "Look here, Therese. It's all quite insane. I don't know anything about you or what your situation really is or why you went through with this, but we are officially married. I'm not such a bad sort apart from my gambling and I think I've been cured of that. I've got the money to clear off my debts. Why don't you come with me?"

"Where to?" she asked blankly.

"Home. It's true that we're strangers, but not any more so than if this were an arranged marriage. Why involve yourself with all these intrigues?"

A strange expression came into her eyes. Their glassy distance softened. He saw that she was much younger than he had imagined.

"How old are you?" he asked.

"Twenty-one."

"I'm twenty-seven. We have both, no doubt, made mistakes. Why don't you cut free? You have a legitimate excuse. You can say that your husband insisted."

She made a sad little movement of her head. "You don't understand—I am not respectable."

"Well, I'm not either for that matter. We could call a moratorium on all that has happened to both of us. Once we're away from Paris—"

He saw that for a moment she was tempted.

"You must go home where you belong," she said more sensibly. "I don't know where I belong. Perhaps one day I shall find out."

She opened the door.

On the threshold he took out his wallet and extracted a visiting card.

"It seems a bit strange to leave a card on one's wife. If you change your mind—"

She looked at the card as though she could in no way relate to the name inscribed on it.

She nodded and said softly, "Goodbye."

The door closed between him and the woman who bore his name.

As she was leaving for her rehearsal, Leonide, finding the drawing room empty, assumed that Therese had left.

She was pulling on her gloves in the foyer when she heard a choking sound from the dining room.

The Marquise de Païva was sitting at the table with her head in her hands sobbing as though her heart would break.

A short while afterward a new occupant moved into Number Twenty-two Chaussée d'Iena.

It was a strangely designed house which had, for some reason, stopped short of becoming a mansion like a novel abandoned after the opening chapters.

An imposing front door opened into a spacious hall, the ceiling of which rose to the roof. Descending from the upper floor was a sweeping staircase with a fine wrought iron balustrade. On the right of the hall was a dining room where sixty guests could comfortably be seated. It looked out at the back onto a narrow and sunless garden with a few mournful statues but no trees. On one side an ell extended containing a kitchen, scullery and servants' quarters. Above the dining room was an equally vast salon, handsomely paneled, with an ornate mantelpiece of red marble. On this floor were also a small sitting room, a bedroom, and a bath, the windows of which looked out across the garden at a blank wall, broken by a window and a door. This led to a capacious carriagehouse with stabling for a team of horses. It was difficult to imagine for what purpose this truncated residence had been built, unless its designer, in a fit of precognition, had guessed that it would one day be occupied by the Marquise de Païva.

She moved in with a great many fine furnishings belonging to her husband who was unfortunately detained in Lisbon on family business. The salon glowed in the soft light of Chinese lamps and an immense Venetian chandelier. Red velvet curtains, Boulle cabinets, gilt sofas and fauteuils upholstered in rich brocades, deep Oriental carpets, combined to create an ambiance of luxury which, if it lacked the charming impulses and mistakes which add charm to a feminine interior, was nonetheless impressive in the manner of an official reception room at an embassy.

Over the mantelpiece was a life-size portrait of an elderly

gentleman of aristocratic appearance. "My father-in-law," the Marquise would casually explain.

The rumor that some connection existed between the Marquise and the Duc de Morny arose, not from those purlieus of pleasure where Therese Lachmann was seen no more, but from the circle of diplomats and politicians who were initially invited to Number Twenty-two by the duke himself and who thereafter availed themselves of the Marquise's hospitality. They were inclined to believe that de Morny was, as he said, a friend of the family who had been designated by the Marquis de Païva to keep an eye on his stately young wife during his absence. The duke's manner toward her was cordial, but distinctly avuncular. From all that was known of this suave debauchée, the Marquise was hardly his type. He preferred innocent young girls he could mold to his tastes. He discovered them and discarded them with equal ease. He was considerate. When he tired of a mistress he married her off to an Army captain or a minor government official. The husbands were flattered and the wives relieved.

If something existed between him and his new protégé, the friends he introduced to the Chaussée d'Iena—"because she knows few people in Paris and needs some distraction"—were prepared to accept it. The Marquise was beautiful, dignified and unobtrusive. If her manner of life seemed unusual, she was under the powerful protection of the Gray Eminence of the Second Empire who did not waste his patronage on nonentities. In that glittering masquerade few people were what they seemed; and success, especially in politics, was seldom achieved by adhering to moral principles, even supposing that ambitious men had any to begin with. The Marquise was acceptable on her own account. She had a handsome home, sufficient means to maintain it, and seemed happy to receive men of some account in the world. Her buffet was excellent and she had no aversion to gambling. There were always two tables set up for baccarat for those who preferred cards to conversation.

In due course, no doubt at de Morny's suggestion, she was presented at court and was graciously received by the Empress. The Emperor conversed with her for a few moments. She was also on friendly terms with the Duc d'Aumale who represented the anti-Bonapartist end of the social spectrum, a fact which did not seem to disturb de Morny. If she did not gain a foothold in the Faubourg St. Germain because her antecedents remained, like her husband, a mystery, she was soon established on neutral ground of her own. Men who were anxious to be on good terms with de Morny were only too glad to partake of her quails in aspic, her Terrine de Foie Gras, her Truffles Blancs Sauce Périgueux, and to drink her liberal supply of champagne. There was a relaxed atmosphere to her Open House that was very agreeable. It was not long before the Marquise's circle was enlarged by friends and friends of friends of those originally introduced by de Morny.

The coterie liked and respected their hostess while doubting her authenticity. Her tact and intelligence, her unflirtatious cordiality, did much to mitigate the questionable nature of her establishment. She was an excellent listener and never interrupted a discussion on some political crisis of the moment. She was, she declared, a serious student of world affairs.

The only woman who appeared at Number Twenty-two was Leonide Leblanc who occasionally swept in after a performance in a great swirl of furs and feathers, bringing into that serious atmosphere a welcome *frisson* from the boulevards. The relationship between this grande cocotte whose reputation had long passed the point of being reprehensible and the young Marquise only added to the general mystery. They would retire to the small sitting room where they could be glimpsed through the open door with their heads together. If some gentleman should knock and inquire if he might join them, Leonide would break off their sisterly confidences with a ripple of that famous laughter that enchanted Parisian audiences. Was there something between them? Was there something between the Marquise and de Morny? After all, did it matter? In a civilized society it was only what appeared above the surface that counted, and what appeared above the surface at Number Twenty-two supplied a need.

If the habitués were prepared to overlook the ambiguities that surrounded the Marquise, they stopped short of inviting her to their homes. They hedged on this delicate issue until her husband returned or until some established social figure should make the first move. The fact that she had been presented at court was not sufficient proof of acceptability. A lot of unacceptable people were presented, for reasons of money or expedience or because it suited the Emperor or de Morny. Meanwhile men harassed by the demands of their professions, grateful to escape the importunities of their wives and mistresses and bored with the formality of their clubs, were glad to drop by at the Marquise's for a quiet respite. She made no demands, asked no favors and never tried to insinuate herself on a personal level. She seemed genuinely gratified to receive men whose company she found worth cultivating and, with good grace, accepted the gifts they brought in lieu of invitations, flowers, books and perfume and game from country estates.

Her official entry into society was brought about by the Empress herself with an invitation to a garden party at St. Cloud.

The Marquise made a distinct impression by the simple elegance of her dress and the cool restraint of her manner. She wore a severe gown of gray silk with a modest crinoline and one green jewel at her breast. A wide-brimmed Leghorn hat with green ribbons cast an intriguing shadow over her marble pallpur in which her amazing eyes gleamed like a cat's. There was an aura of mystery about her which caused heads to turn and questions to be asked. The Empress who, whatever her shortcomings in other areas, was an expert on matters of dress, complimented the Marquise and asked her the name of her couturier.

"I designed it myself, Madame," the Marquise modestly confessed.

"Then you have excellent taste."

"Coming from you that is indeed a compliment," the Marquise replied with a deep curtsey.

Eugenie thought her decidedly decorative. A trifle intellectual perhaps, but a possible addition to her circle. Her grave beauty was further enhanced by the fact that she was not the kind of young woman with whom the Emperor was likely to become enamored.

"I hope that we shall see more of you, now that we have made your acquaintance," the Empress said with a graceful inclination of her head.

With this seal of official approval the Marquise made her way into that section of society that gravitated about the court. Rumors of an involvement with de Morny were more or less silenced when, at a reception, he introduced her to his wife who was known to be insanely jealous. No one who invited her to dinners or musicales had any cause to regret it. She behaved with the utmost decorum. Only the wives of the Empress' circle murmured among themselves, Oh, the so-called Marquise looked well enough, but wasn't she a trifle too— well, how could one put it?—weren't there just too many questions that remained unanswered? She wasn't apparently kept—but who, then, supplied the money? She was ostensibly married, but where was her husband? She lived alone and went about unescorted. She purported to have a salon to which only men were invited and yet, if one could believe one's husband, and naturally, on the score of women, one couldn't, nothing in the least untoward took place. There was conversation, mostly about politics—and a little card playing. It was all entirely respectable.

If it was all so respectable, there could only be one explanation; she must be some kind of spy. But for whom? De Morny? Why should the President du Conseil, with the whole Secret Service to call on, employ that young woman to gather information?

It didn't make sense. Nothing about the Marquise quite made sense, except that she was, however one looked at it, whatever allowances one made, somehow *louche*, suspicious, controversial.

These ladies warned their husbands to be on their guard. At the same time they were very polite. It was just within the bounds of possibility that the Marquise was just what she seemed.

Inevitably, as she moved into these circles, Therese encountered her erstwhile lovers. Lord Stanley was very surprised to discover that the enigmatic girl he had, to his regret, seduced had risen so rapidly in the world. Gramont-Caderousse cut her dead at the races and the Viscomte de Persigny twisted himself into a corkscrew of disapproval when he found himself seated at the same dinner table. He loudly proclaimed next day at the Jockey Club the indignity of including a tart at a supposedly civilized gathering. The fact that she was received at court was only a further proof of the social laxity of the Napoleonides who were, after all, hardly more than upstarts themselves.

If all these rumors caused certain doors to remain closed to her, events at the Chaussée d'Iena confirmed the curious validity of her position.

There was the incident of Leon Gambetta.

The most articulate anti-Bonapartist in France, a passionate republican who seldom missed an opportunity for denouncing the régime and who on many occasions had expressed his contempt for the insidious influence of de Morny, was ushered into the dining room of Number Twenty-two to the astonishment of several gentlemen who were chatting around the table in the casual manner of the house.

They thought the Marquise had committed a faux pas that would cost her dearly. But she appeared as composed as ever and introduced Gambetta as if there were nothing out of the ordinary in receiving a man who had openly accused de Morny of every public offense from nepotism to the misappropriation of public funds.

Gambetta seemed a trifle bewildered to find himself in the house of a young woman he mistook for an aristocrat. She was particularly gracious and made him up a plate of her quails in aspic and poured him a glass of champagne. Gambetta was a man of the people, not used to being fussed over by society ladies, and accepted these attentions awkwardly. He proceeded from nervousness to enlarge on the preparations for the Great Exhibition designed to enhance the prestige of France in the eyes of the rest of Europe. All the crowned heads—whom personally he could do without—were planning state visits to view the marvels of French technology, including the Palace of Electricity and the Hall of Agricultural Inventions. They were building an Egyptian village in honor of the Khedive and a mock Scottish castle with attendants in kilts, murdering Parisian eardrums with national airs on the bagpipes, as a compliment to the English queen. As he munched away at the quail his audience devoutly prayed that de Morny would not put in an appearance. Gambetta had given him repeated grounds for a duel.

"Over a million foreigners will pour into Paris. A tremendous boost for trade, we are told, and a tremendous strain on our security forces. It's to be hoped that our industrialists will take the hint and make a few concessions to the workers. It would look better if our visitors are greeted with fireworks and not barricades."

The door opened. The temperature dropped to zero as de Morny walked in.

He was superbly impassive with the coiled menace of a cobra. The other gentlemen held their breaths for the explosion, the exchange of insults, The Incident.

"Monsieur Gambetta."

Gambetta stood up. With a mouth full of quail he mumbled something and the two arch-rivals bowed to each other across the table.

"May I get you something?" the Marquise inquired. "The quail you so kindly sent are delicious."

"Thank you, I've already dined. But I will take a glass of champagne."

"Monsieur Gambetta has been telling us about the preparations for the Great Exhibition," the Marquise said smoothly. "It seems the only thing missing is a harem for the Sultan of Turkey. Will that be provided?"

"We intend to supply our visitors with every amenity," de Morny replied.

"What an opportunity for the Countess de Castiglione," Gambetta said, returning to his quail.

It was a calculated insult as the whole of Paris knew of the torrid affair the Emperor was having with that lady.

"The position is already spoken for," the Marquise put in

with a laugh. "I've always fancied myself heavily veiled, surrounded by Nubian eunuchs. You won't disappoint me, will you, Monsieur de Morny?"

"What news of your husband?" de Morny asked abruptly, his voice gray and heavy as lead.

"I heard from him yesterday. It seems that at last those tedious negotiations may finally be settled."

"I am glad to hear it. It's been a great privation for you to be separated so soon after your marriage."

The Marquise turned to the others. They were awed by the ease with which she was handling an explosive situation.

"There's a table ready for cards if you feel like a game. Otherwise I shall have to quiz you on ancient Greek. I'm teaching myself, you know, so that I can read the classics in the original."

She piloted them out of the room like a gaggle of willing geese.

As they followed her upstairs they were listening for the raised voices, the pistol shot. The dining room was silent as the grave.

"I must say," Freddie Avondale, an attaché at the British Embassy, exclaimed, "no one but you could have carried off such a meeting. You were superb."

"Oh, but Monsieur de Morny is very broad-minded. He likes to meet people of different opinions. That's why he's a great administrator," the Marquise blandly explained.

"And that's why you're in this house," Freddie thought as he sat down at the card table. "Shall we have a game of whist?"

The Honorable Freddie Avondale, youngest son of the Earl of Mount Drago, had been introduced to the Marquise by another young diplomat from the Netherlands. It was useful, his friend assured him, to frequent the Marquise's "At Homes" because "one occasionally heard things" and one was never certain who one might meet there. Contacts were made.

Freddie had developed a brotherly regard for Therese which, had she not been overshadowed by a Certain Great Personage, he might have allowed to develop onto a more personal plane.

Freddie admired her. He thought her beautiful. He was also sorry for her because her life, as far as he was able to understand it, seemed so unnatural. She apparently had no family and no female friends, if one excepted Leonide Leblanc who came to the Chaussée, Freddie surmised, for other reasons. He had heard rumors about Manoel de Païva's sudden departure from Paris which did not tally with Therese's story of protracted family business in Lisbon. He did not believe in her marriage. He did not believe that anything in the house belonged to her. He definitely did not believe in the imposing gentleman over the mantelpiece. She was, in some way, the dupe of intrigues from which, had his circumstances been different, he might, from sheer gallantry, have been willing to rescue her.

Freddie was a pleasant young man, anxious to acquit himself well in his profession. He was pleasant-looking in an unmistakable English way, country-cheeked, fair-haired with mild blue eyes. He had pleasant manners and pleasant intentions and combined in his nature the practicality and romanticism that were making the British masters of an empire on which the sun was not to be permitted to set. He thought that Therese would make an excellent wife for an ambassador which he intended one day to become, but his practical side warned him that for a variety of reasons she was definitely out of reach.

The night following Gambetta's visit, as Freddie turned off the Champs-Élysées into the Chaussée, he observed a cab drawing up before the Marquise's door. Thinking that this might be one of her circle he hurried forward so that they might enter together. He was taken aback when a squat little gentleman, bundled in a greatcoat with a fur collar and further concealed by a battered black hat and a bristling beard and whiskers, alighted from the cab, paid the driver and rang the Marquise's bell.

By this time Freddie had reached the door. He scrutinized the visitor, unable to believe that he could be who he thought. The plump little person looked at him with two round blue eyes, bright with energy and mischief. He was unmistakable.

The door was opened by the Marquise herself. She glanced at Freddie with the faintest flicker of apprehension and said to the visitor, "Please come in, Monsieur." Ths visitor stepped into the hall. As Freddie was about to follow, the Marquise barred the way.

"I'm sorry. I am not receiving this evening. Perhaps tomorrow."

She shut the door quietly, but firmly, in Freddie's face.

That Mikail Bakunin, the mouthpiece of Anarchy, one of the most dreaded revolutionaries in Europe, who had been involved in an attempt on the Czar's life and had incited riots and written inflammatory manifestos during the uprisings of '48, both in Paris and Dresden, should call on the Marquise under cover of darkness, seemed to Freddie a matter of the utmost significance. Instead of retracing his steps to the Champs-Élysées he crossed the street and concealed himself in a doorway. He was determined to find out for whose benefit a meeting with this notorious agitator had been arranged.

He did not have long to wait. A carriage turned into the Chaussée and drew up before Number Twenty-two. Before its occupant could get out, a man stepped from the recess of the doorway to the Marquise's stables and said something through the window. The carriage proceeded on its way.

To Freddie's dismay the sentinel stepped into the street and walked rapidly toward the embrasure in which he was hiding. Freddie decided that it would be expedient to beat a hasty retreat. As he turned toward the boulevard, the man broke into a run and hailed him.

"One moment, Monsieur."

Freddie stopped. The man had that conspicuous anonymity that marked him as a functionary of the police.

"May I ask what you were doing in that doorway?"

Like most honest people when confronted with the law, Freddie instantly felt that he had been caught committing a felony. "I am a friend of the lady who lives at Number Twenty-two," he said lamely. "I wanted to see who was calling on her at this hour."

"May I see your identity papers?"

"By what right—?" Freddie demanded, his face crimson with guilt.

"I am from the Sûreté," the man informed him.

"I don't carry papers. I work at the British Embassy." He took a visiting card from his wallet and handed it to the detective who lit a match to examine it.

"I suggest that you proceed on your way. It is not advisable to lurk in doorways after dark. The police cannot always protect you."

Freddie held out his hand for the card, but the detective slipped it into his pocket.

There was no purpose in having an argument. With as much composure as he could muster Freddie proceeded toward the boulevard.

He recounted the incident next day to his ambassador, Lord Houghton.

"Are you sure it was Bakunin? It seems most unlikely that he would dare to set foot in France."

"There was no mistaking him, sir. I've seen his picture a dozen times."

"Interesting. Strange. I thought he was living at Putney. I never quite understood why he was granted asylum in England, except that I suppose it's wiser to keep firebrands under surveillance. I shall certainly make inquiries."

"What is, I think, *very* interesting and *very* strange is what the Duc de Morny could possibly have to say to a man who is the archenemy of his régime."

"Perhaps it might have something to do with the Great Exhibition and the visits of so many crowned heads. It's a potential field day for anarchists."

"If Bakunin is planning to throw another bomb at the Czar he'd hardly tell de Morny about it."

"Unless—" The Ambassador swiveled slowly in his chair. "Unless it was something—not pertaining to France."

"Germany, you mean?"

"Very strange." The Ambassador regarded Freddie in a remotely paternal way. "Who exactly *is* the Marquise de Païva?"

"She's a young woman of considerable beauty who seems to be under de Morny's protection."

"One of his mistresses?"

"I don't think so, sir. She's married to a Portuguese who used to work at the embassy here. He left Paris suddenly for unexplained reasons. My impression is that de Morny uses her house as a place where he can meet people it would be awkward for him to meet elsewhere."

"You know her well?"

"I don't think anyone knows her well. She receives in the evenings in an informal way. I thought there was something— well, equivocating about her from the start. It's difficult to explain. She's charming and intelligent, but her whole manner of life—"

"Who pays her bills?"

"Ostensibly she has means of her own or her husband has. She's received at court."

"That's hardly a proof of respectability." The Ambassador smiled. "Without compromising yourself, it might be a good idea if you continue to see her. If you find out anything more by all means come and tell me." He scribbled a note on his pad. "Meanwhile I'll find out if Bakunin is still at Putney. Wherever that man is there's always bound to be trouble."

The Marquise did not refer to this incident when Freddie next appeared at her house.

He thought she looked weary and out of sorts and that her nightly At Homes were becoming a strain.

"You look tired, Marquise."

"I need to get out more," she confessed. "I'd like to buy a horse so that I could go riding when I feel inclined. It's such a bother hiring a hack from the stables."

"There are auctions, you know, where you might find one that suited you. I'll be happy to make inquiries."

"Would you?"

"I'll go with you, if you'll allow me. I know a bit about horses. We hunt quite a lot at home."

"You're lucky, you English," she said with a trace of sadness. "Always so amiable and sensible and settled. Sometimes I hate Paris. People are so insincere."

"Why do you stay here? Wouldn't you be happier in Portugal with your husband?"

"Oh, my husband—!"

It was as close as she ever came to admitting that her marriage was part of the charade.

Therese's life was far stranger than Freddie Avondale imagined.

At nine in the morning two maids appeared who cleared up the debris of the night before, cleaned, scrubbed, polished and put everything in order. They left at noon. At five-thirty a footman-butler arrived and at six a chef who added the finishing touches to the cold dishes sent in from the Café Anglais. At seven Therese dressed. She then waited for whatever guests might choose to appear. Often no one showed up before ten o'clock. Once started, the baccarat upstairs and the discussions downstairs continued till two or three. Therese was forced to remain up in order to perform her role as hostess. From nine to five-thirty her life was a void.

She was aware that the footman-butler had been planted in the house to spy on her and that he, too, sent in reports "To Whom It May Concern."

She had no real position in de Morny's world. The coterie came to the house for reasons other than to see her. She was invited out for reasons other than her company. She was an employee whose activities were less strictly defined than the servants', a puppet whose strings were manipulated for motives not always clear. She received whom she was instructed to receive and relayed gossip that she was instructed to relay. The bills were paid by a firm of lawyers who sent her a dress allowance and a salary that was less than generous.

Her life was a performance in a play that might close at any moment at the whim of the manager.

She had learned certain things in the eighteen months during which she had presided over Number Twenty-two. She had learned that it is easy not to tell the truth and that, even when others knew she was lying, her lies were accepted as social barter. She had learned that men have three genuine drives— vanity, lust, and ambition; that few have scruples and that all are hypocrites. She had learned that kindness is a mask for self-interest and that there are no principles that cannot be abrogated for gain or self-protection. She saw little that was admirable in these facile and adroit climbers who upheld institutions such as marriage, religion, patriotism and political allegiance because these were the props that upheld their careers.

She saw also that these men were not hard to manipulate because they were deceived by their own cleverness and made vulnerable by ambition. They were cynics and sophists who judged the world in terms of intellectual and political abstractions. They endlessly discussed the turmoil that seethed beneath the crust of this age of affluence not in terms of human need or human suffering, but as Socialism, Radicalism, Communism, Anarchism. They supported the forces of injustice, exploitation and repression while pretending to oppose them, because it served their purpose as conservatives, capitalists, imperialists, expansionists. These were the flags they waved over the widening morass of human misery which they chose to ignore while they conspired and struggled for success.

De Morny she recognized as superior both in intellect and guile. He wielded power by dint of an ice-cold grasp of the realities of expedience. Never misled by questions of right or wrong, he was honest in that he made no pretense to honesty.

She had been impressed by Gambetta who, in a rougher, more vigorous way, *was* sincere, and fascinated by Bakunin, the aristocrat turned terrorist, who saw nothing salvageable in a world ruled by privilege and greed. He was as eager to fling bombs at the mighty as a boy to play ball in the Tuilerie gardens.

She knew that that meeting had not been arranged because of de Morny's concern for the crowned heads who intended to visit the Exhibition. His real interests were focused farther afield, on Prussia and the machinations of the Iron Chancellor, von Bismarck. There were two great threats to the Napoleonic Empire, Republicanism and Bismarck, and of the two the latter was more dangerous.

She moved through this prosperous and profligate world as an observer behind a wall of glass, surprised that so much wealth and so much power could be vested in so many trivial people.

There were surprises.

One afternoon during a garden party at St. Cloud, the Empress detached herself from the galaxy of female beauties in which she habitually shone like a moon among the stars and swept across the lawn toward Therese in a great ripple of blue silks that set off her sky-blue eyes and her chestnut-gold hair.

She was very beautiful. Her features, like Therese's, were cold and regular. Indeed they resembled each other and might have been members of the same family.

"My dear Marquise," Eugenie said with that beguiling graciousness which she used as a conscious weapon, "I have been hoping to have the opportunity of getting to know you a little better. Will you walk with me? I should like to show you my little collection of souvenirs."

She started off across the grass toward the white palace that was her favorite retreat during the summer.

"My brother-in-law de Morny has spoken of you so highly. You must not think me intrusive but I know a little of your history. Believe me, you have my greatest sympathy. I intend to do something on your behalf, but we can talk about that later."

Therese was completely taken aback by this impulsive show of interest and by the easy familiarity with which the Empress spoke to her. She followed Eugenie into the palace, through several opulent salons into a smaller room that was arranged like a museum with numbers of objects in glass cases.

Eugenie closed the door.

"This is my sanctuary. Everything in this room belonged to Marie Antoinette. People think it morbid of me to collect mementos of the unhappy queen, but I do so as a reminder. It steadies me. I come in here and I remind myself that everything can be given one, but everything can be taken away. I'm aware that I occupy the same position as she did. They called her the Austrian; they call me the Spaniard. We are equally disliked."

She made these indiscreet remarks as though she was reciting a catechism often repeated.

"Oh, Madame," Therese protested, "you should not let yourself think such things. You are much loved."

Eugenie looked at her sharply. "Not at all. They detest me. I would have liked nothing better than to win the love of the French people. I tried but I failed. The French are not warmhearted. I can say that to you because you're a foreigner. They're led astray always by their talent for dramatics. They turn everything into speeches—" Her voice dropped to a whisper. "Or guillotines."

She was moving among the relics of her unfortunate predecessor, touching them in a nostalgic way. Her fingers lingered on jeweled bonbonnières, fans, a pair of embroidered gloves, a powdered wig, court gowns on dressmaker's dummies.

"This was her spinet. She played and sang at the Petit Trianon at the simple gatherings she loved. This was her harp—and her writing desk."

She sat down at a little marquetry desk.

"Wasn't it strange; I found a love letter in a secret drawer one day. It was from Ferzen, the Swede who loved her. He was the only sincere friend she ever had. Poor queen! She understood too little before it was too late."

The Empress seemed to have forgotten that she was not alone. She spoke in a whisper, quite at variance with her usually polished tone.

"We have so few friends in our position, but perhaps, in the end, that's true of everyone." She turned and impulsively took Therese's hands.

"I have heard how much you have suffered, how greatly you have been wronged. It's important to have a truthful woman friend. I know that from experience. I know what it is to be alone. You think that strange, surrounded as I always am with people."

"You are very kind, Madame," Therese managed to say. "I don't know what I have done to deserve such consideration."

"Oh, I've watched you. I asked about you. You are very beautiful, but I don't need to tell you that."

She got up suddenly and looked 'round the sad little museum.

"Yes, we need friends." Impulsively she held out her beautiful arms to Therese. "Then it's settled? I only ask for one thing—complete sincerity. There must be no pretenses between us. You can always tell me the truth. I'm not inexperienced, you know. I give you my word; I shall always understand."

She kissed Therese on both cheeks. As she turned away, her hand glanced across Therese's breast in a way that was somehow not accidental.

"Meanwhile I'm going to put your affairs in order."

She opened the doors and sidled down the corridor like some wonderful bird of prey.

The Empress kept her word. A few days after her visit to St. Cloud, Therese received a letter from Maître Honoré de Montauban Descases, Président du Court d'Assises, Président du Conseil des Avocats, Cunseiller d'État, Chevalier du Légion d'Honneur Etc. Etc., requesting her to call at his chambers at her convenience.

He was a parchment-dry old gentleman, very gray and Gothic, with the elaborate courtliness of a bygone age. He received Therese in an impressive study overlooking the river on the Ile St. Louis, stationed behind an immense eighteenth-century desk which set the seal upon his eminence.

He permitted himself a smile as thin as whey and placed his spidery fingers together in a gesture that might or might not imply absolution.

"A certain distinguished personage has requested me to consider certain matters pertaining to financial irregularities with which I should esteem it a privilege if you would acquaint me, Madame," he intoned as though reading from a brief.

"Are you the Empress' lawyer?" Therese asked.

Maître de Montauban Descases had never in fifty years permitted himself to answer a direct question. Such an indelicacy reflected upon the arcane science of which he was an established oracle.

"Shall we say that I have been honored on certain occasions

to offer my services in matters of a confidential nature involving the distinguished personage."

Feeling as crass as a fishwife Therese told him the whole story of her relationship with Henri and of Casimir's duplicity.

Maître Honoré de Montauban listened with the inscrutable passivity of an Eastern sage. He raised an eyebrow and then lowered it.

"I am forced to say that it is not altogether a simple matter to substantiate such a claim without the requisite documentation. However, under the circumstances, it might be possible to bring, may I suggest?—certain pressure to bear."

He nodded as though he had already penetrated to the core of a labyrinth of legal technicalities, hummed like an august bee, rose and conducted Therese to the door.

Therese could find no reason for the Empress' sudden interest in her affairs. But Eugenie's motives were no more obscure than de Morny's or Leonide's or any of the other people with whom she was now involved. One could only judge them by their actions which were no more than the tips of icebergs, their real intentions being buried deep beneath the surface of a sea, now smooth and shining, now black and treacherous, according to the weather.

Two events occurred which jolted Therese out of the emotional hibernation in which she had been sunk since Henri's death.

She acquired Saladin and she met Humbert von Bernsdorff at the de Morny's costume ball.

Saladin was magnificent, a coal-black purebred Arabian, with all the pride and passion of his race. The moment Therese laid eyes on him, she knew that he must be hers.

He was making a great commotion at the auction, rearing, striking his hooves in the air, neighing and rolling wild, bloodshot eyes. An ostler was unavailingly striking him with a crop, an indignity that infuriated this prince of this desert. For a moment it looked as though the ostler would be trampled, the auctioneer's stand overturned, and the sale disrupted.

Previous owners had failed to master Saladin. He had a

vicious temper, refused to run in a team and threw the most experienced riders. As an alternative to being shot, he was once again up for sale.

It took three men to maneuver him back to the stables.

Alone in the crowd, Therese raised her hand.

"For Heaven's sake!" exclaimed Freddie Avondale. "He's not for you."

The auctioneer felt compelled to warn the young lady: "I'm forced to say, mam'selle, he's not a suitable mount for a lady."

"Please don't buy him, Therese," Freddie urged. "You'll never be able to manage him."

But Therese nodded to the auctioneer whose gavel came down with a rap. Saladin was hers.

Disregarding Freddie's pleas to reconsider, Therese pushed her way through the crowd, to the stables. Here, too, Saladin was making a great racket, kicking the slats of his stall, whinnying and tossing his head. Confinement was agony to him.

"Don't go near him," an ostler urged. "He's dangerous."

Therese went to the stall and said in a level voice, "Saladin."

Wild eyes, starting from their sockets in fear and outrage, stared at another adversary. The skin on his shoulders twitched as though a swarm of blueflies were running over it.

"Saladin."

He raised his head, trumpeted and bared his teeth. He had backed to the rear of the stall as though preparing to charge.

"You've made a dreadful mistake," Freddie said, trying to draw her away. "You'll never be able to ride him in the city— if anywhere. I do beg you to sell him back. Take anything you can get for him."

But Therese knew. There was an affinity between her and this beast rebellious against a world which had trapped them both.

She had the stable at Number Twenty-two swept and clean straw laid down. Two days later Saladin was brought to the Chaussée d'Iena in a horse van. There was the same prolonged battle as at the auction.

Two ostlers tugged and swore. Saladin resisted with all his

strength. He refused to be coerced out of the van. He was jerked, pulled and beaten, step by obdurate step, into the street.

He saw Therese in the carriage house doorway, whinnied and tried to break loose. One of the men struck him savagely across the muzzle.

"Don't hit him!" Therese cried.

She ran forward and took hold of the bridle. Saladin snorted, nostrils distended, and wrenched away his head.

"Saladin."

The black prince kicked out and reared. One of the ostlers lost his balance and fell to the ground.

It took twenty minutes to get him into the stable.

"He's a devil!" one of the ostlers said, mopping his face. "You watch out, mam'selle. He'll savage you first chance he gets."

Therese opened the carriage house door into the garden and sat down at the far end on a stone seat between two statues.

There was silence for some time and then a noisy gulping of water.

Therese waited.

She could hear Saladin clumping around in the stable. After a while he came to the open door and looked through.

"Saladin."

He hung back, alert to the danger of some fresh attack. At last he came through the door.

He stood there, apprehending the motionless figure at the other end of the enclosure.

Suddenly he reared, splendid and unconquered, as though to demonstrate that he was no more prepared to give in to her than he had been to any of the others.

She remained quite still.

He snorted, unconvinced, whisked his tail in defiance and went back into the stable.

It was the first confrontation.

She watched from her sitting room window. He did not venture into the garden again that day, but the next morning she saw him. He was measuring the confines of his new prison. He was calmer, but his ears pricked at the slightest sound.

She went into the coachhouse at noon to refill his drinking trough and prepare his feed. He was there behind her, blacker than the shadows, flexed and taut, ready for attack.

She did not approach him.

In the afternoon she resumed her silent vigil on the stone seat.

He walked with an air of cautious disdain into the garden. "Saladin."

He was not certain what she was up to. She was plotting something. A trap. Still—she hadn't raised her voice, hadn't struck him, hadn't challenged or demeaned him in any way.

He sensed her vibration. She was a threat, but of a different, more subtle kind.

He remained in his territory, awaiting developments, unwilling to concede an inch.

When she went to the stable to water and feed him, he moved with assumed indifference to the far end of the carriage house. He pretended to ignore her, permitting her to service him as he deserved.

He was becoming familiar with her quick, firm tread, with the clean smell she exuded, with her level voice. He listened acutely for any variation of the tone in which she addressed him. He was prepared for treachery.

He munched, drank and waited. He could sense when she was near.

This uneasy truce lasted for four days.

Now he was ready for something. He wanted her to reveal herself in her true colors.

He was standing at his end of the garden, flicking his tail in warning. She got up and came to him. He stiffened. The skin on his shoulders twitched.

"Saladin, tomorrow we'll go out riding. Then we'll know."

He allowed her to pat his neck. He was impatient for the test without which nothing could be settled.

Before dawn on the fifth day she put on her habit and went down to the stable. Saladin was waiting.

"We're going out. Stand still while I saddle you."

He was tense, but he knew that the moment had come. She

slung her sidesaddle across his back, strapped on the harness, put the bit between his teeth.

She led him to the carriage house door and unbolted it. He sniffed the damp silence of the dark.

He sidled, tempted to bolt. Now! To be rid of his persecutors and betrayers. He trembled. His tail thrashed in defiance. He heard the door close behind him and stood poised for flight. But her restraining hand was on the bridle. She mounted from the curbstone. He judged her weight. It suited him. He would give her a chance—just one.

She guided him into the street toward the boulevard.

The decorations for the Great Exhibition were already up. The gas lamps were festooned with garlands circling the imperial N, that symbol of glory. Flags of all nations hung from poles entwined with laurels and ribbons. These eerie forms disturbed Saladin. Things lurked and threatened under the pools of light cast by the street lights.

The Arc de Triomphe was hung with banners, emblazoned with the Imperial monogram. The golden bees of the Bonapartes swarmed over these immense lengths of blue and terracotta material. They stirred faintly in the chill air of the coming dawn.

Saladin smelled the trees.

He sidled, apprehensive of these strange surroundings, uncertain of Therese's intentions. She remained calm and firm. They made their way up the Champs-Élysées which looked in this hesitant obscurity as though it was prepared not for a celebration of the greatness of France, but for the funeral of Louis Napoleon's spurious empire.

Beyond the heroic arch was another yet larger archway into the exhibition grounds. Immense buildings, domes and spires were dimly perceivable in the shifting half light. Much remained to be done. Great concentrical flowerbeds awaited their plantings. Piles of planking still littered the wide avenue leading to the Palace of Electricity, that wonder of wonders of the modern world.

Then there were more trees, fewer shapes and the scent of open turf.

Saladin needed no further encouragement. He was impatient for movement, hungry to reassert his strength.

They cantered through the Bois de Boulogne, past dim parterres with newly erected kiosks, past phantom lakes soon to be shimmering with the spray of fountains, past a phantom bandstand from which would thunder military marches and patriotic airs.

She steered him off the road onto a stretch of open country and gave him his head. He galloped, intoxicated, no longer aware of the woman who rode him.

He raced, head straining forward, mane streaming, tail extended. The air rushed over them, invigorating as a head wind at sea. The morning poured into their lungs. The turf flew beneath them and the thudding of the hooves vibrated in their hearts. It was resurrection, apotheosis, no longer a horse and a rider, but a centauress riding to greet the dawn.

When she reined him in he reared, splendid, to his full height. He was Pegasus ready to leap from the earth and carry her into the sky.

They cantered up to a small inn, nestled among trees. An old sign hung over the door. The Auberge de la Chèvre d'Or.

Therese dismounted and knocked. After some time a sleepy publican opened the door. He was astonished to find a young woman with flushed cheeks and shining eyes on his doorstep at this hour.

"Is it too early for coffee and something to eat? I'm famished."

"I've only just got up. If you don't mind waiting—" He offered grudgingly, "Come in. I'll light the fire."

"Take your time, Monsieur. I'll wait out here."

He watched her as she led her horse to the drinking trough. A beautiful horse, a beautiful woman. What was she thinking to be out riding alone in the country at this hour?

She drank steaming coffee as dawn broke over the woods. The innkeeper brought her a plate of eggs, fresh butter and warm bread. She had never felt so hungry or so free.

The heavy weight which had lain over her heart since Henri's death had miraculously lifted. This day was a release, a promise and a beginning.

She begged an apple from the innkeeper, cut it in sections and offered them to Saladin.

As he nuzzled them from her hand, he looked at her with a new expression in his deep brown eyes.

He had accepted her as an equal and was content.

The de Mornys' costume ball was to honor the opening of the Great Exhibition. Never since the Congress of Vienna had so many crowned heads been assembled in one city at one time.

The Emperor and Empress of the French were to attend, accompanied by the Kings and Queens of Denmark, Sweden, Portugal and Belgium. Czar Alexander, Queen Victoria, the Sultan of Turkey and the Khedive of Egypt were to make separate state visits later on.

A number of German monarchs had been received with a magnificence that quite surprised them. The Kings of Wurtemburg and Bavaria, the Grand Dukes of Hesse and Baden, and all sorts of confusing rulers from principalities difficult to pinpoint on the map had been established in lavish suites at the best hotels.

The King of Prussia, Bismarck's puppet, was notable by his absence. It was not hard to see why the French were paying court to the less belligerent members of the German Confederation.

A number of Far Eastern rulers had also been invited, together with a cornucopia of Indian Rajas, Sultans, Beys and Nizams. A putty-colored potentate who rejoiced in the distinctive title of the Acond of Swat was fascinated by the plumbing fixtures at the Hotel Continental and ordered his wazir to remove the bathroom faucets as souvenirs.

If such exotic figures as the Kings of Siam and Nepal had been disinclined to make the long journey westward, they had sent embassies, gloriously arrayed and turbaned, who rode about the city in a dazzlement of jewels.

Paris was en fête and the authorities had outdone themselves with parades, bands and pageantry.

The Parisians were tingling with excitement at the prospect of this deluge of visitors. Every hotel and pension was booked beyond capacity. Beds had been set up in corridors and attics and every housewife with a spare room had dusted and polished and was ready to rent at exorbitant rates. As one English wit put it: The exports of France might well be Liberté, Frivolité, Maternité, but the imports were always La Gloire et Le Pourboire.

The theme of the ball was the Court of Napoleon the First and guests were requested to wear costumes of that period. The great ballroom at the Elysée, like the Arc de Triomphe, was hung with terra-cotta silk emblazoned with golden bees. At the head of every column was a panoply of arms, held by a shield bearing the ubiquitous N, that emblem before which the antecedents of the visiting monarchs had once trembled.

Furniture which had belonged to Napoleon and Josephine had been borrowed from Malmaison, St. Germain and the Tuileries. Banks of Josephine's favorite yellow roses screened the orchestra and were displayed in Pompeiian vases in the brilliantly lighted reception rooms.

Not a few sagacious diplomats wondered if this determined evocation of past glory indicated insecurity rather than confidence.

In attics and back rooms young revolutionaries who had not eaten a full meal in many a long week plotted the downfall of this meretricious regime. They printed manifestos and manufactured bombs and were eager for their chance to strike a blow at the Great Impersonation.

Properly organized they could, almost at a single blow, have rid Europe of what they considered its cancerous heritage of royalty.

Leonide Leblanc, like every woman who had received, wangled or purloined an invitation, had been torn with indecision as to how best she could create a sensation in keeping with her reputation. Every dressmaker in Paris was stitching and embroidering Directoire gowns of every imaginable material. Not a single diadem remained in the vaults of any jeweler. Even the Comédie Française had been swept clean of uniforms of the Grande Armée. There would be more Marshals, Generals and Admirals than had ever served in the ranks of the great Napoleon.

Leonide decided to be extravagantly simple. She designed a dress of the finest white chiffon with a low-cut bodice embroidered with silver leaves. She was careful not to wear anything under this diaphanous garment in order to reveal glimpses of her famous figure. She wore a wreath of silver leaves and a cloak of snow white marabou. Her only adornment was a choker of perfectly matched diamonds. Examining herself in the mirror she decided that she was perhaps a trifle too austere and added two or three diamond rings and then a diamond rivière at her breast.

She was not altogether pleased with the result. She took off and put on the rivière several times. As she moved tiny feathers detached themselves from the cloak and floated about like moths. "I look like a moulting swan," she decided crossly. Truth to tell the gown looked like a night dress. Drafts flew up her legs.

Her new Spanish lover arrived, garbed in the sable pomp of an ambassador, with the Order of the Golden Fleece across his breast.

"You look like an undertaker," she informed him.

He removed a marabou feather from his moustache. "Surely you don't need to advertise the fact that you're a *poule de luxe*."

Leonide had the grace to laugh.

"Open the champagne, you beast. I hope the Elysée's well heated. My twot is already frozen."

"Be brave, my dear. It's not a condition likely to last long."

The first guest to arrive was the Crown Prince of Nepal. He had thought, as a compliment to his European host, to break with the custom of his country and arrive on time. He was a charming little figure in a rose brocade tunic, fuschia pantaloons, gold slippers and the neatest of pink turbans from which sprouted a crest of white peacock's feathers held in place by the largest amethyst anyone had ever seen. He was followed by two chamberlains, dressed in equally colorful fashion. They looked like three characters from an Oriental fairy tale.

The Crown Prince was somewhat abashed to find himself alone in these grandiose surroundings.

"I hope you are enjoying your stay in Paris," de Morny said graciously.

The chamberlain translated. "His Highness say where is ladies? Is expecting many pretty ladies, most honored sir."

"They will be here presently." De Morny signaled to the Prince de Sagan who escorted the little prince to the reception rooms.

By the time Leonide and her lover arrived, the great ball-room was already half filled with splendidly attired couples. That air of nervous expectancy hung over the assembly which precedes the success or failure of a great occasion.

As she curtsied to de Morny whose chest was glittering with decorations, mostly bestowed by his brother though not a few by himself, Leonide murmured, "Shouldn't you be wearing the Croix de Guerre lower down?"

She was encouraged by the unbecoming costume of Madame de Morny, a flamboyant Russian, who had chosen a dangerous shade of purple which clashed with her dyed red hair.

"What an original costume!" her hostess declared. "Your dressmaker must have plucked more chickens than my chef."

"They are the breasts of arctic swans," Leonide said grandly as several small feathers detached themselves from her cloak.

A steady stream of guests was making its way up the great staircase, flanked on each step by guards in the uniform of the Grande Armée. The orchestra was playing the dances once popular at the court of Josephine to which everyone had forgotten the steps. Seeing the general confusion the Prince de Sagan sent word to switch to waltzes and soon the immense floor was a whirlpool of multicolored flowers.

The eyes of the little Crown Prince dilated when Leonide entered the reception room where he was gobbling up salmon mousse. He sent his chamberlain over to open negotiations.

The little man made his salaams and politely inquired, "His Highness think most pretty lady. Is available?"

Leonide allowed herself to be presented.

"Is husband?" The Chamberlain indicated her escort.

"No, my dear friend, the Conde de Maribor."

"Oh, then is available?"

The Crown Prince was visibly moved by the glow of Leonide's shapely legs under the chiffon.

"Well, that depends for what?"

Hurried consultations elicited the response, "His Highness like pretty lady come to hotel."

Even Leonide was somewhat taken aback by this precipitous approach.

"I'm sure His Highness will find plenty of female companionship in Paris," Leonide replied as she turned away. "Who is that little sex maniac?" she asked her lover.

"You can hardly blame him," that gentleman replied. "You've made everything plain but the price."

The ball was already in full swing when a subdued commotion on the staircase heralded what the company assumed was the arrival of the Imperial party.

Couples stopped waltzing and turned expectantly toward the door.

A gasp of astonishment rose as a female figure, swathed in pink and lemon saris, rode through the doorway on a jet black charger, caparisoned in cloth of gold and with a golden egret between its ears.

For a moment no one could believe their eyes. Their incredulity was compounded when, at a word from its rider, the Arabian reared to its full height and remained for a moment poised in midair with the splendor of an equestrian statue.

A burst of spontaneous applause rang through the ballroom. Who is it? Who is it? everyone asked. The Queen of India? *Was* there a Queen of India? In what barbaric country was it the custom to ride a horse into a ballroom?

An officer in the uniform of her Brittanic Majesty's Horse Guards stepped forward and helped this vision from the court of the Great Moghul to dismount. She spoke to her black charger who cocked his ears in response and allowed himself to be led away.

De Morny was totally mystified. The majordomo whose office it was to announce the guests had retreated in dismay at the sight of this mounted amazon.

As she made her salaams, palms pressed together, the veil fell from her face and de Morny found himself staring into the brilliant yellow-green eyes of his protégé, heavily outlined with kohl.

"Well!" was all he could find to say. "A sensational entry indeed!"

Madame de Morny was outraged by such effrontery.

"Were you under the impression that this was a circus, Madame?"

"Forgive me for making the mistake," the Marquise murmured impenitently as she made her *révérence*.

De Morny observed her as she made her way into the ballroom where she was instantly surrounded by a group of admiring men. Something had happened to Therese Lachmann. Someone had lit a match to that hitherto dormant powder keg. She would have to be watched from now on.

Therese was the indisputable success of the evening. Everyone wanted to meet her. Everyone wanted to know who she was.

"Whatever possessed you?" Leonide asked, less than overjoyed to be eclipsed by the amateur she had befriended.

"I thought it was time I stopped being an understudy," Therese replied.

"You've decided to be a leading lady? Be careful you cast yourself in the right part, my dear."

Something had definitely happened to Therese. She was dazzling, desirable, with an air of amused nonchalance, as though she had condescended to appear at a ball that was hardly worth her attention.

"She must be having a bang-up affair," Leonide concluded.

The little Crown Prince of Nepal was beside himself. His chamberlain scurried over with inquiries as to the availability of the so pretty lady. Several frequenters of the At Homes gathered 'round the transfigured Marquise, no longer the grave bluestocking with an interest in world affairs, but a challenging charmer well worth the effort of conquest.

The arrival of the Imperial party shortly after came as something of an anticlimax. The Empress, deprived of her billowing crinolines, seemed somewhat denuded in her subtle Directoire gown. She was wearing Josephine's famous tiara which was too heavy and ornate for her smaller, more delicate features. The Emperor, in one of his uncle's much braided uniforms, resurrected from heaven knew what trunk or museum, looked more than ever like a provincial actor not too sure of his lines, his immense waxed moustaches left over from a previous night's performance as a Corsican brigand. The Kings and Queens who followed with their entourages, despite all their jewels and decorations, were, after all, not more impressive than the rest of the company who, in a general outburst of republicanism, decided to enjoy themselves.

Instead of the customary restraint imposed by the presence of royalty, the reception rooms resounded with a hubbub of chatter as though all the bees from the hangings were swarming about the rich food and champagne. These prosperous climbers, intoxicated by their own splendor, danced and drank, laughed and flirted, on the crust of the crater which, if it was destined to collapse like one of Mongolfier's balloons, would surely survive one night's extravagant entertainment.

The Marquise de Païva had set the tone of the ball which suddenly became an immense, if irreverent, success.

Therese was waltzing with Freddie Avondale, her officer of the Queen's Guards who, captivated by her new incarnation, had, during the course of the evening, fallen madly in love with her. An equerry came up to inform her that Monsieur Le Duc de Morny required her presence. It was the summons she had been waiting for.

Eugenie beckoned to her as she entered the salon reserved for royalty and patted the sofa beside her. Madame de Morny was incensed by this signal attention bestowed on a nobody who had dared to insult her.

"My dear," the Empress murmured behind her fan, "I hear you caused quite an uproar. I'm delighted. I was certain this affair would be a fiasco. Don't you detest these costumes? I never cared for the Directoire style."

"You make any style seem beautiful, Madame."

The Empress tapped her with her fan. "We agreed; no court compliments. Everyone, except my sister-in-law, agrees that you are the most beautiful woman present. I gladly concede the palm." She squeezed Therese's hand. "Come soon. I'll send word. We have much to talk over."

De Morny had observed this little encounter. He was not altogether pleased.

"There is someone who wishes to meet you," he greeted Therese coldly. "The Marquise de Païva—Baron von Berns-dorff."

Therese had a swift impression of an elongated, slightly effeminate man with a blond moustache whose eyes glittered in an unnatural way as though they were made of glass.

The Baron clicked heels in the Prussian manner and bowed over her hand.

"As you have demonstrated your skill as an equestrienne you should find much to talk over," de Morny said. "The Baron is the champion steeplechaser of Germany."

Therese found herself dancing with Chancellor von Bismarck's nephew.

"Are you staying in Paris?" she asked.

"For the moment I'm attached to the Prussian Embassy. I've been hoping to meet you. I hear your evenings are the most interesting in Paris."

"Whoever told you that?"

"Everyone speaks of the Marquise de Païva, so beautiful and so mysterious."

"I am not in the least mysterious. But I am at home in the evenings. I hope you will call."

"Also you ride superbly. That's a fine Arabian you have."

"He was supposed to be unmanageable when I bought him. It took some time before we came to terms."

So this was the man who would be the test of her usefulness to de Morny, on whom her future position at the Chaussée could depend. According to de Morny he might or might not be privy to the plans of his uncle, the Iron Chancellor, and might or might not be in Paris on a secret mission.

She was disconcerted by his evident eagerness to know her and wondered how much he was aware of her activities on de Morny's behalf.

At midnight the Imperial party left. People started drifting away and the hubbub in the reception rooms subsided.

"How will you get home?" Von Bernsdorff asked as they waltzed in widening circles over the less crowded floor.

"I shall ride with my escort from the Queen's Own Guards."

"Perhaps you'll allow me to ride with you one day—or one night."

"At night?"

"You ride in the early hours, do you not?"

"How did you know?"

"I've seen you. I'm an insomniac. I often go for a walk or a ride when I can't sleep."

"It is you who are mysterious, Baron."

There was indeed something disturbing and even distasteful about this man, a tension too close to the surface, only just under control.

She was growing sleepy from turning and turning over the great floor.

"What are you thinking, Marquise?"

"Oh, that it's all so unreal, this ball, these people, all this display."

"It's the same game of make believe we played as children, only we are no longer children and the game has less agreeable connotations. Didn't you play at Keeping House with your dolls?"

She thought of Bubilala, Queen of the Goyim and the almond tree in spring under whose branches she had woven so many fantasies about the great world beyond the Muranov. And she thought of another spring, walking with Henri along the terrace at St. Germain, dreaming of the future—all so far away now—another life—

"Did you have a happy childhood," he asked.

"Quite the contrary."

"We have something in common, then."

He held her a little closer. She thought, "This man has suffered in some horrible way."

She was relieved when the music stopped and Freddie came up to claim the last polonaise.

Due to her success at the ball and her friendship with Eugenie, Therese became the catch of the season. She was suddenly deluged with invitations. *Tout Paris*, it seemed, was anxious to cultivate the Marquise de Païva. Her evenings were crowded, mostly with people she had never laid eyes on. These included a number of sharp-witted and sharp-tongued women who clung to the fringes of society by dint of having affairs with well known journalists or second string politicians. They swept up the staircase, scattered a few compliments, made a rapid tour of the house, even peeking into Therese's bedroom, and chattered their way through platefuls of the cold buffet. They pretended from envy to be unimpressed. The Marquise was the passing product of patronage in high places, a shooting star of which they had seen many flash across the Parisian firmament. Who, after all, was she? A fly-by-night, a butterfly, at the most a season's diversion.

The habitués now brought their wives who came more from curiosity than to be agreeable. They conceded that the Marquise was clever and charming in her way and quite acceptable for less exclusive dinners.

A brocade box was delivered from the Crown Prince of Nepal, containing a white silk scarf and a brown cabouchon diamond the size of a plover's egg. The little Prince appeared himself, delightfully attired in white and violet brocade, and hovered anxiously in the hope that the so pretty lady would agree to visit him at his hotel.

Von Bernsdorff became a regular guest to the indignation of Freddie Avondale, who was devoured with jealousy and anyway couldn't abide him. Although it went against his conscience to gossip about the woman he secretly loved, he dutifully reported his observations to Lord Houghton.

"One is beginning to glimpse a certain pattern in the activities of your Marquise," the Ambassador observed. "I am informed that Bakunin did leave England about the time you mentioned. One wonders if there might be some connection with this—"

He pushed a London newspaper across his desk.

STRIKES IN SOUTHERN GERMANY. POLICE QUELL RIOTS IN
BERLIN. OUTBREAKS IN HANOVER.

Disturbances, reported to be the work of Anarchists, are disrupting industry in a number of German cities. During a demonstration in Hanover, shots were exchanged between rioters and the police.

"They blame everything on anarchists," said Freddie.

"It would be interesting to know if de Morny had a hand in these little uprisings."

"That's pretty farfetched, sir."

"European politics are farfetched. Unrest in Germany would keep Herr Bismarck's mind off more ambitious and less convenient schemes."

"One thing I'm sure of," Freddie insisted, torn between loyalty to Therese and duty to his profession, "the Marquise would never waste a moment on Von Bernsdorff by choice. He's insufferable."

It was not altogether true.

Therese found herself in a quandary about "her assignment." With his stiff little condescending manner, his supercilious air of superiority, he systematically antagonized her guests.

His unpopularity was compounded by his prowess in fields traditionally male. He rode, fenced and shot superbly. Frenchmen who considered themselves the most accomplished beings on earth took exception to a Renaissance man from a country they considered inferior. He was better educated, better informed, and had a wider knowledge of music and the arts. He was also irreproachably connected. There was no apparent chink in his armor, except his general unpleasantness, and this made him an object of suspicion and disdain.

To Therese he showed a thoughtfulness quite out of keeping with his general behavior. She treasured the Ming horses he had given her, the beautifully bound volumes of Heine and Goethe from which he would quote at length. Everything about him was at odds with what she sensed him in reality to be. His tight-fitting regimental suits, his high, polished boots, his crisp little upturned moustache, his sleek pommaded hair were the uniform of a Junker aristocrat, but it seemed to her often that behind the false glitter of his eyes a tortured spirit was trying to break through.

She could not repress a warning shiver, if not precisely of fear, when she found him at her door in the early hours, ready for one of their canters into the sleeping countryside.

Was the sensitive and generous side of him only a ploy to win her confidence, as de Morny had warned her? Was he simply what he appeared to be, an adroit diplomat, skilled in deception, who was trying to use her as she had been instructed to use him?

He was also a heavy drinker. He drank steadily throughout the evenings at the Chaussée. She came to know when he was drunk by the glazed fixity of his regard and his bearing which became as stilted as a marionette.

The revelation of the cross he bore, his tragedy and his obsession, was revealed gradually, through hints and evasions, indications suggested and then withdrawn.

They were having coffee one morning at the Auberge de la Chèvre d'Or at that hour she loved best when the world was still innocent and fresh.

He had been silent for some time. Staring off into the distance from which the mists of dawn were lifting, he asked, "Do you intend to go on living as you do now?"

"When my husband returns I suppose my life will become more settled."

"I hope you'll forgive me if I confess that I have not been altogether sincere."

"I don't expect anyone to be altogether sincere."

"I mean that I was not unaware of certain facts about you, even before we met."

"That doesn't surprise me. People have very few secrets in Paris."

"I mean about your marriage—and other things."

They were at last approaching the quicksands that surrounded the purpose of their relationship.

"I think you and I are in much the same predicament. Needless to say it has not made any difference to my personal regard for you. That I would like you to believe."

He shifted on his chair and his thin, wiry fingers, too delicate for a man, stroked his riding crop. "I ask about your intentions—for the future—because I have been asking myself the same thing. In fact it has been on my mind ever since we met. We are both, I think, the victims of circumstance. I was born into a regimented sect whose customs and taboos I have been forced to follow. You will probably not be surprised to know that I detest them. I loathe what my country stands for. I foresee that it carries the seed of something as terrible for Europe as it has been for me." He hesitated, glanced at her as though gauging the effect of this confession. Her attention became fixed on the way he was fingering the riding crop as if it were the symbol of the heritage he hated. "I have, at different times, contemplated suicide. I no longer see that as a solution."

"Why should you think of that?" Therese asked in dismay. "You have everything to live for."

"You think so? What?"

"You're rich, well born, highly intelligent."

He was tapping his boot with the crop, rhythmical little strikes that chilled her. "Do you know what it's like to be an outcast all one's life, to be surrounded by people who represent everything that is abhorrent to one? Perhaps you do. I am not a normal man because of my upbringing. Not only because of my father who was a militarist machine. My mother, in order to make me a proper, God-fearing Junker, used to beat me with a riding crop. She beat me till I fainted. I would come to my senses covered in blood. That was only one of her corrective measures."

Therese recoiled. "Please don't tell me about such things."

He was tapping his boot with greater vigor, sharp little raps that would have cut into his naked flesh.

"Why not? It's your business, isn't it? To report on me?" Therese picked up her gloves.

"I am the nephew of the great von Bismarck," he reminded her. "I am here to make mischief."

He brought the crop down—crack!—across his boot.

Therese stood up. She wanted to escape from this man whose sickness had abruptly come too close to the surface. She started toward Saladin who was peacefully grazing beside the road.

Von Bernsdorff followed her. "Don't run away, Therese. We might as well try to be honest with each other."

She hesitated with her hand on Saladin's saddle.

"Do I repel you? I repel many people. But I don't imagine you *chose* to act as a conduit for that devious adventurer who has never done an honest thing in his life. He is using you as he uses everyone."

"I know nothing about you or what you're doing in Paris. If you want me to be honest, I don't think de Morny knows much more."

"But he'd like to. I know a great deal that would be of interest to him."

Therese was aware that he was trying to bribe her into some sort of intimacy which she had no desire to share.

"Has it occurred to you," he asked, "that there may be a means of escape—for both of us?"

"I'm not looking for a means of escape."

"Shouldn't you? Or are you proposing to spend your life as a hostess for a lot of Parisian riffraff who don't give a damn about you and will drop you the moment it serves their ends?"

She was momentarily thrown off balance by his vehemence. "I'm doing what I have to because I have no choice."

"I am offering you a choice. There are maladies that can be cured, both of the body and of the soul."

"What choice?"

"You have the power to exorcise me, Therese. You are the one person I believe who has that power."

For an instant in that rising light that spread over the landscape like a benediction she saw him clearly, in his isolation and despair.

She said hurriedly, "Perhaps it would be better for both of us if you didn't see me again."

"Why? Because of them? I care nothing for them, the French or the Germans. Let them decimate each other. It's only a matter of time."

She was trapped on the brink of the realization that she could find out everything de Morny wanted to know, but at a personal cost that frightened her.

"What is only a matter of time?"

"You want a detailed account of my uncle's plans? I could give you that."

"I don't want to know anything—anything from you."

He stepped back abruptly at attention as though at a military review. "Will you come away with me? I have a property in Italy, in the hills near Lucca. We are not dependent on them, either you or I."

She was too astonished to react to this proposal.

"You don't realize what you're saying. You hardly know me."

"I am offering you my name and security. You want to be free, don't you? I've seen on your face a dozen times how you despise them all."

"What makes you think I don't include you among them?" she said sharply. "Please help me up."

He turned away as though dismissing her, went back to the table and picked up his riding crop.

She managed to mount unassisted and turned Saladin toward the road.

He appeared a few nights later at Number Twenty-two. Therese had returned from a dinner party and a number of guests had followed her. They were in a lively mood.

There was a disapproving drop in the conversation as the foppish, corseted figure entered the salon. He came straight to Therese and, with a curt Prussian nod and heel click, presented her with a box tied with cerise ribbons.

She led him to the fireplace out of hearing of the others.

"I meant what I said. It would be better if you did not come here again. We have been at cross purposes and I don't want to prolong them. And, please, don't bring me any more gifts."

"What will you tell your mentor?" he inquired with a supercilious sneer.

"That you no longer call. He can draw his own conclusions."

"You are very shortsighted, Therese."

"Perhaps if we had met under different circumstances—"

"The circumstances don't matter. I'm rich. My villa at Lucca is very beautiful."

"Then go there, and leave me to work things out in my own way."

She was about to leave him when he laid a restraining hand on her arm.

"Don't dismiss me. You would have total security for life."

"I don't love you," she said in a low voice. "I don't even like you. Please leave me alone."

"Come and bring me good luck, Therese," Freddie Avondale called from the card table. He had been watching with mounting annoyance the little scene by the mantelpiece.

She went to him, took off her ruby ring and laid it beside him. "There, Freddie. I'll leave you a talisman. If you win a fortune you can buy me the Taj Mahal."

She was halfway downstairs when von Bernsdorff called to her from the landing. She was forced to stop with her hand on the balustrade.

"What is the matter with you?" he asked as he reached her. "You said you are living here because you have no choice. I am offering you everything. I'll make a settlement—anything you want. You can put a stop to this charade by saying a single word."

"I've already said that word."

"I thought you were more intelligent. I can give you a full and varied life. At least you wouldn't be beholden to that criminal de Morny."

"I made one marriage for the wrong reasons. I don't want to repeat that mistake."

He was standing one step above her. His eyes had a glassy fixity that frightened her. "What is it you want? All I know? Is that what you're holding out for?"

"I want you to go away. Now, will you please—" He stepped closer, barring her way. "You fill me with a kind of horror."

He grimaced, his face close to hers. "You don't know what horror is."

She saw Freddie over his shoulder, coming downstairs.

"I have the impression," her rescuer said, "that the Marquise doesn't care to continue this conversation."

Von Bernsdorff swiveled with the speed of a rattlesnake. "I'll make short shrift of you, sir, if you provoke me."

"May I offer you a glass of champagne, Therese?"

She was thankful to take Freddie's arm.

"For heaven's sake," she whispered as they went downstairs, "don't start an argument. He's an expert swordsman."

"If he bothers you again," Freddie declared without lowering his voice, "I'll be happy to blow his brains out."

It turned into an evening like other evenings. She performed her duties, picking up bits of gossip that might or might not be useful to de Morny. But the essential information he wanted only Von Bernsdorff could give.

She was thankful when she rejoined the card players to find him gone.

The party broke up at two. They took their leave with promises of dinners and dances, a weekend in the country, visits to the Great Exhibition. She was popular now. They no longer cared how fraudulent she was. But how much longer would de Morny pay for this nonsense unless she could prove her worth?

Freddie had lingered. "Will you come riding with me soon? It's ages since we had a good gallop."

"That would be nice, Freddie. Thank you."

He was holding her hand a little longer than he needed to. Romantic ardor struggled with English decorum. Would he dare to face his family with this "woman of doubtful reputation?" She rather wished that he would pluck up courage and propose. She would settle for a conventional life in England. No danger there.

She looked 'round the big room in which nothing belonged to her. Essentially her position hadn't changed. She was still a whore who failed to give satisfaction.

The box that Von Bernsdorff had brought her was on the mantelpiece. She sat down and untied the ribbons.

It was the most exquisite object she had ever seen; a small vase of milk-white jade, delicately carved with lotus buds and tendrils.

Suddenly she thought that she had been unjust and unrealistic. Von Bernsdorff was offering her more than escape from an untenable existence in which she was forced to betray everyone, in which every confidence, every gesture of friendship, was the price for a house, clothes and invitations, a fleeting social success that meant nothing to her.

Security. A stable position. All he was asking was to help him banish the ghosts of a brutal upbringing, as Henri had gradually veiled her memories of the Muranov. "There are maladies that can be cured, both of the body and of the soul."

Even if he repelled her physically, she could learn to respect him in other ways. Perhaps in time she would outgrow that distaste. Didn't most women have to? How often did it happen that a woman could marry freely for love as she would have married Henri? But she had been a child then, with a child's trust and gratitude and innocence. Was love even a factor in the rational grown-up world?

He was intellectually far superior to Freddie, for all Freddie's niceness. They had been pitted against each other and their position as chosen antagonists had made it impossible for her to judge him fairly. He had tried to be honest. "I am not a normal man because of my upbringing." Exorcism? Was that perhaps a kind of love?

She heard the click of the door and looked up.

She was too appalled to credit what she saw.

Von Bernsdorff was naked except for his boots. His thin, androgynous body was completely shaved and powdered as white as a clown's face. A disproportionately large phallus dangled between hips as delicate as a ballerina's. It had the repulsive deadness of something preserved in chemicals in a laboratory.

He was drunk, with the fixed stare of a sleepwalker.

She sprang up, dropping the jade vase.

He came toward her without seeing her, compelled by that ponderous phallus to pay homage to the goddess of its obscene desire.

She backed toward the mantelpiece and managed to say, "Get away. Get away from me."

He fell on his knees and, as she tried to dart past him, seized her ankle and started to lick the sole of her shoe like a dog slathering over filth in a gutter.

A ludicrous struggle ensued in which she almost lost her balance and was forced to grip the mantel shelf for support. She wrenched away her foot and kicked him in the face. He fell, pawing at her legs and mumbling, "Yes, kick me. Trample on me. I am the lowest and vilest. Degrade me. Beat me, Therese."

As she rushed past him she saw the long livid welts across his buttocks.

His clothes were lying about the small sitting room. She ran into her bedroom and locked the door.

She was shaking and nauseated.

She couldn't believe that it had happened.

She heard Saladin moving in the garden. He was pawing at the wall under her window.

She heard Von Bernsdorff dressing in the sitting room, heard him going downstairs. She heard the front door shut.

She changed quickly into her riding habit. She wanted to get out of the contaminated house.

On the mantelpiece of the living room was one of her own envelopes propped against the clock.

She opened it and read. "The German Confederation will be dissolved. Wilhelm the Second will be crowned Emperor of a united Germany."

The anonymous functionary from the Sûreté whose duty it was to watch the house saw the Marquise turn her horse, not toward the boulevard, as she usually did, but in the opposite direction. He cursed these people for keeping such late hours. By the time he got back to headquarters and made out his report, it would be three in the morning. Four before he was home in bed.

Therese had taken the other route, the one Saladin disliked. It led through a poor quarter where people lurked about the streets, where there were piles of rubble due to Monsieur Haussemann's demolitions. He was driving a big new boulevard through the slums. There were no gaslights on this murky thoroughfare. The darkness made it difficult to avoid the shapes that suddenly loomed up, threats ready to attack. Saladin was alert to protect her because that was his duty and his desire.

They rode for an hour, encountering no one, to a less congested district where there were old houses with gardens behind high gates.

At the end of a secluded cul-de-sac she reined up before the gates of a small country house which had once belonged to Madame de Pompadour and still bore the imprint of her charm. She dismounted and jangled the bell. A sleepy watchman peered through the bars, recognized her, and unbarred the gate. She led Saladin across the drive to the stables. There were other horses snuffling and shifting in the darkness.

She laid her head against Saladin's neck. "Thank you. I shan't be long."

She went through the garden and by a side door into the house.

The front hall was dimly lit by gas brackets turned low.

She knocked on the study door. A voice answered: "Come."

He was working at his ebony desk strewn with papers. Somewhere in the summer darkness a nightingale was juggling its liquid notes. It seemed incongruously peaceful in this sanctuary where de Morny spun his webs of intrigue and statecraft.

"I'm sorry to come so late, but something has happened." She handed him Von Bernsdorff's note.

"When did you get this?"

"Tonight."

"From him?"

"May I sit down. I have to talk to you."

He motioned her to a chair. The ride had cleared her brain. She was able to see the incident clearly as one may reconstruct the details of a street accident hours afterward when the shock has blurred.

"Why this sudden announcement?" he inquired, indicating the note.

"I don't know how much he knows, if there's anything behind his being in Paris. I only know that I cannot see him again."

"Why?"

"He's unbalanced. He's capable of violence. He has talked of killing himself. I think he's quite capable of killing me."

"For what reason?"

"It's to do with his childhood, degradations he suffered that have resulted in—perhaps a doctor would know the right word."

"Abnormalities?"

"I cannot be involved. He revolts and frightens me. Is that note any news to you?"

"Not entirely. The question is when."

"You must find out some other way."

De Morny laid the note on his desk and considered her.

"Precisely what has transpired between you?"

She was reluctant to tell him because she knew that she was exactly in the position he wanted. The offer of marriage was the lever he would insist on using.

"If you mean have we slept together—no, there's been no question of that. I was subjected—to an exhibition—too sickening to describe."

"And it resulted in this information? Why? As an act of penance?"

"He knows what I do for you. He knew that before we met. But I assume most people do by this time. I think he was ordered to find out whatever I could tell him about *your* plans. It's a double game that I don't intend to play."

After a silence de Morny asked with apparent uninterest, "Do you have any choice?"

"I can leave. There are other women who can do what I've been doing, much better equipped, I'm sure."

"Not women for whom this gentleman puts on exhibitions and then leaves evidence that would incriminate him."

Therese came over to the desk. De Morny had the same impression that he had had at the costume ball; he had under-estimated her strength of will.

"I won't go on with it. You have your Secret Service. Let them find out what you want to know."

"May I remind you that I have spent a great deal of money launching and supporting you?"

"That was your idea. I've carried out your orders as well as I could. But I won't torment a desperate man who needs help and not more deceptions."

"Help him, then."

"So that you can destroy him for leaving notes like that?"

"I have no desire to destroy him. He's much too useful. This and any others like it will be held in the strictest confidence."

He sighed. It was very late and he was not in the mood to argue with a young woman who was suffering from pangs of conscience.

He stood up and said with the loaded indifference that preceded dismissal, "You will be compensated for any shocks he may inflict on your sensibilities."

"It's not a question of money."

"But it is. You own nothing in that house, not a single dress."

"If I leave I shan't be worse off than I was before."

"I suppose you could go back to earning your living as you did. I recall that you were not very good at it."

He went to a sidetable and poured himself a glass of Madeira.

The profound silence of the night that flowed into the room had been undisturbed by this interview. Remote from human concerns and dishonesties, the nightingale warbled in its hidden tree.

"By the way," he said more reasonably, "the Empress is

thinking of making you a lady-in-waiting. She has taken a fancy to you. It would be a good opportunity to make a worthwhile match. She's clever at arranging that kind of thing."

Therese picked up her gloves and crop.

"Perhaps I'll marry Von Bernsdorff. He has asked me to. And then you will find out nothing."

It was at dusk the following day that the anonymous courier who brought her messages from a Certain Great Personage delivered the package. She was dressing for a dinner at the Tuileries to which Eugenie had invited her.

It contained a velvet reticule in which were folded ten bank notes of ten thousand francs apiece.

She counted them slowly. It was a large sum, more than she had ever possessed at one time. Evidently de Morny was not proposing to get rid of her, at least not yet.

A short while later, while she was sitting in the salon wondering if she had the skill to play all these people off against each other, the anonymous butler carried in three large cases in red Morocco leather.

"These just came, Madame. Where shall I put them?"

"On the card table. Was there a note?"

"No, Madame."

The anonymous butler who also reported to a Certain Great Personage took for granted that the *soi-disant* Marquise should receive gifts for services rendered—of one kind and other.

The large box contained a traveling dressing case of crimson tortoiseshell with gold mounts and a gold crest under a twin-headed Imperial eagle. A gold key dangled from a gold lock. Inside, beautifully fitted, was an array of articles in gold and crystal. There were hairbrushes, clothes brushes, combs, scissors, small pots for cream and pommade, bottles for perfume and bottles for toothbrushes and hairpins. The second case contained a standing mirror in solid gold and the third two gold candlesticks.

It was worth a king's ransom.

There was a note attached to the gold pincushion.

Kennst du das Land woh die Zitronen blühn,
In dunkeln Laub die Goldorangen glühn,
Ein sanfter Wind vom blauen Himmel weht,
Die Myrtle still und hoch Lorbeer steht.
Kennst du es wohl?
   Dahin! Dahin!
Mocht ich mit dir, o mein Geliebter, ziehn.

(Knowest thou the land where bloom the citrus flowers,
Where in the leafy shade the golden orange glows,
A softer breeze from bluer heavens wafts,
Still are the myrtles, tall the laurels stand.
Knowest thou that land? O there! O there!
I long to roam with thee, beloved. There!)

She remembered Von Bernsdorff reciting it one day when he had brought her a volume of Goethe's poems.

She stood for a long time staring at these magnificent gifts. It was, in the final analysis, a question of pity. Could she pity him enough to forget the white depilitated body groveling at her feet? Pity for a lost, demented child. Henri had become a child during his illness, the nature of which she had long since guessed. Was there any difference between the two infections? A malady of the body and a malady of the soul. Was pity the thread of Ariadne that could lead the prisoner out of the labyrinth into the normal light of day?

The Empress was particularly charming that evening. She looked radiant in one of her sweeping Winterhalter gowns of pale yellow silk with yellow Gloire de Dijon roses in her hair.

It was an informal gathering of Eugenie's intimate friends, Octave Feuillet, the novelist, Carpeaux, the sculptor, Prosper Merimée who had known her as a girl and had been her confidant during the days when Louis Napoleon had been courting her. The circle of ladies who attended her were statuesque beauties of the type Eugenie admired, including Isabelle de Persigny, the sister of "Par Tout Par Tout." Therese had to step carefully with these favorites who would be only too eager to repeat malicious gossip and who resented the favor shown this intruder by the goddess at whose shrine they served.

Eugenie dispensed with formalities on these occasions. It was a relief for her, in the midst of the endless round of receptions given for dignitaries who were visiting Paris for the Great Exhibition, to gather 'round her those friends with whom she could relax and be herself.

They were discussing Feuillet's new novel which Eugenie pronounced a work of genius. She was girlishly enthusiastic about the productions of her friends and defended them stoutly against all criticism.

"Are you fond of literature?" the novelist asked Therese.

"I read a great deal, mostly the classics. I am trying to teach myself Greek so that I can read them in the original."

"*Quelle phénomène!* A young beauty who studies Greek!"

"Entirely appropriate with her profile," Carpeaux put in.

"The classics are too cold for me," Eugenie admitted. She liked to add a literary tone to her evenings in keeping with her role as a patroness of the arts, though her own tastes leaned toward the sentimental. "Nothing touches me so deeply as French poetry. One day, when history is done with me, I shall retire to the country with Beranger and Prudhomme, de Vigny and Lamartine."

Cupping her hands under her chin like a schoolgirl, she recited,

> "*Si vous croyez que je vais dire*
> *Qui j'ose aimer.*
> *Je ne saurais, pour un empire,*
> *Vous la nommer.*
> *Nous allons chanter à la ronde,*
> *si vous voulez,*
> *Que je l'adore et qu'elle est blonde*
> *Commes les bles.*"

She smiled at the company and her eyes rested for an instant on Therese. Everyone sighed with delight at this example of the Empress' genius for recitation.

Into this enclave of honeyed sycophancy the Emperor appeared with the Prince Imperial, a handsome little boy of serious demeanor. Everyone rose, but the Empress, with a pleasant gesture, motioned them to be seated.

"We don't stand on ceremony among friends."

Eugenie introduced the young Prince to Therese who started to make her *révérence*.

"Pray be seated, Madame," he declared in exactly the same tone as his father.

"And what have you been doing today, my darling," Eugenie inquired, drawing her son to her knee.

"I have been studying military history, Mama. I am resolved to become a great general."

"There is the future of France," Feuillet exclaimed. There were murmurs of admiring assent. Only Merimée regarded the boy with a certain tender sadness. He had lived through fifty years of French history and was less optimistic of the heir presumptive's prospects.

Therese was impressed, on closer acquaintance, by the Emperor's charm. In the family circle, where he was not called on to perform the role to which his strange destiny had called him, he was endearingly simple and unaffected. He went the round of the guests, greeting them with courteous inquiries as to their health and families. "I hear your new book is a sensation," he said to Feuillet. "My wife does nothing but sing its praises, but then I fear she is biased on your behalf. I shall have to decide for myself."

There was a gleam of amusement in his somber, heavy-lidded eyes when he reached Therese.

"This time, I see, you did not arrive on horseback."

"I hope Your Majesty has forgiven that mad impulse."

"You contributed to the success of the occasion."

His inscrutable good manners betrayed no hint of his knowledge of Therese's activities. He was an old hand at conspiracies.

The ruler of France seated himself beside his consort with the heir to the Second Empire between them. It was clear that both parents adored their son who treated them with the liveliest affection tempered by respect. Even at this early age he was imbued with his duty to uphold the traditions of his family.

Seeing them in this interlude of domestic relaxation it was hard to believe that this warm-hearted couple, who seemed in themselves in no way exceptional, could have risen to such a pinnacle in the world. They were like any civilized, well-to-do people, bound by warm family ties, who were enjoying the company of friends.

Glancing down the dinner table Therese noted the Emperor's imperturbable patience. He clearly had little interest in his wife's circle, but his courtesy never faltered. He seemed, in a strange way, to be sustained by an immense fatigue. Despite his lifelong struggle to reinstate his dynasty on the throne of France, he lacked entirely the sublime but terrible egotism of his namesake. Fatigue was his defense against the paranoia of power.

After dinner they played guessing games, devised by Merimée, at which the Emperor displayed a singular ineptness. The Empress was delighted to be the first—which she was naturally allowed to be—to solve these simplistic riddles.

At ten the party broke up. The Emperor made his grave *adieus*, his son followed suit, and the two Napoleons went off to bed.

As she was leaving Eugenie drew Therese aside.

"I'm trying to arrange something which I hope will please you. I have to proceed with a certain caution because one mustn't hurt anyone's feeling or—" she added in English, "tread on anyone's corns. Be patient, will you? For my sake?" She kissed Therese on both cheeks. "Good night, my dear. Sleep well."

She was an adept at the art of being irresistible.

There was some confusion over Prosper Merimée's carriage which had gone to the wrong door of the palace. Therese offered to drive him home.

On their way through streets still crowded with visitors strolling back from the Exhibition, the old writer sighed. "Such charming people! I have the warmest affect for them *as* people. But I sometimes ask myself, 'Can it last?' Louis Napoleon has done far more for this country that his vainglorious uncle ever dreamed of. But are they grateful for all this prosperity? I am a Frenchman. I admire the genius of my country, but I deplore its insincerity. It will take history to make the French realize how fortunate they were to have this Emperor. He is a great man *malgré lui*."

As they were approaching his house Merimée took Therese's hand. "May I give you a piece of advice, my dear child? Eugenie has her faults—as who hasn't. Hers are mostly impulses which damage herself more than others. But of one thing I can assure you; she is absolutely pure of heart. Trust her. Be true to her. There is nothing she will not do for those she loves."

She saw him, a phantom among the phantom mists as she turned Saladin toward the Chèvre d'Or.

For a moment she was on the point of avoiding another confrontation, but then she thought that she owed it to herself and to him to make a final effort to bring this ill-fated involvement to an end.

He looked up but did not move, as though he had been expecting her. Even from a distance she could sense the weight of his shame and sadness.

She dismounted and led Saladin to the drinking trough. It was a chilly dawn, heavy with moisture. Mists floated over the fields, pierced here and there by shafts of pallid light.

He did not move, did not dare to look at her. He was wearing a dark coat with the collar turned up and a peaked cap pulled down which gave him the air of a student who had been expelled from his university.

"Have you had coffee?"

He shook his head.

She went to the door of the auberge and knocked. The innkeeper had got used to her appearances in the early hours and assumed that she was a married woman who was having an affair with this German.

"I'll bring it out in a moment."

She steeled herself and sat down. Von Bernsdorff seemed

paralyzed, either by shame or by his failure to make clear his true intentions.

"That was a very beautiful dressing case you sent me and a very beautiful vase. You must know that I cannot accept them."

He made a small movement of distress, raising his hand and letting it fall on the table.

"I told you that we must not meet again. Nothing can come of it but what is embarrassing to me and might be dangerous for you."

No response.

"I gave the note you left to de Morny. Naturally he wants to know more. If you tell me more I shall be forced to repeat it. I am asking you not to put me in that position."

Only the pale silhouette, cut off by the peak of the cap and the upturned collar.

"You send me things to prolong a situation I am trying to end. I don't want to be bribed in that way."

"They are not bribes," he said in a scarcely audible tone.

"All you can do for both of us is not to see me."

He raised his head and said as though to an invisible judge in a court of law, "There is going to be war. He won't wait for a crisis. Any trumped up excuse will do. They routed the Austrians in six weeks. They will rout the French in a month. It will be the end of France as a great power."

He looked at her suddenly and said with an intensity that was patently sincere, "Can't you understand that I tell you these things for your own sake? If the Empire falls de Morny will fall with it. You will be left with nothing. I don't care what they do to me. There's not much left they can do. I am trying to save you, Therese."

"If it falls I shall suffer like everyone else."

"You are counting on something that already does not exist."

The innkeeper came up with the tray of coffee. "Will you have the usual? I have some fresh mushrooms. An omelette perhaps?"

"That would be fine."

"And you, monsieur?"

Von Bernsdorff shook his head.

"There's no point in my offering an apology," he said when the innkeeper had left them. "I'm not sure what I did. When I'm drunk I don't always remember. It's another self that I carry in me—that breaks out—an alter ego I can't control."

He was staring again into the distance because he could not trust himself to look at her.

"I have always been alone. I have become—quite horribly alone. Sometimes the fantasy of my other self takes over. If there were *someone* I could outgrow it. I don't expect love. There's doubtless very little worth loving in me. But without—someone—I fall back into the past—into a terrible repetition of things that happened then—things I detest but that compel me."

"There must be some doctor or priest who could help you."

"It can only be someone I love—someone altogether above that—truer and finer—"

The coffee was waiting between them. It seemed incongruous to perform the mundane task of pouring coffee in the midst of this confession.

"You despise me. Granted. But do you admire de Morny? Are your sympathies roused by that man who has pilfered millions from the treasury for his children and mistresses? You know that he personally ordered the massacre of hundreds of people in the coup that put his brother on the throne and he, as we know, is no more a Bonaparte than you are."

"What has de Morny to do with you?"

"Not with me—with your sympathies—with your misplaced loyalty—your readiness to believe—"

He picked up the pot, poured out the coffee and pushed a cup toward her.

"I am really trying to be honest with you. It necessitates saying disagreeable things. I know that I am—unbalanced in certain ways. I don't try to excuse it. It's been a component of my life—much as I loathe it. But that could change. I ask you to believe that there is a great deal more in me that hasn't found an outlet—for lack of a purpose, of encouragement. If there were someone—if I were not always alone—I would have a reason for strengthening, for building on the better part of myself."

He glanced at her quickly. She had reached for her coffee and then not touched it.

"I know how you earned your living before de Morny found you. I accept that. I know your sins, if they were sins, as you know mine. We don't have to go through life condemning people for things that, for the most part, they couldn't help."

"You condemn de Morny," she pointed out.

"Because his whole life has been built on fraud. You can't be so naïve as not to know what these people are. They're thieves, liars, criminals on a colossal scale."

"That's ridiculous. They've done a great deal for France. Anyone who reaches that position—"

"You think they believe in France—as an ideal? Were you impressed by that outrageous display we were subjected to at the Elysée ball? Are you really impressed because that Spanish lesbian makes a fuss over you?"

"Don't speak of her like that. She's a kind and generous woman."

"She's not a woman at all. Ask her husband. Ask any of his mistresses. Paris is littered with his illegitimate children."

"I know them, I've been with them, at home, with their son." She stood up and said in white anger, "You think you can win my sympathy by slandering them? I find that more disgusting than your behavior the other night."

"I'm trying to save you, Therese," he insisted doggedly. "Doesn't it mean anything to you that you are the only woman I've ever loved?"

"I don't know what you mean by love," she retorted. "I'm not even sure that I want to know. Why can't you leave me alone to work out my life as best I can?"

She fled to the protection of Saladin, mounted, and rode away.

She was lying down before dinner, studying her Greek lexicon. She was training herself to memorize ten words a day. She had been invited to the Moradiers. He was a journalist who had just returned from making a survey of industrial disturbances in Germany. De Morny wanted to know his private opinions and Moradier wanted to know de Morny's views on the same subject. Moradier counted on the fact that Therese was new to politics and that with a good dinner and a few compliments she might be tempted to be indiscreet.

De Morny was shown in.

Observing him in the sleek opulence of evening dress she saw that he lacked entirely the basic good nature of his brother. He was a political machine.

"Thank you for sending me such a large sum of money," she said without rising to greet him. "What do you want me to do with it?"

"Keep it against a rainy day. I can't promise there may not be one."

He sat down, lit a cigar and considered her. It was a pity that he had never desired her. It would have made it much easier. But she was like Eugenie, essentially cold, unstirred by physical passion.

He had never understood why his brother had been seduced by his wife's shallow enameled charm. If one was going to marry an insipid woman one might as well make a dynastic marriage. People admired Eugenie, but very few liked her. The French were anyway too cynical and too sensuous to put up with a "good" woman who was only good because she was frigid. They preferred warmhearted whores like Du Barry and Pompadour.

"Have you seen him?" he asked, exhaling a long snakelike coil of smoke.

"Yes."

"What did he tell you—if anything?"

"He said there would be war with Prussia. That he—I suppose he meant Bismarck—would not wait for a major incident, but would use any trumped-up excuse. He said that France would be beaten within a month."

The snake slowly uncoiled and dissolved before this blast of disagreeable news.

"He also said that it would be the end of France as a dominant power and that it would be the end of your dynasty."

"Did he give any indication when all this was likely to happen?"

Therese shrugged. "At any moment, I gathered."

Was she lying? Had Von Bernsdorff said any of those things? Had he written the note about Wilhelm the Second? Was this calculating bitch taking advantage of him? Or was Von Bernsdorff telling her these things in order to lead her on? It seemed incredible that a Prussian, so close to the seat of power, should reveal so much unless he was really bewitched by this arctic Rhinemaiden.

He took a long draw on his cigar and examined the glowing end as if it were a two-way mirror.

"I want specifics. When and where. We don't need to know why; that's obvious. I have reason to believe—" But no, why tell her that Von Bernsdorff had been making certain calls on certain people of questionable loyalty, fodder, no doubt, for a Wooden Horse if this conflict should come about?

"How do you imagine that I can get him to be specific?"

"Play him along. Use your fatal allure."

"I told him that I wanted nothing to do with him and asked him to stay away."

"A sure way to stoke his ardor." His manner abruptly changed. "I don't need to tell you that this little game has gone far beyond political gossip. Even in the most general terms this concerns the security of France."

"I have no loyalty to France. I'm Polish."

"And, of course, Jews are internationalists."

"And equally not all nationalists are legitimate."

Their mutual dislike was now in the open. They could insult each other with perfect politeness.

"May I remind you, once again, that I took you from nowhere and that I can as easily send you back there."

"If Von Bernsdorff is correct, that may happen to both of us."

De Morny conferred with his cigar. He was on the point of ordering this bitch out of the house.

"Have you no loyalties, Therese?"

"Perhaps to the Empress. She has been very kind."

"Then do what I ask for Eugenie. Once you have found out all you can, I will release you to the gilded banalities of court life."

Very slowly and deliberately the great intriguer stubbed out his cigar.

"Let me give you a word of advice. I have learned one thing in the long struggle to reach the position which my brother and I now occupy. To survive it is necessary to cast one's lot with one side or the other. Even in my life, even with all you have doubtless heard about me, I am loyal to certain principles, to certain people—not many, but a few."

"What do you believe in—except your brother?"

"In France—if that doesn't strike you as too pretentious."

Therese closed her eyes. He thought, "She's beautiful and intelligent and she has courage, but there's something missing. If she could ever find out what that is, she could be someone of importance. She is also dangerous because, in her way, she's honest."

"It's difficult for me," Therese admitted, "to believe in abstract principles. I came from nowhere and I have no one."

"Then be like your friend Leonide. She also came from nowhere and had no one. She, at least, believes in herself."

The evening at the Moradiers dragged on till midnight. The riots in Germany were discussed at length. In the journalist's opinion they were not spontaneous outbreaks, but had been organized by transient agitators well supplied with funds.

"On the surface the issues are obvious; profits make poverty and poverty makes revolution. It's the same everywhere. But there's another more dangerous element. The great nations meddle in each others affairs and they meddle to play for time. What they choose to call the Balance of Power is really the imbalance of unrest. Obviously neither England, Russia nor France wants a united Germany. It's to their advantage to keep Germany disunited. But I very much fear, if things get worse, if these uprisings continue, that Bismarck may resort to more stringent measures to protect his plans."

"War?" Therese asked.

Moradier looked at her sharply. "There's nothing like war to unite a nation. If Prussia goes to war the other German states will support her as they did against Austria—with the results we know. What do you hear, Marquise, in the exalted circles you move in?"

"I hear that the Exhibition is a great success, that there will be a boom in trade and, let me see—I hear how prosperous we all are."

As he was saying goodnight Moradier realized that he had revealed far more than the beautiful and enigmatic Marquise. Whatever else she was not, she was an accomplished listener.

Therese was tired when she got home. She didn't feel inclined for her usual nocturnal ride. She would say goodnight to Saladin, make out her report on the Moradier's dinner and go to bed.

There was a single lamp burning on the hall table. For some reason that night the emptiness of the house oppressed her. Other women came home to husbands or lovers, went into nurseries to see if their children were safely sleeping. It seemed part of the strange pattern of her fate that she should be alone.

She went into the garden. Saladin was waiting for her by the stable door.

He was her refuge, her support, her one true friend.

Something was troubling him. He nudged her toward the stable.

"I don't feel like a ride. We'll go out early tomorrow."

But he nudged her again, snuffling urgently at her shoulder.

She glanced up at the silent house. There was a light in the salon. A faint, elongated shadow moved across the ceiling. It must be de Morny, she concluded, waiting to give her some fresh instructions or to hear an account of her evening. She felt disinclined for another interview at that hour, but at least it would save her the trouble of making out a report.

She gave Saladin a push toward the stable. "Go to sleep now. I'll see you in the morning."

Saladin was reluctant to let her go. He followed her to the door into the house and tried to block her way.

The deep lambent eyes were full of love and concern as she pushed past him and shut the door.

As she went upstairs instinct told her that it was not de Morny. But who else had access to the house?

Von Bernsdorff was standing by the fireplace. He had on the same black coat with the same turned-up collar. His face was unnaturally pale.

"How did you get in here?"

"I bribed your servant to let me wait."

She thought, "That isn't true. He has somehow got hold of a key." Was there someone in de Morny's employ who was playing a double game?

"I don't like you or anyone to come into this house without my permission," she said coldly. "Besides we have already said everything there was to say."

He took an envelope from the mantelpiece, one of her own envelopes which, as before, he had propped up against the clock.

"You left before I was able to make the situation entirely plain."

"It was plain to me."

He handed her the envelope.

"What is this?"

"You can read it or not as you choose. If you read it you will be faced with a clear-cut decision."

"I've told you my decision on several occasions."

She opened the envelope and took out a single sheet of paper. "There will be an attempt on the life of the Emperor during the visit of the Czar."

"What does this mean?"

"What it says, Therese. If you choose to disregard that information you will be free of them. If you hand it on to de Morny you will be committed. That means you will share their fate."

She folded the note and put it back in the envelope. "You persist in playing this game in order to force me to agree to something which I have no intention of agreeing to. Besides—how do I know there's any truth in this?"

"Everything I have told you is true. That's why you find it so hard to believe me."

"You expect me to believe that your uncle—"

"It's not him. At the most he would let it happen."

"The Czar isn't due in Paris for three weeks."

"Those sort of plans are made a long time in advance."

She sat down with the letter in her lap.

He took a step toward her and said with an authority he had not shown toward her before, "I want you to give me six months, Therese. Six months to show you the kind of life I can make for you. If you tear up that letter now I will hand in my resignation tomorrow and we can leave for Italy. It will be a complete break for both of us. If you choose to give that to de Morny there's nothing more I can do for you and you will learn nothing more from me. That is my ultimatum."

He was offering her an escape, but it was the one escape her heart warned her not to take.

"You're very sure that France will lose if there's a war. Suppose they win?"

"What I offer you won't be affected one way or the other." He was standing over her now. "I'll make a settlement on you anyway so that you will never again be in the position you're in today. I will take that risk. You risk nothing but six months. If at the end of that time you find that you still dislike me, you will be free to go."

There was no flaw in his offer except for what he was and the fear and distaste he inspired in her.

"I wish you hadn't given me this. It's unfair to test my loyalty in this way. Whatever they may be, they have kept their promises to me."

"How much will their promises be worth if France is defeated? Can't you bring yourself to trust me? You trust them—when you have overwhelming proof of how dishonest they are." He went back to the mantelpiece and stood with his hands on the red marble shelf, staring into the empty grate. "You find it so hard to believe in love, in the power of love to transform—

I never knew it existed. Now it seems to me the simplest thing in the world."

Through her mind ran the words of the poem, *"Kennst du das Land woh die Zitronen blühn?"* After all, why couldn't she trust him? Henri had been transformed by the feeling he had had for her. Perhaps it was all true. Perhaps this man, because of his long and terrible isolation and the suffering his demons had caused him, was capable of change. Six months. Was it so much to risk on the chance of the happiness he believed in? She would have a purpose then, instead of this endless improvisation, playing with days and nights like counters at a roulette table? Saladin had fought the world because he had no one to trust. She had shown him patience and forbearance. Could she do the same for this lost and unhappy man?

Beyond the silence of the room she could hear Saladin moving in the garden and, beyond, the dim murmur of the city. There were still carriages passing along the Champs-Élysées, people going home from late parties, people who were secure and occupied and happy. Was it possible that all this would be swept away?

"It isn't love that I find hard to believe in," she said quietly in a changed tone. "I've led such a strange, disjointed life for the last two years. I know that it's a life without foundations. I see one facet of it and then another like the prisms of a chandelier. All different and conflicting. Sometimes I feel that I'm incapable of judging what is true and what isn't any more."

"Then give me six months, Therese. It's beautiful at Lucca. An old red villa with orange groves. You can take your beloved Saladin and ride in the hills to your heart's content. It's not far from the sea. There's a little resort, hardly more than a fishing village, called Forti dei Marmi—"

She hesitated. Hesitated. Was this what she had hoped to find beyond the gates of the Muranov in the great world she had thought was only Poland? Was this the substitute that fate offered for the life she might have had with Henri?

The sickening episode that had happened in this room was not, after all, important. It was no more disgusting than her first experiences with men like Stanley. They were the bits of wreckage cast up on the sands that were washed away by other tides.

"Thank you," she said humbly, "for offering me so much."

She looked at him, trying to see him clearly. It was impossible to assess what the love of such a man might mean.

She handed him the envelope which he took with mingled surprise and hope.

"It would not be, either way, because of that."

With an unwelcome impulse of submission and desire he dropped to his knees and held her. She was aware of the predatory power of his weakness that could drain her of all her strength.

"I'll let you know tomorrow," she said, disengaging herself.

"Can't you decide tonight?"

"Tomorrow."

She saw wha she did not want to see, the tears of a dog hungering abjectly for its master.

"It's my life, Therese. Try to think that it may be yours."

She watched him from the head of the staircase as he was going down.

"*Do* you have a key to this house?" she called after him.

He looked back, pained that in spite of everything she still doubted him. "I told you. It was your man."

In the hall he put on his black peaked cap that made him look like a student.

She stood there above him in her white and lonely beauty, with her flaming hair and the barbaric green jewel, like a third eye, at her breast. He wanted with all his being to rescue her from the insecurity against which she armed herself with so much pride and coldness.

"*Dahin! Dahin! Mocht ich mit dir, o mein Geliebter, seihn!*"

The anonymous functionary from the Sûreté who spent his nights cursing the nocturnal habits of the Marquise de Païva noted the Prussian as he emerged from Number Twenty-two. He did not walk off in the direction of the boulevard, but crossed the street and secreted himself in a doorway. The Marquise evidently did not inspire much confidence in her admirers. How much longer would he have to wait there, watching them both? It was almost 2 A.M.

It was still dark when she reined up before the villa at St. Cloud. She jangled the ball and the disgruntled doorkeeper let her in. She left Saladin in the stables and went by the garden door into the house. The gaslights in the hall cast their usual subdued shadows. The house was always waiting, perhaps for its first owner, the enchanting Pompadour.

She knocked at the study door. There was no answer. She went in.

The desk at which de Morny usually sat was unoccupied, neat and impersonal. The pens, the blotter, the scarlet sealing wax, all the accessories of his spider industry.

She sat down. She was suddenly very tired.

She had betrayed Von Bernsdorff as she had all along known in her heart she would. She thought of him with impersonal pity as someone who would no longer play any part in her life.

The dream of the Italian villa in its orange groves had no more validity than the poem that had evoked his longing. *Kennst du das Land?*

She was woken by someone entering the room.

It was the Emperor in a black frock coat and black silk breeches that revealed his shrunken calves. His sallow features were held together by the great moustaches.

He seemed unsurprised to find her there. Nothing in the known world still had the capacity to surprise him. He motioned her to remain seated.

"My brother will not be here tonight. I come over some-times—to get away." He spoke slowly as if his mouth were full of stale cake. "You are fortunate to sleep. I haven't slept for years."

"I came, sire, because I have something of importance to tell Monsieur de Morny. He gave me permission to come here if it was urgent."

"My brother thinks highly of you, so does my wife. You have made quite a conquest of my family." He looked vaguely toward a sidetable with glasses and decanters. "Will you join me in a Madeira?"

"Thank you, sire."

He brought her a glass with that courtesy that, even in the face of death, would never desert him.

There was something impressive in the exhaustion of this monarch who had long since passed the point where he could be stirred by fear or hope or any recognizable emotion. Power and exhaustion were the achievements of his long and tortuous career.

He filled his glass and sank into a chair.

"You had something urgent to tell my brother?" His dark voice echoed from some mausoleum in which his illustrious forebears, more fortunate than he, were laid eternally to rest.

"Baron von Bernsdorff told me tonight that an attempt would be made on Your Majesty's life during the visit of the Czar."

The extinguished eyes regarded her.

"Oh?"

"He seemed quite certain. He said that his uncle, the Chancellor, was not responsible, but that he knew about it and would let it happen."

"And who is—responsible?"

"He didn't say."

It was impossible to tell the Emperor's reaction to this news.

"Why did he tell you this?"

"It is a difficult situation, sire. Baron von Bernsdorff appears to be—or thinks he is—in love with me. He wants me to go away with him to Italy. He has given me various pieces of information—"

"To lead you on?"

"To convince me of his sincerity, I think."

"What else did he tell you?"

"He's convinced that Prussia will declare war and that France will lose. He told me tonight that if I repeated this I would share your fate."

The black eyebrows partially revived and rose about the lusterless eyes. "My fate?"

"Because, in his view, it would mean the end."

The Emperor withdrew into a profundity of silence that seemed to fill the room.

"I have lived through forty years of prophesies about my end. Everyone with any knowledge of European politics has always assured me that my end was near." The effigy stirred sufficiently to take a sip of Madeira. "And you came at this hour to tell my brother that?"

"I thought it was important, sire."

"It is important. It is also not important. But I thank you, Therese, for your concern."

The mummified architect of the Second Empire closed his eyes. A voice that rose from the grave addressed posterity. "There have been many attempts on my life. Every day someone or other threatens me. Not without cause, I'm sure. What can I do? Tell the Czar to postpone his visit? He, too, has had attempts on his life. It is one of the hazards of our profession. Like the best trapeze artists we perform without a net. There will always be enthusiasts, madmen, crusaders. They are justified in their way. They are also not justified because they don't know—they have not experienced—what it means to rule."

A great silence enfolded him.

"Some things I achieved. Other things I did not achieve. They do not understand, those men with bombs and pistols, that one cannot achieve everything. They fire at my defeats."

The eyelids opened but the eyes remained closed.

"Destiny is a great mystery, Therese. We cannot define our destinies. I thought I could. I believed, in spite of everything, in my star. Sometimes I look into the darkness and I see nothing. I think perhaps my star has fallen. But I go on and then, in the same darkness, I see it once again. Only age makes one wonder if it is really there or if it is only vanity or hope or the will to endure that has added that speck of light to the enigma of the firmament."

"Monsieur Merimée said that you are a great man, sire, and I believe that."

"Merimée is a poet. I challenged history to a duel. Only history will know the outcome."

He looked at her as though seeing her for the first time.

"How old are you, Therese?"

"I am twenty-two, sire."

"A child: What was my brother thinking of to involve you in this kind of life?"

He put down his glass and stood up. It seemed astonishing that he could still find the energy to do so.

"Sometimes he is overzealous on my behalf. It is not right. I shall speak to the Empress. You know that she wants you with her. We'll arrange that. Now it is very late, my dear, and you must go to bed."

She was baffled by his change of manner which was abruptly as familiar and as solicitous as though she were a member of his family.

"My horse is in the stable, sire."

"You rode here? But I remember—you ride everywhere. No, my dear. It is quite unsafe for you to ride alone through that district. Sleep here; there are a number of unused bedrooms. Tomorrow I'll send a groom to see you home."

He found a candlestick, lit the candle, and, with an avuncular hand on her shoulder, led her to the door.

"Thank you again, dear child. We creatures of destiny must stand together."

She was so overwhelmed by his kindness which made him suddenly accessible that she curtsied and kissed his hand.

"I love you, sire."

The Emperor's turgid gaze followed her as she went upstairs.

She had not been asleep long before she was awakened by someone's climbing into bed with her. The waxed moustaches adhered to her mouth. Her pillow was soon greasy with a pomade that smelled disagreeably of nutmeg.

In the embrace of history Therese discovered that it was not only the Emperor's moustaches that had retained a spark of life.

She watched the speckled deer come from the thicket as she was drinking her morning coffee.

He sniffed the air to assure himself that there were no marauders lurking in his green domain and summoned his doe by pawing the ground with an elegant hoof. She emerged from a screen of foliage with her fawn. The little creature, as delicate as porcelain, with legs so spindly that they were scarcely able to support it, nuzzled its mother's side, its tail twitching with antic joy.

Therese watched this pristine family as they ventured forth to enjoy an environment they neither soiled nor shamed.

They were the Empress' pet deer that she loved to feed by hand.

Therese looked at the rumpled bed. The pillows were smudged with dye from the Emperor's hair. A sickly hint of nutmeg lingered in the room.

She had made her choice. They would keep their word. She would live at the Tuileries, share Eugenie's confidences and sleep with the Emperor when there was no one else at hand. The lies and posturings and betrayals would go on under the brilliant lights where history waited, as he had said, to pronounce its verdict. She did not resent the Emperor. In a way she was grateful to him; he had robbed her of an illusion. She saw that to live without illusions was the wisest precaution in a world where the citrus flowers only bloomed by imperial command.

The groom was waiting in the courtyard. Saladin had been rubbed down and saddled. He nuzzled her neck in greeting. He was pleased with her that morning.

They rode back through the slums which she had never seen by day. A subhuman race pollulated in these ruins like maggots upon a carcass. Haggard women with babies wrapped in sacking, burned-out men, vacant but for a dull despair, crouched in the doorways of dwellings that were no more than shells. Half-naked children ran beside her with grimy hands outstretched, begging in whining falsettos, and cursed her as she rode by.

She was so sickened by this wasteland that she barely noticed the more prosperous section of the city where worthy citizens were embarking on the business of the day.

When they reached the Chaussée d'Iena the groom dismounted. He opened the stable doors which she had forgotten to lock the night before.

On the threshold Saladin stopped, shuddered, twisted his head and whinnied. He refused to budge.

"What is it? There's nothing there."

Peering forward to see what it was that frightened him, she detected in the gloom the obscene object hanging from the rafter. The face, grotesquely angled by the dislocated neck, was purple as an eggplant. A swollen tongue protruded from a gaping mouth—a buffoon's last comment on the world.

Never in her life had day dragged by more slowly. Interminable moments stretched to interminable hours. She lay on her bed trying to grasp that the unspeakable had happened.

Everything was ominously still. It was as though the corrupting horror in the stable had swollen to gigantic proportions until its abomination filled the house.

What was de Morny doing? She had caught him that morning as he was leaving the Elysée. He had immediately assessed the consequences. "Go home. Stay there. See no one. Keep all the doors locked. I will arrange matters."

Why hadn't she listened? Why hadn't she at least *tried* to understand Von Bernsdorff? Some stubborn perversity had shut her mind against him. She had no longer been able to judge between his truth and the Emperor's falsehood. She had chosen the lie and the truth was hanging there, irrevocably damned and lost.

Was it her fault? Had any of it been her fault?

Henri's friends had laughed at her at the Pavillon because she always spoke the truth. In her innocence she had known what the truth was then. She was no longer innocent. That inner perception had been blurred and tarnished by all the untrustworthy, expedient, ambiguous people who had passed through her life since then. It was so clear to her now when it was too late. The risk of trusting Von Bernsdorff had been all along far less than trusting the Emperor and de Morny. "I love you, sire." That moment of belief in his sincerity had resulted in contaminated embraces not any less repulsive than the sight of Von Bernsdorff's white clown's body, his hangdog tears.

And then it seemed to her that her treatment of him had been an unconscious revenge against all the men who had substituted their gross desires for love and had never considered her as a woman. She had rejected the very thing she had wanted because in her inmost heart she hated men. She was not to blame for what they were. She was not to blame for having defended herself with the contempt they merited. Perhaps it wasn't even herself and them as individuals but something else, something larger and more mysterious. That nemesis called destiny. "We cannot divine our destinies," the Emperor had said. Somehow she must carry in her tainted blood, like the seed of a contagion, a fatality that reached out and struck down those who came close to her; the murders in the Muranov, Henri—and now this.

She dragged herself into the sitting room and lay down on the chaise longue, picked up her Greek lexicon and tried to concentrate. The words meant nothing.

She was listening.

There were people downstairs. Footsteps passed to and fro across the hall. Not the anonymous butler or the anonymous chef. De Morny's secretive associates were "arranging matters."

He would get rid of her now. She was certain of it. She had become a liability, the only link between *them* and Bismarck's nephew. Would this be the trumped-up excuse the Chancellor had been waiting for? Would they see to it that she was blamed?

Her life in that house, which had never been her life but only a performance, was drawing, moment by moment, to a close.

The light was fading from the wall across the street. A sudden terror seized her that they had taken Saladin away. She looked down into the garden. He was standing there, head bowed, under her window. Why hadn't she been able to know things as clearly as Saladin? There had been no questions or doubts or hesitations in that strong and constant heart once he had known that they belonged together.

She had never belonged anywhere. She had no place anywhere in the world.

Someone was coming upstairs.

A man in a trench coat came into the room. An anonymous functionary like everyone associated with de Morny.

This was the man who had spent so many nights in the doorway opposite. He knew everything about her. There was nothing to know about him. He was a cog in de Morny's immense, invisible machine.

"Madame de Païva?"

"Yes."

"I have an order from the Chief of Police. You are to leave Paris at once, within the hour. I have a carriage waiting. It will take you to Orleans. I was instructed to give you these."

He held out a document and an envelope. She recognized the envelope: it contained banknotes. The document was the order of her dismissal.

Von Bernsdorff had been accurate in every detail.

"I will not go anywhere by carriage."

"Those are orders. I am here to see they are carried out."

"I will not set foot outside this house unless I can take my horse."

The man was just human enough to be exasperated.

It occurred to her that, once in the carriage, they could strangle her and dispose of her body in the same way as the corpse in the stable.

"I will go on horseback or not at all."

"There's no time to argue. Pack."

She said quite calmly, "If you force me into a carriage I will write to every newspaper in Paris and tell them exactly what has happened. I will tell them everything I know. I leave you to imagine what that would mean."

"That is ridiculous," the man said sharply. "No one is going to harm you. Now, get ready. There's not much time."

The tortoiseshell dressing case, the gold mirror, the two

gold candlesticks were still in their Morocco cases. Von Bernsdorff had not sent anyone to collect them.

"Go into the salon," she said firmly. "There's a white vase
on the mantelpiece and two Chinese horses. Bring them to
me."

The man hesitated, annoyed. It was a reversal of procedure
that she should give him orders. But he had had altogether
enough of the Marquise de Païva who had robbed him of so
many nights' sleep. He wanted to get the matter over with.

She sat down at her desk and hurriedly wrote a note to
Leonide.

> *Dear friend, I have to leave Paris. There is no time to
> explain. Please keep these things which I am asking them
> to bring to you until I am able to return. I thank you for
> all you have done for me. Always your affectionate Therese.*

The man from the Sûreté returned with the vase and the two
Ming horses. All that belonged to her were the things the dead
man had given her.

She brought a suitcase from the bedroom and, stripping a
sheet and the pillow slips from the bed, wrapped up the jade
vase and the horses.

"You are to take this suitcase and these three red leather
boxes to Madame Leonide Leblanc. At that address." She handed
him the envelope. "Do you understand? You can read the note.
There's nothing in it that's incriminating."

She had the money de Morny had given her a few nights
before. She stuffed the new envelope into the same reticule
and scooped up the few pieces of jewelry she had acquired in
the last three years. There was a set of rubies and diamonds
that de Morny had rented for her to wear on important occasions. He could pay for dismissing her in this way, without a
single word. She put on the heavy ornate necklace under the
high collar of her blouse and dropped the pendant earrings into
the reticule. This she tied 'round her waist under her riding
habit which she had not taken off all day, and secured it with
a tasseled cord which held back the bedroom curtains. She put

on her gray tricorne which she wore out riding, a cloak lined with gray fur, and went back into the adjoining room.

"I'm ready."

The man from the Sûreté had been trained not to show emotion. "Aren't you taking anything with you?" he asked in surprise.

"You can send my clothes to Madame Leblanc if you want to. I don't really care what becomes of them."

She went downstairs for the last time.

Neighbors who had observed through their lace curtains the carriage and the two mounted policemen waiting in front of Number Twenty-two were surprised to see the Marquise de Païva about whom so many rumors circulated lead her black Arabian out through the front door. She mounted at the curbstone.

A man in a trench coat followed her and got into the carriage. It almost looked as if the Marquise were being arrested, except that no one would ride horseback to the police station.

The strange cortège made its way down the street.

Dark had fallen by the time they reached the Porte d'Orleans. The barrier was down.

One of the mounted police roused the *douanier*.

The man from the Sûreté climbed out of the carriage and said to Therese, "I hope you understand clearly; you are forbidden to return until further notice. You are to send your address to the gentleman you know. I don't need to warn you that you will pay heavily if you try to cause any trouble."

The Marquise looked at him with contempt.

The barrier was raised and she rode through.

The Man from the Sûreté thought, "I've made a mistake in letting her go like that. She should have been confined somewhere till the whole thing blows over." That was the trouble with de Morny and the Emperor. They were too civilized to have the courage of their convictions.

They watched as she spurred her horse to a canter and disappeared down the road.

To nowhere.

Callers at Number Twenty-two were informed that the Marquise had left for Portugal to rejoin her husband. She would not be returning for an indefinite time. They thought it strange, but then there had always been a great deal that was strange about the Marquise. As the Duc de Morny offered no explanation and her name was no longer mentioned at court, it was assumed that she had fallen from favor. The deck of imperial playing cards had been reshuffled and the game went on.

The body that was dragged from the Seine lay unclaimed for some days at the city morgue. It was curious that a man who had died by drowning should have had so little water in his lungs and what appeared to be the marks of a noose about his neck. But it was difficult to be certain due to the advanced state of decomposition.

When the identity of the deceased was established, the Duc de Morny wrote a personal letter of condolence to Chancellor von Bismarck deploring the untimely end of a young diplomat of such marked promise and distinction. The fullest investigation had revealed no suggestion of foul play. It was with the most profound regret and with the deepest commiseration et cetera et cetera.

Paris was a graveyard of mysteries. They came and went like the spring fashions.

When Czar Alexander arrived on his state visit the whole city turned out to greet him. He was a popular monarch who, though an autocrat, persisted in showing a misguided concern for the welfare of his people. He rode through cheering crowds, escorted by crack French regiments, feathered, caped and helmeted.

On the day when the two Emperors set forth from the Tuileries for the Great Exhibition, the Champs-Élysées was jammed with enthusiastic spectators. The chestnut trees burgeoned with youngsters who climbed to the topmost branches. Every balcony was a flowerbed of flags, handkerchiefs and pennants.

By an ironic coincidence which Therese would have noted had she been there, as the open carriage passed the entrance to the Chaussée d'Iena, a man broke through the cordon of Gardes Civils and, before anyone realized what was happening, fired at the Russian monarch. The bullet hit a horse immediately behind. The animal, crazed with pain, screamed, reared, crashed into the crowd, and stumbled to the ground, its legs jerking in the air.

A number of people rushed forward and seized the assassin who, in the general melée, managed to fire two more shots, the second of which ripped through one of Louis Napoleon's epaulettes.

There was the wildest confusion before order was restored.

Czar Alexander with admirable sang-froid insisted on proceeding. The cavalcade reformed and the two emperors continued up the avenue to deafening acclaim.

The would-be regicide was revealed to be a member of the Polish Resistance, fighting to free his country from Russian rule. It was not established, however, who had provided him with the large sum of money found in his hotel room.

A Certain Great Personage in discussing the matter with The Man with the Moustaches wondered how it was that Chancellor von Bismarck's nephew had known about the incident three weeks before it happened. Of course, the attempt had been made on the Czar and not on the Emperor of the French. Were the other two shots, then, merely accidental?

Therese read about it in a week-old newspaper. By that time she and Saladin were far away.

Part Four

Radoom

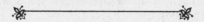

*P*RINCE AUGUSTUS OF Oppeln-Piast was in a very bad temper. He had never trusted the French and now he deplored them.

His carriage was hopelessly stuck in a dense crowd that filled the Place de l'Opéra. Parisians could never resist the opportunity for dramatics. They had screamed themselves hoarse over the Great Exhibition, that conglomeration of hideous inventions and even more hideous buildings. They had wept cataracts at the funeral of the Duc de Morny, that meretricious intriguer. Now they were yelling *"A Berlin! A Berlin!"* bawling the Marseillaise and stampeding the government into war.

As the carriage swayed under the impact of the press of bodies, Prince Augustus prayed that none of these besotted patriots would notice his coat of arms on the door. Although he detested the Prussians even more than he mistrusted the French, he was, due to the vagaries of history, a Prussian citizen. His family estates which had for centuries been where they were supposed to be, in Poland, had been ignominiously squeezed inside the Prussian border. *"A Berlin! A Berlin!"* A lunatic parade of gargoyles from a painting by Heironymus Bosch bobbed and leered and grimaced at the carriage windows. The Prince recoiled.

"How shall we ever get out of this?" he asked his secretary, Vittorio, who was sitting across from him.

"They're starting to move toward the Tuileries," the handsome Italian replied. "There's nothing to do but wait."

Above the clamor the terrified horses were neighing and whinnying. The coachman, precariously perched above this human inundation, tugged at the reins and shouted, "Whoa! Whoa there! Hold still!" The horses feared that at any moment they would be crushed to death and the Prince feared that the carriage would be overturned and that he and Vittorio would be torn limb from limb. Only the Italian preserved his calm. Theirs was not the only carriage trapped in this maelstrom of screaming fanatics.

Bismarck had engineered it with a trumped-up excuse to crush the intemperate French, who for the second time in a century had appointed themselves the dominant power of Europe. The prospect of a Europe controlled by Prussia was infinitely worse. The Prussians were gross and the Prince feared the German mystique of power. There was a terrible new composer called Richard Wagner who was glorifying the German disposition to muddled thinking in a series of thunderous epics about Rhine maidens and dragons and pots of magic gold, the idiocy of which defied description.

The thought crossed his mind at this alarming moment, when the Parisian mob was about to smash up his carriage and possibly smash him as well, that he would have been wiser to settle in England. The English were also gross and muddle-headed, but less offensively so than the Prussians. They were too phlegmatic to strike attitudes, too stolidly bourgeois to be carried away by exaggerated emotions. English complacency was an advantage in times of peril.

Had it not been for his sister's marrying an English peer he might have settled in London. But he had always wanted to keep the greatest possible distance between himself and his siblings, except for Ellamine, the youngest, a hummingbird hatched by accident in a henhouse. He had lived in Paris on the safe side of the Channel for twenty years.

That very evening the Prussian ambassador, a Junker whose acquaintance he had steadfastly avoided, had suggested, had, in fact, practically ordered, that he leave. War would be declared at any moment. The Embassy was packing up and all Prussian citizens should do likewise.

Leave? How could he leave? Who would look after his collections? He had been collecting since the age of sixteen.

He was now fifty-six. The Hotel de Piast was stacked with paintings and porcelains, books and objets d'art of incalculable value. And there were the dogs. He couldn't possibly leave the dogs. He had six little Maltese terriers whom he cherished almost as much as the celadon lovingly displayed in the great glass-fronted cabinets that lined his study. Nothing in his life had given him more delight than those jade green bowls and vases, infinitely graceful, with a purity of line that was poetry transmuted. He could certainly *not* leave the celadon or the dogs to the mercy of any hooligans who might break in if the house was deserted.

It was infuriating. It was inexcusable because it was senseless. The French would go to war and the Prussians would beat them. Thousands would be killed and what recourse did he have but to defy the Ambassador and stay to protect his dogs and his celadon? And of course the magnum opus on which he had been engaged for fifteen years, that illuminating history of the Piast family who had been Kings of Poland and were related, in one way or another, to all the crowned heads of Europe, not that that was always a matter of pride considering the dolts and despots produced by some of the ruling houses.

The old Prince tapped Vittorio with his cane. "We're not moving. We can't stay here all night."

"Patience, Altesse."

"The Rue de Rivoli will be impassable. We must cross the river and come back another way."

Vexations! The Prince's head withdrew into the sable collar of his greatcoat like a tortoise retreating into its shell. The Prince resembled a tortoise. An early attack of meningitis had deprived him of all his hair, including his eyebrows and eyelashes. His high, domed skull was polished like a baroque pearl and his little gray eyes blinked rapidly all the time like a hen prospecting for grain. He suffered constant discomfort from dust and his eyelids were always pink and puffy. He had a small petulant mouth like an angry cherub. He was a great eccentric, much laughed at by his servants behind his back. He had the reputation of being a pederast because he only employed sturdy young men to look after him. In point of fact he was innocent of such tendencies. His young servitors mocked "the old codger" behind his back, but they respected him and were fond of him and did their best to protect him. He gave them handsome settlements when they married and was mildly gratified when they brought their offspring for his inspection. He was constantly prodding babies and complimenting their parents. If people chose to have children that was their business. It was a commonplace human failing, but people *were* commonplace. That was why he chose to remain a recluse.

And he would not leave Paris. He would certainly *not* leave. If the servants were mobilized he would stay with Vittorio who was fortunately Italian. He relied on Vittorio. Although Vittorio was of humble stock he had the bearing of a Roman senator. That often happened in Italy where the classic strain prevailed.

The carriage was edging along the Avenue de l'Opéra. Although one could not commend Haussemann for the style he had chosen to inflict on Paris—the Opéra and the Bourse were vulgar in the extreme—nonetheless the new boulevards were a blessing.

The Prince tapped Vittorio on the leg. "We should turn off. We'll get caught by the Louvre and that will go on all night."

Vittorio stuck his head out of the window. "Try and turn off somewhere. The side streets may be less crowded."

He respected the Prince's orders. He had made himself indispensable and intended to remain so. That the Prince had no heirs and was immensely rich augured well for the future. In his way like the other servants he was fond of "the old codger." Crazy, of course, but a true nobleman.

The Avenue rang with the wild refrain to the strains of which the mob had conquered Paris in 1789. It was the proudest, most passionate hymn to freedom in the world. They had sung it again behind the barricades in '48. Now it had broken through the shell of the Second Empire. The Marseillaise was France at her most courageous, her most triumphant. *"A Berlin! A Berlin!"* and the Marseillaise! The Prince hunched down into his sable collar. Much good would it do them!

Suddenly there was a scream and the carriage lurched to a halt, precipitating the Prince into Vittorio's lap.

The old gentleman gasped. "My God! What's happened?"

Vittorio restored his master to his place and got out. The Prince banged irately on the floor with his ebony cane. "What is it? What has happened?"

Oh, the vexations! The shocks! Barbarians!

Vittorio stuck his head through the window.

"An accident. Someone's been knocked down. A woman."

"What woman?"

"A streetwalker."

There was a sudden outburst of shouting. A wild-looking ruffian shook his fist at the window. "Bastards! You've killed her. Dirty aristocrat!"

There was a great commotion. A woman wailed, "She's dead! The horses ran over her!"

The ruffian banged on the window.

"Butcher. Millionaire! You think you can run down innocent people? Murderer!"

His face was distorted with hatred. More shouts. "Dead! Yes, she's dead! She fell right under the wheels."

Frenchwomen screamed and Frenchmen hurled insults. It was all just noise. The Prince heard Vittorio's commanding Italian tenor. "Stand back, please. She's not dead. Get out of the way."

The hubbub subsided slightly. There were exclamations of distress and sympathy. Now they would turn the incident into a wake. Everyone would start weeping.

Vittorio and the coachman had lifted the woman up. The Prince saw a stream of red hair.

"Open the door," Vittorio called. The Prince leaned forward and pushed the door open with his cane.

To the Prince's utter dismay Vittorio laid the woman across the seat and then got in and lifted her head into his lap.

It was an outrage. The Prince shrank into his corner. A streetwalker covered in blood in his carriage!

People were crowding about the windows, eager to drain the excitement and tragedy to the dregs. "Drive to the Invalides," Vittorio shouted to the coachman.

Those freaks were jeering now. "Look at them! Bloodsuckers! What do they care? Some poor creature crushed to death!"

The old revolutionary continued to shake his fist at the Prince. "Murderer! Millionaire! You deserve the guillotine!"

The Prince was profoundly shaken. Such a thing had never happened to him before. Vittorio, in his well-organized way, had taken the accident in his stride. His calm, his superior strength, were infuriating. He had taken matters into his own hands without asking permission, without even consulting—

"For God's sake, get a move on. Get a move on!" the Prince insisted.

The carriage started again.

Well—! Well—! What could you expect when the whole city had gone mad? People surging about, blocking the streets, screaming like maniacs! Someone had pushed her. She hadn't been run over. Pushed!

"Is she—?"

"She'll recover. She may have a few broken bones."

A few broken bones? The Prince blinked rapidly in great agitation. But then he noticed something which of all the untoward things that had happened on this untoward night startled him the most.

This woman, this streetwalker, was wearing a ring. Her hand had slipped down and was dangling in front of him. A carved ruby ring. The Prince peered at it through his lorgnette. Unmistakable! A crown with the letter S.

There was only one family in Europe that, in its supreme self-esteem, considered itself above bearing a coat of arms.

The Prince stared at the ring and then at the woman. She was haggard and deathly pale. Come to think of it, she didn't look like a streetwalker, nor a woman of the people, not with that profile, that high forehead, that mass of astounding hair.

What to make of it? Perhaps she had stolen the ring. Or found it. It was all too distressing and confusing. All in all, it was the most distressing and confusing night he could remember.

He shut his eyes. He refused to think of it.

The carriage clattered down a side street.

Where now? Where were they? He refused to look.

At each cross street the carriage slowed.

"There's no chance of getting to the Invalides," Vittorio said. "We'd better take her home. I'll send for Dr. Cottard."

Waves of distant cheering broke against the Tuileries. People were running down the street to join the demonstration.

The drive to the Hôtel de Piast seemed interminable.

The Prince kept his eyes firmly closed.

The woman was moaning softly. He couldn't stand the proximity of sickness. He shrank from physical pain of any kind.

At last! Was it possible? They had reached the Rue St. Honoré.

"Hurry! Hurry!" the Prince kept muttering.

At last the carriage stopped before the street entrance. The coachman climbed down, rang the bell, and then resumed his place. What a time it took!

The carriage rattled into the courtyard.

The moment it stopped before the main door, the Prince climbed out and, disregarding the two footmen who darted forward to help him, hurried into the house.

All too dreadful and disturbing!

He pattered on his little feet through the main salon, through an anteroom, into his study.

Home!

At once there was a joyous scampering as six little white terriers jumped from chairs and sofas and rushed to greet him.

The sight of them restored his sanity.

"Oh, my dears, my dears, what a night! What a dreadful night!" He scooped up his favorite, Nichette, who covered his face with kisses. "Yes, my dear. It has been most, most upsetting!"

The little Maltese were dancing about him, balancing on their back legs with their paws outstretched.

He opened the French window. "There you go! Out with you! *Promenade!*" He kissed Nichette on the nose. *"Veux tu faire tes petits besoins, mon ange?"*

Nichette wriggled in assent. He put her down and she raced off after the others. He watched the six balls of fluff disporting themselves about the garden and turned back, exhausted, into the room.

A brandy! That would restore him. As he picked up the decanter his eye lit on the Duccio Madonna.

How beautiful she was! He went over and paid homage to this exquisite work which he had rescued from oblivion.

He had known all along what lay under the crude over-painting, the spurious crown and the blue cloak. Now she was restored to her original glory, with her rich austere beauty, the somber Mother of God.

One could almost believe in God when one looked at her. How far removed she was from all the sordid follies of mankind! He sighed with relief as the room with its treasures reclaimed him. In the great glass cases along the walls the celadon plates and bowls and vases glowed as pure as jade.

Only these things mattered. Only the inspired artists who had created such matchless beauty were worth considering.

Yes, he would stay. This was his sanctuary, his joy, his *duty*.

Vittorio would attend to the rest.

When, two hours later, Dr. Cottard knocked on the study door and was bidden to enter, he found the Prince huddled over his desk, absorbed in the Magnum Opus.

He always wore a sable cap indoors for fear, with his baldness, of catching cold.

The Prince looked up as though he had never before seen Dr. Cottard. He had just made an astonishing discovery. Ernestine Delphina of the Palatinate who had married Carolus Hamilcar of Oppeln-Piast in 1642 was a granddaughter on her mother's side of Gustavus Johannsen who had become King of Sweden and was thus a cousin by marriage, though twice removed, of Gustavus Adolphus the Great. It added an entirely new dimension to the family tree. He was thunderstruck that, in all these years of research, he could have overlooked a connection of such importance.

"Am I disturbing you, Altesse?"

The Prince remembered who he was. A nice man with

pretensions to culture. But what was he doing there at this time of night?

"Well, not exactly." Could he have summoned the doctor for some reason he had now forgotten?

"I came to report on your victim."

"My victim?" The Prince blinked his little hens' eyes.

"The woman who was knocked down by your carriage."

"Oh, that—yes, of course." That ugly, unnecessary incident. But hadn't Vittorio taken her to the hospital?

"She's not seriously hurt, a dislocated shoulder which I have set and a broken wrist."

"Ah, yes—I see." Well, that was settled, wasn't it?

"She has suffered a slight concussion, but quite apart from the accident, she appears to be in a generally rather weak condition, due, I fancy, to malnutrition."

Malnutrition? Why was the doctor giving him a medical report on a woman he didn't know?

"Vittorio will see to it."

"In normal circumstances I would not advise that she be moved."

It was very annoying, very inconsiderate to have interrupted him at the moment of his great discovery.

"Where has Vittorio put this person?"

"In one of the servants' rooms."

"Well, she's all right then. You and Vittorio must see to it."

That ended it. He wanted the doctor to go, so that he could return to his researches. But the doctor did not go. He was looking at the Madonna.

"I see you have had her cleaned."

At once the Prince was all attention.

"Isn't she beautiful? The crown and robe, as I surmised, were completely extraneous. That was obvious from the start. Added, I should guess, at least a century later. There she is— exactly as Duccio painted her."

He toddled over to the painting which was resting against a cabinet.

"How daring they were, those early masters! No painter of

later times would have had the courage to say so much with apparently so little. Almost no detail. And yet what depth, what splendor!"

Amused as he always was by the Prince's eccentricity, Dr. Cottard had a great respect for his taste and knowledge. The Hôtel de Piast was crammed with marvels. This passion for collecting was not the vainglorious plundering of a Napoleon or the vanity of a wealthy man who wanted to gain prestige. It was a true dedication to what was finest in art, supported by an instinct that seldom faltered.

"What do you intend to do with all your treasures?" the doctor asked.

"Do with them?"

"War will probably be declared tomorrow. Won't you be forced to leave?"

This question amounted to an impertinence.

"I don't intend to do anything," the Prince replied haughtily. "I live here and I shall stay."

"The temper of the city is violently anti-Prussian."

"I am not a Prussian, except by default. I consider the subject ridiculous."

"War generally is."

He was trying to warn the Prince that governments in wartime had the habit of requisitioning the property of enemy subjects. The French government would like nothing better than to find an excuse for nationalizing the Piast collection.

"If it would be of any help I could give you a medical certificate."

"A certificate? What for?"

"That you are under my care and cannot travel—for reasons of health."

The Prince looked straight at the doctor and blinked his puffy eyelids.

"Thank you, but that will not be necessary."

He wished to bring this intrusion to an end and pointedly returned to his desk.

"Well, if I can help in any way—" Dr. Cottard said to the Prince's back. "Good night, Altesse."

Impertinence! The Prince dismissed the matter and returned to the important question of Ernestine Delphina's ancestry. "Now *she*—" he murmured, "was the daughter of Lizalotte of Anhalt-Zerbst, a cousin of the Catherine who married Paul of Russia. And *her* mother appears to have been—let me be quite sure—a Maria Cornelia Johannsen—"

But the doctor's implied warning troubled him. He looked up through the open window. Out there in the subdued clamor of the city, history was on the march, that nemesis, draped in her blood-stained tricolor, who had so often stalked the streets of Paris in this unruly century.

He got up with the intention of drawing the curtains against this unwelcome presence, but, instead, went out into the garden. He could hear it, even here, that distant roar of lions.

They were still demonstrating before the Louvre.

Nichette looked up from her embroidered cushion, her bright eyes alert with inquiry and concern. She hopped down and joined her master. At once two other heads were raised. Ce Monsieur and Murmurine trotted after her.

The Prince was not given to introspection. All his life because of his name and fortune he had done whatever he wanted.

Suddenly, for the first time, he felt threatened and alone.

Vittorio heard her cry out as he came down the passage with the tray.

She had woken, bathed in sweat, and was staring at some horror across the room.

"Are you in pain?"

Her enormous eyes, dull as frosted glass, found him but remained unfocused.

She was gasping for breath and luminously pale.

"Dr. Cottard left some laudanum. But you must take this first. It's nourishing."

Her left shoulder was bandaged and throbbed violently. Her left wrist was in a splint. He came 'round to the other side of the bed and bent over her with the glass. She averted her head and warded him off with her good hand.

"Drink this. Dr. Cottard said you need strength."

She moaned like a wounded animal and covered her mouth.

He stood there, defeated, with the glass which contained two raw eggs beaten up with cream and brandy.

"You must try."

Her torso heaved and she vomited. Yellow bile streamed down her worn bodice, over her marvelous hair.

Vittorio took a towel and wiped away what he could. She appeared to have fainted. He felt her forehead. It was clammy with tepid sweat.

It occurred to him that she might die. That would be awkward. The police would have to be informed. He had seen many people die at the hospital where he had worked as an orderly when he first came to Paris.

The room already had the rank smell of sickness. He opened one of the small windows that overlooked the courtyard. A distant clamor rose from the city. War had been declared that morning and the streets were agog with patriotic crowds. It was the human hunger for carnage that had echoed all through history. Vittorio had no taste for violence. It offended his sense of order.

He went down the passage to his room and brought back a bottle of lemon verbena which he sprayed on the sick woman's breast, on the pillow and on her hair.

Even in her present state of dereliction, haggard, delirious, and in pain, he could see that she was no ordinary woman. There was something disturbing about her, a sort of magnetic power. Somehow this accident and the tumult in the streets were augeries of the march of events that were about to engulf their lives, his, the Prince's, perhaps this unknown woman's.

He sat down and waited. He did not know what he was waiting for.

Therese was rocking on murky waves of nausea. On the table the terrible needles, long and lethal as hatpins, gleamed. The old hag seized one, brandishing it in her face, and then drove it into her womb. She tried to scream. A thin bile trickled across her chin.

Vittorio got up and wiped her face. She groaned and shifted. Where was Saladin—the kind schoolmaster—the little nuns? Why was she in this room?

The Corsican brothers knocked at the door of the Prince's study. They felt awkward out of livery, in their ill-fitting suits, but they could not leave without saying goodbye to the "old codger."

The Prince was at his desk as usual. He had convinced himself during that morning that the Johannsen from whom Ernestine Delphina of the Palatinate was descended was probably not the senator who had been raised to the throne of Sweden. Johannsen, after all, was a fairly commonplace name.

The two brothers stood stiffly by the door waiting for permission to speak. For a moment the Prince could not grasp what they were doing there.

"Yes?"

"Mon Altesse," one of them began, "we have come to tell you—that is we would like—"

"Yes?" The Prince blinked rapidly.

"Mon Altesse," scarlet with embarrassment the youth blurted out, "we have come to say goodbye."

The Prince turned 'round in his chair and considered them.

"Where are you going?"

"We are volunteering for military service—with your permission."

Military service? Absurd!

"Why?"

"France is at war, Mon Altesse. We must do our duty."

They looked so young, so innocent and so stupid that, in spite of his annoyance, the Prince was touched.

"Can't you wait a little?"

"Mon Altesse," the spokesman floundered. "We want to be with the first to reach Berlin—begging Your Highness' pardon."

The Prince snorted. "I can think of no reason why anyone should be anxious to reach Berlin. It is a most disagreeable city." But he realized that, after all, however absurd, this was a serious matter. "How old are you?"

"Seventeen, Mon Altesse."

"Wait till you're eighteen. The war won't last that long."

"We want to contribute to the victory—with your permission."

"Of course I don't give my permission," the Prince retorted with familiar tartness. "You are far too young. Don't you have families—parents?"

"Yes, Mon Altesse." The brothers devoutly wished that they had not embarked on this interview. After all "the old codger" was Prussian and couldn't possibly understand.

"Our grandfather was with Napoleon at Moscow," one of them blurted out.

"And you want to emulate him by assisting at the retreat from Berlin?"

The brothers were torn between indignation and respect.

"We shall take Berlin and crush the enemy." For once they did not add, "with your permission."

The Prince shook his head. It was useless to tell these decent, trusting lads that they would be killed or crippled for nothing but the satisfaction of Bismarck. He went to a cabinet, opened a drawer, and took out two Louis d'Or.

"My permission I do not give. But I wish for your safe return."

He solemnly handed each of them a gold piece. They were suddenly very much upset. In spite of being a Prussian, "the old codger" had always been decent to them, had allowed them holidays, and had never punished them when they made mistakes.

They bowed. They were close to tears, but they felt that to show emotion at this moment was beneath the dignity of Frenchmen.

The two boys blundered out.

The old Prince called the dogs who scampered from their baskets, chairs and cushions, and went into the garden.

He was depressed by the probable fate of the twins. Youth was so short and the chances of happiness so fleeting. He thought, as he seldom did, of his own lost youth on the gloomy estate in Silesia, of his parents, two mummified figures who moved in stiff brocades through stiff formalities, of his two strident sisters who had made his childhood a misery and of the lovely, wayward Ellamine, who had danced and laughed and wept her way out of his heart.

Life was a wilderness. He had built a fortress of art against a disillusion learned too soon.

One by one the servants departed. By the end of the first week of war there were only the Prince, Vittorio, and the chef, an Austrian, in the great mansion on the Champs-Élysées— and, unbeknownst to the Prince, the sick woman on the servants' floor. With the tacit consent of Dr. Cottard, Vittorio had decided not to refresh the Prince's memory. He knew his master well. He quickly forgot things that did not concern him personally. If something annoyed him he could be as unpredictably cruel as he was capable of being kind.

She was improving, but she was weak with something more than physical depletion. The unhappy eyes which had recaptured something of their enigmatic clarity watched Vittorio when he brought her food. She watched him as though he belonged to an alien race with which she was no longer connected.

"Whose house is this?" she had asked.

"A private house. You can stay here till you're well."

Dr. Cottard, on his rounds, stopped by to see how his patient was progressing. She asked again, "Whose house *is* this?"

"Prince Augustus of Oppeln-Piast on the Champs-Élysées."

"The big house near the British Embassy?"

"Yes. You live in Paris then?"

"I did. Not far away."

"Is there anyone you wish me to inform of your whereabouts?"

She shook her head.

"Clothes? Things you need? Vittorio could fetch them."

"If he could change the sheets. I think I'm bleeding."

"In that case I must examine you."

He was shocked by her condition. Black and clotted blood had soaked through the sheet into the mattress.

"I have to ask you this as a doctor; have you had an abortion?"

She nodded.

"How long before the accident?"

"I was on my way home. I think I fainted."

"You're running a serious risk of blood poisoning."

After he had attended to her, he wrote out a prescription. "It's essential that you take this. And you must apply the medicated pads. I'll send Vittorio to the chemist."

It was another of the sordid little tragedies that happened all too frequently in a big city.

Her weary eyes implored him. "Please don't tell them. They've been so kind."

Dr. Cottard went in search of Vittorio and returned with fresh linen. He had practically to lift Therese from the bed. She could hardly stand.

She sat swaying on a chair while they stripped the bed, turned the mattress and changed the sheets.

She sank back with relief against the pillows. "I have a little money in my bag. Please take whatever there is."

"That is not important." Dr. Cottard tucked her in. "Surely there must be someone in Paris who is concerned about you?"

She was too spent for explanations. Besides—what explanations could she give?

"Rest, then. Eat all you can. I'll come back tomorrow."

It was always strangers who were so kind.

Vittorio came in a little later. He looked at her with concern in which there was also suspicion.

"I'm going to the chemist. Is there anything else you need?"

She tried to smile. "Yes, but it would take you at least an hour."

"I can spare the time."

She made the great effort of giving him instructions. "At the end of the Rue du Temple in the Marais there's a restaurant called the Provençal. Beside it there's a high iron gate that leads into a garden with a house. Under the piano lid in the salon I left a reticule with some money and jewelry. The key to the house is in my bag. Or did I lose that when I fell?"

"No, the coachman retrieved it." He brought her a mud-stained purse that had been lying on the dresser.

She managed to open it and took out a key and a few small notes.

"Take them to pay for the cab."

As he took the money he looked straight into her eyes which he thought were the strangest, but the most beautiful, he had ever seen. Who on earth *was* this woman?

"Would you like me to bring you some clothes as well?"

"I have put you to so much trouble."

She wanted him to go so that she could sleep.

As the doorkeeper had also left to join the army, Vittorio let himself out by the main door. It was a heavy August day and the city seemed to be en fête. One might have thought it was a public holiday. Festive crowds milled about. Every window was draped with flags. There was a general feeling of excitement, of anticipation.

When he reached the Place de la Concorde he found himself on the fringe of a dense throng cheering a parade of soldiers bearing their regimental pennants. As the cavalcade passed, cries of *A Berlin! A Berlin!"* drowned out the rhythm of marching feet.

It was dangerously unreal, he thought.

He made his way along the Rue de Rivoli to the Pharmacie Albert, presented the prescription, and told the druggist that he would be back in half an hour.

He found a cab by the Place Vendôme.

He thought the Prince had been very unwise to remain in Paris. It would have been far more sensible to pack up the most valuable things, store them in the attic and close the house for the duration. Whatever the outcome of the war the Prince's position was precarious. A great many foreigners had been in the habit of calling at the Hôtel de Piast. They were dealers mostly, some German, others Italian and Swiss. It was impossible to know how much the authorities had noted these comings and goings. Although the Prince was a recluse and seldom, if ever, went into society and seldom, if ever, entertained, he was, without knowing it, a legendary figure in Paris. There was never an auction he did not attend, every art dealer vied for his patronage, and any number of important people, including the Empress, the Duc de Morny and the Duc d'Aumale had written for permission to view the collections. The Hôtel de Piast was well known to be a treasure trove and now that the Prussian Embassy was closed, the Prince had no protection of any kind. He was isolated—by choice—but also by circumstances far more dangerous than he supposed.

Vittorio knew that once the old autocrat had made up his mind it was useless to argue with him. He was impervious to reason and could only see one thing, his absolute right to have his own way.

He had reached the Marais, a quarter of the city he barely knew. He peered through the cab window looking for the restaurant, Le Provençal, spied the sign, and called to the driver to draw up.

The shutters of Le Provençal were drawn, the door covered by a typically Parisian sign, "Closed during rearrangements of the map of Europe."

There was the iron gate. Vittorio lifted the latch and went into the garden. He was surprised by its size and beauty. The roses were at their peak, pale yellow and white and pink. Within their neat box hedges the beds were bright with flowers. Doves strutted and cooed about the fountain. Not a leaf stirred on the four great chestnut trees.

There was a strange, sad magic about the place, of something lost but remembered, which deepened the mystery of the sick woman who apparently lived here.

He let himself into an unfurnished house. The octagonal salon was empty but for a grand piano and a large carved sofa. The walls and floors were bare. The nymphs on the ceiling floated above an abandoned temple.

He found the reticule under the piano lid. But where were her clothes and other things?

He looked through empty rooms. Upstairs, in a dismantled bedroom, he found two dresses hanging on a door and a few underclothes lying on a rush-bottomed chair. In a corner was a carpetbag such as country women used. He packed the clothes into it with a pair of cheap slippers. In the bathroom two pairs of cotton stockings had been hung up to dry. He retrieved a plain brush and comb.

In the hall closet hung a well-worn riding habit, a gray velvet cape and a tricorne hat with a green plume. He supposed that she must have sold her riding boots.

The sick woman, whoever she was, had been reduced to the brink of abject poverty and yet this was not the house of a poor person. In his five years with the Prince, Vittorio had developed a shrewd sense of social values. A grand piano was an instrument that only the wealthy owned.

He locked the front door and looked back at the garden. Was she the wife of some man of means who had died or the mistress of someone who had tired of her and given her this property as a parting settlement? Whatever the changes of fortune which had reduced her to a few poor possessions, it made him reconsider his own position.

He had thrown in his lot with the old Prince because it had proved to be a secure job. It paid more than he could have earned elsewhere. He lived comfortably and he had learned a good deal about that privileged world into which the Prince had been born. But he may have counted too much, he thought now, on the Prince's favor.

Fate took away with one hand what it gave with the other. He was not, in fact, much more secure than the woman who had lived in this strange retreat and who was now virtually penniless. What would happen to her when she left the Hôtel de Piast? If anything happened to the old man what would happen to him?

Vittorio was confident of his assets, but equally aware of his shortcomings. He was handsome, he was superbly built. He was aware that his appearance gratified the Prince. He had cultivated a quietly deferential manner. He was observant, efficient and discreet.

Beyond that he had little with which to make his way. He came from a humble background; he had no education to speak of. He knew that many young men with his physical endowments made a good living off rich women who sometimes married their lovers rather than lose them. Such a career did not appeal to him. He enjoyed women, largely as targets for self-approbation. He liked to dazzle them, he liked to arouse desire. He was careful to avoid commitments. He had risen from house servant, to valet, to majordomo, a position that carried responsibility. He had envisaged a time when the Prince, grown old, would depend on him entirely and would, as a bribe for his continued services, make him financially secure. After his benefactor's death he would return to his village near Florence, buy a small property, marry, raise a family. What else was there?

But if the Prince died before all this came about, if the misfortune of war disrupted these plans, he would be worse off than this woman who, at least, had this property that could be sold for money.

He thought of her beautiful rich hair with its copper glints as he had smoothed it across the pillow. Disturbing rather than desirable. Why had he taken pity on her and kept her presence a secret?

It was not enough to know how to behave, to wear tight enough trousers to show off one's splendid thighs. She, too, may have counted on her beauty. What good had it done her?

It would have been easier if the rumors about the Prince's taste for young men had been justified. He would have had a hold over him then.

Debating the problem of his future, Vittorio had made his way down the Rue du Temple. At the corner of the Boulevard Sevastopol he encountered a group of people shouting and laughing and hugging each other.

"What's going on?" he inquired of a passerby.

"Victory! We've crushed the Crown Prince of Prussia's army. Rubbed his nose in good French shit. That's what!"

People were celebrating all along the boulevard.

"Victory! French army triumphant! Victory!" the newsboy screamed at the corner.

Strangers were running about embracing each other as if it were Mardi Gras.

It was dusk when Vittorio reached the Hôtel de Piast. The

great house had the same look of abandonment as the pavilion in the Marais.

The old codger didn't even know how to turn up the lights! Vittorio knocked on the study door.

He was greeted by the usual yapping of the dogs and the Prince's testy demand, "Where have you been? I've been left here quite alone."

"I went out to see if there was any news," Vittorio said as he turned up the chandelier. "There's been a big French victory, it seems." He handed the Prince a newspaper.

The Prince glared at the headline. "Nonsense, I don't believe it. Well, true or false, it may get the thing over with." He said sternly, as though Vittorio was to blame, "Anton has left."

Anton, the Austrian chef, had expressed a concern that his reputation might suffer if it became known that he had remained in the employ of a Prussian in war time.

"He announced without so much as a by-your-leave that he was returning to Vienna. A lie, of course. He's going to work for some French profiteer. The Austrians were never reliable, with all their whipped cream and waltzes."

"Don't upset yourself, Mon Altesse. I will prepare the meals."

"Can you cook?" the Prince demanded, amazed.

"Not as well as Anton, but enough."

"Well, that's something."

Vittorio stood by his master's chair.

"If I may say so, Mon Altesse, considering the general uncertainty, I think it would be advisable to lay in a stock of food."

"Oh? Why is that?"

"Prices are going up. There may be shortages if the war continues."

"It won't continue. Well—very well—do as you think best."

"I shall need money, Mon Altesse. And if I may further suggest, I think it would be wise to withdraw a considerable sum."

"Eh? Why? What for?"

"We do not know what restrictions may be imposed on enemy citizens. They may very well freeze your assets."

"Freeze? Nonsense. I've had an account at the Banque de France for twenty years."

"We are at war, Mon Altesse. A fact which you don't seem to take seriously—as far as it affects yourself."

The Prince was on the point of taking umbrage, but when he looked at Vittorio's handsome face, as perfect in its way as Michelangelo's David, he demurred. He was forced to keep on the good side of his majordomo because if Vittorio, for some unaccountable reason, took it into his head to leave—

"I'll think of it. It seems quite unlikely, but I will think of it."

Vittorio dared to employ a word which he had never used to the Prince before.

"You must think of it. I can fetch the money in the morning. Otherwise we shall most likely starve."

The Prince was startled. He picked up Nichette and held her against his face, like a muff, for protection.

"Very well, I will think of it—tonight."

Vittorio left in his lordly way. The Prince would never have admitted it, but he felt a sincere attachment to his Italian. Of all the young men who had served him he liked Vittorio best. It pleased him to watch Vittorio moving about the room with his steady feline grace. Vittorio gave him reassurance, a sort of pride, a sort of regret, perhaps a postmortem stirring of some paternal instinct, something close to what he had once felt for his sister, Ellamine. Vittorio made him feel that there was some order to things, a progression. And he was honest. He had often pointed out how grossly the tradesmen took advantage of him. He had argued over the bills and brought money he had reclaimed, laying it out carefully to the last penny. The Prince had no interest in money, but this was a proof of Vittorio's sincerity. It warmed him to feel that perhaps Vittorio had some affection for him as well.

When the Italian entered the invalid's room she was sleeping. He put down the reticule and the carpetbag and looked at her. It annoyed him that he could not define why this woman disturbed him.

She opened her eyes and for the first time saw him distinctly.

He was a servant who deserved to be something more. De Morny would have put a young man of such remarkable good looks and bearing to good use. Somber, steady eyes, a finely sculpted head, a light but powerful physique.

There was born in that silent appraisal a mutual respect and mistrust. They recognized in each other a capacity not only for manipulation but for sustained antagonism. They were, in certain other undefined ways, alike.

"I found what you asked for and I packed a few things I thought you might need."

"Thank you."

She managed to draw back the strings of the reticule and extracted a few notes which she offered him.

"Will you allow me? Please?"

It was a bribe, but also an armistice. "That isn't necessary." He examined the bottle he had collected from the pharmacy.

"You are to take two of these every few hours."

He shook two pills into his hand and stood over her while she swallowed them.

"That is a very unusual house. Does it belong to you?"

"I inherited it from a man I was going to marry."

He wanted to ask if the man were dead or if he had deserted her.

"The estate fell into the hands of a lawyer who embezzled the money. The house was all I got."

"It has no furniture."

"He stole most of it and I had to sell what was left. I thought I would sell the house, but it seems that people are not investing in property now."

"Will you go back there?"

"I suppose so."

It occurred to him that she had made up her mind to stay and that she could cause him trouble.

"I don't know how much longer the Prince will be allowed to remain in Paris."

"Because of the war?"

"He's a Prussian. Shall I unpack something for you?"

"A nightdress, please—if there is one."

He put the carpetbag on a chair, opened it and extracted a plain cotton nightdress.

"Can you manage?"

She undid the bodice of her slip and worked her right arm free. He helped her slide the other sleeve over her bandaged shoulder. As he did so he glimpsed her breasts, full and widely spaced.

"Don't be embarrassed. I worked in a hospital before I came here."

He helped her into the nightdress and from the foot of the bed drew it down over her body. His hand glanced along her chilly thigh.

"I'll bring you something to eat in a little while."

At the door he looked back.

"May I know your name?"

She didn't answer. He waited. She had decided to remain a mystery. He was sorry for her, but he thought, "She can stay here, but not for long."

Her mind was working more clearly now. She was dimly able to review the events of the past weeks as if she were sitting in the back row of a theater watching a play.

She had seen at once when she entered the office of Maître Descases that Casimir was determined to bluff it out. He was more offensively theatrical, more unctuously dishonest, than he had ever been. Five years had bloated his mannerisms into cirrhosis of the ego. He greeted her with a smile that would have shamed a crocodile.

"My dear Therese, I am delighted to see you. What a blessing that under such fine auspices we can at last resolve our misunderstandings. You know, or perhaps you don't, that I have never wished you anything but well."

He was performing, of course, for Maître Descases whose good opinion, as the Empress' lawyer, was valuable to him in his profession.

He saw that Therese had been ill and that things had not gone well for her since her fall from grace and this encouraged him to be patronizing.

"I am only too glad for your sake to reach an agreement. I know it's useless to try and convince you that poor Henri's financial position was never what you thought it was," he said.

"Since you never furnished me with proof I have only your word for it. As for your good intentions, I have had ample opportunity to regret them."

Casimir hunched his shoulders and made the wide gesture of an innocent man accepting the martyrdom of an unjust verdict.

"So be it; you have taken a stand. I shall not seek to dissuade you. Shall we, cher Maître, outline the terms which, for purely humanitarian reasons, I am ready to accept."

"I want no humanity from you, Casimir," Therese said sharply. "If I had been less innocent and less unhappy at the time of Henri's death I would gladly have seen you in jail where you belong."

Casimir stood up with a fine show of indignation. "I assure you, Madame, that I did not come here to be insulted."

Maître Descases de Montauban emerged from his smoke screen of legal eminence sufficiently to clear his throat. He had no interest in the matter now that the Marquise de Païva was no longer under the protection of his august client.

"Monsieur Fabre-Marquet is ready to cede you the property known as—" he consulted a document, "the Pavillon d'Armide on the Rue du Temple, in return for a guarantee that you will drop all further proceedings against him."

"It is a contingency that has been forced upon me," Casimir assured that pillar of official rectitude, "out of regard for my late client and friend and to save myself the infinite amount of paper work involved in providing an audit of accounts going back ten or fifteen years. It is a concession, I wish to make it plain, but in no way an admission."

Maître Descases was not impressed by either of these litigants. He had no desire to soil his hands with a matter so far beneath him.

"Are you ready to sign the agreement, Madame?"

Therese glanced through the document.

"What about Henri's things? His piano and furniture and other possessions?"

"Understand," Casimir said, pointing a judiciary finger, "that you have no legal claim to anything. Despite your contention that Henri Herz intended to marry you, he left no testament to that effect. I do this solely to end a matter which is extremely distasteful to me."

"You are a contemptible liar," Therese retorted. "Please give me the pen."

In a stormy silence, potent with accusations, she signed the deed.

"There will be certain disbursements that have accrued," Descases murmured, as though the question of fees was hardly worth mentioning.

"I'm sure that Monsieur Marquet has enriched himself sufficiently to take care of those." Therese rose. She was white with anger. "Where do I get the key?"

Maître Descases handed the deed to Casimir who signed it with an indignant flourish. He remarked with a grandiose display of magnanimity which his expression clearly belied, "I will, of course, be responsible for any financial obligations pertaining to this matter."

Their voices receded as her head clouded. The dizziness that had come over her lately forced her to steady herself against the great jurist's desk.

The two men saw her sway. With an effort she regained control. "Just give me the key and let me go."

She was aware that Casimir had handed her something and that they were staring at her. She must say something coherent. "I hope you will never forget how much trouble you caused me. Henri trusted you and you betrayed him."

She felt sick and thought, "Oh God, I am going to faint."

"I shall need a week to vacate the premises," she had heard Casimir say.

The floor rocked and then rose to strike her as she fell.

It was after that meeting, back in the sordid little hotel, that she realized the worst beyond the worst had happened; she was with child.

She could barely even bring herself to think of it. It had all happened to someone else. The malign fate that lurked in the wings of her life had once again intruded in the shape of a hired hand, a brutalized Caliban, who had come to the village with other itinerant laborers to help with the harvest. He had seen her riding the country roads as he swilled his wine, half stripped and grimy with sweat, after a hard day's work in the fields. He had seen her as, by ill chance, he had lunged out of the inn, dead drunk, when she was passing. He had seized the bridle. "You Paris bitch, where do you think you're going?" She had struck him with her crop and spurred Saladin down the road. He had shouted obscenities after her. Red eyes like the rat that had once crawled up her in the Muranov, broken, diseased teeth, dehumanized dregs of something that had once been a man. Fabrice, the schoolmaster, her only friend in the village, had lodged a complaint with the police. But what did the police care? She was as much an enigma to them as to the rest of the village. Why had they hated her, those hardheaded, mean-spirited peasants? She had kept to herself as much as possible in the cottage she had rented by the river. All she had wanted was to be left alone. For a while, in those first months, she had found peace, even happiness, in that simple retreat with the few bits of furniture she had bought at Angers, with the books the schoolmaster lent her, with Saladin safely ensconced in the barn where former generations of peasants had kept their hay and pigs and chickens.

The river enabled her to dream. She wandered with Saladin beside those placid waters, along the sedges starred with meadowsweet and iris. Sometimes in the evenings she would dine with the schoolmaster and his invalid mother. Good people. Gentle and undemanding. She would read to the old lady who taught her to embroider. She was grateful for such placid company when Fabrice was teaching school. The old lady had grown fond of her and had hinted at marriage with her son. She wouldn't last forever and was worried by the thought of Fabrice being left alone.

Sometimes it had seemed to her that she could find contentment there, away from all the intrigues and deceptions of

the city. She had discussed with Fabrice on their Sunday walks
the idea of buying a bookshop in Angers. After all, why not?
He was a good man. He revered her. He was kind.

Her mind balked at the memory of that night when the three
men had come pounding on the door. There was no escape
from that room. They had ripped off the shutters, smashed the
window, climbed in and ransacked the cottage for hidden gold.

Hell had struck her down on the bed. The weight of Hell's
body pinioned her, screaming. Hell's foul breath in her face.
Saladin trumpeting in the barn. A hand over her mouth. Her
legs held. Shouted encouragement at the outrage. And then the
other—And the deafening crash as the door burst in and the
great black bulk of her avenger scattered the bodies. She saw
Saladin rear and plunge and heard the body fall by the bed.
She came to with the rough tongue licking her throat, reached
for the dear black head and fell away.

She remembered a blurred journey to Angers in a cart and
Saladin trotting alongside. They had lifted her up steps into a
convent. Pale faces of nuns peeping from black coifs and the
commanding figure who gave orders, who set everything
straight, who was the ultimate reassurance. Saladin had made
a great commotion at the door. "Don't hurt him," she had cried
out as they carried her upstairs. "He saved my life."

It was the Mother Superior, an angel disguised as a stout,
imperturbably capable woman who had allowed Saladin into
the courtyard to the consternation of the nuns. "He's here, my
child. Under your window. Sleep."

One man they found on the cottage floor with broken legs
and a crushed rib cage. The other two had fled with the money.
Only the reticule with the jewels remained where she had hidden
it in the chimney.

The schoolmaster came every day and sat disconsolately by
her bed. She only wanted the Mother Superior, that bulwark
against pain and despair who restored broken limbs and broken
spirits by an inner force beyond faith or pity.

"My child," this good woman said to her one day, "you
were the victim of an outrage. There is no consolation I can
give you. Your only redress is courage. You must live."

She must live because she had no choice, because the days came and went and she was still there. She watched the Mother Superior on her rounds and marveled at her fortitude, at the simple totality of conviction in what was right.

Fabrice brought her the letter from Maître Descases. Casimir had agreed to relinquish the Pavillon. She must go to Paris and sell it. She needed money.

It was all there unchanged, except that everything had changed.

As she heard the click of the latch of the iron gate, she had said to herself, "Your only redress is courage." She saw, without seeing, the garden in all its unbearable sweetness. The roses, the little paths, the white table and chairs where she and Henri had so often sat. The doves were still cooing by the fountain. Were they the same doves she had tamed so long ago?

There was little left in the house. Casimir had seen to that. Only the piano, a sofa and a few chairs and, when she lay down, the flying figures on the ceiling. Euterpe with her lyre and her angels, white clouds that never moved.

It was no longer an irony when the jeweler informed her that de Morny's rubies and diamonds were paste, that the other items were not of the first quality, and the Prince of Nepal's diamond had no marketable value because of its size and bizarre color.

She took what was offered without comment.

On her way back from the jewelers she passed Sophie's pastry shop. It was now called La Belle Etoile and sold ribbons, laces and stays. The woman behind the counter regretted that she knew nothing of the former owner. Sophie had gone to the Midi—to the sun.

She asked in the neighborhood if anyone wanted to buy the Pavillon and posted a "For Sale" sign on the gate. The proprietor of the Provençal remembered her.

"But, of course, you were Monsieur Herz' friend. I often wondered what had become of you. Indeed I would love to buy the Pavillon. It would be ideal with the garden for summer trade. The fact is, times are very uncertain. There's talk of war. It's not the moment to embark on new ventures."

The beauty of the garden was another sadness. It gave her a deadened peace to break off the dead roses, to feed the doves, to scatter feed for the fish that rushed to the surface in a scarlet and golden swirl.

She put off going to see Leonide to the last because with Leonide there would be so many explanations. But she needed the things Von Bernsdorff had given her, the gold dressing set and the jade vase. She needed money to get rid of this thing inside her, money against the future that no longer existed. "Your only redress is courage." Even more than money she needed that.

Leonide was starring at the Gymnase in a revival of La Dame aux Camellias. She had scored an immense success.

Her astonishment was complete when Therese walked into her dressing room. She prolonged it as though she were having her photograph taken.

"I can't believe it! You!" She smothered Therese in a scented embrace. "Oh, you wretch, I've wondered so often where in God's name you were. You fell off the edge of the world without even a word. I can't believe that you're here!"

This outburst gave Leonide time to decide how to deal with this exile who was no longer part of the scene and was likely to prove a nuisance.

She led Therese to a chair and sat down, knee to knee. The glare of artificial light revealed that her looks were fading and that forced vitality and ambition were her chief weapons of survival.

"Where have you been? Why did you never write?"

"I did—from Angers and from the village where I've been living."

"I never got a word, not a word. I didn't know what to believe. De Morny refused to discuss you. I thought you must have murdered someone or been caught in *flagrentio* with the Montijo. Wasn't it a shock the way he died? A chill caught out hunting at Compiègne. Three days in bed and—pouff! Everyone was appalled. They gave him a tremendous funeral.

Everyone came, even Bismarck. That was a laugh! The Emperor had aged terribly, poor man. He looks a hundred."

"I read about it in the paper."

Leonide was suddenly all intentness. She grasped Therese's hand. "Now tell me—what happened?"

"Didn't you hear about Von Bernsdorff or was all that hushed up?"

"One heard he'd jumped in the river. He lay at the Morgue for days because no one knew who he was."

"Was that the official version?"

"Wasn't it true? *Wasn't* it?"

"Not exactly."

"Then what? You can tell me. You must. With my awful memory I'm a perfect reservoir for secrets."

Therese sighed. She didn't want to go into it.

"Actually—he hanged himself in my stable."

"No! Oh, my dear, how ghastly! So that was it! They covered it up. Those fiends! It was they—Can you imagine? Yes, I suppose, because of Bismarck. To prevent a scandal. But why? Why did he do it? And why didn't you come to me?"

"I didn't have time. De Morny sent an order for me to leave Paris within an hour. I took what money and jewels I had. I was forbidden to return."

"Typical! They're ruthless when it comes to protecting themselves. Why did he do it, Therese? Was he in love with you?"

"It's a long story, Leonide. He was a very unhappy, tormented man. I was caught between him and de Morny. I made the wrong choice, that's all."

"You poor girl! Oh, my poor Therese, what a story! And now it's all over for de Morny, too! I remember Von Bernsdorff at that costume ball. He danced with you most of the evening. I thought he looked strange and sick. People said he was 'that' way, you know. He did not have a savory reputation."

She broke off and with a gesture of genuine sympathy touched Therese's cheek.

"Perhaps I didn't do you such a good turn after all when I introduced you to all that."

"It wasn't anyone's fault. It just happened."

"And what are you going to do now? Why have you come back?"

Therese was on the point of asking where she could rid herself of her unwanted child. But she was too embarrassed and too weary and said instead, "I really came to see you about my things."

Leonide was prepared. She asked with perfectly simulated surprise, "What things?"

"The gold dressing set and the jade vase. I wanted to sell them because I'm short of money."

"I don't understand, Therese."

"When I had to leave I packed the things that belonged to me and had them sent to you. There was a gold and tortoise-shell dressing table set, a mirror and two gold candlesticks in red leather cases. And a white jade vase."

Leonide's bafflement was too perfect to be convincing.

"Well, I never got them, my dear."

"I gave the man from the Sûreté your address."

Leonide shook her head.

"I knew nothing about what had happened to you. I called one day at the Chaussée and found the place boarded up." She was all too genuinely distressed. "Oh, Therese, I am sorry. But surely you can reclaim them. The police have no right to keep them if they belonged to you. Those bastards! Why don't you write to the Empress? She was so fond of you."

Therese knew that it was useless. Whatever Leonide knew she was not going to reveal it.

"No, I can't do that. I thought—"

It no longer mattered what she thought. The barriers against her were unsurmountable.

"Well—!"

Leonide sat down again, finished her champagne, glanced at the small clock on her dressing table and said in her old practical way, "It's no use having pride. If those things were yours they should certainly be returned to you. They treated you badly enough. Write to Eugenie. She's a good-hearted woman with all her faults. After all, you were totally blameless, a victim of their rotten intrigues. I'm sure she'll do something and if she doesn't, I'll put on my thinking cap." She glanced at the clock again. "I'm truly relieved to see you, Therese. I really have worried. But I'm dreadfully late for a supper. You know how it is—the old whirl goes on."

Therese could not even find it in herself to be angry. "Do you still have the same admirer?"

"That Spaniard? Certainly not. He turned out to be a complete fraud. All that talk about his estates in Cuba! I practically kept him. He made love like an angel but one can't live on love at my age. Now I've got my hooks on an American, immensely rich and immensely simple."

She was up again. The reunion was over.

"It was nice to see you, Leonide. You were very kind to me in the past. I haven't forgotten."

"Kind? Nothing! We're friends, aren't we? Listen, my dear—" She darted to a table, opened an embroidered purse and took out a roll of bank notes. "Take this, darling, till you get things settled."

"No, really. I didn't come here to borrow money."

"I know that. We've all been through it. Things will change now you're back in Paris. Besides I'm flush. This play's going to run forever." She thrust the money into Therese's hand. "You need to buy some clothes."

In the warmest, most sisterly fashion she escorted Therese to the door.

"Come and see me soon. We'll have tea and talk things over." She embraced her unwelcome friend. "After all, last time we didn't do so badly, did we?"

She opened the door.

"Goodbye, dear Leonide, and thank you."

"It's nothing—between us girls." She patted Therese on the shoulder. "You know who was mad about you? That nice boy from the British Embassy—Freddie—Freddie Avondale. He was broken-hearted when you disappeared."

She had got rid of her. She had made the best of an awkward situation. After all, she could afford to be generous. The gold dressing set was her prize possession.

She was terribly late. As she flung herself into a whirlwind of dressing, she thought, "There was always something wrong with that girl. Well, she had her chance and muffed it."

Life went on.

It went on whether one wanted it to or not. Lying in the drab little room at the Hôtel de Piast, reviewing the events that had befallen a woman named Therese Lachmann to whom she was dimly related, Therese thought that, along with the many harsh blows that Fate had dealt her, it had also, by way of atonement, slipped her a few trump cards. There was her chance encounter with Henri at Warsaw, her meeting with de Morny, and the fact that she had fainted before that particular carriage.

When Vittorio presented himself next day at the Banque de France, impressive in his well-cut black suit and black fedora, he found the main floor besieged with frantic customers.

The news of the French victory had proved to be false, a deploy of certain speculators who were trying to rig the market. The truth was quite the opposite; the French had suffered a serious defeat, the Prussian armies were advancing and had already crossed the border into Alsace-Lorraine. There was a run on the banks as the value of government bonds was plummeting.

It was useless to present the Prince's draft at any of the tellers' windows. They were under attack by an hysterical throng, waving withdrawal slips and demanding instant attention. It was an ugly and ludicrous reversal of the previous day's jubilation.

Monsieur de la Rue who handled the Prince's account had an office above. Vittorio had had dealings with him before. Bypassing the scrimmage which threatened to turn into a riot, he made his way up the stairs. Halfway up he was stopped by an agitated cashier who gripped his arm. "You can't go up there. That's private."

Vittorio threw him off and, in his imperturbable way, proceeded to the first floor and, without knocking, walked into de la Rue's office.

The havoc below, like a rising flood, had already infected

the upper floor. Officials were running to and fro with sheaves of paper in a futile attempt to avert a panic. De la Rue was barricaded behind his desk, barking out orders, and generally giving an expert performance of the Establishment under fire.

Vittorio stationed himself in front of the desk and, seizing a moment when the harassed submanager was mopping his brow, announced in a firm voice, "Monsieur de la Rue, will you kindly attend to this draft?"

De la Rue glanced up as though he had been insulted. "What? Who are you? Go downstairs and wait your turn."

"I have brought this draft from His Highness of Oppeln-Piast."

"What? Impossible! Come back tomorrow. I can't attend to that now."

Vittorio said levelly, "The Prince wants this money now."

"I said later. Tomorrow. Be off with you. Can't you see I'm snowed under?"

"*Now.*"

De la Rue, with a gesture of outrage as if he were confronting an anarchist, snatched the draft from Vittorio's hand. He was about to cast it aside when he noticed the signature and the big red seal which the Prince affixed to his correspondence.

"Oppeln-Piast? You don't mean to tell me he's still in Paris?"

"He intends to remain here. His sympathies have always been with the French."

"I don't care what his sympathies are. He's an enemy subject. I shall certainly not honor this draft. He's lucky that his assets haven't been frozen and they may well be at any moment."

"As long as they are not frozen he has a right to his money and I will thank you to fetch it, Monsieur, at once."

A note of menace in Vittorio's voice caused the bank manager to reconsider. It flashed through his mind that if things took a turn for the worse that damned old Prussian might be a useful contact. It might not be unexpedient to have a foothold in the enemy camp.

"It's most inconvenient. Everything's in confusion, as you can see."

"I'll wait."

De la Rue shouted, "Dubois! Carnal! Where are those idiots?"

Two men dashed out of an inner office.

"Attend to this. You may give the money to this man." He initialed the draft and handed it to one of his underlings. "And tell the Prince of Piast that's the last he can count on. I don't know from moment to moment what's been decided. And don't come bothering me again."

Ten minutes later Vittorio left the bank, his pockets stuffed with notes.

Outside everything seemed quite normal. People were about their daily business. Only from the distance, a curious humming filled the air, persistent as the drone of a turbine engine. It was the steady drumming at the Champs de Mars across the river where fresh regiments were assembling for the front.

Vittorio crossed the avenue and made his way to Roos', the English butcher.

He bought a large Bradenham ham, three game pies and a number of tins of meat and pâté. All these he stowed in a large string bag which he had carried under his coat.

He called at other charcuteries and brought more provisions, including cheeses. A number of other customers were also laying in stores against an emergency. He was careful to avoid shops where he usually did business, as he thought it wiser that as few people as possible should be aware of the Prince's continued presence in Paris.

People were standing at street corners shaking their heads over the morning papers. It was dawning on the populace that this war might after all prove to be more than a national holiday.

The drumming from the Champs de Mars grew louder as he approached the Hôtel de Piast. He noticed that a number of houses on the street were shuttered. People with a sounder grasp of events had already left for the country. He wished that "the old codger" had shown such sense. They could have been safely at Bordeaux by this time or, better still, in Italy.

He stowed away his purchases in the well-stocked larder. They could manage for a couple of weeks or so. He would go on buying up what he could. It occurred to him that the sick woman might prove a drain on their resources and that he would broach the subject, today or tomorrow, of her returning to her house in the Marais.

He made coffee and took it to the Prince's study.

"Well, what news?"

"I managed to get the money, but Monsieur de la Rue warned that it might be the last for some time. There's a run on the banks due to the morning news."

The Prince opened the paper and snorted. "Fools! They'll find out that Bismarck means business. He's been planning this for a long time."

"It's not too late to leave, Mon Altesse. The trains are still running to the South."

"I can't leave. It would be courting disaster."

"Do you really think that you and I could defend this house if a mob broke in? You should have seen them at the bank!"

"It will be over in a few weeks. It's better to sit it out."

He poured himself a cup of coffee while Vittorio held the tray.

"Then at least we should pack up the more valuable things. They can be stored in the attic. They'll be safe up there."

"I will not give into hysteria. I have never done the French any harm. There's no reason why they should harm me."

"If things go badly with the war, you will be in danger."

"I refuse to discuss it." The Prince took his cup and retired in a huff to his favorite chair. The dogs danced 'round him in the hope of a biscuit, balancing on their back legs and waving their paws in the air.

There were moments when the Prince exasperated his major-domo. It was the blind pigheadedness of aristocrats who had always had their own way.

Each time he brought the invalid food, Vittorio tried to broach the subject of her returning to the Marais. But she looked so pale and seemed so listless and was so grateful for his attentions that he lacked the courage to do so. Practical as he was, Vittorio was sympathetic by nature. He knew what it was to walk the streets of Paris alone, to be without friends or the price of his next meal. He had worked as a waiter and as a valet de chambre at a hotel and as an orderly at a hospital, before a chance tip from a shopkeeper had led him to apply for work at the Hôtel de Piast. The Prince had taken a fancy to him for reasons which he had misunderstood at the time. He would have been willing to accommodate an old pederast, the need for security being greater than distaste. Fortunately things had not turned out that way.

This woman was becoming a problem. Dr. Cottard had warned him that she was very weak and needed care, but he wondered, as the days passed, how genuine her pallor and languor were and whether she was deliberately trying to drag out her stay. But then he thought of that empty house and her few poor dresses, her general air of tragedy and abandonment, and he thought that it was little enough to let her lie there in that huge mansion in which there was now only himself and his master.

She had propped herself up in bed and greeted him with the same sad smile. He had cooked her a little entrecôte and a portion of string beans.

"I thought it was time that you tried to eat something solid," he said as he set the tray on her lap.

"I don't know how I can ever repay you for all you have done for me."

"It was we who knocked you down. It's the least we can do."

"I don't think it happened like that. I fainted."

She tried to cut the meat but her strength failed her.

"I don't think I can—just yet."

"Let me do it."

He cut up the meat and said gently, "Try. You must gain strength."

She forced herself to eat a few pieces. He sat near the bed and watched.

She said as though facing an eventuality which she had avoided, "I must pull myself together and try to sell the Pavillon. And there's the piano. It's a very fine instrument."

"When you're better. Perhaps I can help you."

"How long have you worked here?"

"Five years."

"Is there any news? I don't even know what day it is."

"Things are not going well. The Prussians have invaded Alsace. Strassbourg has fallen."

"When was that?"

"It was in the papers this morning."

"I can't eat any more." She pushed the tray away from her. "I must try to get up tomorrow."

He took the tray and set it down on the dresser.

"What have you done about selling your property?"

"I put a notice on the gate. Someone may call."

"Where will you go when you do sell it?"

"I don't know. Are you going to stay here—I mean if the war goes badly?"

"The Prince refuses to leave. We'll stay—well, until—" He shrugged.

She was staring at her hand, very white on the blue bedcover. "I would like to give you something. You've been so kind."

"Don't think about that. It's not important."

"Does the Prince know I'm here?"

"I haven't told him. He gets upset. He's a very strange man."

"I used to hear about him when I lived on the Chaussée d'Iena."

"Across the way?" He was surprised because only rich people lived in this neighborhood.

"I was married then—to a Portuguese. The Marquis de Païva."

"You're a Marquise?"

"For the little good it has done me."

He was more mystified, but more intrigued, than ever.

"Don't you have any family? Relatives?"

She shook her head, and then sighed deeply.

"It's a problem, isn't it? Why we have to go on struggling when we don't even know what we're struggling for. Well, that's not your concern. I've been a big enough trouble as it is."

The natural gallantry of his Latin nature prompted him to say, "I'll help you sell your house and I'll speak to the Prince. After all, he owes you something."

"Please don't. I'll manage somehow. It wasn't his fault I fell in front of his carriage."

They had crossed a subtle boundary and were prepared to risk compromise. For the time being Vittorio shelved the doubts he had had about her. He felt, not an obligation, but a desire to help.

"You must take your pills."

He shook two tablets from the bottle and brought them to her with a glass of water.

She grimaced and swallowed them.

"Thank you, Vittorio."

"Well, at least I know now who you are."

"For you I am Therese."

News and rumors of news continued to pour in. Government refusal to reveal the facts compounded the general confusion. No one for certain knew what was happening at the front. There were reports of victories, but the victories evaporated with the smoke of battle. There were reports of grave defeats. The Prussians were advancing; they had retreated; they were digging in. The war would last six months, a year; it would be over in a week. The Emperor was at the front, which was encouraging. What was less encouraging was that the Empress, as Regent, issued a daily snowstorm of decrees which she instantly rescinded. With her highly emotional nature Eugenie relished to the fullest her role as Joan of Arc. She displayed immense energy, courage and lack of judgment. She mistook obfuscation for diplomacy and was afraid of being honest with a people whose loyalty she had never gained.

Meanwhile life in the capital veered between the old laissez-faire extravagance and a harsh rapacity disguised as "taking precautions!" There was a run on foodstuffs. Sugar was suddenly unobtainable. The price of wood and coke skyrocketed.

Wise citizens hoarded, but the wiser profiteered. The Bourse fluctuated wildly. Fortunes were made and lost on the strength of information obtained from "irrefutable sources" concerning the progress of hostilities.

The serene summer weather continued into autumn. Paris had never looked more lovely. The theaters were full, the gardens thronged with happy children. When the boulevards were not blocked by military parades and patriotic demonstrations, they were impassable with the carriages of society ladies hastening to inspect Worth's winter collection.

Paris was Paris, war or no war.

As these days of forced normality passed into September the Prince found himself unable to concentrate on the Magnum Opus. Although Vittorio kept up a semblance of routine, the Hôtel de Piast seemed vaster and more desolate than the palace of Diocletian. He found himself listening, either for distant cheering, the drumming on the Champs de Mars or the toxin of the front doorbell. He listened to the silence and for the bell that didn't ring.

He was beginning to have doubts about his decision to stay, doubts about what would happen to his collections. He shuffled about the rooms, followed by his six little white familiars, looking at the vast accumulation of treasures which he had gathered in his life. Suddenly they oppressed him. Their value appalled him. There was nothing to protect them but a garden wall on one side and the street door on the other.

No one scaled the wall. No one beat down the door. Instead there was silence, dreadful and intimidating. It threatened him because he was alone and rich and old and because he was, by accident, a Prussian.

There were the Rembrandts that had belonged to his father, the Tintoretto, the El Grecos, the great Cimabue altar piece, the Bronzino portraits, the two Van Eycks—so many others. There were cases and cases of snuff boxes and bonbonnières, all these exquisite trifles of a century he had always felt akin to. There were rooms full of Chinese porcelain, Meissen, Delft, Sèvres—and books, rows upon rows, cases upon cases, of rare, beautifully bound books. There were paneled rooms and painted rooms he had had transported from places as far away as Bohemia. There was Catherine the Great's bedroom from the Tauride Palace in St. Petersburg. So much! So much! So much! A huge necropolis of *things*.

His only links to the living world were Vittorio and the dogs.

He was horrified by his isolation.

Passing through the main salon on this depressing assessment of his possessions, he noticed someone in the garden. *Was* there someone or was he imagining things? Was it the forerunner of a horde of anti-Prussian savages who would swarm over the wall and exterminate everything?

The figure was motionless, in complete repose. The afternoon sunlight accentuated the extraordinary color of the hair, like some exotic and dangerous plant blooming among the subdued greens and grays of the garden. Where had he seen such hair before?

And then he remembered. Could that be the streetwalker with the ring who had been knocked down by his carriage?

Had she died and returned to haunt the garden?

It was extremely strange.

The Prince ventured through the window onto the path with his convoy of little dogs.

She had seen him and stood up slowly. She was tall and, as she moved toward him, he noted a certain rather stately grace. But what struck him, as they drew closer, was her resemblance to Vittorio. They came from the same classic mold.

"You must be the Prince de Piast," she said in a low and agreeably modulated voice, extending her hand on which he again glimpsed that tantalizing ruby ring. "I owe you my thanks for your very great kindness."

The Prince had taken her hand without intending to. He was dumbfounded.

"I'm afraid—I am at a loss—"

"You must not be annoyed with Vittorio. I think he kept my presence a secret for fear of annoying you. He has been so wonderfully kind."

"Vittorio? You mean you have been here—in this house?"

"On the top floor. I was so weak I couldn't stand or I would have gone. But today I feel much stronger. I do thank you and I can never repay Vittorio. He literally saved my life."

It was astonishing. All the time when Vittorio had been going about his duties, cooking the meals, putting out his clothes, he had been ministering to this mysterious creature.

"I have often heard of you. I used to live across the avenue on the Chaussée d'Iena."

"Ah yes, indeed—" The Prince was unable to gather himself together. "But I fear—I very much fear—it is I who owe you an apology."

"For the accident? No, not at all. It was just that; an accident. No one was to blame."

"A terrible accident. I was very much upset. I remember Dr. Cottard saying— Well, I am shocked, I am embarrassed, that Vittorio didn't tell me."

"It was only to protect you. You must have so much on your mind with this stupid war."

"Yes, stupid. It is stupid. But where have you been sleeping? On the top floor, you say?"

"Overlooking the courtyard."

"But—how quite unsuitable! There are much pleasanter rooms on this side."

"What darling little dogs!" The Maltese dogs had been sniffing Therese's shoes, making inquiries, darting pert glances through the fringes that hid their eyes.

"They are my dearest friends. This is Nichette. I presume to call her my *maîtresse en titre*. She is a regular Pompadour. That is Ce Monsieur, Murmurine, Tizane, Noisette and Aubépine."

Feeling that they had now been introduced, the little dogs barked their greetings and hopped about.

"Since I had no need to introduce myself, may I inquire to whom I have the pleasure of speaking?"

"I am the Marquise de Païva."

"Ah!" the Prince exclaimed, greatly relieved. After all, he was *not* annoyed with Vittorio. Vittorio had shown good sense.

She was a Marquise, someone one could receive, someone respectable.

"My dear Marquise, you will permit me to speak severely to Vittorio all the same. He should have put you in one of the nicer rooms. I shall see to it."

"No, please. If you'll allow me to stay where I am for a few more days, I shall be quite well enough not to bother you any further."

"I insist." The prince was charmed with the elegance of her manners. "You must stay till you're completely cured. And now, my dear Marquise, I have an impertinence to inflict on you. Allow me." He took her hand. "This ring. I noticed it that night when they lifted you into the carriage."

"My father gave it to me."

"Your father! Ah, that explains it. Then I have something to show you."

He led her back into the house to a small salon next to his study. Resting against a cabinet was a magnificent silver tray flanked by two candelabra. It bore in the center of an elaborate design the letter S surmounted by a crown.

"I have a complete service. It came into my family through my great-great-great-grandmother. So, you see, in a round-about way, we must be related."

"I don't want to sail under false pretenses. My parents were forbidden to marry. My father was forced to make what was considered a more advantageous match."

The Prince was impressed by her honesty. "Well, that happens in such houses. Dynastic alliances cause a great deal of unhappiness. But that is no reflection on you, my dear. And now you must join me for a glass of Madeira or we can get Vittorio to make us some tea."

He was quite elated at the prospect of company after so many days alone.

Half an hour later Vittorio found them comfortably ensconced in the study. He was amazed at the easy conquest Therese had made of his irascible employer. He found that he did not resent it. In fact he was relieved.

"Join us, Vittorio. I was going to reprimand you for keeping the Marquise shut away on the top floor. Now I can only thank you for providing us with such charming company. I drink to the speedy conclusion of the war."

As he raised his glass with a courtly little bow the Prince thought that Vittorio and the Marquise made a remarkably handsome couple.

They felt remarkably handsome when they set out next morning to sell Henri Herz' piano. Vittorio, in his smart black suit and black hat, felt proud to be a member of the male sex with a beautiful woman on his arm. Therese, who still had to walk slowly, was grateful that for once she had a man of such simple strength to lean on.

The city looked as it always had. The shops were doing a brisk business. Smartly dressed people were about their daily affairs. Carriages rolled by. The flower seller at the corner of the Place de la Madelaine had a pretty display of asters and dahlias. The usual customers were at their usual tables at the cafés, dipping their brioches into their coffee—as usual. The streets exuded that pleasant animation that made Paris the most civilized city on earth.

Pleyel et Fils had their showrooms on the Boulevard des Capucins. Therese had been there in the old days with Henri who was a friend of the son of the house, Fernand Pleyel.

He was in his office and received her warmly.

"My dear Therese, how charming to see you! It must be quite five years."

He recalled various rumors about Herz' protégé, but life took many strange turns. He assumed that she had taken up with this handsome Italian whom he put down as a tenor. Handsome Italians usually were.

"Do you remember the piano you made for Henri?"

"Indeed I do. It was one of our finest instruments. A rose-wood case and the best African ivory. I remember how wonderfully he played on it at those evenings he used to give."

"It's still at the Pavillon and I would like to sell it. Would you be interested?"

"Most certainly." He recalled some gossip about Herz' lawyer's getting possession of the Pavillon, but it was not his business and he decided not to refer to it.

"I would like to keep it, but I'm trying to sell the Pavillon and it's a pity that it should not be used."

"I'd have no trouble in disposing of it. How much did you have in mind?"

"I'll leave that to you. I know that you'll give me a fair price."

No doubt she'd had a hard time after Herz' death and the muddle, whatever it had been, over the will.

"Would twenty thousand suffice?"

"When could you send for it?"

"Wait. I'll see if any of our men are available."

He left them. It had been a pleasant surprise to find someone willing to be so generous after all the haggling she had had to endure over the jewelry.

Pleyel returned after some moments.

"We have two movers who could pick it up at noon if you could be there to let them in."

"I'll go there now. Thank you so much, Monsieur Fernand."

"Delighted to be of help." He handed her an envelope. "No need to go through the formalities of invoices between old friends."

He escorted them to the street.

"I'll bear the Pavillon in mind. It's a wonderful retreat for a musician. That was a sad loss to the world of music. He was a gifted and charming man."

On their way to the Marais Therese said, "Will you have a coffee while I do one small piece of business? I shan't be long."

Vittorio had been impressed by the treatment Therese had received in the music shop. This little outing opened up for him the charms of a steady relationship with a woman which he had never seriously considered. He had been too intent on establishing himself in the Prince's graces because security had seemed so important, but that cloistered existence, catering to the demands of a volatile eccentric, had deprived him of the normal pleasures of life. The girls he had had affairs with, seamstresses or lady's maids, had not been worth sacrificing anything for. But Therese was different. There was much about her that remained equivocal, but she had style, she was someone, she complemented his self-esteem.

Therese had gone into a jeweler's. "I'm looking for a birthday present, something suitable for a man."

She examined some watches and cigarette cases, a gold bracelet, and finally selected a pair of cufflinks made of two carnelian intaglios set in gold.

They were expensive, but she wanted to give Vittorio something that would express her gratitude for all he had done for her. Besides, she needed him as an ally.

The jeweler found a smart little box for her purchase. As she approached Vittorio, sitting bareheaded at the café, she thought that she must be careful to strengthen this relationship, as yet too tentative to be counted on.

She was already tired. They took a cab to the Marais.

The garden was undisturbed, though the grass needed cutting. The unbearable sadness she had felt when she first returned had dimmed to nostalgia. The life she had lived there seemed so remote that she was already losing touch with it.

She found a basket in the toolshed and a pair of clippers and went 'round the beds cutting the roses that were in their final glory. Henri had always loved the deep yellow Gloire de Dijon. All the bushes he had planted were in full bloom.

As he watched her moving along the paths, Vittorio thought how agreeable it would be to live in such a secluded place with a woman like Therese. He had worked hard all his life and had never experienced leisure. He did not know what he would do with it, but it seemed to him that with such a woman he would soon learn.

Of course, he was a servant and she was a lady. She belonged to the Prince's world. The old man had recognized that at once. He did not know if good looks and physical strength were enough to overcome those social barriers that people of that class were so aware of. There were so many subtleties of behavior and status by which they judged. Even if he were able to make her love him would those differences remain?

He was vain. He did not want to be regarded merely as a handsome stallion. Would he remain a servant in her eyes if he and Therese became lovers?

She brought the basket, now filled with roses, and set it on the table.

"I thought they would look nice in the Prince's study."

He nodded. She thought that he was a truly beautiful man. She couldn't tell if his slowness and diffidence were signs of stupidity.

"Vittorio, I have something for you. It's quite unimportant, but I wanted to give you something—for your birthday, if you like, or simply with my thanks."

He opened the little box. He was acutely embarrassed and, for some reason, annoyed because this gift put him at a disadvantage. He saw it as a substitute for the money she had offered him, a tip that a lady would give a servant.

"No." He shut the box with a snap. "I don't want to accept it. There's no reason for you to give me anything."

"There is for me. You have been very good to me. I would like you to have them because I am grateful."

"There's no reason. Whatever I did was because—well, I wanted to do it." He flushed and said harshly, "I don't need thanks."

He held out the box. He saw that she was hurt and that he had misjudged her intentions. But it was too late to relent.

"Please, Vittorio. It's only a small thing."

He looked offended and put the box on the table.

"You were sick. What I did I would do for anyone." She should have had the tact to see that to give him something expensive spoiled the balance between them.

"I didn't think," she said, turning away, "that I was merely an object of charity. I hoped that perhaps we were friends."

He stood up. He didn't know how to justify his position.

"Just because—because of that."

"Do you think it would be wrong for me to give the Prince these roses?"

"That's different."

"Why?"

"Because it's his house and I work for him. I am his valet."

He thought he detected a hint of disdain in her reply. "I'm sorry; that didn't occur to me."

At this moment, when the pleasure they had found in each other's company had been marred by cross-purposes, two workmen came through the iron gate.

"We've come to collect a piano."

Therese led them into the house.

The beautiful instrument stood isolated in the center of the empty room.

"Oh, it's a big bugger," one of the movers said. "We really need three for that."

Vittorio had followed them in. He took off his coat as though deliberately to impress on Therese that he belonged to the working classes. "I'll give you a hand."

They turned the piano on its side and unscrewed the legs. With two men at the keyboard and Vittorio at the case, they maneuvered the piano through the door, through the gate, and loaded it onto the back of an open wagon.

Vittorio went back to retrieve his coat and found that Therese had returned to the garden. She was feeding grain to the doves.

"We'd better be going."

"Will you give the roses to the Prince with my thanks?" she said coldly without turning.

"You're coming, aren't you?"

"No. I may as well stay here now to sell the house."

He was angered. "You can't stay here alone. You're not well yet."

"I shall manage."

"The Prince made it clear last night that you were to stay with us till you were better."

"I'm declining the kind invitation. Thank you."

"Stop playing the fool!" he exclaimed, exasperated. "You have nowhere to go and no one to look after you. You can't stay in that empty house."

"I stayed there before."

"Well, you're not staying there now."

He picked up the basket of roses and then scooped up the little box with the cufflinks.

"All right, I'll take them. Does that make you feel better?"

"You're rude and unreasonable." She suddenly burst out, "Go away! I've had enough trouble lately. I want to be left alone."

He controlled himself, gulped and managed to say in a level voice, "I said I'd accept them. I thank you. It is not my birthday, but I accept them. Now please come along."

She had won and he knew it.

He started off down the path. She hadn't moved.

He called back in a normal voice, "Therese!"

She gave in and followed him in silence. Therese compounded her perversity by going into the restaurant. She wanted to make arrangements for someone to feed the doves and the goldfish.

Vittorio stared glumly at the "For Sale" sign fixed to the gate. He produced a gold pencil from an inside pocket—he had a schoolboy's love for smart gadgets—and wrote in careful capitals at the foot of the notice: Apply Piast, 10 Fau: St. Germain."

The men had just finished securing the piano.

"Can you give us a lift as far as the Capucins?" he asked.

"You'll have to sit in the back."

Therese reappeared, stony-faced. He lifted her onto the back of the wagon. She stationed herself on the lid of the piano without once looking in his direction.

The movers whipped up the horse and they trundled down the Rue du Temple.

As they were about to enter the Boulevard Sevastopol, Vittorio said in an offhand way, "Look, they're beautiful. I'm grateful. I shall wear them."

"I was hurt and offended, but I forgive you."

They declared a truce.

As they rumbled along they became aware that something had happened in the last hour. An ominous silence had fallen over the city. People were moving along the sidewalks, but everything had slowed down. Crowds were gathering at corners, standing and staring, as though they had forgotten where they were going, as if it were no longer worthwhile to go anywhere.

They turned onto the Boulevard des Capucins to find it impassable. A dense throng was immobilized as far as the eye could see.

The pigeons, circling over the rooftops, settled as though they, too, were awed by the silence.

Nothing stirred.

And then, at the far end of the avenue, a figure in scarlet appeared from a side street, standing in a carriage and holding aloft a blood-red flag. Her harsh voice like the cry of a kestrel carried over the sea of motionless heads. *"Vive la République! A bas l'Empire! Vive la France Libre!"*

The crowd parted for her like the Red Sea before the advancing Israelites.

"What has happened?" Therese asked, frightened by the sound of her own voice.

One of the movers said over his shoulder in an uninterested way as if he were announcing the winner of the three-thirty at Longchamps, "The army's capitulated. The Emperor's been taken prisoner. It's all over."

In the wake of that scarlet nemesis, waving her flag, a shudder passed through the multitude as if the earth were trembling beneath them. There rose from those thousands of throats an inarticulate cry. It gathered momentum like a tidal wave as the whole avenue surged forward.

"Vive la République! Vive la France Libre!"

The red flag had reached the Madeleine. The crowd poured after it.

One of the movers lit a cigarette. "Well, those bastards! It was only a matter of time."

Was he referring to the Emperor or the government or the Prussians? Defeat, in some way, made them one.

"We'd better get out of this," Vittorio said.

He jumped off the back of the wagon and lifted Therese down.

"My roses!"

He reached up and retrieved the basket. They made their way to the sidewalk.

It was as if the whole city had lost its sense of direction. Vittorio bought a paper from a newsstand. An old woman came timidly up to him as he was reading the headline and inquired, "Excuse me, Monsieur, but will this affect the value of government bonds?"

A man was leaning against a shopwindow, crying.

It took them nearly an hour, by taking small side streets, to reach the Faubourg St. Honoré.

People were wandering aimlessly like owners of lost dogs who felt compelled to go on searching long after they knew it was useless.

Little groups had gathered near the entrance to the Hôtel de Piast. Vittorio took Therese's arm.

"We'd better not go in yet."

They turned back and sat down at a café. After a normal interlude in which nothing happened, a waiter appeared because waiters are supposed to ask customers what they want because if you sit down at a café you are supposed to want something.

"Two coffees, please."

The waiter retreated. The coffees were not forthcoming. A woman at the next table asked her companion, "What will happen to the Prince Imperial? Has he been captured, too?"

"He'll abdicate like his father."

"Will they execute him?"

"They'll execute the lot."

"It's terrible. We should have bought more sugar."

Dusk fell. They returned to the Faubourg St. Honoré to find it almost deserted. They sauntered past the door of the Hôtel de Piast and then ducked back. Vittorio had the key to the gatekeeper's lodge ready. They slipped inside.

The courtyard was as gloomy as a battlefield.

As they entered the study the Prince jumped up in dismay. "Where have you been? I've been here alone! For hours! I thought some disaster had happened."

Vittorio handed him the paper.

He glanced at the headlines and crumpled into a chair. "Poor France! What ignominy! Oh, my poor France!"

"We've no means of knowing what will happen now," Vittorio said.

"They'll sign a peace treaty. There will be some kind of peace." He crumpled the paper. "That monster Bismarck!"

Therese was looking at the roses. They were so full and lovely. A few petals had fallen. It seemed immensely important that they, at least, should not suffer from the debacle that had engulfed the city.

"Is there a bowl or a vase?"

"I'll find something."

The Prince had picked up Nichette and was holding her against his cheek. That was always a sign of distress. The other little dogs, sensing that something was amiss, had gathered 'round him.

He said unexpectedly, "The French are too intelligent. They are always betrayed by their intelligence. They grasp the moment but not the hour."

Vittorio went 'round the house closing all the shutters. By nightfall even the windows on the servants' floor were closed.

He lit candles in the study and brought the Prince his usual glass of Madeira.

"You must not turn up the chandeliers, Mon Altesse. I will prepare dinner."

Therese and the Prince sat in the darkened study.

"Do you have any cards?" she asked. "We might play patience."

They would have need of patience now.

The following morning Vittorio started carrying valuables to the crawl-in under the roof that was reached by a ladder from the attics.

With Therese's help, impeded as she was from the use of her left hand, he carried the celadon, piece by piece, upstairs and stowed it carefully away. The Prince stood disconsolately at the foot of the main staircase. "Oh, do be careful. Be careful!" He was saying goodbye to twenty years.

It took them the whole day to clear the cabinets in the study.

They moved into the adjoining salon and together packed up the snuffboxes and jeweled bonbonnières. They packed the fans and the figurines, the Meissen, the Nympenburg, the Sèvres. They dismantled the miniature theaters with the original scenery painted by Boucher that had come from Versailles. They wrapped up the Renaissance jewelry, the enamel mermaids riding baroque pearls, the tiny dragons breathing ruby flames at heroes with diamond swords. They wrapped up the silver embossed with the letter S under the crown, the Russian coffee set of white agate, the Chinese tea set of rock crystal, engraved with the poems of Li Pu. The endless parade of the Prince's treasures overwhelmed them. It was incredible and it was appalling that one man could own so much.

The Prince padded after them from room to room, followed by his flotilla of little dogs, renewing love affairs with forgotten objects only to say goodbye.

Vittorio worked steadily, pacing himself, never dropping anything, climbing up and down, up and down the ladder with bundles worth a king's ransom, disappearing into the crawl-in on hands and knees, while Therese stood below holding a candelabra for the feeble light it gave.

They ate by candlelight on a small table in the study and were to some extent consoled by the Prince's excellent wines.

At night Vittorio would venture forth in search of news which was always contradictory. The government was about to fall; the Empress was holding the government together. There would be revolution; the threat of revolution had been averted. Then Marshal Bazaine, the last hope of the French armies, surrendered at Metz and the capital was left defenseless.

Would Paris hold out or would it fall?

A feeling of fatalism gripped the city. Things would happen or they would not happen. Torn by so many conflicting rumors no one exactly cared.

In that cavernous mansion, dark and silent as a tomb, Vittorio and Therese continued their work of saving collections whose beauty and value now seemed of little consequence. They were not even sure why they were going to such lengths, except that to do something, to exhaust themselves physically, was better than sitting in semidarkness waiting for the end that didn't come.

They had become intimate like people who had shared a shipwreck. Vittorio took the Prince to bed and roused him in the morning. Therese read to him aloud. She read Montaigne and Montesquieu and St. Simon. The Prince barely listened, but he was grateful.

The little dogs, deprived of their garden, became irritable and relieved themselves sulkily in corners. Nichette, the best beloved, never left her master's side.

They began to lose the sense of night and day.

It happened at last, not as a result of some great cataclysm, but because some nerve of national patience snapped.

A group of firebrands broke through the palings of the private gardens and marched on the entrance to the Tuileries. The guards on duty, fearful that they were confronting the enraged populace of Paris, gave way and a small crowd broke into the Imperial residence.

They marched up the stairs determined to face the Empress and demand her abdication, if not her life.

Eugenie was in conference with the Austrian and Italian ambassadors when a servant burst into the room. "They're here! They've broken into the palace!"

Eugenie fled through the great gilded rooms in which she had known her glory, followed by her reader, Madame Lebreton, and the two ambassadors. They reached the door into the Louvre; it was locked. They could hear the mob yelling and rampaging through the anterooms. Fortunately these brave republicans were awed by so much splendor and, like tourists, stopped to gape.

An old doorkeeper tottered up the stairs waving a bunch of keys.

Eugenie hurried through the immense shadowy chambers filled with Greek and Roman statuary and the relics of other vanished empires, followed by the distraught ambassadors. They reached a small stairway that led down to the Quai du Louvre.

"Don't show yourself, ma'am. It would be fatal," the Austrian urged. "Wait here. I'll try to find a cab."

Eugenie's courage did not desert her. She stepped out into the sunlight of a balmy autumn day. Men were placidly fishing along the river. By a lucky chance a cab came ambling by. Eugenie hailed it and got in with Madame Lebreton, who was on the point of fainting. A small boy who had been snaring sparrows recognized her and ran alongside shouting, *"Mort à l'Espagnole! A bas l'Empire. Vive la République!"*

He threw pebbles after his retreating sovereign.

They went to Prosper Merimée's; he was away. They went to Feuillet's; he was out. At last, in despair, they called at Dr. Cottard's. He secreted the two ladies in his dispensary and went in search of the Empress' American dentist, Dr. Evans.

Eugenie spent her last night as Empress of the French on the sofa of Dr. Cottard's waiting room. At dawn Dr. Evans appeared with a carriage and accompanied them on the long journey to Boulogne.

The Empire was over. It had ended without a great national upheaval, without a revolution or even an election. It was there one day and gone the next like a word erased from a blackboard at the end of class.

Vittorio found Therese in the study trying to read by the light of a single candle.

"Well, it's over," he announced. "The Empress has fled. A Republic has been declared."

She sprang up. "And Paris?"

"They are going to hold out, it seems."

She gave a low cry that was half a sob and fell into his arms.

It was anything but over for the three refugees marooned in the Hôtel de Piast.

Their subterranean life continued like early Christians in the catacombs.

A routine was established which they adhered to like a religious rite.

The Prince, fearful of sleeping alone on the second floor, had moved to the servants' quarters. He occupied a room between Vittorio and Therese.

When she awoke, assuming that it was morning in that outside world from which they had been banished, Therese with her candle would feel her way downstairs through that ominous emptiness where each footstep resounded like a drumbeat, down and down to the kitchen where she would start to prepare the coffee and warm the bread which the ever resourceful Vittorio had baked the day before. They had long since run out of butter and breakfasted on bread and Brie.

Vittorio would get the Prince up, dress him, shave him, and conduct him to the study. The Prince, to his credit, never complained. He was continually thanking his two protectors. He had come to accept Therese as part of the phantasmagorical life he was now leading. They would breakfast. Therese would then put the kitchen in order, noting, with sinking heart, their rapidly diminishing supplies. The dismantling of the collections continued. Many of the pictures had been taken down. Following the Prince's instructions, they were removed from their frames, unnailed from their stretchers, rolled in linen sheets and swathed in blankets. Masterpieces became indeterminate rolls of milliner's materials. They vanished to their calvary under the roof. Only the two Rembrandts, a portrait of Saski and "The Woman Paring her Nails" the Prince refused to relinquish. Wherever he went, whatever became of him, they would share his fate. The Duccio Madonna still rested against an empty cabinet in his study. It consoled him to have her near him.

An incident occurred that was to have unfortunate consequences.

On going out one night Vittorio's coat caught on a nail in the door of the porter's lodge. In trying to extricate himself without tearing the material, he almost collided with a shopkeeper who was on his way home. The man recognized him and glared.

"Are you still here, you and that damned old Prussian?"

"He left long ago," Vittorio assured him. "I'm just acting as caretaker."

"Why didn't you go with him? I thought all foreigners were ordered to leave Paris."

"I'm Italian. I decided to stick it out."

The man squinted at him, unconvinced.

"He should have been strung up and all filthy Prussians like him. And you, too. Foreigners!" He spat contemptuously on the Prince's door.

Paris was digging in for a siege. The Prussians were moving up. The National Guard and what remained of the army were to defend the city.

Every day food became scarcer. Horsemeat was a staple. Soon even this was rationed. Parisians who had hitherto held tinned food in contempt consulted each other as to the relative virtues of Bully Beef or Pickled Herring. The animals in the Jardin des Plantes became cadaverously thin and lowed piteously at the bars of their cages. They were regarded by passersby with a certain salivary interest. Yaks and buffalo vanished and then Minnie the elephant, for twenty years the childrens' favorite. Culinary experiments produced ragouts of rats, pronounced more delicate than chicken. At fashionable restaurants such exotic items as camel's kidneys or monkey's brains no longer caused raised eyebrows among experienced gourmets.

And then the first shells crashed.

They fell haphazardly, knocking the pediments from doorways, decapitating statues, gouging holes in the façades of public buildings. St. Sulpice was hit and then the Sorbonne. Part of the Hôtel de Ville was demolished.

The bombardment struck harder at the poorer districts. One house would be hit and, having waited for the opportunity for a hundred years, a whole street would collapse.

Paris shuddered, made sour jokes, but held.

The tension of waiting for some unspecified denouement brought Vittorio and Therese to a mutual dependence that was closer than love. They were no longer the valet and the Marquise, they no longer questioned or doubted. They had been tested and had not found each other wanting. If in the course of her checkered life Therese had ever found in a man the qualities of Saladin, courage, loyalty and endurance, she found them in Vittorio. He was a tower of resourcefulness and reliability. She was touched, and often amazed, by the patience he showed with the old Prince. No son could have been more concerned, more constant or more responsible. If he was taciturn, he was untiring. If he fell asleep in a chair, worn out from his exertions, it was like a watchdog with one ear cocked for any untoward sound or threatening footstep.

She knew that it was only the abnormality of their present circumstances that impeded any further development between them. He wanted her and only a sense of formality and fitness, acquired through domestic service, held him back. He was proud but conventional. To take advantage of her under the stress of their present situation struck him as unworthy. At the same time, whoever and whatever she really was, he thought Therese remarkable.

The final break in that tension of days that were nights and nights that were weeks, endless as outer space, occurred, not by a shell crashing into the Hôtel de Piast, but by a prolonged jangling of the bell at the main door.

The sound reverberated through the whole house like a thunderclap.

They had just finished a meager meal of bread with the last scraps of Vittorio's English ham and were wondering over wine how they could possibly replenish their supplies.

The scream of the bell electrified them. It was Revolution! It was the summons of an infuriated mob who had finally come to drag them to execution.

They listened to the ringing, accompanied by a violent pounding on the door.

"Take the Prince upstairs," Vittorio said quietly. "Lock the door and stay there until I come."

"What about you?" the Prince queried in alarm. "Suppose they take you away?"

"They won't. I'm Italian. Call the dogs, Your Highness."

Therese took the Prince's arm and led him down the passage. *"Venez Ce Monsieur, Tizane, Aubépine. Venez, tous. Venez,"* the Prince twittered.

The little dogs scrambled after him. Vittorio waited by the stairs until they had reached the top floor. He went out into

the courtyard. It was raining. It seemed extraordinary that anything as normal as rain could still occur in Paris.

He shouted above the racket at the door, "Who is it? Stop
making such a din!"

"Open this door!" a voice answered. "It's the police."

Vittorio went into the gatekeeper's lodge and opened the
side door. All this thunder had been caused by a man in a
trench coat and four gendarmes armed with rifles.

The man glared at him. He was gray and wet and insignif-
icant.

"What the hell are you playing at? Why don't you answer
the bell?"

"I was on the other side of the house."

"I've come for the Prince de Piast."

"He's been gone for weeks. I'm only the caretaker."

"So we've been told. Out of my way!"

The gendarmes were fingering their rifles. They would gladly
have shot someone if only as a relief from getting so wet.

The five custodians of the law pushed Vittorio aside and
tramped into the courtyard. The mansion loomed above them,
a citadel of detested Prussianism.

It seemed so vast and dark and powerful that these ordinary
fellows felt obscurely intimidated.

"Light some candles," the police officer ordered.

Vittorio, taking his time, produced several candlesticks and
lit them.

"Search the house. And when I say search, I mean *search*!"

The house which had grown accustomed to its own morose
silence was reluctantly roused by tramping feet, banging doors,
oaths and shouts of official authority. This unwelcome disturbance echoed in a void.

Vittorio waited in the hall.

The gendarmes peered into rooms in which huge pieces of
furniture stood abandoned like prisoners awaiting a firing squad.
There was nothing to smash or knock over, no objects upon
which to vent their patriotic scorn. And no cowering Prince de
Piast.

The men converged in the hall, put out and bewildered, and

were joined by their officer in the trench coat. "Upstairs!" he commanded like a general ordering an assault on a fortress.

They charged upstairs. Vittorio followed, his attention riveted to the silence on the floor above.

The men barged in and out of bedrooms, poked under unoccupied beds, challenged armoires to disclose themselves, delivered death thrusts to curtains. The emptiness refused to surrender.

It was the dogs that betrayed them.

Alerted by the racket below, they started to bark in defense of their master. The officer whirled to a standstill in front of Vittorio. "Ah, he's up there! You thought you could obstruct the law. You are under arrest."

"I've been looking after the Prince's dogs," Vittorio insisted.

The officer signaled to the men with one of those dramatic gestures that come naturally to the French and which are reproduced for posterity on equestrian statues.

There was no stopping the dogs. They barked in a frenzy, intent on putting the whole French army to flight.

The officer pounded on the bedroom door. "Open!"

He was in for a shock. The door opened and he found himself face to face with the Marquise de Païva who, on so many winter nights, he had cursed for keeping him out of bed.

"You—?" he exclaimed like an actor in a third-rate melodrama. "What are you doing here?"

"I am staying here," Therese replied, blocking the doorway.

"You were ordered to leave Paris. You have no right to be here."

"That order was revoked when Monsieur de Morny died."

"I heard nothing about it." He had not forgotten his outrage at this woman who had insisted on riding her black charger to the Porte d'Orleans. "You're under arrest."

He overheard the Prince surreptitiously warning the dogs to stay quiet and pushed past Therese into the room.

"So!" He advanced on the miscreant, that miserable example of the race that was now destroying Paris. "You left weeks ago, did you? Are you aware that you stand in violation of the law?"

"I am not aware of any such thing," the Prince replied with surprising calm.

"Are you aware," the officer thundered, "that all Prussian citizens were required to register with the Police? Did you register?"

"Certainly not. I have nothing to do with the police."

"Well, the Police will have plenty to do with you. If you're not out of Paris within an hour I have orders to take you to the Conciergerie."

To everyone's surprise it was the Prince who took control. He was not used to being addressed in such peremptory tones. Indignation took precedence over the danger confronting him.

He took a step forward and, with a ridiculously inappropriate gesture, raised his lorgnette and examined the officer as if he were a small boy caught pilfering the larder.

"You will have the very great goodness not to speak to me in that manner. This is my house. I have a perfect right to be here. I have not broken the law and you, sir, are not going to order me to the Conciergerie or anywhere else."

The man from the Sûreté was taken aback by this unexpected display of aristocratic defiance.

"We'll see about that," he replied with a faltering inflection. "I have a carriage downstairs. You will leave now or you will go to jail."

Vittorio, in his reasonable way, tried to put an end to this altercation. "We had better go, Mon Altesse. It is useless to argue."

"And you," the man from the Sûreté turned to Therese, "will come with me. We'll soon see if that order was ever rescinded."

The Prince brushed Vittorio aside. He had picked up his ebony cane and now gave the police officer a sharp rap on the calf which caused him to jump and swing 'round.

"This lady is my guest. She is under my protection. She will either come with me or we will go to jail together. And I warn you, sir, that when the siege of Paris is over, as it soon will be, it will go very ill with you if you attempt to obstruct me now."

"Don't give me orders," the officer snapped. "I am not impressed." But he was nonetheless sensible of the possible validity of the Prince's threat. "You will do as I tell you."

"From now on," the Prince informed him icily, "it is you who will do what I say—precisely."

They were all dumbfounded. He was at all times an extraordinary figure, with his high, domed head, puffy eyelids and fussy little mannerisms; but now, outrage transformed the Prince into the apotheosis of an autocrat. A long line of Piast rulers who had ordered the deaths of countless serfs and traitors with a nod stood embodied in that elderly art collector.

"Be so good, Therese, as to get your things. Vittorio, my coat."

Vittorio was delighted and proud of his master. It confirmed his respect for the aristocratic tradition.

The Prince put on his fur-lined coat and his sable hat. The man from the Sûreté, deflated by this superior show of force, retreated to the door.

"The dogs."

Vittorio, who had never been known to forget anything, produced two wicker traveling boxes. Into one he stuffed three of the dogs who protested with little barks and whimpers. Two others were bestowed in the other box and Nichette, the maîtresse en titre, was secreted in her place of honor under the Prince's arm.

Therese put on one of the Prince's brocade waistcoats which she had taken the habit of wearing against the cold, and over it her cloak. Her old tricorne with the green plume. Her reticule. She was ready.

The Prince proceeded down the passage, lit by the raised candlesticks of the gendarmes who had abruptly been elevated to a guard of honor.

Vittorio handed Therese the lighter of the wicker boxes with a significant look in which there was a certain amusement. At least, whatever lay ahead, their confinement in the Hôtel de Piast was over.

They went downstairs.

In the hall the Prince, not to be hurried, signaled to Vittorio. "The trunk and the pictures."

Vittorio hurried into the study. The one object that had not been wrapped was the Duccio Madonna, due to the Prince's insistence on keeping his talisman near him.

Vittorio wrenched the fine linen cloth from the dining table, sending plates and dishes crashing to the floor. He folded it 'round the wooden panel and tied it securely at the back. He shouldered a small tin trunk containing the Magnum Opus, loose money in gold and notes, and some jewels that had belonged to the Prince's mother and joined the others in the hall.

"I'll take the Madonna," the Prince said.

"Hold it this way by the knot." Vittorio placed the Duccio under the Prince's arm. "Can you manage?"

"Perfectly. Therese, will you bring the others?"

He made his way carefully across the hall.

The two Rembrandts proved to be of unwieldy proportions. Therese contrived to hold them by tucking them under her left shoulder and crooking her damaged arm around them. She picked up the basket with the two dogs in the other hand.

The gendarmes had watched these preparations open-mouthed. The Prussians were not only devils incarnate, they were lunatics as well.

A desultory sort of hackney cab with a dispirited horse was waiting in the rain.

The Prince got in unassisted and placed the Madonna beside him with the dogs on top. He was curiously calm. The Rembrandts were too long to lay on the seat and, after various maneuverings, were balanced between Therese's and the Prince's knees. The man from the Sûreté squeezed himself in on the other side.

It was a night for incongruities. As Vittorio was securing the tin trunk to the luggage rack, a neat little gentleman with an umbrella, a smart top hat, an overcoat pinched in at the waist and pointed patent leather shoes, appeared out of nowhere and asked one of the gendarmes, "Excuse me, but is this Number Ten Faubourg St. Honoré?"

The gendarme looked at him as though he had been asked something in Chinese.

"Yes, it is," Vittorio replied with one foot on the carriage step.

"I am inquiring about a property on the Rue du Temple. I would have come earlier, but I had to wait for the bombardment."

Therese put her head through the door. "Do you want to buy the Pavillon?"

"It would be admirably suited to my requirements," the little dandy replied. "May I present myself? I am Etienne Perroneau de Roose. I give lessons in Terpsichore."

"Have you got a visiting card?"

"Indeed yes, Madame. Delighted." He produced a wallet and from it withdrew a card which he presented with a bow. Therese, in turn, had taken the key to the Pavillon from her reticule.

"Take this. Feed the doves and the goldfish and please prune the roses. We can do the business by post."

"By post! Admirable! By post!" Monsieur Perroneau de Roose raised the key in salute with his feet in the fifth position.

Vittorio got in. There was barely room for him beside Therese.

The carriage started. They looked at each other. Therese burst out laughing.

The Prince looked surprised, Vittorio smiled, the man from the Sûreté was shocked.

"That little man—on top of everything! Did you see his feet? In the fifth position! Oh, it's all too absurd!"

Therese laughed till she cried.

They drove through a dead city without lights or people, desolate as the ruins of Pompeii. Here and there were gaping evidences of the bombardment, a lamppost twisted into a hairpin, boarded up windows, a pile of rubble where the façade of a house had fallen into the street. The populace seemed to have retreated to the cellars to the now familiar company of the rats.

They were driving eastward, away from the river. At an intersection they were held up by a long convoy of carts bearing wounded into the city. Figures that had once been men lay piled on straw with their faces upturned to the rain. They passed slowly, because the horses that had escaped being turned into steaks and stews were overworked and weary.

"Where are we going?" the Prince asked.

"To the city limits. From there you can make your way to the Prussian lines."

"How are you proposing we shall do that?"

"You can walk."

"How far is it?" Vittorio inquired.

The man in the trench coat shrugged. "Two miles."

"I am not a young man," the Prince pointed out. "And this lady has been ill. We shall need this carriage."

"I have my instructions."

"Sir," the Prince insisted, "we have six dogs."

"Leave them behind. Someone will be glad to eat them."

The Prince shuddered. "I must commend you for making the most repellent suggestion I have yet heard."

The full horror of their expulsion had now become clear to them. Vittorio and Therese were thinking, "He'll never be able to walk two miles with the Madonna and Nichette."

The Prince was thinking, "They are barbarians, the French police. Well, if I have to walk two miles I will walk them." He gave Therese a sickly smile. "I'm sorry, my dear. Do you think you can walk that far?"

"We'll manage somehow."

The Prince sighed. "These are very peculiar times."

"They're not of our making," the police officer put in. "France was forced into this war."

"France was not forced into the war," the Prince replied in a level tone. "The French wanted war. It appeals to their sense of the dramatic. One would have thought that Napoleon would have taught them a lesson."

"Listen, you Prussian bastard," the man exploded. "You're lucky to get out of this with your life."

"You may be thinking the same thing in a few weeks," the Prince said, concluding this exchange of civilities.

They had entered a poor quarter where the full brunt of the war was painfully evident. They passed shell after shell of abandoned houses. Great piles of uncleared rubble impeded their progress. Pitiful rooms were exposed with bits of broken-down furniture. Pictures still hung at odd angles on half demolished walls.

They reached the end of what had once been a street. The hackney stopped.

The Prince peered through the window. "I don't see anything."

"This is as far as I'll take you."

Vittorio got out. They were at the crest of a hill. A muddy, pockmarked road descended into darkness. Far away on the opposite heights he could make out the faint glow of the Prussian encampment.

He helped Therese out with the two Rembrandts. She realized as her feet sank into the icy mud that she had forgotten to put on walking shoes.

The Prince descended. Nichette had wriggled her head free and was peering anxiously about. She found this experience very upsetting.

Vittorio unstrapped the tin trunk from the rear and lifted out the Madonna and the two wicker baskets. The man from the Sûreté raised not a finger.

"You're wise to sit there," Vittorio informed him through the window. "If you dare to get out I'll break your neck."

The man from the Sûreté muttered the vilest oaths and barked an order. The hackney turned with difficulty and trundled off.

They were alone.

"It has stopped raining," the Prince observed.

"Well, there's nothing for it," Vittorio said. "The German lines are over there. We must get to them somehow."

He stowed the Rembrandts under Therese's arm and gave her the box with the two dogs. Her feet were already cold.

"Would you rather carry the Madonna or the dogs?" he asked the Prince.

"The Madonna."

They were equipped for their journey through Hades. Vittorio shouldered the tin trunk. "I'll go first. You follow directly behind, Altesse. Then you, Therese. We must stay as close to each other as we can."

They made their first tentative steps down the long hill.

There was no road, only mud. It was pitch black. They had nothing to guide them but the faint glow on the distant bank.

They slipped and floundered, but managed to keep their balance. The dogs, now thoroughly frightened, whimpered.

Therese was chiefly concerned with not falling down on her broken wrist. The mud sucked at her slippers.

"*Du calme, ma belle. Du calme,*" the Prince was whispering to Nichette as he picked his way through the slush. "*On arrive. Tu vas voir. Bientôt.*"

They had not gone far when the Prince gave a cry, careened wildly, dropped the Madonna, and slid on his backside into a puddle.

"Oh, my God, it's outrageous," he shrilled as though the road had been guilty of *lèse majesté*. "Oh, my God. *Calme toi, Nichette.*" For the first time, he gasped as Vittorio helped him to his feet, "I hope the French are reduced to rubble."

Vittorio retrieved the Madonna and the sable hat which he restored to the Prince's head.

"Thank you, my dear," the Prince said in a conversational tone. "I must say the state of the French roads leaves something to be desired."

Therese loved the staunch Italian at that moment as he replaced the wooden panel under the Prince's arm. "Hold it by the knot. It will help you to keep your balance."

"Yes, precisely. The knot. I have it. Excellent, my dear."

"Are you all right, Therese?" Vittorio called. They could barely see each other in the hellish darkness, but the strength of his voice reassured her.

"Yes, I'm all right." Her feet were now insensate. The cold, like rigor mortis, was creeping up her legs.

She wished the dogs would stop whimpering and that they didn't weigh so much.

"*Alors, on avance*," the Prince announced. "*On avance, ma belle.*"

They advanced, step by slithery step. Something loomed up on the left. It was a ruined farmhouse which bore on its one remaining wall an advertisement for Levoisier's beer. The rest of the building had capsized into the dark, the eternal dark, the Prussian dark that was Bismarck's final anathema on France.

Suddenly a screech tore through the night above them.

The bombardment had resumed.

"What was that?" the Prince queried.

"A shell, Altesse."

"Oh, really?" He was unable at that moment to cope with the significance of shells. "It was a shell, Nichette. Nothing, my petite. Precisely nothing."

Therese's feet had ceased to be part of her. They were stumps of ice on which somehow she stumbled forward.

They were reaching the bottom of the hill.

Voices and a bobbing candle somewhere down there in the pit.

A young woman in agony. "But it's not there. I tell you it's not there!"

A coarse middle-aged woman: "Yes, it's there. I dropped it there. *Zuchen sie es! Zuchen!*"

There came on a vixen in a fur coat holding a candle that shed no useful light. At her feet a servant girl was crawling in the mud, knee-deep, wrist-deep, in mud.

Behind them a portly figure in an overcoat with an Astrakhan collar was guarding a pile of suitcases.

"I tell you; never mind!" he shouted. "Leave it. You can get another in Berlin."

"You think I'm going to leave an earring of thirteen carats in the mud? *Got in Himmel, Du dorf trottle Du!*" She gave the girl a prod with her shoe. "Zuchen! Zuchen! It's there, you stupid creature!"

The girl sat up and, losing control, screamed at her mistress, "I tell you it's not there, you bloody bitch."

The woman in the fur coat raised the candle. Her face was livid with indignation. "You hear? You heard what she called me? Ungrateful slut! I've a good mind to send you back to Paris."

As the girl staggered to her feet and was about to hurl herself at her tormentor, she became aware of the three specters who had materialized out of the darkness. She gave a shrill little scream of fear.

"Where are you going?" the middle-aged woman demanded as though they had no right to be there. "To the German lines? You, too?"

"Yes," Vittorio grunted and kept going.

"Ah, they turned you out, too! Well, let me tell you, they'll live to regret it. I have their names. I'll see they pay dearly for this outrage. My husband is an important man. We are people of consequence, let me tell you."

"You? You're nothing," the maidservant screamed. "A fat slug! I hope you die right here in the mud."

"It's nothing, Nichette. Precisely nothing," the Prince murmured, shielding Nichette's sensibilities from such vile abuse.

The man with the Astrakhan collar stepped forward and raised a yellow kid glove.

"Herman Mendelsohn, Mendelsohn and Fishbein, importers of fine gems, Thirty-three Avenue Hoche."

The Prince glanced at him, unimpressed by these credentials. "Yes, precisely," he muttered keeping as close to Vittorio as he could.

They started to climb the opposite slope.

The dogs had stopped whimpering. They huddled, chilled, in their rocking cages.

The maidservant's shrill voice followed them from the abyss. "Wait! I'm coming with you. Wait for me!"

They went on for a while until the Prince suddenly exclaimed, "I can't. I can't go a step farther."

He let go of the Duccio which slithered away behind him. Vittorio put down the trunk.

"I'll come back for it later. Take my hand."

Therese had managed to stop the Duccio with her foot. She

lowered the dogs and the Rembrandts, retrieved the Duccio and set it against the bank. She no longer cared about the paintings. Masterpieces they might be and worth a fortune, they had encumbered her long enough. She laid them beside the trunk, squelched back for the dogs, and proceeded up the hill.

The servant girl had caught up with her. She was dripping with mud and incoherent.

"I'm not going to stand for it. Let her find her own rotten earring. I should have stayed in Paris. I don't know what we're doing here. I don't know what this stupid war is about. But I have rights. I'm a citizen. I have my rights."

She kept up a stream of hysterical chatter, until miraculously, at the end of eternity, they reached the summit.

A wood. Campfires. Burly, blond soldiers warming themselves, swilling beer.

Vittorio left the Prince by the fire and met Therese on his way back.

"Stay with him. I'll fetch the things."

Never in her life had she found the sight of fire so beautiful.

The servant girl staggered forward with her arms extended as though to greet a lover and fell on her knees beside the flames.

The Prince had withdrawn Nichette from his coat.

"Get warm, *ma petite*. Get warm now, my treasure. It's over."

Nichette did not respond.

The other dogs now broke into a frantic yapping. The Hanovarian soldiers had recovered from the shock of these apparitions and gathered 'round.

Therese said gently to the Prince, "I'm afraid it's too late to warm her."

"Eh? Too late? Nichette—?" The Prince was holding the little body toward the warmth. Under the tangle of white hair the mask was already set in the ugly grimace of death.

"Nichette? *Ma belle?* No—you couldn't. Oh no— How can that be?"

He stood holding the inert body. Tears trickled down his

cheeks. Of all that had happened in the last weeks, the disruption of his life, the loss of his treasures, this was the cruelest blow.

"I don't understand—how? Was it when I fell? The cold—?"

Vittorio returned with the trunk and the paintings.

"I'm afraid it's Nichette," Therese warned him.

Vittorio did not intrude on the Prince's grief. He summoned one of the blond soldiers.

"Can you take us to your commander?"

The soldier grinned, shrugged, not understanding.

"The Herr Comandant."

"Ja, naturlich, Meine Herren bitter folgen sie mir."

He obligingly shouldered the trunk and one of the dog boxes. Together they escorted the stricken Prince through the wood, onto a country road where, at a short distance, was an inn that was now the Prussian headquarters.

It was loud with the tramping of boots and that jubilant activity that accompanies a victorious army.

The Prince recovered himself sufficiently to say to an orderly, *"Ich bin Prinz von Oppeln-Piast. Ich Möchte mit ihre komandant sprächen."*

An immensely tall officer with an eyeglass and moustaches waxed to needle points appeared unimpressed by the Prince's titles until Vittorio advised him in an undertone, "He is a cousin of your King Wilhelm."

The result was immediate. Orderlies clattered upstairs and the Prince was shortly after shown to a room, hastily vacated by two officers who were less importantly related.

Therese found herself in the restaurant bar of the requisitioned establishment. A group of officers were gathered around a fire, toasting their successes. They gallantly offered her a chair.

The heat of the fire which had seemed infinitely desirable seared her. The unthawing of her legs was an agony worse than their iciness.

One of the officers clicked heels and courteously asked, *"Kan ich besorgen etwas fur ihren, Genedige Frau?"*

"A brandy, please."

She fell into a sort of trance from which she was woken by Vittorio. "I've put him to bed. Poor man, he's quite worn out. I don't wonder after that journey."

"Poor Nichette!"

"He refused to be parted from her. We'll have to bury her in the morning."

She took his hand. "You've been so wonderful, Vittorio. We should never have got here without you."

"I don't even know where we are."

They sat hand in hand by the fire. They were both falling asleep. "There's only one other room, I'm afraid."

They went upstairs, undressed like a married couple and got into bed. She was too exhausted to feel apprehension at risking proximity to a male body. She was grateful to sink into the quiet strength of that harbor. She thought vaguely that it would be nice to love again, nice to be protected.

They slept through the rest of the bombardment and were woken by the uncanny stillness that fell afterward.

"Should you look to see if he's all right?"

"Let him sleep."

He spread out her hair across the pillow.

She shivered, repelled, as she felt him stir against her.

A moment of panic and then of horror as the male weapon rose against her. "Your only redress is courage." She resisted terror and, at the moment of penetration, gritted her teeth to prevent herself from screaming. She thought wildly, "Saladin—Saladin—where are you? Far away in Fabrice's barn. She had no one—"

He wasn't aware as he thrust toward climax that she had fainted.

They woke to silence and winter sunlight.

He was stroking her breasts, drawing her nipples between his lips. She wanted to feel, wanted to respond. "It should have been like this long ago, with someone as good as this." Could she ever conquer her fear? Would she ever be able to relax with a man, to trust a man sufficiently to accept love?

She was amazed by the beauty of his body.

She shut her mind and allowed her body to function. She felt nothing; at least it was better than fear. Afterward, as they lay there, she said, "It's all so unreal. I don't know why I'm here or where we're going."

"He has estates in Germany. I suppose we'll go there."

"It all happened because of you."

She forced herself to look into those somber Latin eyes that concealed the light. There was nothing to be afraid of in this gentle giant. But he was still too close to the past, to the others, to that horror and the hag with the needles. Courage—yes. But much more. There was so much to forget.

She would have to forget her whole life to be able to love this man.

They buried Nichette, rolled in a pillow slip, under a tree in the hotel orchard.

"She was a good little soul," the Prince said. "It is sad to leave her without a mark."

A decrepit pony cart had been commandeered with an orderly to drive them to the nearest station.

They rattled along a country road through woods and orchards from which the last leaves had fallen. It was a pale and peaceful day.

They reached Nogent. As he alighted the Prince said crossly, "Mendelsohn and Fishbein! I've never heard of them!"

After a long wait in a chilly stationroom, they boarded a train crowded with German troops.

The countryside through which they passed had the alienated look of land that no longer belonged to its rightful owners. This part of France was now in enemy hands.

All that day the train resounded with the singing of soldiers returning home in triumph. German songs roared from German throats. Soldiers laughed, drank, embraced each other, impatient to be marching down avenues decked with flags, with bands blaring, to the cheers of multitudes, their helmets crowned with flowers.

"A new era," the Prince observed gloomily. "The Pax Germanica. And, incidentally, Vittorio, I am not related to the

King of Prussia. That is one family I am honored to exclude from my family tree."

"It got you a room, Altesse."

"You are a sly fellow." The Prince withdrew into his sable collar. "Strange to be an expatriate, but I suppose I have never had a country. One thing is certain; I shall never return to France."

He had added to the Prussian victories his personal condemnation of the country that had betrayed him.

Toward evening they reached Metz. Sometime during the night they crossed the border into Germany.

Radoom, the country home of the Piasts, was in Southern Silesia, twenty miles from Breslau.

Whenever the Prince traveled he made a great many purchases. On this occasion they filled two coaches, which followed the one in which he and his two companions were bumped and shaken from that gloomy medieval city, surrounded by factories, to the estate which he had not seen for thirty years.

He had laid in stocks of linen and blankets, pillows and quilts, bearskin rugs, foodstuffs of every kind, and crates of the bitter local wine. Shopkeepers did not presume to ask for payment. The name of Oppeln-Piast was equal to a royal command.

This remote corner of Europe was, in its lugubrious way, impressive. Dense forests of fir repelled intruders. It was the territory of bears, wild boar and wolves. Glacial streams flowed sluggishly through stretches of farmland that bore the imprint of centuries of penury and invasion. Marauding armies had robbed the land of its identity. It had never had much charm. Grimy villages clustered for refuge against the forbidding hills and the local populace, depleted by undernourishment and moronism, observed the passing of this alien convoy with indifference.

The region subsisted under an evil spell.

After two hours the road forked abruptly and came to a stop before a high iron gate surmounted by a faded escutcheon. A group of peasants in smocks and muddy leggings ran forward to open it, bowing to the ground as the three coaches rumbled through.

They passed up an avenue of immense old trees, many of which were revealed by the winter to be in a sad state of decay. Parliaments of rooks rose with a startled cawing.

The avenue ended before a vast gray pile built in the manner of Polish and Russian country houses. A central building on two floors in a vaguely classic style was flanked by wings that abutted onto a courtyard, the open side of which was contained by a high iron paling with an ornamental gate. A family of caretakers, scared out of their wits by the appearance of their legendary employer, hurried forward to bow him into his ancestral home.

He stood for a long moment gazing at the house which confronted him like an edict, neglected but still censorious.

The Prince proceeded into the central hall. It was icy cold. Marble statues in rigor mortis stood in niches, their heads and fig leaves swathed in cobwebs. The walls rose to a glass rotunda. He looked up as the light of yesterday fell on him without a blessing.

The progress through the house, unlived-in for a generation, revealed that the caretakers, ensconced, they had imagined, for life, had allowed it to fall into lamentable disrepair. They had pilfered many of the furnishings, many others had been despoiled. Valuable tapestries were slung on ropes across rooms to keep out draughts, others were nailed to ceilings against the rain. The roof leaked in a dozen places. The long procession of rooms, leading out of each other, were perishingly cold and damp. Chairs were worm-eaten, curtains tattered by rats, walls bore traces of missing pictures and mirrors.

The caretakers, in a cold sweat of fear that they would be flung into jail or beaten senseless, followed the Prince on his tour of inspection, unrolling a feeble carpet of excuses and explanations. He paid them no heed; his silence grew more and more alarming.

They climbed to the second floor. It was a shambles of fallen plaster, broken windowpanes and rotting floor boards.

When they returned to the hall the Prince said without raising his voice, "You are dismissed from my service. Before you leave you will light fires in every room, unpack the things I have brought and bring down three beds from the upper floor. I do not wish to lay eyes on you again."

They groveled, terrified, and vanished.

The Prince stationed himself in the main drawing room in a high-backed chair the brocade of which was in ribbons. He was deeply shaken but grimly resolved.

Therese was looking through the window at a large walled garden that stretched the length of the house in which she could not detect a single living thing. She turned, incredulous, as the Prince announced, "It seems that we must be prepared for a period of discomfort."

"Surely you don't have the intention of staying *here*?"

"It is a fine old house. It deserves to be tenanted."

"It will cost a fortune to put it in order," she protested. "You could rent a palace in Italy, near all the works of art you love—with a good climate and servants who know how to run things. Why on earth would you want to live in this depressing, half-ruined place?"

"This depressing, half-ruined place, as you choose to call it, happens to be my home."

"You can't have any attachment for it. You haven't seen it for thirty years."

The Prince was affronted by such obvious common sense. It was exactly the insurmountable obstacles that appealed to his pride and perversity. He had always hated Radoom; now it presented a challenge. It had been desecrated; he would restore it. It had haunted him; he would exorcise it. As it stood it was an insult to the manner in which a member of his family had the right to live.

"You will allow me, Marquise, to make my own decisions."

"You have the whole civilized world to choose from—"

"Yes, and I have chosen Radoom."

The ukase had been issued.

For once even Vittorio was on the point of rebellion.

"You realize, Mon Altesse, what it would mean? There's nothing here. Even the beds are unusable."

The fact that they were both against him only determined the Prince to enforce his will. "I consider it my duty."

"You've dismissed all the servants. How are you proposing that we shall manage?"

"We managed in Paris; we can manage here."

"We lived like that for a few weeks because we had no choice," Vittorio insisted. "At least the house was properly equipped. It had a roof and running water and kitchens— windows with panes of glass. Do you realize what it will be like here in the winter?"

The Prince lost his temper. "I refuse to discuss it," he squealed. "Go and make some tea."

Vittorio approached him. He delivered his trump card. "You leave me no alternative, Mon Altesse. I must offer my resignation."

The Prince shot from his chair as though released by a spring. He was galvanized by indignation. "You want to resign? Then resign. Leave with the others. If I have to live here alone, then I'll live here alone. You are dismissed!"

He stomped out of the room.

The little dogs looked at each other in consternation. They had never heard their master's voice raised to such a pitch. They followed him dutifully, keeping a safe distance.

"What are we going to do?" Therese asked. "It's madness."

Vittorio looked 'round in despair. He foresaw a purgatory of renovation, an onslaught of carpenters, plasterers and painters, a Sisyphean unpacking and moving of furniture, an endless and unavailing struggle with servants.

It was the aristocratic principle carried to lunacy. For the first time he bitterly resented the loyalty that chained him to this petty despot who could understand nothing but the right to get his own way.

Therese was relieved when Vittorio slipped into her room.

They had chosen two small bedrooms that were in slightly less disrepair in the right wing. The Prince had been installed in what had once been his mother's sitting room.

Nothing further had been said.

Despite a moth-eaten tapestry that Therese had flung over the bed, she could not escape from the cold and the smell of decay that clung to everything.

Vittorio threw off his dressing gown and went naked to the window to see if it was as tightly shut as it could be. The sight of his nakedness, of that superb male body, reassured her. With the other men she had known the shedding of clothes had been an embarrassment, hastily ended by a dimming of lamp and a swift escape under the bedcovers. Vittorio's body was an affirmation of life, of normality, of sanity, in the demented situation in which she found herself.

He pulled the covers over them and then exclaimed, "Peugh! This stinks." And threw the tapestry onto the floor.

He was warm. He smelled of bread and hay. His abundant health stood between her and her demons. His strength was a panacea for the past.

He drew her nightdress over her head. She was suddenly not afraid.

They talked in low voices, holding each other close.

"Did he say anything?"

"No. He will never admit he's wrong."

"But what is it with him? Is he mad?"

"He has all this money. He can do whatever he wants."

"Where does it come from? It seems to be endless."

"Silver mines in Mexico. The silver's sent over in bars because the Mexican money's no good. It's a family monopoly."

She was aware of him erect against her. It was part of the natural order of things in the sane physical world he belonged to. There was no sickness, no grossness or deception. She thought, "It should have been like this all along." He was simple, God-given, human.

"He can't be serious. This place is a nightmare."

"He lives by whims. You can't judge him like other people."

He was kissing her throat and breasts. His tongue found her navel. She stretched back. She wanted him to love her. She wanted to banish the last vestige of her disgust. She scarcely trembled when he entered her. She received him willingly. She wanted him in her, to his full length, to her deepest point of surrender, the point beyond fear.

"You're wonderful, Therese—"

He thrust. She was flowing. The past flowed out of her like the long residue of an illness.

"I don't understand," she said afterward. "Are you going to give up your life to him?"

"I haven't much choice as things are."

"You could do anything."

"I have no education."

"You could marry a rich woman—any woman—with your looks."

"Where would I meet her? There were a few at the hotel where I worked. All they wanted was a quick fling. Men, too. It's not very well arranged that he has everything without lifting a finger."

"Has he always lived like this? I could understand it in Paris because of the war."

"He lives as he wants. He hasn't seen his relatives for years. He has no one but himself to consider."

"Who are his friends?"

"He hasn't any. Dealers and art collectors—a few people who came to see the collections. He can be very gracious—and very mean."

He was stroking her neck, slowly combing his hand through her heavy, silken hair.

"The mysterious Marquise—"

She recognized in Vittorio's nature the inherent passivity that goes with great physical beauty. There were two kinds of people; those who accepted Fate, who were creatures of circumstance, who swayed like seaweed with the tides; and there were the few who wrestled with it like de Morny and gained the upper hand. It wasn't easy to meet Fate head on. Fate hid and stalked, an invisible hunter, played tricks and concealed the future. But she dimly perceived that it was not mere accident that had involved her with the Prince and Vittorio. There was some kind of concealed pattern that had led her to this point. Fate was spinning another skein.

And meanwhile, instead of Saladin, she had her gentle giant to protect her.

While they were sleeping, warm in each other's arms, the Prince was huddled in a bearskin rug beside a dying fire.

The past was palpable in this room. He thought of his mother in her severe black dresses with high lace collars, boned under the chin, stiff as an effigy at her eternal needlework. She had never thought to caress him, never given him the least token of affection. Had she felt anything under that hard veneer of habits and conventions? He thought of his father with his thunderous looks and great fur coats, always hunting in the forest. Who had he really fired at when he brought down the soaring birds, the blameless deer? Into whose body had he thrust the lance when he cornered the wild boar? They had both despised him because he was weak and ugly and loved books and graceful objects, instead of the bleeding carcasses of animals.

He thought of his angry sisters, one always rescuing creatures her father had failed to kill, in a pathetic defiance of brutality, the other climbing the tallest trees to escape to a kinder realm. And Ellamine, singing and weeping, a bird beating its wings against a cage. She had vanished one day in Berlin leaving an incoherent note full of love and pain and regret. He had never seen her again.

The past overwhelmed him. Could he conquer it by rebuilding this barrack according to his own desire? He was no longer angry with Vittorio and Therese. He knew that they wouldn't leave him. How could they? They were dependent. And he knew that they were right. A villa in Italy would have led to a richer and happier life. But it wasn't happiness he wanted. He wanted to do battle with the past, to rub the past into the open wound of all he had lost, long before Paris and the war, here in this terrible fortress of family pride of which he was finally master.

The rebuilding of Radoom occupied the Prince's complete attention. It was an undertaking after his own heart which enabled him, among much else, to demonstrate his skill at making things as difficult as possible for everyone.

Regiments of workers were commandeered from Breslau and the neighboring town of Oppeln. The great house like a supine Gulliver was assaulted by a swarm of Liliputians scaling ladders and erecting scaffolding. It resounded to hammering and the tramping of workmen's boots. Every passage was impassable with planks and boxes of tools, every room a maze of canvas sheets, more ladders and more tools, and men daubing and scraping and plastering and chipping and chopping and banging in nails. The smell of mold was replaced by the sharp odors of size and varnish and unseasoned wood.

Through this satisfactory hubbub the Prince padded like Frederick the Great reviewing his army, rapping carpenters on the legs, summoning roofers from their perches, hiring, dismissing, issuing a stream of instructions and reproofs and generally exercising his authority. He impressed everyone and annoyed everyone, but in general got his way.

Vittorio spent his days rattling along the roads to Breslau and Oppeln on impossible missions to procure impossible things. He cursed his master, but did his bidding.

Therese was put to screening the men and women of all ages who tramped to Radoom from farms and villages in search of work. Communication was impeded by her lack of German and, even had she been proficient in that language, these stolid, slow-witted peasants would scarcely have understood. They were Sudetans and spoke their own guttural tongue.

She selected the few that appeared to have a modicum of sense and set them to scrubbing and scouring. She hired cooks who could only roast joints and make blood puddings, manservants who could only lift and carry, girls who could only make beds, dust and drop things. She unpacked trunks locked for thirty years and unearthed china and glass and tableware and a plethora of household objects.

Gradually she made some order. She had little knowledge of domestic matters and none of running a house this size. She functioned by common sense, Vittorio's council and the Prince's constant demands for better service and better food.

Her attitude to the Prince fluctuated between exasperation, outrage, amusement and a certain reluctant admiration. He was inconsiderate, arbitrary, quixotic and impenitent. He was also, when he thought of it, generous. He made no offer to pay her for her efforts and appeared to think it a privilege that she should be allowed to participate in the reconstruction of his home, but he gave Vittorio a large sum for her to buy some winter clothes. Part of this she sent to Fabrice, the school master, for the care and maintenance of Saladin.

The five little terriers were in their heyday. They scampered all over the house, barking at ladders, diving at workmens' legs and romping in dust and wood shavings.

It was with immense relief that Therese welcomed Vittorio into her bed at night. After the follies and frustrations of the day, their lovemaking was a reaffirmation of sanity, a renewal of their status as human beings. From Vittorio she was learning the pleasures of sensuality. He was more than her lover; he was her physician. He was curing her of her demons. He was restoring her lost youth.

She came to know lust and gratified it with a new hunger. Vittorio's untiring body was the alter at which she worshiped a profane god. As they became physically attuned they prolonged exquisite torments that drove her to frenzy. She devoured him, a succubus of delights.

He bore the marks of her teeth; she assuaged these wounds with her kisses. They drained each other in a passion that precluded love.

In their respites of repletion, huddled in their chrysalis of rugs and blankets, they would discuss the madness in which they were helplessly involved.

"He's not going to give up. He's determined to see it through."

"This is only the beginning. When the house is finished there'll be a new garden, a new park. He'll start traveling in search of carpets and furniture."

"This avalanche of wasted money!"

"Take courage, *cara*. There's a mansion in Berlin, too."

"It's horrifying—a disease of *things*."

"There's no alternative for us—the way things are."

There was no alternative *now*. What disturbed and came to irritate her was that Vittorio could not see, and perhaps did not want to see, any alternative in the future. Their nights were their only solace, but even of these Therese came to have her doubts.

"If you loved me you'd be willing to leave him, to try something else—to make something for us."

"Where? We can't go back to Paris with the war on."

"You'd think of something. You'd be ready to take risks."

"Don't I give you sufficient proof of what I feel?"

"I don't mean that." She wanted the assurance that she possessed not only his body but his heart. "You think of me as someone to sleep with because there's no one else."

"That isn't true. I think of you very highly—more—"

His hesitation frightened and angered her.

"You're wonderful, Therese. The most wonderful woman I've known. I don't know if I love you yet—in the way you mean."

She looked into those deep, lusterless eyes unsparked by the fires of risk or impulse. Had she found in this man that bald honesty she had lost that could only see things as they were?

"Why? Why not?"

"I still don't know who you are."

She sat up in bed, indignant. "Who else could I be? This is me—this—!" She held his hand over her breast. "How can you say you don't know me?"

He drew her down. "I shall probably love you if we stay together. Is it so difficult to wait a little to be sure?"

His mouth closed her uncertainty. He guided her hand down to the proof of returning need.

"Doesn't that tell you enough?"

"No, it doesn't. I'm not just an animal."

She wanted to hurl him out of bed. She wanted to kill him. She was no more to him than she had been to the others. She struggled; he held her. She resisted and then fell back with a cry.

"Why? Am I so difficult to love?"

* * *

Although she devoted her energies to fulfilling the Prince's wishes, her position was no less ambiguous than it had been at the Chaussée d'Iena.

She was the mistress of the Prince's valet and the Prince apparently accepted her as a friend, as much as he was capable of friendship. But the Prince was as complex and unpredictable as Vittorio was steadfast and phlegmatic. Vittorio had the woman he wanted, but what the Prince wanted or might, on some pretext, reject, was never to be anticipated. He judged relationships solely from personal need. Therese was useful. She was intelligent and efficient and she was decorative. What she might be in herself, what his obligations toward her might become, he did not consider. He had the obstinacy of the weak and the selfishness of the very rich.

Vittorio, who did not question his position and did not aspire to social status, knew how to handle him. When the icy anger flared he waited. Therese, with her sharp sense of injustice and her insecurity, found it hard to control her temper. The Prince was often insolent to Vittorio from whom he expected absolute obedience. Vittorio overlooked what seemed to her a flagrant abuse of his self-esteem. She expected him not merely to resign and then do nothing, but also to resign and leave. She wanted a show of temper as proof that Vittorio was a man and not a slave.

Instead there were electric silences when Therese's eyes became cold as glass, when her mouth set, and she had to bite back her natural propensity to sarcasm. The Prince, like all bullies, accurately judged his power. He recognized an element in Therese that he could not entirely manage. He tested her, but did not quite push her to the brink. They were the subtlest of adversaries, the wariest of friends.

The bone of contention which emerged when the snows came, the winds blew, the forest soughed, the wolves howled, when their isolation and interdependency drew them together over the fires in the still cold and drafty rooms, was their rivalry over Vittorio. Therese knew that she could hold him as long as she satisfied his sexual needs. She wanted to be certain, if she and the Prince fell out, that Vittorio would come with her. The Prince was equally determined, if the Marquise grew tired of her duties, that Vittorio should stay. He did not know that they were lovers. Because of his total innocence in such matters, he did not judge people in sexual terms. It was a matter of control.

Vittorio navigated these occasionally stormy waters. He carried out the Prince's orders and quelled Therese's recalcitrance in bed. He knew that he was essential to both of them and, in his impassive vanity, felt secure.

Sometimes at night when they sat over the fire in the Prince's sitting room, with the old despot mummified in furs, his hands in thick mittens slowly turning the pages of a book in the wavering light of candles, with Vittorio seated at a respectful distance, staring into the fire, Therese's old contempt for men would return to mock her. She would look at Vittorio's matchless profile that belonged to a classic hero, a leader of men, and was wasted on this unenterprising fatalist, at the Prince, an ivory tortoise, encased in egotism, and an impotent rage would fill her. She wanted to bang their heads together, to scream and smash things and make a scene.

It would be so still that she could almost hear the snow falling. And then the wolves would start howling in the forest, calling to her, it seemed, in her desolation.

The work continued despite the winter. Bundled in furs, gloves and gaiters, the Prince made his rounds. By March the results were noticeable. The roof was mended, the upper floor more or less in order. The great tiled stoves gave off a reluctant warmth. Fires blazed. Plaster was replaced by paint. The rooms reeked. Numbed by cold and fighting sniffles, the three protagonists in this drama of willfulness and cross-purposes performed their daily chores, seethed at the importunities, drank hot toddies and longed for spring.

An unexpected setback curtailed the renovation.

One of the new footmen, still awkward in ill-fitting livery and white cotton gloves, presented His Highness with a letter.

The Prince's eyebrows rose. The inconceivable had happened. "It seems," he announced, "that I have no more money."

It was the ultimate irrationality. The entire banking system of Europe had taken leave of its senses.

"I shall go to Berlin and arrange matters. Vittorio, start packing at once."

There was the familiar flurry, the familiar firing of orders. The Prince was once again galvanized, prepared to annihilate the House of Rothschild which had had the effrontery to withhold his funds.

"I expect you to see that the work continues," the Prince cautioned Therese who had pointedly not been invited on this journey.

"How long will you be away?"

"A week at the utmost."

The Prince climbed into the carriage. Vittorio spread a fur rug over his knees. He caught the cold fury in Therese's eyes.

She hated them both. She hated the Prince for flaunting his authority over the man she considered hers and she hated Vittorio because he was inescapably a servant, destined by choice and lethargy to acquiescence.

Vittorio had a last disturbing vision of her standing on the steps in a gray cloak with a gray fur hood that framed her white face and brilliant hair. Radoom should have belonged to her. She was an exiled queen, deprived of the station she was meant to occupy. It was this that prevented him from loving her completely as she wanted. She was always above him. There was always something in her he could not possess.

She watched the carriage rumble across the courtyard from which the last snow was melting. There was only one weapon that could give her power over men, one whip she could crack that would bring them to heel, that would force them to respect her as she desired.

It was money. And she had none.

In May the war with France ended. Wilhelm the Second of Prussia was crowned Emperor of Germany in the Hall of Mirrors at Versailles. It was Bismarck's triumph. German regiments marched down the Champs-Élysées. Not a single cheer, not a single flag, greeted them. The avenue was deserted. Every shutter of every house was closed.

Peace brought civil war. The Commune which had held the capital through the siege was followed by insurrection. A new government was formed under Gambetta. The brave soldiers who had failed to slaughter enough Germans turned their patriotic energy on fellow Frenchmen. Twenty thousand were shot down in the streets or at the barricades.

After this salutary bloodletting the Third Republic was declared.

The Prince began to dream of his possessions hidden under the roof of the Hôtel de Piast.

He had returned from Berlin with a considerable sum, advanced by the House of Rothschild against the next shipment of silver from Mexico. He decided to be benevolent.

He presented Therese with a bundle of notes. "Please accept this, my dear Therese. It is little enough after all you have done for me."

She counted the money in her room. Should she leave? But where could she go? There was nothing for her in Paris, nothing for her in France except Saladin.

She longed for Saladin as the Prince longed for his paintings and celadon.

She wrote a long letter to Fabrice, the schoolmaster, enclosing money, and asking for news of her beloved friend.

Her affair with Vittorio had entered another phase.

When he came to her room as usual, after his return from Berlin, and took off his dressing gown, she observed him objectively. He was still beautiful in her sight, no doubt the most beautiful man she would ever know, but that body no longer held surprises. She had experienced everything it had to offer.

He was about to get into bed. "Not tonight, Vittorio. I'm tired and would like to sleep."

"What's happened?"

"Nothing. I want to sleep."

"Well, you can sleep with me."

He took hold over the covers which she did not relinquish.

"No, Vittorio," she said calmly.

He was annoyed and puzzled. It was the first time she had rejected him. He sensed a change in her, a deliberate challenge.

"We can sleep together at least. We haven't been together for a week."

He disliked the appraising way she was looking at him.

She shrugged with perfect indifference. "Very well."

He got in beside her and slid his arm under her head. She did not respond.

"Haven't you missed me? I thought of you every night."

"At night?"

"All the time." His hand slid up her leg and cupped that part of her which she had learned to surrender with such abandon. Not a muscle moved.

"Whenever I thought of you I was like this."

She turned on her side. "You seem to think that's all there is."

"I thought a great deal, Therese. I didn't realize how important you'd become to me. You wanted me to say that and now I can." He was stroking her breast, caressing her nipples. "I love you. I had to be away from you to know for sure."

He was drawing her nightdress over her head. She felt the head of his phallus against her thigh.

"Let me in, Therese. I've wanted you so badly."

The old fire stirred in her, but with sadness. She turned over to receive him. He made love with the ardor of return.

When he had spent, shuddering, and lay still in her, she thought, "Was this all there was—this coupling of bodies? There should have been something more."

It was she who withdrew. The organ that was his identity slipped from her. Was that all he could ever be?

She thought back over the men she had known. There had been a pride and splendor of strength in Saladin which she had never found in men. She had been mastered by passion in the first weeks with Vittorio, but she found that it had not changed her. Her mind, that part of her that had looked for a complete awakening as a woman, remained separate, still functioning alone.

He slept for a while and then asked drowsily, "What did you do here alone?"

"Read. Walked. Tried to drum some sense into the servants. They're a hopeless lot, these Sudetans."

"He thinks you've accomplished wonders. He'd never admit it, but he admires you greatly."

"I'm tired of that subject."

"You're unhappy. What happened while we were away?"

"I'm not unhappy. I see no outcome. Are we going to give up our lives to him and this house?"

He sighed. He had no comment. He had long since accepted what she refused to accept.

She wished he would go. She wanted to sleep alone.

She had changed. He watched her, perplexed and troubled, as she went on her rounds, instructing the servants, when she dusted the worm-eaten books in the library, when she sat down at table. The three of them ate together in the new yellow dining room. She was distant, uninterested, and made no comment on the Prince's plans for fresh improvements. He had hired a chef in Berlin who would be arriving soon. He had ordered some decent wine. He had found some fine Persian carpets for the drawing room. She nodded. "That will make it nicer." And sighed.

She was withdrawing, drifting out of reach like a boat that had slipped its moorings. He was maddened because she had never looked so beautiful. He exercised all his charm and kindness, drew her behind doors, kissed her tenderly and whispered, "I love you, Therese."

She disengaged herself with the same enigmatic smile.

He was determined to win her back.

He still went to her room at night. She pretended to be asleep. He lay on top of the covers, stroking her hair, feeling shut out, not knowing how to approach her or what to say.

She neither objected nor welcomed him when he got in beside her. She allowed him to do what he wanted like an obedient wife forced to accommodate a husband she no longer cared for. He was frustrated and then exasperated.

"What is the matter with you, Therese?"

She refused to answer.

In a fury he threw back the covers.

"Take it!"

"No."

He seized her by the neck and forced her head down.

"Why not? You couldn't get enough of it before."

They struggled. She wrenched away her head and hid her face in the pillows.

He went back to his room, defeated, and raged at her inconsistency.

He had brought himself to the point of confessing that he loved her. Even if it were not entirely true it could easily have become so. She had led him on with her wiles and mysteries and then driven a knife into the core of his male pride. She was the bitch of all bitches. The doubts that he had had about her in the beginning returned to taunt him.

They didn't speak to each other for two days. They passed in the passage in a current of hurt feelings. In his unhappy restlessness he would go in search of her and find her reading, stretched out on a sofa. She would look at him as though from a peak in the Himalayas. He longed to smash the wall of glass between them, to be reconciled, to be part of her again. Her indifference tortured him more than rage.

He would shrug and leave.

He suffered from more than wounded pride, from the calculated slight to the lengths he had gone for her, to the care he had taken of her when she was ill, to the trust he had placed in her. It was the shabbiest repayment for which there was no excuse.

She was always polite at meals, listening as she might to an estate agent when he discussed with the Prince some change of plan. This detachment riled him more than any outburst which would at least have been human, however unjustified. He saw in it the condescension of a woman of higher birth toward a servant. He felt reduced in her presence to a level that he accepted from his employer, but would not accept from her. She made him feel that he was no more than a sexual machine which had afforded her passing pleasure.

Therese knew that she was committing a human wrong and could not resist it. She knew that she made him suffer, that she humiliated him, that she was merciless. She pitied him and despised him. And if in her heart she struggled against an attachment that stemmed from all they had shared together, she could not forgive him for having, in the final analysis, failed the test.

The Prince was aware of a shift in the atmosphere between the two young people. His attitude to the Marquise, in the process of his tactics of self-protection, had also shifted. The time was approaching when Vittorio would leave for Paris to rescue the treasures at the Hôtel de Piast. No one else could be relied on. When this eventuality came about he did not wish to be left alone. The settlement of his affairs in France, the sale of the house to which he had vowed never to return, might take some months. The Marquise's continued presence was essential. He needed her, as much as it was possible, to take Vittorio's place.

He noted the change in her, questioned her apathy and listlessness. Could she be debating whether to return to whatever life she had been leading before the war?

The triangle which had formerly revolved in the Prince's favor now reversed its orbit. Self-interest alerted him to the fact that he was now dependent on these two young people, far more so even than he had been in Paris. At Radoom there was no possibility of finding substitutes should either of them leave. He had committed himself to the restoration of this house as a permanent residence and, in doing so, had, in a way he had not anticipated, put himself at their mercy. He needed them now more than they needed him.

When he finally brought himself to broach the subject of the Paris collections, Vittorio, to his surprise, made no objection.

"It has to be done, Altesse. The longer the things are left there the greater the risk of theft."

"Are you prepared to undertake it?" the Prince asked with unusual diffidence. "I'm afraid it will take some time. I'm afraid you will think it an imposition."

"I can go whenever you please."

He wanted to go. He wanted to get away from this damnable house, from the eternal palaver with workmen and servants, from this countryside that, even in spring, exuded autumnal gloom. He wanted to get away from Therese.

"If, perhaps, you could get it done by August, you could come back here to help with the unpacking. And then, perhaps, when everything is in order—" he said, risking the supreme concession, "we might go away for the winter, perhaps to Italy."

He had, of course, no intention of going to Italy. Vittorio knew this and nodded. But what had happened, the Prince wondered? Was it possible that both Vittorio and the Marquise had lost interest in his great undertaking? Could they—was it conceivable—be making other plans?

"How will you manage here when I'm gone?"

"Well, I—I shall not be alone entirely. The Marquise—"

"Are you certain that she will stay?"

The Prince became quite alarmed. "Well, I assume—I haven't asked—"

"Perhaps you had better ask. She may have other ideas now that the war is over. It was only because of that she stayed so long."

Because of the war?—Only because of that—? Then she hadn't been interested—she hadn't felt the importance—?

"After all," Vittorio reminded him, "we know very little about her."

"Well, that's true— We left together because of circumstances. But I regard her—I have come to regard her—"

"I wouldn't count on the Marquise, Altesse."

The Prince was now very agitated. He saw himself threatened by total abandonment.

"Perhaps it would be better if you came with me," Vittorio suggested. "You might even change your mind about living in Paris. In which case the Marquise can be left to her own devices."

"No, I can't go back. I said I would never go back. I will never live in France again—after the way they behaved."

It was all most disturbing. To live alone in this immense house—with the snow and the wolves. Couldn't they see— couldn't the Márquise *see*—?

"I will speak to her," the Prince said hurriedly. "I will sound her out." He took the final plunge. "I will make it *worth her while.*"

"I'm going to Paris," Vittorio announced at dinner. Therese looked at him, startled.

"When?"

"Soon. To settle up. Everything has to be packed and crated. His Highness has decided to sell the house."

She seemed unexpectedly shaken and asked quickly, "Why? It was your home."

The Prince was also flustered. It was presumptuous of Vittorio to have brought up this delicate matter so bluntly.

"Well, I feel—I've decided, you see—to live here—now that things have advanced so far. I don't feel inclined—after what happened—"

"But that was the war. Those things happen in war. There's a stable government now."

She was looking at Vittorio in consternation, as though she suddenly couldn't bear to be parted from him, as though the very thought of him leaving made her frightened and unsure.

"I told His Highness that you may be thinking of going back yourself," Vittorio said with a certain implied menace, "now that the war is over."

"I haven't thought—" she replied nervously—"I haven't made any specific plans—"

"I am glad to hear of it." The Prince seized the opportunity to settle the matter. "I was hoping that you could spare the time to remain—at least till Vittorio returns."

She glanced from one to the other.

"It will take months—to pack those things—"

"Three at least. Don't you have to attend to the sale of your house in the Marais?" Vittorio challenged her.

"You can do that by mail," the Prince said sharply. "You are quite—may I say—quite indispensable here."

She got up suddenly, seemingly on the point of tears, and with a murmured "Excuse me," hurried from the room.

"You should have left me to discuss the matter," the Prince said tartly. "I am very much displeased."

Vittorio wasn't sure why he had acted in this way or what Therese's reaction signified. Perhaps he had wanted to call her bluff or to hurt her, to make it plain that she had no hold over him and that, after her recent behavior, he felt no obligation to her at all.

He found her in that room at the far end of the ground floor to which she was in the habit of retreating. It had been the library in years gone by. Many of the books that remained were worm-eaten or waterlogged, their fine old bindings rotted. Those that were salvageable she had been drying out and treating with saddle polish. There were editions of old sermons, military histories of obscure campaigns and memoirs of minor German courts.

She was working on an edition of Casanova which she had been trying to save.

She did not turn when he came in, but went on applying the polish to the binding that bore the elaborate arms of the Bishops of Wurtsburg.

"Can you bring yourself to discuss what you intend to do?" he asked in a tone more like the Prince's than his own.

She turned then. Her eyes were streaming with tears.

"I've been so wrong. I've behaved so badly. You were so good to me always. I can't bear that you should go—like this—when I've hurt you."

She sat down and covered her face with her hands.

"I simply don't understand."

"I know. You think I don't know? It's not you—anything you've done. I damage everyone who tries to love me. I thought with you it would be different. I can't help it—I've been so twisted by things that happened."

Her obvious and inopportune grief put him at a disadvantage. It was theatrical and unnatural and he thought suddenly, "It's because we've been couped up here all winter. We none of us mean what we say."

"I don't ask you to forgive me. I don't deserve it. I want to feel and I try—but something in me makes everything cruel and ugly."

"Nothing has happened, Therese. I told you when I came back from Berlin—"

"I know. It's me. It's in *me!*" She moved away in a passion of self-condemnation and wept, her head against the shelves of old books.

"I know that things haven't been easy. The old man gets on your nerves and this place is enough to drive anyone mad. But as far as I am concerned—nothing has changed. Why can't you believe that?"

"You're good. You are always good—to him and to me. Things happened before I met you. I've tried to forget them. You almost saved me. Oh, if I could tell you everything you'd understand."

She stood before him defenseless and pitiable and yet there was something about her plunge into guilt that annoyed him. It was irrational and uncalled for and had no part, as far as he could discern, in what had existed between them.

"We all have things in the past we wish hadn't happened. But we go on, don't we? What else can we do?" He thought of the blood-soaked sheets in Paris and of how she had lain there for days in a trance like death. But he wasn't responsible for all that. She was blaming him for a tragedy, whatever it had been, in which he had had no part.

"Anyway, that's over, Therese. What I'm asking now is whether you are going to stay here or whether you are coming back to Paris with me?"

A glimmer of hope shone for a moment behind her tears.

"We can't leave him here alone, can we? One of us has to stay."

"Then it's settled? You'll stay until I get back."

"Yes—unless—"

"Unless what?"

She was pleading with him to make the one offer that even now could have saved them both.

It was not forthcoming. It hadn't occurred to him, she saw.

Perhaps it was not in his nature or perhaps it was because she couldn't eradicate from herself whatever it was that held him back.

"All right. If you want—I'll stay."

If he wanted? That wasn't the point. He was upset and baffled by her unfathomable feminine illogic that put the onus of this decision on him.

He sighed, nodded, and left her. Her shifting game of loyalties, needs and passions was too complex for him to cope with.

She came to his room that night, ghostlike in her nightdress, and knelt by his bed. She was as humble as a child who had earned disfavor and was begging to be taken back into the familiar comfort of home.

"Don't kneel there. You'll catch cold."

He moved over and held back the covers. She got in beside him. From habit he put his arm 'round her and she leaned her head gratefully against him. Their silence, the lull after an unwarranted storm, soothed them until she slept.

In the dawn she stirred and reached for him. They made love with a sad sort of tenderness. It was balm and a remission of the rift between them, but the rift remained.

During his last days at Radoom she was all gentleness, sweetness and concern like a young wife whose husband was for the first time forced to leave her. She slept with him each night, giving him what he wanted without hesitation. It was married love after the first passion has faded.

They never referred to her outburst in the library and, in their nocturnal exchanges, only discussed the practical aspects of keeping the Prince content. The new housekeeper received instructions from the departing majordomo. Under these placid councils was a sense of saying goodbye.

The Prince showed Vittorio many small attentions. This break in the routine of his life was perplexing. He was loathe to part with his stalwart Italian on whom he had depended for so long. It was not in his nature to thank anyone, but he expressed his gratitude for Vittorio's unswerving devotion, for his tireless capacity for surmounting obstacles, for his years of dedicated service, by deluging him with instructions concerning the packing and shipping of his treasures, the sale of the house, and his requirements from the Banque de France, and many other cautions and admonitions to all of which Vittorio listened respectfully, most of which he intended to disregard.

The last he saw of them as he climbed into the coach, was the Prince with his unwieldy torso bent forward on his spindly legs, his sable hat aslant on his grotesque domed skull and his puffy eyelids blinking in agitation. Therese stood at his side, very straight and expressionless, a washed out caryatid.

He thought as he drove out of the courtyard of that mansion that no amount of restoration could ever make it into a home, that he had never understood Therese and that he would never learn any more about her than he knew at present. It occurred to him that she had always intended it to end like this and that all her quixotic behavior had been part of a plan devised long ago in Paris. Perhaps if he had been a different sort of man who could have penetrated her mystery she might have become the permanent woman in his life.

He left with the sense of a phase ended, of a profound but unresolved experience, with sadness but with relief.

If a phase of Vittorio's life had ended, a phase in the Prince's life had begun.

He had never been left unprotected in the company of a woman. Women were to him semimythical nuisances, nymphs or furies, who played, by choice, no part in actual life. He was uncertain, querulous and flustered and felt himself to be the target of Therese's dark designs.

She was assiduous in her attentions and if, at first, he bridled at the unfamiliar and the presumptuous, his vanity was gradually assuaged. She sent emissaries about the countryside, as far as Oppeln, in search of flowers. Bowls of roses appeared in the red salon, posies bloomed beside his morning coffee. When she greeted him each morning she pinned a rosebud or a scented pink to his lapel. He thought it absurd and bothersome, but permitted it to please her and then found that it pleased him. He was indignant when he found the Magnum

Opus all sorted and in order on his desk, the inkwell filled, new pens in readiness. No one had ever presumed to touch the Magnum Opus, that sacred document that he had rescued from the siege of Paris. He thought it a gross intrusion and could not put his hand to anything because everything was there.

Imperceptibly the house became more livable, the food improved, the servants were more adept at their duties. The sheets were properly aired. There were sachets of herbs beneath his pillow. His slippers and dressing gown, his cane and walking shoes, were in the right place at the right moment. The dogs were washed and combed and sported topknots decked with colored ribbons. He noted, bridled, then condoned.

He was forced to admit that the presence of this efficient and distinctive woman had advantages. He could converse with her on subjects that had evinced no response from Vittorio. The Marquise spoke Greek. She quoted Plato and Democritus. She asked perceptive questions about art and history and made reflective comments. As they paced up and down the terrace she offered suggestions about the garden and won his consent to have the weeds and wasted plants, the dead and dying trees, removed.

He savored the unfamiliar graces of female companionship, female conversation, and female expertise in domestic matters. He conceded, when reviewing the situation, that, in certain areas, Therese was an adequate replacement for Vittorio.

After his birthday he succumbed.

The Prince, Therese discovered, on coming across an old family Bible in the library, was not nearly as old as he appeared. He was fifty-seven and not, as she had assumed, near seventy.

He had never celebrated his birthday. It had never been celebrated even as a boy. It was a date that came and went and neither added nor subtracted from the pall of middle age that had settled over him in his mid-twenties.

He was dimly aware on that July morning that something was afoot. There was an air of expectancy about the house, a scurrying and tiptoeing in the passage, a subdued bustle in the dining room. Therese had not appeared. There was no rosebud or scented pink. By noon he was beginning to feel neglected.

The footman appeared with an ill-concealed grin on his foolish peasant face.

"Luncheon is served, Your Highness."

Where was Therese? They had not had their usual preprandial glass of sherry. He disliked it when a custom once established was ignored.

The dining room was transformed. It had been decorated with swags of leaves and flowers. He stopped and stared. On the table stood a miniature triumphal arch entwined with roses and carnations. What was the significance of this most singular embellishment? Peering at it through his lorgnette he saw that it bore an inscription: FELICE NATIVITATUS DIE AUGUSTO.

Suddenly, as he struggled with his surprise, a choir burst forth outside with loud hosannas, accompanied by violins and trumpets. The air rang with shouts and loud Te Deums. He was flabbergasted.

And then Therese came through the window, all in white with flowers in her hair. She bore on a white cushion what appeared to be a wreath of laurel. He gaped, torn between indignation and astonishment.

She curtsied deeply and proffering the pillow announced, "Happy Birthday, dear Prince Augustus."

He stood there, the helpless butt of a joke he didn't know how to share.

She placed the wreath on his head. He felt supremely ridiculous. She took his hand and led him through the window. A resounding cheer greeted him from the servants gathered on the right. "Vivat! Vivat Augustus!" On the left the choir and orchestra of St. Stephen's in Oppeln were singing and playing their hearts out. "Hosanna! Hosanna!" they sang in chorus. "Vivat. Vivat Augustus!" the servants responded. He was deafened by the din.

The five little terriers danced about in the greatest excitement. They sported large bows and bells around their necks.

"Hosanna! Hosanna! Vivat! Vivat Augustus!"

Those infernal trumpets!

He felt altogether weak and bewildered. He hated music.

He hated demonstrations. He could find no connection between this ill-conceived commotion and himself. His birthday? What was his birthday? The Marquise had taken leave of her senses. They were all quite mad.

A small, golden-haired boy in a white surplice separated himself bashfully from the choir. The kappelmeister held up his hand. Silence fell like a thunderclap.

In a piping treble the boy read from a scroll an address of welcome and congratulations, extolling the Prince's virtues, thanking the hereditary ruler for returning to his realm. His loyal subjects wished him a long life, health and happiness.

More cheering followed.

The Prince realized at last that all this clamor and jubilation was for him.

Eight hundred years of Piast patriarchy came to his rescue. He thanked the little boy. He thanked the kappelmeister. He thanked the choir and the servants. He scowled at Therese, the perpetrator of this tomfoolery, and retreated, deeply shaken, to the dining room.

He sat down. The triumphal arch confronted him.

He managed to proceed with luncheon. Champagne was poured. He drank. A cake appeared with candles. He gazed at the ten flickering flames. It was a pretty white cake encircled with strawberries. He was a small boy recapturing a joy that had been denied him, a joy that he had long denied himself.

He blinked. The flames blurred.

Therese was offering him something, a long thin object wrapped in paper.

Why had she done all this? Why had she gone to such lengths to upset and mortify him?

He was unwrapping the long thin object because he was expected to. It was a walking stick the like of which he had never seen. Ebony with a brass spiral hammered in the length of the stem and a brass head set with a brown cabochon stone that gleamed like topaze or molasses.

He looked at it without grasping what it was or why she had given it to him.

"Yes. So. What is it?"

"A brown diamond from Nepal."

He nodded. A walking stick with a brown diamond. What did it signify?

He was blinking rapidly. He couldn't see the Marquise clearly. She was blurring like the candles.

"It's for your birthday, Augustus. I had it made in Breslau."

She rose. She was bending over him. She was kissing him on the cheek.

He was shocked. He had never, in his long memory, been kissed before.

Afterward, when he had partially recovered his equilibrium, he went into the courtyard where the servants and the choir of St. Stephen's were enjoying a country feast.

They all rose as he appeared. He looked down the long table, at the beaming foolish faces, assembled to do him honor. He saluted them. He smiled and nodded, mystified. He distributed gold pieces from a purse provided by Therese. She had thought of everything.

They raised their glasses.

"To the Prince! Good health! Happiness and long life to the Prince!"

He acknowledged their good wishes. He was deeply moved.

Later there was dancing. They brought him out a chair. He sipped his wine and watched.

He looked at the exotic walking stick with its strange, mesmeric stone. After all, to be given something—a token of something. He couldn't recall being given anything before.

He watched Therese as she danced with the country people, tall and graceful, with her burnished hair. The violins scraped and screeched, the children ran in and out, the dogs barked. They were all happy.

It was Therese who had overcome the past. She had swept it all away like cobwebs.

She had brought Radoom to life. He could not comprehend this phenomenon which had crashed like a meteor into his empty life.

A week later they left for Dresden.

She had accepted with alacrity his proposal that they should visit the capital of Saxony in search of furniture. It was a great cultural center where he would be sure to find interesting things and she would enjoy the architecture and other refinements of this most beautiful of German cities.

They set off by coach on a fine August morning.

The Prince was in very good humor. It was an entirely novel experience to be traveling with this beautiful and intelligent young woman who took such a lively interest in everything. It was as though his sister Ellamine had been miraculously restored to him or he had, by divine dispensation, acquired a daughter.

They rode side by side with the five little dogs on the seat across from them and a large hamper of food which Therese had packed so that they could picnic if the mood seized them.

They passed through the foothills of the Sudetan Mountains, very grand and gloomy with their dense forests, rushing streams and small watering places clustered about mineral springs.

They lunched under heavily scented pines. The silence was so profound that their conversation sank to whispers. The dogs, at first joyous to be free, soon realized that there were somber mysteries out there better not investigated. They stayed close and yapped for tidbits.

The Prince seemed quite content, but he said sadly when the meal was over, "How Nichette would have enjoyed this!"

They spent the first night at Franckenstein, a haunted medieval town. A seven-foot stuffed bear with fiery eyes and menacing claws threatened to devour travelers in the hallway of the inn.

On the second day the scenery began to change. The forests were green and gave way to placid lakes. Stretches of lush farmland and spotless villages with windowboxes bright with flowers relieved the monotony of mountain peaks and gorges.

They reached Gerlitz. They had left Silesia and were now in Saxony. Colors lightened. The people were blond and welcoming, the food rich, the wines buoyant. They crossed the broad Elbe with its wooded islands and baroque chapels. They had returned to civilization. And there at last, in a great sweep of the river, splendid, serene and spacious—Dresden.

Therese's heart lifted as they crossed the Augustusbrücke and passed through the Georgentor Gate into a city of baroque palaces and churches, cream and gold, turreted and domed, graceful and gracious, and all with that endearing familial charm that surpassed the chill and formal elegance of France. She was reminded of her first sight of Warsaw, but here the fine buildings were not restricted to a few streets of the very rich. The charm spread everywhere. It embraced everything. Even the elaborate lampposts expressed a joyous freedom of design.

At the Drei Kouiqeu Hotel everything was pleasant, comfortable and well ordered. Therese couldn't bear to waste a moment in her room. She splashed water on her face and hurried out into the winding streets that offered so much to the eye and to the soul. She found her way to the Hofkirche, that apotheosis of the rococo with its swirling draperies and sunbursts, its smiling, seductive madonnas, and sugar-stuffed angels soaring to heaven on clouds of cream. The whole church was a jubilation.

She looked 'round, enraptured, and wondered, "Why didn't Augustus decide to live in Dresden?"

They dined by an open window. Even in the hotel garden, filled with pink and white flowers, the statues seemed to be flying away, released from their pedestals.

"This is the most entrancing place I have ever been to."

"Tomorrow I'll show you the great collections. The Kings of Saxony were always mad collectors, madder even than I. One of them exchanged a platoon of grenadiers for a Meissen dinner service."

"Did you come here when you were young?"

"Every year. My father and the old king were cousins."

He was tired, he said, and would see her in the morning, but Therese would not hear of his retiring. She cajoled him into an open carriage and they drove around the city. He pointed out the landmarks on the Weiner Platz, on the Haupstrase, the twin-towered Sophienkirche, the Altmarkt, the Royal Palace. He knew all their dates and histories and architects.

"Shall you tell the present king you're here?"

"Oh no. I have lived out of the world too long."

"Why, Augustus? Why did you become a recluse? You have so much knowledge, so much to offer."

"It was a habit and like all habits hard to break. I never had much liking for society. And time passes—"

"You were disillusioned. It's not hard, most people being what they are." She slipped her arm through his. "But there's still so much beauty in the world."

Was there so much? She thought of Henri playing on those summer evenings at the Pavillon, of Vittorio as he moved naked across her room, of Saladin racing through the mists. Glimpses of the unattainable. Against that weighed the perpetual void of insecurity, of not belonging anywhere, of having no human roots. And there was this selfish, isolated, obstinate old man who had everything and had so little instinct of what to do with it.

They drove back in silence to the hotel.

He was in his element next day, galvanized by one of those bursts of energy that occasionally possessed him. He conducted her 'round the Zwinger Gallery, stopping before familiar pictures, pointing out details of style and composition. His erudition was as profound as his knowledge of life was limited.

He stood before the crowning jewel of the collection, Raphael's Madonna di San Sisto.

"Of course, it's beautiful, but it's a beauty that cloys a little, that reveals too much, a beauty perhaps for the young and the profane. I prefer my Duccio. She has a greater force because of a greater reticence."

And then he forgot about Therese. He was lost in a private paradise of Chinese Blue and White, of the finest Meissen and majolica. As he passed from case to case, peering through his lorgnette, she overheard his running commentary. "Yes, first-rate. Remarkable! Well, that has no right to be here! An obvious copy. So-so. I can't quite allow it. As to that—superb! One has to admit; superb."

He emerged into the lesser light of day, refreshed and stimulated.

They proceeded to the Semper Gallery. It was past noon.

He had no thought of food. He was absorbing the one pure nourishment that had sustained him for thirty years.

At the Georgenschlosse, the royal residence, they signed the visitors' book and wandered along corridors of Roman and Greek statuary, through rooms of armor, coins and astronomical instruments.

"All very handsome and all quite boring," the Prince pronounced. "Now, I will take you to the Japanese Palace. You will enjoy that with your taste for books."

It was a magnificent library stacked with rare manuscripts. Here the Prince appropriated a chair provided for the guard on duty and fell asleep.

She was entranced by the illuminated Missals, the Books of Hours and bestiaries with their tiny illustrations bright as jewels.

She woke him gently. "Aren't you hungry? It's almost four."

They drove across the river into the Dresdener Heide where they bought sausages and pears from a stand. The great woods, already touched with gold, rang with the voices of young men hiking.

Therese longed to be riding these paths with Saladin.

On their return to the hotel they found an invitation from the King of Saxony to attend an informal musicale and supper.

"How did he find out we were here?" the Prince asked crossly.

"We signed the visitors' book."

"I don't want to go. He plays the trumpet."

Therese cajoled.

"It would be the greatest bore. I know those evenings and I hate music. Besides we have no clothes."

"It says an informal musicale. It's not a court occasion."

"No, I won't. He was always a noisy boy. Can you imagine anything more absurd than a king who plays the trumpet?"

Finally, for her sake, he agreed.

The King of Saxony was immensely tall with the bluff and blustering manner of a grenadier. He advanced toward them like a Titan descending from Valhalla.

"My dear Prince Augustus! I am delighted to see you after

all these years, but I must reprimand you for not letting us know you were to visit Dresden. Is this your daughter?"

"May I present the Marquise de Païva who has been staying with me at Radoom."

As Therese made her *révérence* the king gripped her hand in a lethal paw. "Come, I'll present you to my wife and daughters. And what are you doing in Silesia, Prince?" he shouted as though his cousin was hard of hearing.

"The Marquise and I were forced to leave Paris because of the hostilities."

"What about your treasures? You still have your father's Rembrandts? You should come to Dresden. I'll build you a wing on the Zwinger. I'll build you a gallery of your own."

They had reached the Queen whose obesity equaled her husband's stature. "Amalia, this is my cousin, Augustus of Oppeln-Piast," he bawled in her ear. "He has a great collection which I'm telling him he should bring to Dresden."

The Queen, who after thirty years of marriage was impervious to sound, bobbed her head, partially submerged in three double chins. "Very welcome. Very welcome."

"I disapproved of the war," the King shouted. "All Bismarck's doing. Now we're to be an empire, but not Saxony. I shall resist. My father supported Napoleon. I shall resist."

Therese curtsied to the Queen who responded with her double nod. "Very welcome. Very welcome."

The King beckoned to his three plump and rosy daughters, charmingly dressed in white and blue. "My three girls, Adelaide, Adelphia and Antonia. They all play instruments. We are all musicians in this family. Now, find places and we'll begin."

He waved the Prince and Therese away. They found chairs among a group of guests, self-satisfied burghers with their hausfraus, very complacent, cordial and well to do. The Queen embedded a violin between the first and third of her chins, the daughters took up their instruments, the first a flute, the second an oboe, the third and prettiest a harp.

The King blew a warning blast on his trumpet that would

have roused the dead and announced, "Suite in D Minor by Telemann."

The royal family and the small court orchestra played with vigor and enthusiasm. The King, while keeping time by stamping with his foot, his cheeks distended like Boreus, the North Wind, produced enough noise to drive a windmill. The Prince cringed, gritting his teeth. It was an appalling demonstration of the German love for "making music."

The Telemann was followed by a Mozart concerto. Two more trumpet suites followed. The concert ended with the Handel Harp Concerto. The charming Princess Antonia executed the solo part with dexterity while the King conducted, waving his arms like a general transmitting commands by semaphore.

"Well, that's it!" he declared. "Let's have supper."

The bourgeois monarch helped his wife to her feet which were so tiny that she could only waddle like a mechanical doll and strode into a handsome baroque dining room where the table was spread with an array of cold roasts and poultry and serious puddings and pies suitable to the capacious appetites of Saxons.

When it was time to go the King boomed, "Now, cousin, don't bury yourself in Silesia. We'll find you a suitable residence in Dresden. And remember, I want your collections here. I'll build you a gallery; you have my word on it."

"I am sensible of the honor, Majestät."

"Very welcome. Very welcome," the Queen mumbled, her mouth full of whipped cream and walnut cake. The Prince and Therese bowed themselves away.

The three princesses clustered about Therese at the door. "You will come to see us, won't you? We have lots to show you. We each have our own collections. Adelaide collects dolls, Adelphia musical boxes and Antonia miniature furniture. Please come. We do hope we shall be friends."

They found the Marquise quite the most beautiful and distinguished person they had met for years.

"They're charming!" Therese laughed as they settled themselves in the carriage. "I think the king's quite right. You should come and live in Dresden."

"Provincials!" the Prince said with a sniff. "I should never survive that racket. And the food! No wonder they're fat as oxen."

Truth to tell he had enjoyed himself. It had been borne in on him during that evening that to go into society accompanied by a graceful woman who knew how to behave was a distinct improvement on going out alone. It made everything easier and more civilized. He had observed how perfectly Therese had conducted herself, as though she belonged quite naturally in such circles. He was forced to admit that she was an asset, a distinct asset, the mysterious Marquise.

The next morning the Prince embarked on an exploration of the art dealers and *antiquaires*.

Therese was once against amazed, as he prodded and pondered on this serendipitous expedition, at the infinite amount of trouble he put people to in his determination to satisfy his whims. Sometimes he would spy in a dark corner the cornice of a cabinet hidden behind a mountain of furniture. It would take two workmen twenty minutes to excavate the desired object. The Prince would glance at it and turn away without a word of thanks to the men who had strained every muscle to oblige him.

At noon he vanished into the Lethean obscurity of a warehouse. She was stifled by this accumulation of discarded things, the residue of so many lives and habitations. It reminded her of Solomon endlessly locking and unlocking doors to guard his piles of rubbish.

"Tell his Highness I will see him at dinner," she said to an assistant and escaped into the sunlight of the real world.

She walked about the spacious city. Everywhere she encountered students, singing and strolling arm in arm, in the enchanted ignorance of youth, families stuffing themselves with pies and sausages at the beer gardens, old people peacefully sunning themselves in the public parks. All part of something, all belonging somewhere, all sharing a common life.

The Prince was edgy at dinner. She had deserted him; he thought it inconsiderate.

"I would never disturb a priest at his prayers or a collector on a treasure hunt. Those are sacred occupations."

He grunted, unamused.

She watched him as he spooned up his soup. Could she put up with him? She was fond of him in a way and even at his worst he was never commonplace. It would take infinite guile, patience and self-restraint to trap him. The last two virtues did not come easily to her. His egotism, unpredictability and willfulness were obstacles it would be difficult to overcome. She thought of de Morny and the Emperor. They had waited, planned, connived and finally conquered. Fate had presented her with a challenge in this eccentric but immensely rich old man.

It would mean the slow death of the heart. But what had the heart given her?

Only longings and regrets.

She made the first move in her campaign of encirclement on their return journey to Radoom.

"Write my memoirs?" The Prince's mouth fell open. "What gave you that idea? Who would be interested?"

"A great many people. You have this vast fund of knowledge and experience. You are known to be a great collector."

"I have no literary gift. It would be a most tedious undertaking."

"I could act as your secretary. You could dictate. We could work for an hour or two each day. There's plenty of time at Radoom, heaven knows."

"It does not appeal to me. Besides I have other more important things to think of."

"Your memoirs as a collector would be read all over Europe. I'm certain of it."

He humphed. He wasn't interested. It was his nature to denigrate any suggestion made to him.

She returned to the subject the following day as they were rumbling toward the forests of Silesia.

"All you would have to do would be to sit in a comfortable chair and talk aloud. I would write it down and return it to you for editing and correction. The story of your discovery of the Duccio alone—"

"Well, yes, I dare say; that *was* unusual— And there were others, many others. You know how I came across the models for the royal productions at Versailles? They had been packed away, my dear, after the death of Louis the Fifteenth." He told her the whole story.

"You see? That's fascinating. And all your porcelains—the celadon. There must be a hundred stories attached to your discoveries."

"Well, yes," he conceded. "I suppose there are."

He pretended to have dismissed the subject, but she knew that he was mulling it over in his strange, rabbity warren of a mind.

As they turned up the long derelict driveway to Radoom the Prince said casually, "I might—I don't say I will, but I might—because there is a great deal more pressing business on the agenda—but I *might* consider a *short* account of *some* of my experiences as a collector."

"Well, I'm ready," she said next morning. They had gone into the study after breakfast. "Let's begin."

"Begin?"

"The Memoirs. Let's start at once."

Before he could think up a suitable list of objections, she had settled herself at his desk, *at his desk*, if you please! without asking his permission, without even considering his feelings in the matter. She was facing him with a pen threateningly poised. He was quite taken aback. He had intended to debate the matter back and forth, over a period of days, to arrive, one way or the other, by gradual degrees at a possible decision.

She had completely taken the wind out of his sails.

"But I—I haven't thought. I haven't arranged things in my mind. It would take me a considerable time. No, no, not yet. Not yet."

"Just begin at the beginning. You can sort it all out later. What was the first thing you every bought, the very first thing that gave you the idea of forming a collection?"

He was too flabbergasted by her importunity to protest. She

was there, with her dreadful dictatorial pen and her dreadfully intent and dictatorial manner.

He gaped. He shuffled about. He hemmed and hawed. He could think of nothing. Thirty years tumbled through his head in an indescribable muddle of purchases and places, pictures, people, porcelains.

"I don't know. I don't remember. We had always, to some extent, collected. People did."

"Your father?"

"Well, yes—he, too. He had, of course, no interest in art, but from time to time he bought things. It was the custom. As a young man he went on the Grand Tour. He was expected to take an interest in cultural matters. In those days works of art, spurious or genuine, were available in quantities. He bought some paintings. Atrocities, of course, in the manner of Guido Reni. And then, somehow or other, I forget the circumstances, he acquired the Rembrandts, The Portrait of Saskia and The Woman Paring her Nails. In settlement of a debt, perhaps. Yes, probably—from the Sigmaringens who were always short of funds."

He was exhausted already. He sat down. A Pandora's Box had been precipitously opened. He looked at her in consternation. She was busily occupied in writing.

"What are you doing?"

"Putting down what you said. Was it the Rembrandts that first inspired you?"

He sank back. He had been deposited in the past against his will as though by a Montgolfier balloon that had suddenly deflated.

"The Rembrandts? Had it been—?"

"I used to look at them. They were marvelous to me. I recognized, without understanding, their importance. I was not, you see, the son my father would have wanted. I had no interest in hunting and the usual gentlemanly pursuits. I was ill much of the time and was forced in upon myself. Those two paintings offered me what religion might have, had I been of a mystical disposition. As it was—"

He talked as though in a trance, as though she were not

there and the pen was not busily scratching across the paper, as though once embarked on this odyssey of reminiscence he had no choice but to follow where it led—back and back to the beginnings.

It was the dogs who jolted him into the present. They were yapping for their midday walk and scratching at his legs.

He looked at them, dazed and disoriented. What had been happening in the last few hours?

"Look what we've accomplished in one morning." Therese held up a sheaf of foolscap. "I told you it would be easy once you started."

Easy? It wasn't easy. It was painful, it was extraordinary. He dimly perceived that by this method of recollection he could unburden himself of the weight that seemed always to have lain upon him, that he might discover what his life had meant and why it so often seemed to him that he had created out of so many dreams and disappointments such a wilderness.

The next morning he pretended that he had forgotten about the project, that he had more important matters to consider. He puttered off on a tour about the house. He had to decide where to put the new cabinets that were being built to house the objects that, sooner or later, would arrive from Paris.

She was still there, waiting, at his desk. She was presumptuous. She was inexorable.

"No, no. Not now. Some other time."

"Come along, Augustus," she said calmly like a nurse to a disobedient child. "You have just reached the point where you discovered the El Greco on the back of one of your father's pictures."

"I said not now," he snapped. He sat down, sulking, and gave her to understand that he was deep in thought. He wished she would have the politeness to vacate his desk. He felt just in the mood to do some research about Delphina of the Palatinate. But she did not vacate his desk. She sat with that maddening pen and all that maddening paper.

Waiting.

"The El Greco, Augustus—"

He snorted. Oh, very well! It was disgraceful that he couldn't

have peace and quiet in his own study, to do what he wanted
at his own desk, just because she had conceived the notion—

"One day," he started crossly, "I happened to notice some
paintings that had just been revarnished. It was an unfortunate
habit at that time to overlay every painting with coat after coat
of varnish that gradually turned yellow so that it was impossible
to see—"

He talked steadily till noon.

He felt surprisingly refreshed, even exhilarated. It was
amazing all that he could remember. It was enthralling, this
saga in which he was always the leading character.

She brought him his outdoor hat and cane.

They walked slowly up and down the terrace.

As she had rightly estimated, once the routine had been
established, he became addicted to giving her dictation. By the
end of the first week he was all ready in his chair after breakfast,
impatient because she took so long to settle herself at his desk
with her secretarial equipment.

She was spinning a web around him and, day by day, he
was becoming more and more dependent on her. There was
the morning buttonhole, the work on the memoirs, the pre-
luncheon glass of sherry, the afternoon nap, the stroll about
the park, the glass of champagne before dinner, the evenings
when she read aloud to him or they discussed the manuscript
that was rapidly piling up. She had developed her own kind of
shorthand and presented him each morning with a clean copy
of what he had dictated the day before.

The Prince was in excellent humor. He never thanked or
complimented Therese on her efforts, but he admitted to himself
that, high-handed as she was apt to be, all in all, the Marquise
was remarkable.

Letters arrived from France.

There was a long missive from Vittorio, penned in a careful,
schoolboy hand. Everything was progressing at the Hôtel de
Piast. Nothing had been touched or damaged. One of the Corsican boys whose brother had been killed at Strasbourg had
returned and was helping him. Most of the porcelains and
pictures were already packed.

The Prince was elated. "That Vittorio! He's a marvel. Always to be relied on."

"I've sold my property in the Marais!" Therese exclaimed. The first of her two letters contained a bill of sale from Etienne Perroneau de Roose, the dancing master, and a draft for a hundred thousand francs.

Therese's second letter was from Fabrice Broussard, the schoolmaster in the village where so much that was good and so much that was terrible had happened to her.

My dear Therese,

I was greatly relieved to receive your letters, even though their postmark revealed that you are so far away.

I have not written to you before about your beloved Saladin, as there was nothing I could have told you that would not have distressed you. Even what I am able to tell you now, I am afraid, is far from good.

After you left for Paris Saladin became increasingly restless and unmanageable. One morning when I went into the barn to feed him, he broke out, almost knocking me over, and vanished in the direction of your cottage. I went there at once, but he was nowhere to be found. People in the village told me that he had been seen galloping along the Angers road. It occurred to me that he might have gone back to the convent, knowing that you had been there. Sure enough the nuns had seen him. The Mother Superior, whose wisdom exceeds even her goodness, had tried to lure him into the courtyard, but he sensed a trap. Efforts were made to catch him to no avail.

Finding you gone, not knowing, I suppose, where you were, he took to the woods. Reports reached me that he had been seen, here and there, even wandering by the river. A farmer succeeded at last in trapping him. He put up a tremendous fight as you can imagine. It took three men to drag him to Ingouville where the farmer unwisely attempted to harness him for use in the fields. He proved so intractable that the farmer decided to shoot him. At the sight of the gun Saladin rampaged, kicked the man over, and vanished. He was several times seen in the vicinity of your cottage and by hunters in the woods. He became a sort of legend in the neighborhood. People were afraid of him. Possibly that saved his life.

Last week I had gone into Angers to fetch some medicine for my mother whose health, I am sorry to report, has not improved. On an impulse I turned down the lane toward your cottage where we spent so many agreeable hours. I don't know what prompted me; nostalgia perhaps. Saladin was leaning against the door. He was in a very sorry state, dreadfully emaciated, his coat a mass of cuts and sores. I do not want to distress you, my dear Therese, but I think he had come back to die.

I managed to induce him into the barn where he collapsed. I am not familiar with the treatment of horses, but it seemed obvious that what he needed most was nourishment. I bought what meat I could in the village, pressed the blood from it, and fed it to him through a funnel with a little brandy. He seemed grateful for my efforts though perhaps he was simply too weak to resist. I was afraid he would make off again, so I locked him in and went to consult the Curé—you remember him; he is the same—who has some knowledge of animals. Together we applied salve to Saladin's wounds and have continued to dose him regularly.

If he has not visibly improved, his condition remains stable. My feeling is that it is more a breakdown of spirit than physical dereliction which has reduced him to this condition. He lies there, apparently asleep and stirs but slightly when I visit him. He is, at least, warm and safe. I am caring for him as best I can.

I have nearly all the money you sent me for his upkeep and have only spent what was needed to save his life. Please advise me, my dear Therese, of your wishes in this matter and rest assured that I will do all in my power for Saladin meanwhile, as I know how much he means to you.

Life goes on, dear friend. It has been a painful year, what with the war and the privations resulting from it. My mother often speaks of you and always with great affection.

There was more which she was too upset to read.

The Prince was startled when she knelt beside him and thrust the letter into his hand. He had never seen her cry.

"Read this. Please try to understand, Augustus. I'm going to make arrangements to have him sent here. If I can nurse him I know he'll be all right." She kissed him swiftly. "Try, please try, to understand."

She ran out of the room.

The Prince glanced at the letter. What was it all about? He wanted to discuss the shipment of the things from Paris. Saladin—her horse? How did that concern him?

He was distinctly vexed. He finished his breakfast and went into the study.

She wasn't there.

He waited.

She didn't come.

It was thoughtless. He was annoyed. He had a number of important things to tell her which had occurred to him during the night.

He rang the bell.

"Where is the Marquise?"

"She rode off to Oppeln, I think, Your Highness."

"To Oppeln? Whatever for?"

"I don't know, Your Highness."

He was very annoyed. She had no right to ride to Oppeln when he was waiting to start dictation.

The whole structure of the day went wrong. There was no one to bring his hat and cane. No one to walk up and down the terrace with. No sherry before luncheon.

He did not feel inclined to take a nap. He padded about the house which seemed unnaturally large and silent. He didn't feel inclined to take his usual walk. The constant yapping of the dogs annoyed him.

When, at long last, it was time for dinner he refused his glass of champagne. It was an absurd whim of hers to drink champagne *before* instead of *after*. One of many absurd whims.

He had allowed her altogether too much of a free hand. Managing. Sitting at his desk, forcing him to write his memoirs.

He wanted Vittorio back. At least Vittorio knew his place.

He was in a vile mood when he sat down alone to dinner. She appeared suddenly in a rush, without leave or warning, in her old gray riding habit, covered in dust, with her lovely hair disordered, like a gypsy, a baccante, and compounded her unacceptable behavior by kissing him and then, to make matters worse, by reaching for his hand across the table.

"I'm sorry I was so long. They were so stupid at the Post Office. Nobody spoke French. It took hours to send two cables. I've asked Vittorio to have Saladin shipped to Berlin as soon as he's strong enough to travel. I know if I can nurse him myself that he'll get well. You do understand, Augustus; I love him more than anything on earth and I owe it to him because he saved my life."

She looked so beautiful, her cheeks vivid from the open air and that brilliant mane about her shoulders, that for a moment he relented.

"Eat your dinner. Your soup is getting cold."

The summer bloomed into autumn. Even the somber landscape about Radoom glowed in a golden haze.

Something was happening to the Prince which he had never experienced before. He had known contentment with his books and treasures and the secretive excitement of acquisition, but now he awoke with eagerness, anticipating the attentions and enthusiasms with which Therese surrounded him.

He was ready in the morning room and pushed out his chest a little for the rosebud or scented pink and held up his cheek for the morning kiss. He no longer bridled when she took his arm because she wanted his special attention to explain some idea about the memoirs that had occurred during the night. He knew that she labored long into the early hours to present him with a perfect copy and he noted the order she brought to his haphazard thoughts and memories.

She had procured somehow or other workmen who had dug up the garden and removed the dead and dying trees. She had procured somehow or other lists and catalogues of plants and bulbs from as far away as Holland. She made him consult them. She made him discuss the layout of the garden. She made him decide whether he preferred white or pink tulips before his windows, white or pink or yellow or vermilion roses, white or pink or violet rhododendrons. He had no notion of what a rhododendron was. Somehow or other she had discovered that the estate of a horticulturalist near Berlin was being sold. She made arrangements to have plants dug up and shipped. She consulted with botanical gardens in Germany and England for advice on unusual trees. His mind buzzed with Latin names. Didn't he think the back wall of the garden was a little bare? Didn't he think a small pavilion or gazebo would be agreeable—where he could have tea in the summer and dictate on fine mornings? She thrust pencils and paper into his defenseless hands and begged him to design something—in the classic manner—or perhaps Chinese—or perhaps a Gothic ruin. What was his opinion about fountains, about water gardens, about cascades? He protested, she persuaded. She was a whirlwind of ideas.

Often in the afternoons, after his nap, she would suggest that they go hunting for trees and bushes in the neighborhood and beyond. It was entirely against his inclination but he preferred to go with her than to be left alone. He would grumble and make objections. There were his stick, with the mad diamond and his outdoor hat. There was his carriage. They were off!

"Isn't this fun?" she would exclaim, tucking her hand under his arm.

He would humm and humph a little, but, after all, why not admit: it *was* fun. He enjoyed these expeditions. She brought everything to life. She was full of curiosity. Like passive souls in general he began to thrive on her vitality. She was the oil that lit his timid and lethargic lamp.

More and more he turned things over to her. "Ask the Marquise," "The Marquise will know."

He was amazed at the speed with which the manuscript

piled up. In six weeks more than half the projected volume was completed.

"You have enough material for a dozen more," she announced. "The Memoirs of the Prince of Oppeln-Piast will become famous!"

It was absurd, of course. Perfectly absurd. She was a child with a child's optimism. He was prepared to humor her. And yet, why not? Perhaps with her help he would be famous.

Suddenly the blow fell, the spell was broken.

She did not appear for breakfast. There was no rosebud or scented pink. No kiss. Instead he found a letter before his plate.

My dear Augustus,

I have gone to Berlin. Saladin arrives on Tuesday. I want to find the best doctors for him. I shall be back as soon as possible. A few days at the most. Be patient. Meanwhile, the pavilion, please! And ideas for the memoirs. Ideas and more ideas!

Soon, dear Augustus.
Always,
Therese.

He couldn't believe his eyes. He could not bring himself to believe that she had had the callousness, the effrontery. His old anger welled up in him. She had dared to leave without telling him, without even having the courtesy to say goodbye.

He was unable to drink his coffee. His eggs congealed on the plate before him.

He marched into the morning room.

To leave—in *his* carriage—without a word!

He was so put out, so altogether mortified, that he could not think what to do, on whom he could vent his anger. He stomped out onto the terrace. Some workmen, some of *her* workmen were planting some of *her* roses.

"What are you doing there?" he shouted.

The men looked up, startled. One of them pulled off his cap and replied sheepishly, "We are planting the roses, Your Highness."

"Then stop! Stop this instant! Get off my premises!"

They looked in horror at this scarecrow, waving his arm like a madman. They dropped their tools and beat a hasty exit.

Roses! Gardens! *Her* ideas. All *her* ideas. A pavilion! What right had she to tell him to design a pavilion? He didn't want a pavilion. She had taken over everything. She had coerced and flattered and maneuvered him—to do *her* bidding, to carry out *her* schemes. And then, when the mood seized her, she made off. She vanished! On account of a horse. She cared more for a horse than for him, more for a sick animal than for him, more for this Saladin than for her obligations—after all he had done for her, all he had put up with, all he had suffered. Without a word!

He went back into the house. There on the desk lay the manuscript. That damnable manuscript of his damnable memoirs. Part of her arrogant, insufferable campaign to run his life, to reduce him to the level of a servant who could be dismissed when the impulse seized her.

He swept the manuscript off the desk. A cascade of papers sprayed over the floor.

He would never finish the memoirs. He would never dictate another word. He would never give in to another of her suggestions, her designs, her plots. Against *him*! To dominate *him*!

He found himself in his bedroom, sitting on his bed. She had gone. She had disrupted the routine. She had spoiled everything And oh! the silence that replaced her, the silence of this room, of the whole house, the silence within himself!

The little dogs had followed him about and now stood in a circle gazing at him anxiously.

"Go away!" he shouted. "Go away."

They retreated, frightened. He had never shouted at them before.

Thirty years before he had found a similar note from another woman he had allowed himself to care for. Ellamine had gone and the Marquise had gone. Women! Abominable, mendacious creatures! He was back where he had been then and all that those two vixen had given him was the knowledge which he had carefully hidden for so long of what it felt like to be, in one's inmost self, alone.

He would certainly not weep. He had never allowed himself to weep for any human being. For Nichette, yes, but for no human being.

He would have a great many harsh things to say to Madame the false Marquise when she returned!

It proved to be no easy matter to find Saladin.

At the Berlin railroad station she was passed from one official to another. They consulted documents. The Germans had a deep respect for documents. It appealed to their sense of order to consult them. It enhanced their sense of importance and efficiency. Yes, certainly the express from Paris had arrived on schedule. Everything in the new German Empire arrived on schedule. No, they had no record of a special car containing a special horse. They had no idea onto what siding such a car with such a horse might have been shunted. There was no requisite document and hence no car, no horse.

The higher the official in the hierarchy of the Berlin railroad the more grandiloquent his title. The Germans had a deep respect for titles and insisted on being addressed by them—in full. It was all part of the new structure that rose, rank upon rank, title upon title, to the sacred person of the All High, Wilhelm the Second, Emperor of Germany.

If some mistake had been made it could only have been made by the French on the French section of the line. In the new German Empire no one was permitted to make mistakes. Hoch Der Kaiser!

Therese was desperate. It was extremely hot. The car in which the unfortunate Saladin was stranded was somewhere, on some siding, waiting to be identified by the right official with the right document. It must be stifling. She was terrified that the heat would kill him.

She resorted to Vittorio's ruse. "This horse has been shipped by order of Prince Augustus of Oppeln-Piast, a first cousin of the Kaiser. If anything has gone wrong I can assure you it will cause a great deal of trouble."

A tremor passed through the offices of the Berlin Railroad. Officials clicked heels to their superiors and the superiors gave orders to their inferiors. A document, *the* document, the one and only and essential document, was discovered in exactly the right place in exactly the right dossier in exactly the right office. It had lain there awaiting official recognition of its existence.

As a result of this display of Teutonic efficiency Therese had mislaid Captain O'Higgins, the trainer from the Austrian Riding Academy who had volunteered to examine Saladin and prescribe a regimen. Captain O'Higgins needed no prompting to offer his assistance to a beautiful woman who was so concerned about her Arabian. The world was divided into two categories, those who prized horses above all God's creatures and those who didn't.

She found him in the station bar brooding over the lamentable, sickly, watered-down concoction that passed in Germany for whiskey.

He was a ruddy-cheeked, lively Ulsterman with a twinkle in his eye, a gallant manner toward the ladies and a healthy contempt for all continentals except the Austrians who justified their existence by breeding the beautiful, graceful Lippizaners.

They were led through various purlieus of the station to an area of sheds and warehouses where freight cars waited to be unloaded.

At last the minor official who nonetheless had one toe of one foot on the lowest rung of the ladder that led to the All High, located a car whose number corresponded to the number designated on the document. He required signatures. One, two and three.

Therese was by this time in a fever of impatience and anxiety. At last the car was ceremoniously unbolted, and O'Higgins lifted Therese on board.

It was, indeed, unbearably hot inside.

For a moment in the gloom she could make out nothing, but then, with a sudden catch in her throat, with a pounding of her heart, she made out the beloved form lying supine in the straw.

"Saladin!"

A convulsion passed through the stricken animal. He whinnyed feebly and tried to rise.

"Oh Saladin! My darling Saladin!"

Her arms were around his neck. He was trembling, struggling to drag himself up, overcome by a turmoil of emotion.

Captain O'Higgins was much affected. It seemed the most natural thing in the world that two such fine-bred creatures should be overcome by this reunion.

While Therese soothed the struggling, groaning beast who was mortified to receive his mistress in this condition, O'Higgins ran his experienced hands over the emaciated body.

"He's a beauty, sure enough, poor lad! But terrible undernourished. His coat's in a shocking way. Now let's see if I can find any broken bones."

During a thorough examination, Therese held Saladin's head in her lap. Only his tongue weakly tried to express his joy. Finally O'Higgins said cheerfully, "As far as I can judge, ma'm, it's not organic. He needs a lot of care and building up and more than that, I fancy, he needs you."

"Will he be well again? Can he get back his strength?"

"I wouldn't be surprised if it's yourself that looks after him. They're very emotional craytures and the better bred they are the more emotional they be."

"I'll do anything. Anything at all."

"Don't worry about his coat. That'll improve with his general condition. Now you stay here, ma'm, and I'll be back in a jiffy with O'Higgins' special remedy, guaranteed to bring the dead back from the grave."

He hopped out of the car.

She sat there, cradling Saladin. Nothing in her life had meant as much to her as this animal. The horror and sadness that had separated them only reaffirmed this love. He would be well. She would pour into him all her energy. She would *will* him back to health.

"Oh my dear, my dearest friend, you suffered so much for me."

O'Higgins returned in an hour with a sizable keg that had

once contained brandy and was now filled with the various ingredients essential for the recovery of the "dear crayture."

"Now listen to me well, ma'm. In this barrel is my elixir. You must give him a syringe full three times a day for ten days. After that twice a day for another ten days, with a little food if he has a mind for it. A good bran mash. Then once a day until the barrel's empty. Now I'm giving you the recipe which has never left me hands before. If he needs more of it you can make it up yourself."

The components of the elixir consisted of malt, honey, raw eggs, beef's blood and a large quantity of Irish whiskey.

"And when I say Irish whiskey, ma'm, I mean the real thing, not the measly abomination they call whiskey in this country. This is an ointment for his cuts. Apply it till they're healed. It smells like hell itself, but it works wonders. When he's back on his feet just walk him about at first, don't take him out. And keep him warm. I've written down my address. If there's anything more you need I'm at your service."

"I can never thank you enough," Therese said with tears in her eyes. "You don't know what this means to me."

"Och! He deserves the best. And now I'll make inquiries from these German turds, if you'll forgive the term, and see they put you on the right train tomorrow. Breslau, isn't it?"

"What do I owe you, Captain O'Higgins?"

"I wouldn't accept a thing, ma'm. It was a pleasure." He patted Saladin. "You do as your lady tells you and you'll be as good as new in no time."

He held out his hand with a grin. "Good luck to you. And stay with him all you can. That'll do him more good than anything."

She kissed him fervently on both cheeks. O'Higgins blushed and beamed and jumped out of the car.

He strode away, whistling, as though he were walking across the green turf of his native Armagh.

Therese resumed her place by Saladin. As she stroked his neck and whispered to him, his ears twitched in recognition.

Toward dusk, worn out by so much emotion, they both slept.

* * *

The Prince was sitting by the fire in the red drawing room. Already in the afternoons a damp chill fell. In a few weeks the long ordeal of the Silesian winter would begin.

She was utterly weary and disheveled. She hadn't eaten since they left Berlin. But she was triumphant. Saladin was safely in the stable. He was *there*! He had managed, at her urging, to stumble from the cart in which they had jolted the interminable distance from Breslau. She couldn't believe yet that this miracle had been accomplished.

She dropped down at the Prince's side and laid her cheek against his hand.

"It's done. He'll be all right. I got to him just in time."

It was a moment before she realized that there was no response. She looked up at the pinched, eunuch face. The little eyes were hard as flint, the petulant mouth puckered like the tied end of a balloon.

"I met the most wonderful Irishman in Berlin, a trainer from the Austrian Riding School."

He refused to acknowledge her return.

"What is it? Aren't you glad for me?"

He got up and stomped past her to the desk on which lay the neglected manuscript, her pens, her paper.

"What is the matter with you, Augustus?"

"It is a little late, don't you think, to consider my feelings?"

Everything drained out her. She got up.

"I don't understand."

"I will explain," he replied acidly, prodding the manuscript. "You have kept me waiting for four days."

She was too exhausted to be angry, even to realize that he could possibly be offended.

She said evenly, "You are the most spoiled and the most selfish man I have ever known."

She did not appear at dinner. The Prince ate grimly, steadily chewing every morsel as though he were extracting retribution. He had no intention of forgiving her. She had repaid his immense kindness with a total lack of consideration.

He ate everything that was placed before him. He did not

bestow a single tidbit on the dogs, grouped, as usual, hopefully around his chair. He ingested what was his.

He finished his wine and placed his napkin beside his plate. He retired to the drawing room for coffee.

There was nothing to do and nothing to be said.

He let the dogs out and walked back and forth along the terrace, prodding the pavings with his cane. Her cane. The vulgar and bizarre gift which she had had the temerity to give him at that ill-conceived and humiliating birthday party, with the diamond that was not a diamond, with the spiral of brass which would not have been acceptable even had it been gold.

He went in. He sat.

The fire went out. He went to bed.

The Marquise did not appear next morning. She denied him the satisfaction of dictating the terms of an armistice. There would be no armistice. He would consider nothing but a full apology.

He went into lunch. Alone.

He ate what he was able to eat without interest. He ate because it was a formality which she had chosen to disregard.

He returned to the drawing room. He had coffee.

The coffee was removed.

The afternoon dragged on. He tried to console himself with the thought of how badly he had been treated. He had offered a refuge to a young woman of whom he knew nothing, for whom he was in no way responsible. Because of a ring. Because of Vittorio. Vittorio had conspired to keep her presence in the house a secret. They had conspired together. She was an adventuress. Clever and conniving. She was able to charm and to deceive. She had charmed him. She had charmed the King of Saxony. She had doubtless worked her wiles on Vittorio, that simple fool. Sending telegrams as though Vittorio was her servant and not his.

He reviewed all her ploys. The morning kiss. The rosebud or scented pink. The Memoirs. He saw through her maneuvers. They would avail her nothing.

Because of a horse. A horse!

He summoned a footman. "Inform the Marquise that I am expecting her for dinner."

The footman returned. "Your Highness, the Marquise will not be taking dinner."

Not be taking dinner! When he had asked, when he had been prepared—

A further insult!

He ate alone.

He did not want to eat.

He despised this ill-cooked food. The wine was unfit for a cultivated palate.

He refused dessert.

He threw down his napkin. "Inform the chef he must do better. An inedible repast."

The coffee was bitter, too. Where was Vittorio? Nothing had been right since Vittorio had gone away. But Vittorio had deceived him too. He had kept her hidden in that upper bedroom. They had plotted, they had intrigued. It was part of a plan to infuriate him, to take advantage of him. They would see!

He was tired. Tired of this emptiness, of feuding, of doing nothing. Tired of Radoom.

How could he face a winter in this house alone?

The dogs were disgruntled. They missed Therese. They had not been brushed or combed for days. They wanted to be fondled, to have their ribbons changed.

He stared at the Duccio Madonna. That stern and tragic face, unyielding like his mother.

There had been moments with the Marquise when he had felt something like happiness seeping into his heart. Bitter illusion! There was no happiness to be had from women.

Her wiles, her sweetness!

How *could* she behave like this?

She did not appear for breakfast or for luncheon. The war of attrition continued.

He had no appetite.

He had been abandoned. The past had conquered. In the end his parents always had. Even death hadn't made much difference. Strong, inflexible, self-righteous! What had happened to his sisters? The one in England, the one in Baden? They had children he never saw. He had never wanted to. They would be impossible like their mothers, rescuing animals and climbing trees!

Spoiled and selfish? By no stretch of his limited capacity to make concessions could he think of himself as spoiled and selfish.

She had been cruelly unjust. Hadn't he rescued her from the Siege of Paris? Didn't she owe him at least *some* gratitude?

He held out till four and then capitulated.

He stomped down the passage and rapped with his cane, her cane, upon the door.

"Come in."

She was lying on the bed in a room he had never seen before eating a bunch of grapes.

"I have come for an explanation."

"What do you want me to explain?"

"Why, for three days, you have not appeared. You have ignored—"

"I've been busy looking after Saladin. I know that means nothing to you. It means a great deal to me."

"A horse—!" he exclaimed contemptuously.

"Yes, a horse. The one living thing I care about."

She continued with quiet defiance to eat the grapes.

"I am forced to remind you that you are my guest."

"I thought I was your housekeeper and secretary until Vittorio returns."

"I am not referring to Vittorio. You have not had the politeness to put in an appearance for three days."

"I don't intend to. I have given notice. I am no longer in your employ."

She had not once looked at him. Now she leveled at him a look of cold and insolent contempt.

He rapped the floor with his cane. "And what do you intend to do here, may I ask?"

"I intend to get Saladin well and then I'll see."

"I find your behavior unacceptable, Madame."

"Then don't accept it. You weren't able to accept my going to Berlin. You're not able to accept anything that doesn't concern yourself."

He banged on the floor. He was white with anger. "Don't speak to me like that. I will not be insulted in my own house by an—an adventuress."

She smiled. It was not an agreeable expression.

"Yes, I'm an adventuress. And what would you be without your silver mines and houses and works of art? This avalanche of wealth you dissipate? Have you ever done anything for anyone? Have you ever given anything to anyone? Oh yes, money—when it occurs to you—when it pleases the Prince of Piast to distribute largesse to the serfs."

He couldn't believe his ears. He was unable to comprehend that anyone, anyone he knew, anyone in his debt, could utter such words in his presence, to his face.

She got off the bed like a pugilist preparing for attack and placed the remainder of the grapes on a dresser.

"You do not impress me, Augustus. Neither does your anger at my daring to desert you for four days. I am not like Vittorio. I am not your slave. What I tried to do for you I did because I wanted to, because it pleased me, because I wanted to please you. I could have spared myself the trouble. Whatever anyone does for you results in the same thing. You give orders. Vittorio gave you six years of his life. Your gratitude was typical; you gave him orders. Well, to me you do not give orders. That is the difference between us. I do not take orders from you— ever!"

He stood there trembling, but bereft.

"A small thing. One small human thing. I thought you would be glad that I was able to save the life of something I loved so much. But even that you couldn't find, in your small, mean heart, to give."

She dismissed him as though he were not worth her anger, as though he were beyond the effort of redemption.

"Oh, don't stand there. Go and have your dinner. As soon as Saladin is well, I'll leave."

He was in the passage. His rickety legs carried him down

the passage of this house that had always been a prison. Her voice rang in his head.

She spent many hours in the stable, sitting on a milking stool, with her head against Saladin's shoulder. He was able to stand now with his head bent down to hers. They drew strength and resolution from each other. She felt no regret at having fought with the Prince. There was a sort of relief in not having to be constantly agreeable. After all the obstacles between them had proved too great and her schemes had come to nothing.

She had no idea where she would go when she left Radoom; Breslau or Berlin—or even Paris—it didn't matter.

When she was with Saladin she trained herself not to look ahead or to remember. There was this one brief segment of the present that they could share in peace, a communication of souls unmarred by words.

It was almost dark in the stable.

"Now you must sleep."

She put away the stool, slung a blanket over Saladin's back and whispered to him, "I'll see you in the morning."

He nuzzled her neck and snorted softly.

As she was crossing the courtyard the young footman with the flat peasant face came out of the house.

"Meine Gnägiste, will you come, please? The Prince is ill."

"Since when?"

"Yesterday. He's in bed. He won't eat anything."

It was an obvious ploy to make her feel guilty.

"I think you should go to him, Meine Gnädiste."

She steeled herself, went to his bedroom and knocked. There was no response.

He was lying on his back like a cadaver on a funeral slab with the blankets pulled up under his chin and an absurd nightcap that flopped down to one side like a rabbit that had lost an ear.

His eyes were firmly shut.

"Are you really ill, Augustus?"

For answer he turned on his side with his back toward her. She was mildly irritated by such childish tactics.

"You must eat. I'll get you something."

She went to the kitchen, warmed some soup, and carved a breast of chicken, added some beet and potato salad, and carried the tray to the Prince's room.

She sat down on the side of the bed.

"Come. Drink a little soup."

He refused to budge. She tapped him on the shoulder with the spoon.

"Turn over, Augustus."

He was angry and still deeply wounded. He debated whether to do as she demanded would be an admission of defeat.

"Please. I can't sit here all night."

He turned over, scowling, keeping his eyes shut because he didn't want her to see that he was hungry.

She brought a spoonful of soup to his mouth.

"Open."

He consented to open his mouth a little. He had small crooked teeth like a rodent.

She fed him the soup, spoon by spoon, as though he were an infant, and wiped his chin.

She cut up the chicken and placed the plate on his lap.

"You can eat that. It's light."

He extracted his arms from beneath the covers and condescended to prod, piece after piece, the breast of chicken and convey it to his mouth. He did not once glance at her.

When he had finished he withdrew his arms and closed his eyes again. The whole charade was so pathetic and ridiculous that her irritation turned to pity.

"Do you want anything else?"

He raised a haughty eyebrow.

As she was picking up the tray he darted a flinty glance toward her in which she detected an appeal.

"You want to do some work on the Memoirs?"

He shrugged. It was beneath his dignity to admit that he wanted this more than anything, not merely on account of the manuscript, but to reestablish their routine.

She took the tray to the kitchen, went to the study, collected the wretched Memoirs, the wretched pens, the wretched inkpot and blotting paper, and returned to the bedroom. She arranged herself at a small table near the bed.

He observed these preparations covertly through lowered lids.

"I was strolling one day in the gardens of the Palais Royal in the summer of 1860," she read out, "when I noticed in a shop an obscure canvas, much yellowed with varnish, which struck me as being in the style of Murillo."

After a pause, in which he struggled not to appear too eager, as though he were only bringing himself to do this out of a disagreeable sense of duty, he resumed where he had left off ten days before.

"Although Murillo is not a painter I hold particularly dear, I bought the picture for a few francs. When I examined it at home I saw that it was at the most a studio copy, but something struck me as unusual. The back of the canvas was covered by a thin layer of gesso."

The voice droned on. The pen scratched across the paper. After an hour the candles wavered and he stopped with a long drawn sigh.

She moved the table away so that he would not fall over it.

"Are you ready to sleep now?"

He nodded.

At the door she was surprised by a muffled clearing of throat and a hesitant inquiry. "Hm! Is your horse getting better?"

"Yes. He's able to stand now."

"I am glad to hear it."

It was the most he could concede.

"Good night, Augustus."

"Good night, Therese."

The routine was resumed. She was ready at his desk when he came in from breakfast. She did not eat with him now, but had her meals in her room. She was polite and formal.

He dictated. She transcribed. But the pleasure had gone out of it. It was no longer a collaboration.

The days, in between these sessions, seemed dreadfully long. He disliked eating alone, sitting alone in the study, walking the dogs alone. He watched the light change and wondered what she was doing.

And when she had gone—what then?

One afternoon a cold gray rain was falling. He noticed her in her garden. She was actually planting the abandoned roses, digging holes with a shovel, and then, on her knees in the mud, pressing them in and tramping down the soil around them.

He watched her for some moments in mounting disbelief.

He padded out and stood uncertainly beside her.

"Don't do that now. You'll get soaked."

"They'll die if they're not planted."

"Let the men do it."

"The men have gone."

He hovered, distressed and helpless, and then went in.

He watched her from the window. The rain was falling steadily. She was doing it deliberately to mortify him. He rang for the footman.

"Tell the Marquise to wait till the rain stops. She's sopping wet already."

The footman joined her in the garden. They conferred briefly. To the Prince's annoyance and dismay the man picked up the shovel and worked along beside her. The rain was streaming from her head. Her cloak clung limply to her body.

They went on doggedly planting the roses in the mud.

The rain swelled to a deluge. At last they desisted and, bedraggled, went indoors.

It was outrageous. If she wanted to kill herself in order to prove he had been wrong.

What could one do with such a woman?

The next morning she had a streaming cold. She worked with a handkerchief pressed against her mouth. She sneezed constantly. He was distracted.

"You'd better go to bed. You're ill."

She leaned forward as though at the end of her tether, with her hand across her eyes.

"Why do we do this? Why do we fight and hurt each other?

I never wanted to hurt you. It's always the same. People tear at each other as though we were all wild beasts."

She stood up. He couldn't tell whether her eyes were red from weeping or from the cold.

"A nun in a convent said to me, 'The only redress is courage.' I've tried to find courage. But for what? For what?"

She left him without defenses. It *was* all senseless, all a waste. He sent the footman to Oppeln for the doctor. "You are not to return without him, understand?" He went to the kitchen and told the chef to make the Marquise some soup, a hot toddy, whatever was beneficial for a cold. After an hour, beset with worry that she might be seriously ill, he went to her room and sat down awkwardly by her bed.

She was sleeping, her face flushed, her breathing heavy and irregular.

After a while she woke and turned her head. She said with difficulty, "Will you tell someone to give Saladin his medicine? Listen, Augustus, I'll explain what must be done."

He tried to listen, but his mind wandered. How ill was she?

She said without rancor, "You didn't listen."

To his dismay she started to get out of bed.

"Therese, you mustn't. You must stay there. Please—go back to bed."

"It doesn't matter."

He protested. She slid her feet into slippers, pulled on a dressing gown, a coat.

"Don't. Please don't. I will see to it. I'll see the horse is fed." He followed her into the passage. "I've sent to Oppeln for the doctor. At least wait till then—"

He followed her across the courtyard through the rain.

In the stable the black horse was leaning against its stall. Its ears pricked when she came in. He whisked his tail in greeting. She filled a big syringe with a dark substance from a keg and, lifting the horse's lower lip, slowly ejected it down his throat.

The horse seemed to know exactly what was expected of him.

She leaned against him, spent.

"Please now—will you come back? You can't stay here."

Instead she folded in on herself and sank down on the straw. The horse moved closer and bent his protective head down over her.

The Prince was totally helpless. He noticed blankets folded across the stall. As he laid them over her, he thought, "This woman has disrupted my whole life."

He trudged back across the courtyard. This enormous house with all its empty rooms!

In the hallway he stood for a moment, listening to the rain, drumming on the glass roof of the cupola.

The most unexpected, the most staggering thought occurred to him. It came to him as a revelation, at once incredible and obvious. Obvious! The one solution.

The news of the Prince's marriage did not come altogether as a shock to Vittorio. At the back of his mind he had sensed that this might have been, from the start, Therese's ultimate objective. What was astonishing was that she had accomplished her aim so quickly. By what persuasion or guile or necromancy had she been able to reverse the habits and inclinations of a lifetime? It was incredible. At the same time there was an odd kind of inevitability about it. Those two strong-willed, obstinate, opinionated people belonged to the same breed; they were rulers determined never to be ruled.

"The old codger" had at last met his match in that woman of icy fire. It was the triumph of willpower over willfulness. He was lucky to have escaped in time!

Vittorio had lingered on in Paris until the last crate had been removed from the Hôtel de Piast, until the final deed of sale had been signed by the Argentine Embassy, until the Banque de France had completed the last transfer of the Prince's funds.

Paris had recovered her former charm and animation after the rigors of the Siege and the horrors of the Commune. The superficialities of life had again proved more durable than the grim realities. The shops and restaurants had reopened. The smart *équipages* promenaded in the Bois. The Opéra announced its winter season. Worth had reopened his salon with a new collection designed about the new color he had created. "Ashes of Paris," a delicate smoky gray with lilac undertones. It took the French to wear mourning with such éclat.

Vittorio had taken up with a midinette, named Adèle, a pretty, light-headed creature whose room under the eaves, where she perched like a perky sparrow, he had refurnished with things from the Hôtel de Piast which the old man would never miss. He had piled a cart with a Venetian bed, a dressing table, a chest of drawers, painted all over with flowers and ribbons, a Persian carpet, silk curtains, chairs, mirrors and two handsome Meissen parakeets, all of which he appropriated without a qualm.

Adèle was in ecstasies. Her room was a jewelbox fit for a queen. No one had ever been as good to her as her "gros choux," her Italian Midas. She prepared her little dinners behind a Spanish leather screen and served her lover on Sèvres china decorated with pink roses and angels with rosy bottoms. Vittorio was her angel, her divine "joujou."

He would stretch his great length naked before the fire while she sat at his feet caressing his legs and bestowing kisses on the source of her greatest joy. He basked, catlike, in adoration. There was nothing more soothing to the soul than a thoroughly stupid woman.

He had felt no inclination to return to Silesia and the Prince's exacting temper. He felt reluctant to resume his relationship with Therese which, because of her violent and incomprehensible moods, could never be established on an even keel. Adèle suited him better; he never thought about her.

He was enjoying a well-earned respite as a gentleman of leisure, a boulevardier who ate in good restaurants, wore good clothes and had a charming and undemanding mistress.

But this extraordinary marriage altered everything.

The Prince had written a long and rambling letter full, as usual, with instructions. There were a hundred details he wanted seeing to. There was a reference to his concern about the Mexican silver mines which the Princess would explain in a covering letter. The Princess! She had been promoted and had got down to business soon enough. Vittorio smiled and shook his head. Fantastic!

Therese's letter was written in her clear, inflexible hand, as regular as an accountant's.

My dear Vittorio,

No doubt you will be surprised to learn that P.A. and I are married. There is no time now to explain the circumstances that led to this decision. Whatever you may think of it, I ask you to believe that I did not take this step easily nor without some doubts as to the consequences. I am all too much aware of the difficulties involved. My motives, while selfish, were not entirely so. I will try hard to make something of this strange union that will be of benefit to both of us.

I have been trying to bring some order into P.A.'s affairs. As you know he has never paid the slightest heed to business. His finances will take a long time to untangle.

In the first batch of papers to arrive from Paris I came across a sheaf of statements concerning the Mexican mines. As far as I am able, at this stage, to understand no positive accountings have ever been provided by the present overseers. There are two mines, one at Cusco and one at Villadama. Don't ask me where either of these places are. Nor do the statements hitherto provided correspond to the bills of lading from the shipping line which has handled the transfer of the silver bars to Paris. And, further, the bankbooks from the Banque de France do not coincide with either of the above. It would appear that P.A. has been systematically robbed for years. There are glaring discrepancies in all these accounts covered by unspecified "expenses." I fancy that a number of people along the way have been making fortunes at P.A.'s expense.

There are other accounts in Berlin at the Rothschild Bank, at Coutt's Bank in London and at the National Bank in Mexico, but these I have not yet examined.

I want to try and clarify this confusion, extending back over years and to seek redress on P.A.'s behalf.

You know, my dear Vittorio, and in this I am perfectly sincere, that I always believed you were wasted in your

*position here. It was unworthy of your capacities and offered
you little to look forward to. If you can bring yourself to
believe that the altered circumstances have not diminished
my regard for you, I beg you to consider the following
proposition.*

*Would you be prepared to go to Mexico and look into
the whole matter of how the mines have been for so long
mismanaged, how much silver is actually extracted, how
much sent to Europe and who has been responsible for so
much illegal appropriation? I know nothing of that country,
but it might please you to visit it, if nothing else, and if, as
I firmly believe, it will be necessary to find some honest
person to run the mines, might this not be worthy of your
consideration? You can trust me to see that your interests
are protected at this end. You have everything, Vittorio, but
ambition and it would give me immense satisfaction to feel
that I might be partially instrumental in giving you an opportunity commensurate with your talents.*

*Think it over and let me know. If you are willing to
embark on this adventure I will set the ball in motion and
send you the necessary authorization, a draft of money, and
whatever else is needed.*

*P.A. is well and eager to have around him the things
from Paris that he loves. My Saladin has fully recovered
and it is once again my greatest joy to ride with him in the
afternoons. There again I am in your debt. But there is so
much more that can never be repaid and which I do not
and never shall forget.*

Believe me always your sincere friend,

Therese.

I can't bring myself now to write the rest.

He sat for a long time in the dismantled study with this
letter in his hand.

Was she sincere? Had she ever been? Their intimacy had
arisen from blind chance and what he now saw to have been
her instinct for self-preservation. Very clearly his presence at
Radoom would be a threat to her new security. Their former

attachment would become clear, sooner or later, even to some-one as innocent in such matters as the Prince. It was in her interest to have him as far away as possible.

One had to admire her gall!

He was taking Adèle to the Opéra Comique that evening. He let himself out of the empty house and strolled slowly in the direction of the Place de la Concorde.

He would always be haunted by that mysterious woman. He did not blame her for seizing the opportunity of extricating herself from her former life, whatever it had exactly been. He had come close to loving her, though even in her moments of tenderness and passion there had been something equivocal, something he couldn't reach. No, he didn't blame her. She had been honest in her deceptions, in her anger and pain and what he supposed had been her terror of the future. She had done well for herself, the Princess of Oppeln-Piast!

He had walked for some time and found himself on the Boulevard Sevastopol, crossed it and continued along the Rue du Temple. This was the way they had walked together, the day she had cut the roses.

The Restaurant Provençale had reopened. It was unchanged but for a freshly painted door.

As he lifted the latch of the iron gate into the secret garden, Therese's image returned to him in all her vivid and enigmatic grace. He would have given anything to know her secret. But she was a Chinese box of secrets, each one concealed another.

A little gentleman in a black suit with knee britches was taking tea in a pool of yellow leaves fallen from the chestnut trees.

He rose with his feet in the fifth position, assuming that this handsome young man had come to inquire about dancing les-sons.

"Excuse me, I am a friend of the Marquise de Païva from whom you bought this house."

Etienne Perroneau de Rousse was politely mystified. "No, Monsieur, I purchased this property from Madame Therese Lachmann."

Was that her real name? Lachmann? Had the Marquise de

Païva been a bluff, a *nom de guerre*? He wondered how much the Prince had found out about her.

He thought of her on that day over a year before, moving along these paths, clipping the roses. He would never know who she really was, this chimera under whose spell he had fallen. Had it been love? Had they loved each other for a while?

The yellow leaves drifted down. Moments—moments from his life.

Mexico? Why not? There was nothing for him here.

In the second year of Therese's marriage two events occurred that were to have a marked impact on her future.

The first was a visit from two of the Prince's nephews, Otto and Sixtus of Baden-Oldenburg.

Otto, the youngest of the three Baden brothers, occasionally read the papers "to keep in touch." He had been greatly surprised by a laudatory review of a newly published work, *Memoirs of a Collector*, by Prince Augustus of Oppeln-Piast. Otto had purchased a copy of this handsome volume, profusely illustrated, with the Piast coat of arms on the title page. It was the dedication that struck him like a thunderbolt.

"For my wife Therese."

His *wife*? Uncle Augustus had a *wife*? Impossible!

The Baden brothers had only seen their uncle a few times, having been instructed by their alpinist mama "not to associate with him because of his dreadful habits." This warning had been confirmed by the number of handsome young men who ran the Prince's establishment in Paris. The Baden brothers naturally condemned inversion on moral grounds; in this instance they condoned it as a safeguard for their inheritance.

The news that their relative had compounded his "dreadful habits" by taking a wife pulled from beneath them the rug on which, by right, their feet had been firmly planted. Their mother having fallen down a crevasse in the Himalayas, they stood to inherit millions, even taking into account their English cousins, the Hadleys, whose mother was still extant but deemed insane. Uncle Augustus was immensely rich. He had mines in the New World and the New World, which civilized people did not condescend to visit, justified its discovery by providing the fortunate with Niagaras of wealth. In a fit of something far more heinous than inversion Uncle Augustus had betrayed them. He had fallen into the clutches of an unscrupulous adventuress ready to overlook his "dreadful habits" in order to defraud them of what was theirs. She was obviously as depraved as he was.

The brothers conferred. They wrote a guardedly congratulatory letter on the publication of *Memoirs of a Collector*. The dedication had surprised and, if they might say so, pained them. Had their dear uncle taken a step which for reasons of his own and perhaps by a mere oversight he had neglected to inform them?

They were surprised to receive a cordial invitation to visit Radoom from the new Princess, their aunt, as they were forced to consider her, by marriage.

Maximilian, the eldest brother, a Colonel in the Hussars and a close friend of Crown Prince Wilhelm, declined to have anything to do with it. He could not allow the faintest breath of scandal to touch his name. Otto and Sixtus, more daring and more dependent on their prospects, being seriously in debt, agreed to spend a few nights at Radoom on their way to Hungary for the hunting season.

Their first impression was not encouraging. In the falling snow the long gray pile looked distinctly sinister. It seemed the perfect setting for "dreadful habits," far from the prying eyes of respectable society.

Servants handed them into an impressive hallway with classic statuary and an enormous chandelier suspended from a cupola obscured by snow. They were escorted upstairs to adjoining bedrooms, warm and well appointed. Steaming canisters of water appeared and hot toddies on silver trays.

So this was Bluebeard's Castle where the old sodomist persued his gross desires with the connivance of his evil, scheming wife!

"When Your Highnesses are ready the Prince will receive you in the red drawing room," the footman informed them. The footman deepened their uncertainty. He was not at all good-looking.

They changed, washed and, correct as blueprints, went downstairs. They were shown into a large room, entirely covered in red damask. Their unspeakable relative was seated beside a blazing fire. A number of little dogs greeted them with disapproving yaps.

He had changed very little since they had last seen him. He still looked like the Chief Eunuch at the Court of China, but they saw at a glance that he was in good health and in full command of his faculties. He had a curious sable hat on his high domed skull and was holding a curious cane with a curious brown stone. He was altogether most curious and most distinguished and not, the brothers realized, to be trifled with. They had calculated en route that he must be about sixty. He looked no older; it was discouraging.

He waved them to chairs on which they planted themselves stiffly. They were faultless examples of caste and of tradition.

"Did you have a good journey?" the Prince inquired.

"As far as Breslau, yes. After Breslau the road was nearly impassable with snow."

"We have had a lot of snow this year."

"We had no idea," Otto ventured, "that you had come back to live here. We only learned of it by accident through the preface to your book."

"I left Paris because of the war. Thanks to my wife this house is now quite habitable."

His wife! How could they broach the subject of the most dangerous of his aberrations? They had mutually conceived the image of some middle-aged Brünnhilde, rapacious and overbearing, who had terrorized this helpless eccentric into marriage, possibly by threats of exposure of his "dreadful habits."

The Prince seemed singularly relaxed and spoke of his wife quite simply. It was disturbing.

"We were surprised to learn of your marriage," Sixtus said, "also by accident from the dedication of your book. As your nearest relatives we would have liked, at least, to send you some token of our esteem."

"I wasn't aware that you esteemed me," the Prince said dryly. "Your mother didn't."

It was not a promising beginning. Fortunately a footman entered with glasses of champagne, followed by a second footman with caviar. They did themselves well, the unspeakable uncle and his unspeakable wife.

"You're going to Budapest, I think," the Prince said, helping himself to caviar.

"To Jaszapati—for the hunting."

"Where is Jaszapati?"

"It's the Esterhazy's estate in northern Hungary. We go there every year."

"Which Esterhazys?"

"Count Ferdinand."

"Ah yes, the lesser line."

When the footmen withdrew the conversational void was bridged by the Prince who asked abruptly, "How is your mother?"

The brothers were shocked. "She died—five years ago."

"Oh yes, I forgot," the Prince admitted unperturbed. "She fell off a mountain somewhere."

"She was lost in a tragic accident—on an expedition," Sixtus corrected.

"She always liked climbing. She used to climb trees. She was very daring."

This lapse of memory renewed the brothers' hope that perhaps their uncle was not in such mint condition as he appeared.

"And the others, your English cousins, you see them?"

"We visited the Hadleys for the hunting two years ago."

"And how are they?"

"Both well."

"And how is *their* mother?"

"She is well, too."

The Marchioness of Hadley was hardly a topic for conversation. It had been on their last visit that she had threatened an equerry of the Prince of Wales with a shotgun. There were distinct drawbacks to being related to the Piasts.

"I'm surprised she had children," the Prince reflected. "She was only interested in animals. She kept a menagerie. Anything her father failed to kill."

"She is still interested in animals."

The Prince gazed into the fire. "Neither of my sisters could be described as normal."

The door opened. What faced them was disaster.

The new Princess was young. She was shockingly young, elegantly gowned in Nile green which set off her astonishing hair and her astonishing eyes. She was no middle-aged Brünnhilde. She was infinitely more dangerous. She was, to their horrified gaze, superb.

She was disarmingly gracious. She greeted them with queenly warmth. They saw in this Hyppolyta the awful likelihood of a whole new generation of Piasts, each one of whom would put them at a further remove from their inheritance. They prayed devoutly that their mother had been right in her estimation of the Prince's incapacity.

As the evening progressed their doubts deepened. There all too obviously existed between these two disparate people, the Frog Prince and the Snow Queen, an accord, a sympathy, a secret communication. They were unable to diagnose the nature of the empathy between them.

The Princess sat at the left hand of her husband, the two brothers catty-cornered at the other end of the table.

She was so much at her ease, so charming, so quietly in command, that they found it difficult to be disapproving. She spoke about the Prince's renovation of Radoom, his knowledge of architecture and gardens, the success of his Memoirs which were now in their third edition and were being translated into French and English, she took such obvious pride in his accomplishments that they were hard put to it to believe she was not sincere.

The old man kept glancing at her with an admiration tinged with awe and evidently preened himself in the sunshine of her praise.

"It was all her doing," he acknowledged. "I would never have thought of writing memoirs."

"I'm bullying him into a second volume. And there'll be others. I'm ruthless when it comes to all he knows."

Was it a well-rehearsed performance? The brothers were

used in their world to couples who for financial or dynastic reasons were forced to keep up a front before the world. What confounded them with Uncle Augustus and his bride was that rare phenomenon, a seemingly happy marriage.

And yet it could not be, not between an elderly recluse who, according to their mother, had never evinced the slightest interest in women, and this self-assured enchantress. In moments during dinner when they had the chance to scrutinize her, they detected a veiled strength and firmness which she kept well sheathed like the claws of a deceptively domesticated panther. They saw that the Prince was aware of this and deferred to her and was possibly afraid of her.

After dinner, at his wife's suggestion, the Prince showed his nephews 'round the collections, now handsomely displayed in glass-fronted cabinets in the redecorated rooms. They knew little about art, but were impressed by the old man's enthusiasm and erudition.

"My wife arranged things so that I can lay my hand to any object when I need a point of reference."

He showed them into a smaller room where all the models for the Versailles theatrical performances had been set up on little stands.

"My wife devised this way of lighting them with hidden gas jets. One really has the impression of looking into miniature theaters."

The Prince toddled from room to room, pointing out items of special interest.

"I never knew how much I had. My Paris house was always in great confusion. My wife has put everything in order. She has genius for organization. Shall we rejoin her?"

The paragon was reclining on a sofa with a book. She suggested nightcaps.

"I'm afraid we don't have much to offer in the way of diversion at Radoom, but I hope you'll enjoy the little boar hunt I've arranged for you tomorrow. Neither Augustus nor I hunt, but I've rounded up some beaters. It may serve to whet your appetite for Hungary."

As they said good night they noted the conspiratorial smile

that passed between husband and wife as though they shared a secret that particularly amused them.

"What do you think of her?" Sixtus asked as the brothers started to undress, wandering in and out of each other's rooms as they exchanged impressions.

"I can't find anything against her," Otto admitted. "She couldn't have been more charming."

"She's a consummate bitch. God knows where he picked her up or rather where she picked him up which is more likely."

"I'm not so sure." Otto was better natured than his brother and had been genuinely taken with Therese. "It's no easy matter for a woman of her age and looks to live with an old crank like Augustus, especially marooned out here."

"She knows which side her bread's buttered on and where the skeletons are hidden. A calculating bitch is my conclusion."

"We've only mother's word for it that he's peculiar. Perhaps he's changed."

"Mother knew him. She grew up with him. Besides, all the Piasts are odd—look at the Marchioness. She's certifiable."

"If she makes the old boy happy—what's the harm in it? I'd say he's jolly lucky."

"One thing's certain; I've got to tackle her about our position before we leave."

The following morning Therese rode out with the brothers to the edge of the forest. She looked very stylish on her black Arabian. "She's just too bloody perfect," Sixtus thought, "to be convincing."

That day, after a hard day's hunting, Sixtus bearded his new adversary in her study, the former library at the end of the corridor on the ground floor.

The room was in itself a sort of affront, a statement of her taste and independence. The walls were covered with white watered silk. She sat at an imposing ebonized desk across a lake of emerald green carpet. The only point in the room that was not white or green was her brilliantly burnished hair.

She was working on a great pile of documents. Stacks of documents of a legal sort were piled on nearby tables, awaiting scrutiny.

"I am interrupting you."

"Not at all. I'm almost finished for today."

She set down her pen, but did not rise. He felt a little as if she were considering him for a position. As the son of a reigning duke he was practiced in the art of condescension, but for once he felt obscurely at a disadvantage.

"I'm delighted that you had a good day," she said cordially. "It's given Augustus so much pleasure to see you. It's a pity that he's been estranged from his family for so long. Of course you live at some distance from each other, but still—you're his nephews. It's important for you to know each other. I don't think he's seen the Hadleys since they were children."

"You're right," he agreed. "It is important."

"Now that you've found your way here I hope you'll come often. I think in time Augustus will reopen the Berlin house and then he'll be more accessible."

"These all look very official and imposing." He indicated the legal documents.

"I'm trying to bring some order into his affairs. Like most artists he has no head for business. And he is an artist, not creatively, but through appreciation."

"All this has to do with business?"

"It's a terrible tangle. Nothing has been sorted out or itemized for years."

She appeared so detached, so without ulterior motive, that for a moment he was tempted to believe in her.

She was perfectly aware of what he had come to discuss and the purpose behind the visit.

She took the wind out of his sails by saying in the same unforced and casual manner, "I've come across a number of family papers, including your grandfather's will which I'm sure Augustus has long forgotten. But I expect your mother had a copy of it or at least told you about its contents. I don't want you to think I'm intruding on matters that don't concern me. I just happened to come across it."

Sixtus said quietly, "I don't recall my mother discussing my grandfather's will."

"Would you care to see it? You have the right to as the next of kin."

Her daring was disgraceful. He would not allow himself to be led into betraying his burning interest.

"Really—I dare say it isn't necessary."

Her hand strayed among the papers. She failed to produce the all-important document. She seemed for the moment to have mislaid it.

"Well, it was here. I'm sorry, but you can't conceive the muddle. All this goes back for years and years."

He caught her eye. He wanted to make it plain that he was not taken in by this maneuver.

"I know what you must be thinking," she continued in the same guileless tone, "but you needn't be alarmed. This will was drawn up long ago under conditions that no longer apply. It should have made provisions for other contingencies. I'm sure that Augustus will rectify it."

Sixtus flushed. Her effrontery was beyond belief.

"My dear *Princess*." He underlined her new title with careful sarcasm. "We did not come to Radoom to discuss a possible inheritance."

"No, of course not, but you have a perfect right to be concerned. Provisions should have been made and they must be. I'll remind Augustus to attend to it."

She rose and Sixtus rose. They confronted each other with deadly cordiality across the desk on which the will was tantalizingly within and not within his grasp.

"It was a pity that the estate wasn't entailed in the usual way. That saves so much trouble. As it is, unless Augustus has a son he's free to dispose of it in any way he wants. Had it been sensibly entailed it would have gone to the eldest of his nephews, I suppose. I'm not sure which of you that would be."

"Maximilian," Sixtus said darkly.

"I don't suppose he'd be interested in the titles. He has titles of his own. But one has to consider the financial aspects which are considerable." Her poise was insufferable. She actually came 'round the desk and touched his arm. "That's really why

I'm so glad you came. You should be on good terms with Augustus. It will make it much easier for him when he decides how he wants to dispose of everything."

He was not going to let this insult go unchallenged. "I find it hard to understand why my uncle should hand over his financial affairs to someone as young and as presumably inexperienced as yourself."

"You don't know Augustus. He has never in his life taken the slightest interest in money."

She had glided, this Medusa who already had her claws on everything, to the door where she turned and smiled at him with an amused condescension that was his right, not hers.

"I hope you don't think of me as an interloper," she suggested. "My motives are less obvious than they may seem."

"I don't think I have misjudged your motives."

"You may have. I wouldn't blame you. As it happens Augustus has a great deal more to offer me than may seem apparent. He's a quite remarkable man."

She held out her hand which, despite his burning resentment, he was forced to take.

"I do hope," she concluded as a parting thrust, "that we can become good friends."

The brothers left next morning.

They had accomplished nothing.

The consummate bitch had made their position plain.

The snow fell. Great winds soughed through the forests and moaned around the house. At dusk the wolves howled.

Therese and Augustus dug in for another Silesian winter.

What had emerged from her unaccountable marriage had come as a surprise as great to Therese as it had appeared to the Baden brothers. She and Augustus were singularly well suited.

The isolation of Radoom was no great privation for the Prince. He was not much more cut off from the world than he had been in Paris. For Therese this absence of human involvement came as a relief. There were no promises, no threats and no deceptions. Her days were occupied with running the great house, taking dictation, editing the Prince's inexhaustible memories, caring for Saladin, and with her new and absorbing passion; money.

As the Prince was preoccupied with Art, so Therese became increasingly fascinated by finance. Her talent for mathematics, her clear deductive mind, which had flummoxed Mr. Willing at the Pavillon, opened for her an immense and complex sphere, unmarred by the fallibilities of human nature, as abstract as science and as unlimited. Money, divorced from its purchasing power, fired her imagination as nothing had ever done. The making and manipulation of money, not as a means for self-indulgence as it would be for Augustus or as a weapon of power as it had been for de Morny, intrigued her like a physicist who combines certain properties in a test tube and evolves mutations of hitherto unsuspected value. Simple mathematica developed along immutable lines to the pure dynamics of Euclid. Money was a source like opium of infinitely varied possibilities. As she labored to untangle the Prince's assets she came to see the Piast fortune as a foundation as vast in its potential as the Great Pyramid of Cheops.

It was at night, with the chores of the day behind her, with Augustus and Saladin safely in their quarters, and the great house silent, that she delved, item by item, into the accumulated muddle that had resulted from mismanagement and neglect. She prepared long lists of queries concerning discrepancies in bank statements and unjustified deductions from bills of lading. She estimated that at least a third of the Prince's income had been siphoned off under spurious pretexts and by all sorts of nefarious means. Once in command of all the details she planned to launch an offensive against all these officials who had been illegally enriching themselves for years.

Vittorio was proving an invaluable ally. He liked Mexico. He had shouldered the responsibilities of management with surprising ease and was gaining control over the ramifications of mining and shipping silver. He was honest and he was capable. As Therese's life had entered a new phase, so Vittorio's had swung into a wider orbit. They were accomplices by post, but their conspiracy had a larger purpose than self-enrichment. They worked to set the Prince's fortune on a sound and viable basis.

Their letters made no reference to personal matters. They exchanged facts and figures and not endearments. It was wiser and more rewarding so.

Sometimes it would be two or three in the morning before Therese had finally tracked down some deposit debited instead of credited, some dividend mysteriously unpaid, some rental uncollected, some miscalculation in the sale of silver that did not tally with the market price.

Augustus never interfered. The success of Volume One cemented his trust in her. He was admirably looked after and he was stimulated, under her aegis, by a new ambition. If occasionally the old temper flared and he resorted to his former quixotism, Therese waited. He knew the danger signals. When the green eyes turned to glass and the mouth set, he wavered and quieted down.

It was more than tolerance derived from mutual benefits. They enjoyed each other's company. Out of their personal isolation an equable companionship emerged. Augustus fed on her suggestions, her efficiency, her concern for all he did. She, in turn, never forgot the enormous debt she owed him. He had given her the one thing that Fate had always denied her. She was, at last, secure.

But there were nights, when the great gales seemed to be tearing up the landscape, when the old terrors possessed her. She was haunted by fearful dreams—the crone with her needles, the body hanging from the rafter. She would run down empty streets in strange cities, crying for Saladin. She would ride up flights of steps into vast ballrooms crowded with jibbering puppets. Solomon was locking all the doors, locking her out. She was searching, searching for Henri by the river.

She would wake in an icy sweat. Had it all really happened? Was she still really there? She would wait, frozen and shivering, for the horror to return, the dread footsteps echoing on the terrace, the crash of the shutters. She would force herself out of bed, tiptoe to the window, and peer through the curtains at the white expanse of the abandoned garden to glimpse the specter of a wolf with yellow eyes.

There was the haunting dread that, in some unforeseeable fashion, Manoel de Païva would reappear to invalidate her marriage, to disprove her lie that he was dead.

Bundled in her fur-lined robe, with her candle casting great shadows on the walls, she would creep back to the study and resume her excavations into bank books and accounts. There were no phantoms in mathematics.

The second event that was to change her life occurred the following spring when she was out riding with Saladin.

The peasants were ploughing the drab fields. She noticed beside the furrows what looked like the bodies of small blackbirds. Wherever foundations were being dug or burrows hollowed out for the storing of turnips or potatos, these black deposits were turned up. She even noticed them in the forest by the winter's uprooted trees.

She examined these fragments of mineral with their iridescent specks and sent them to Berlin for analysis.

By the early summer, when she and the Prince left for Florence, she had all the evidence she needed.

The Piast estates and the surrounding countryside covered one enormous field of coal.

Part Five

---

3 Parisplatz

*I*N THE COURSE of his career as a journalist, Valentin Zorn had occasion to meet many of the famous and infamous who lived in Berlin around the turn of the century. By far the most fascinating was the Princess of Oppeln-Piast who was reputed to be the richest woman in Germany, if not one of the richest in the world.

She was one of those equivocal personalities around whom legends gather like clouds around mountain peaks. Not that she courted publicity; she was indifferent to the world's opinion and did nothing to dispel the rumors, increasingly sinister as time passed, that arose from her activities in the worlds of industry and finance and, later, politics, that is to say the dark underside of politics seldom reported in the press.

Valentin first saw her as a boy at Marienbad where his parents went every year for the cure. He was immediately struck by an extraordinary couple making their way to the Kursale. The old Prince of Piast, bundled in furs, although it was the height of summer, advanced with little short steps, bent over a black cane, as frail and nervous as a spider. At his side his stately, patrician wife patiently adjusted her pace to his. She would have been a great beauty but for the coldness of her expression and her general air of remoteness.

The Piasts occupied a suite at the Grand Hotel and took all their meals upstairs. They apparently saw no one and went nowhere. Their isolation—or was it their exclusivity?—was complete.

They were always together, except in the afternoons when the Princess went riding on her superb black Arabian. Valentin was vastly intrigued to learn that this horse traveled everywhere with the Piasts in a specially constructed van attached to the back of their private railway car.

Ten years later he was to meet them in Florence where he was staying with an aunt who fancied herself as a devotee of the arts. She collected painters more than their paintings and was a determined social climber as well.

She took Valentin with her one afternoon to the Demidoff villa in the hills below Fiesole which the Piasts rented each year. The impression made on him at Marienbad was intensified when he saw them again at close range.

He was an observant youth and it was clear to him that the Prince of Piast, as cadaverous in extreme old age as the mummy of Ramses III, was completely under his wife's thumb. It was her strength of will which kept him alive at all. She was a sort of Svengali who had created this apotheosis of an internationally revered expert whose word on matters pertaining to arts was law.

She had arranged this gathering with the Prince as the star attraction. He was enthroned in a high-back chair like a monarch ready to receive ambassadors. The Princess introduced connoisseurs and curators, supervised the conversation, and cut it short when she saw that the Prince was tired or no longer interested.

"He is *the* authority," Valentin's aunt assured him. "People come from all over the world to consult him. No museum will buy a really important work without his seal of approval. His *Memoirs of a Collector* are the definitive work on the subject."

Valentin, always interested in books, had drifted off to the library and was placidly browsing when the Princess suddenly came in.

"Have you seen Mr. Berensen?" she inquired.

"I'm afraid I haven't," Valentin answered, having no idea who Mr. Berensen was.

"He must be in the garden."

On her way out she paused and asked, "Have you found anything interesting? I'm afraid the owners of this place regard books as something to fill up the shelves."

"There's an edition of Goethe in Italian which somehow seems rather strange."

"*Kennst du das Land woh die Zitronen blühn?* There are so many lemons and oranges in the garden perhaps this is the Promised Land. What do you think?"

She smiled and, without waiting for an answer, went outdoors.

Valentin longed to detain her, to talk about books, about anything. He was dazzled by something superb and regal in her manner. But she was a very great lady and he was only a college student.

Twelve years were to pass before he saw her again.

At twenty-seven Valentin joined *Die Zükunft*, a controversial paper edited by Maximilian Harden, an intrepid crusader for causes with which Valentin did not always agree. Harden's passion for sensationalism occasionally warped his judgment. *Die Zükunft* was the standard bearer of reform and how better to promote reform than by uncovering corruption? In his later years Harden came to believe that corruption lurked everywhere, except in his own conscience. Like many reformers he ended by doing more harm than good.

Valentin served his apprenticeship covering fires and railroad accidents, was promoted to murder trials and society scandals and started to make a name with celebrity interviews, unusual in that they were incisive without being malicious. His innate good nature inclined him to give his subjects the benefit of the doubt.

One day Harden summoned Valentin to his office.

"I'm giving you an assignment which I'll admit in advance is impossible. You know who the Princess of Piast is?"

"Of course. I met her once years ago."

"You met her? How the devil? Nobody meets that woman. She's as shrouded in mystery as the Sphinx."

"I was taken to her villa in Florence, a long time ago when her husband was still alive."

Harden leaned forward across his desk. He was a commanding figure of immense energy with a shock of iron gray hair and the self-hypnotic eyes of a fanatic.

"I want to get to the bottom of what she's up to. We all know she made a fortune out of the coal mines, but her activities go far beyond that. She has some sort of hold on Eulenberg and through him she's lent huge sums of money to the Kaiser in return for concessions—railroads and timber—or so it's said. And she's hand in glove with Talaat Bey, the Sultan's henchman, one of the most unsavory characters at large in Europe. Whenever there's some shady political maneuver or an underhanded deal that ruins a lot of people she's had a hand in it. I'm not expecting that she'll reveal any of her secrets to you. Just try to see her. Find out anything you can."

"How do you propose I should do that?"

"That's your business. You're a journalist. There's a gold mine there if we could ever tap the vein."

It was impossible to get an introduction to the Princess. Eulenberg, the Kaiser's confidential adviser, was far beyond Valentin's reach.

In the end he was forced to resort to the obvious expedient of writing a letter, giving his credentials and asking if she could spare him half an hour of her time. He was specially interested, he stated, in labor-management relations and would value her opinions as the owner of the largest coal mines in eastern Europe. He reminded her of their precious meeting which he was quite certain she would not remember.

While he was waiting for an answer he embarked on a program of research. Considering the extent of her achievements there was precious little information available. Even that little was staggering.

It seemed that, having found coal on her husband's estates, she had spent ten years quietly buying up the surrounding countryside until she owned over two hundred thousand acres of southern Silesia. Farms, villages and forests passed into her hands. All these purchases were apparently financed out of her husband's money.

The Silesian Coal and Coke Company expanded rapidly and the profits were soon enormous. Experienced industrialists predicted that the sheer impractibility of transporting coal from such a remote region would cripple further progress. The Princess built her own railroad over her own territory. Coal continued to flow to Breslau in a never ending stream and from Breslau to Berlin and throughout the German Empire.

It was outrageous, but everything concerning the Princess of Oppeln-Piast was outrageous. In the 80s any woman in business was suspect, but a woman in industry was ipso facto notorious. Furthermore the Princess introduced innovations that were considered revolutionary, in the exact meaning of the word. She was a capitalist with the wildest socialist ideas. At conclaves of industrial magnates and financiers where she was the target of ceaseless discussion, she was condemned as a threat to the economic system. What was inexcusable was that while defying accepted standards, she continued to pile up gigantic profits.

She paid her miners double the normal wage. As a result the Silesian Coal Company was besieged by workers from all over Germany, Austria and Poland. It was Holy Writ that cheap labor protected profits. The Princess proved that the opposite was equally true. She instituted reforms that exceeded anything remotely considered by such established firms as Krupp. Apart from building a model village, she provided her workers with free medical care and accident insurance, a school for the children, a hospital with a resident staff and a lending library, all housed in the former Piast mansion, Radoom, now entirely surrounded by smoke stacks, trolly lines and factory buildings and shrouded in a perpetual pall of smoke. Workers were encouraged to hold meetings, to present complaints, to offer suggestions. There was even a maternity ward where miners' wives could have their babies under medical supervision.

The trade Unions and the Socialist Party resented the Princess quite as much as rival industrialists. She was taking the ideological bread out of their mouths. If Capital voluntarily conceded that labor had the right to live decently what future was there for Socialism at all?

So much for the coal mines! The Princess' subsequent activities were concealed by an impenetrable smoke screen. Valentin was unable to unearth a single clue that corroborated Harden's suspicions of her dark designs.

As he had half expected he received no answer to his letter and, taking the bull by the horns, presented himself at the Piast Museum in the hope of, somehow or other, gaining admission to the top floor where the Princess lived.

It was the most elegant museum in Berlin.

In the spacious lobby a lady, discreetly stationed behind a desk, presented one with a visitors' book which one was required to sign.

Most museums at that time were a hodgepodge of miscellaneous objects crowded into cavernous, ill-lit rooms. Here care had been taken to group examples of different styles and periods with sufficient space between them so that their individual qualities could be enjoyed. There was never too much of anything so that the attention became fatigued.

Down the center of the rooms on the ground floor, glass-topped cases displayed a dazzling array of little boxes for snuff, cosmetics and bonbons, many set with precious stones, with miniatures on their lids. Along the walls were cabinets of celadon, Chinese blue and white, Sung vases and a marvelous array of Delft and Meissen. Valentin was specially charmed by a small anteroom of miniature stage sets, perfectly lighted and ready for a performance by elves and pixies.

The upper floors of the old Piast mansion were given over to paintings and a library which offered comfortable chairs and desks for historians and scholars.

The Piast Museum was a fitting memorial to the Prince's remarkable taste and to the Princess' organizing skill.

Valentin had wandered into a room overlooking the garden which contained fine examples of the early Italian school, including a superb Duccio Madonna. With a start of delighted surprise he recognized the Princess who was consulting with two guards over the hanging of a picture. They were holding it up for her at various levels while she considered it in relation to its prospective neighbors.

She had changed very little with the years, the same lithe, statuesque figure, the same imperious poise of the head. Only her features had set into the chiseled pallor of a Canova marble.

Great wealth had given her the authority of a queen and perhaps, Valentin thought, of a commanding general as well.

He waited until the painting had been hung to her satisfaction and then went boldly over and introduced himself.

"I had the pleasure of meeting you once at Florence. I am the journalist who wrote to you a week ago."

"Oh yes," she replied without interest. "I should have answered you, but you know I never give interviews."

"I assure you I'm not interested in gossip. What concerns me are the innovations you introduced at Radoom which have given rise to such controversy."

"There's really not much to say. It seemed to me obvious that men who have to spend most of their lives underground have the right to a decent living. I pay them little enough as it is."

"You've been branded as a humanitarian who is also mad. That seems to be the worst stigma you can earn in the eyes of Industry."

"I try to run my business in a practical way." She added with a smile, "I think what annoys my competitors is that Radoom is the only industrial center that never has strikes."

She was about to leave when he insisted, "Couldn't you give me ten minutes? It would mean a great deal to me."

She relented with a touch of impatience. "All right; I'll give you ten minutes. Do you mind coming upstairs?"

She went to a side door which she unlocked. It led into the private section of the mansion. Valentin congratulated himself on the ease with which he had crashed the barrier.

The top floor was divided into her private apartment and offices where secretaries and accountants worked. Her living room was sparse and businesslike, the walls lined with maps like a military headquarters. The rattle of typewriters could be heard from an adjoining room.

She took off her hat and went to the window.

"I have to keep an eye on my old horse, Saladin. He's twenty-three now, but he still enjoys the garden on sunny days."

Saladin was leaning against a statue in a contemplative mood.

"Is that the Arabian you used to ride at Marienbad?"

"Did you see us there? Yes, we're very old friends. We've been together for nineteen years."

For a moment he glimpsed behind that formal mask a more human, even vulnerable, self. She went to a wide executive desk on which were piled an array of newspapers in different languages such as one finds in a man's club.

"Which paper is it you work for?"

"Die Zükunft."

"Then I must be careful what I say."

"My editor is inclined to favor anyone who dares to affront the Establishment."

"I never set out to affront anyone. What seems to annoy people is that my methods produce results." She had opened the *London Times* and was glancing across the headlines. "I wasn't always rich. Before I married the Prince I had no money at all. Poverty is the greatest human indignity. It drives people into taking all sorts of desperate risks. I determined when I started the coal mines that no one who worked for me would ever have as little as I had at one time."

"Not many people remember the bad times."

"There are things one never forgets."

She looked up past him toward the window and beyond.

"What made you embark on a career as an industrialist?" Valentin asked.

"Chance. When I discovered coal on our estate I studied mining. It didn't seem too difficult to start a company. I studied management as well. Half the disorders that disrupt industry are due to shortsightedness. Why fight over salaries when, by giving workers a fair wage and decent living conditions, you save the time lost in strikes? I never lost any money by recognizing that miners are human beings."

"Do you think of yourself as a Socialist?"

"No. All capitalism is essentially exploitation. If one is going to exploit people one may as well sugar the pill."

"That sounds as if you're a cynic."

"Life made me into a realist. I don't approve of society as it is, but I'm certainly not a financial Joan of Arc."

She got up and went back to the window.

"People always try to put things in categories. One is supposed to be either a Conservative or a Radical, an Imperialist or a Republican. What does all that mean? Any system works if it's run by dedicated, selfless men. Such men seldom exist so that all systems turn out to be much the same. We're not born free and we can't achieve freedom. The poor are the victims of the slavery that poverty imposes, the rich are victims of the system that made them rich. Capitalism breeds Socialism; it's inevitable. As a capitalist I see no reason to hasten the day of judgment."

She broke off abruptly as though realizing that she was not alone.

"Have I told you anything you wanted to know?"

"Has it made you happy being a female Midas?"

"It keeps me occupied."

"And interested?"

She shrugged. "It's a game—like chess."

She stared at him without seeing him as if he were one of the maps on the wall.

"I suppose I am a cynic. I sometimes think that I miss what's inside people because I can't help seeing what's outside so clearly. Perhaps I miss what poets and churchmen call the soul."

She brought the interview to an end abruptly. "I have to get through all these papers before dinner. They never tell the truth, but I try to piece the falsehoods together to find out what's going on."

In the course of this short meeting Valentin had completely fallen under the spell of this strange and compelling woman.

He asked on an impulse, "Do you ever accept invitations?"

"Not when I can help it. Why?"

"Would you have dinner at my home one evening? I'd like you to meet my wife and son. I know they'd find you as fascinating as I do."

"Take them to the circus, Mr. Zorn. They'll find the performing seals more amusing."

"I give you my solemn word that nothing you say under my roof will be used against you."

The invitation was so unexpected and, on the face of it, so impertinent that she looked at this young intruder with surprise. He was a distinct cut above the average journalist, both well bred and well mannered. A combination of enthusiasm and kindness gave him the appearance of good looks. He reminded her a little of Vittorio as she had first known him in Paris, except that Valentin Zorn was more intelligent and obviously ambitious.

She was about to refuse when she thought, "Oh, why not? It's years since I went out. There must be some limit to isolation."

"I am not asking you as a journalist," Valentin assured her. "It would be a very great honor."

She stood up and held out her hand in an odd, almost military way.

"Very well. I accept."

"You mean it? You'll really come?"

"When do you want me?"

"Would this Friday suit?"

"What time?"

"At eight."

"You had better write down your address."

The Zorns lived in the Charlottenburg district in a pleasant, rambling apartment filled with plants and books. Valentin's English wife, Dolly, was used to her husband's impulsive invitations which sometimes turned into friendships that were useful to his career.

"She'll have to put up with an English dinner," Dolly declared. "Mulligatawny soup, steak and kidney pudding and a raspberry fool."

"She's a most unusual woman, not half as overbearing as she first appears. I fancy she has very few friends."

By an irony that Valentin always slightly resented it was not he who became the Princess' friend but his son, Hugo, who was then nine years old.

Hugo was a rather withdrawn boy, serious to the point of solemnity. He had his English mother's peaches and cream complexion and his German father's respect for learning. He kept his own counsel and had a good deal of self-respect.

Up to the last minute Valentin expected a note from the Princess begging off on the grounds of a previous engagement. To his surprise she appeared promptly at eight o'clock. She was simply, but elegantly, dressed in Nile green taffeta with one large green brooch and a double strand of jade beads. "Dressing 'down' for the middle classes," Dolly thought.

She proved disarmingly simple. She found the Zorns an agreeable change from the financial tycoons she was occasionally forced to go out with. They were warm, unpretentious and obviously devoted.

Hugo was dressed up for the occasion in his Eton suit and collar. He thought the Princess the most marvelous person he had ever seen, especially as she treated him without any of the condescension adults usually display with children. He brought her a glass of sherry and a napkin and offered her a plate of canapés. Hugo's manners were ceremonious.

"What are you studying at school?" the Princess asked.

"The usual. Greek is my favorite subject."

"Ah, how nice! Mine, too. What are you reading?"

"We've started the Iliad."

To Hugo's astonishment the Princess quoted a complete passage in Greek, the description of Helen's first encounter with Paris.

"You know it all *by heart*?"

"Only the parts I like best. You must go to Greece one day. When you see the temple at Sunion on that cliff above the sea, in that sunlight that falls straight from the sky without casting shadows, you'll understand why the Greek ideal is imperishable."

"What ideal is that?"

"Light and space, beauty and reason. That's the world I would have liked to live in."

Hugo was captivated. When dinner was announced and it was time for him to leave them, he looked so dismayed that the Princess intervened. "Oh, but I shan't have an escort. Can't he stay up this once?"

"Oh, please, please, Mama!"

Dolly, of course, gave in. Hugo offered his arm to the Princess and conducted her into the dining room, a proper cavalier. He drew up a chair and sat beside her. All through dinner he hung on her every word.

What Dolly had feared would be an ordeal turned into a pleasant, relaxed, almost family affair.

Afterward Dolly sang some of the Schubert songs she loved and a few Scottish airs in her flutelike choirboy soprano. She had retained the easy charm of her English upbringing. She brought fresh air into the house and trod, not on carpets, but the soft green lawns of home.

At ten-thirty the Princess rose to go.

"I have truly enjoyed it," she said to Dolly. And to Valentin, "If you're going to write about my endeavors you'd better go to Silesia and see for yourself. I'll send you an introduction to the foreman. He can show you 'round."

Hugo was loath to part with her and insisted on bringing her cloak and seeing her to her carriage. As she was getting in she gave him her hand.

"Come and see me, Hugo. I'd like you to meet Saladin."

She waved good night and drove away.

After Hugo had gone to bed in a daze of first love, Valentin flopped down on the sofa beside his wife.

"Well, what do you think of her?"

"She's very gracious and very intelligent."

Valentin detected a note of doubt. "But—?"

"I don't know; she frightens me a little."

"Why?"

Dolly had no pretensions to being an intellectual, but her intuitions about people were generally accurate.

"Something has died in her—where the heart should be."

"I thought she was particularly warm, especially to Hugo."

"I mean as a woman." She would say no more.

The following day a large box of roses arrived for Dolly, the promised introduction for Valentin, and a beautifully bound copy of the *Iliad* for Hugo. It was her personal copy, bound in green leather and stamped with a crown over the letter S.

It was the beginning of a branch of the Piast library that was to occupy a treasured place in Hugo's room.

Armed with the Princess' letter Valentin left for Radoom.

Coal mines are not uplifting to the spirit, but Valentin found Radoom particularly depressing.

The gloomy countryside was a network of tracks along which trolleys rattled, laden with coal, huge sheds and chimneys belching smoke. Inroads had been hacked through forests and one could hear in the distance the crash of timber and the dull boom of explosives. Everything was coated with a film of soot.

The model village was neat enough; rows of uniform dwellings with grime-encrusted plots in which washing hung on lines, as dirty by the time it dried as when it was stuffed in the washtubs. There was a desultory general store, a gin shop and a church. All other necessities were brought from Breslau.

In the midst of this hive of industry the old palace of Radoom stood shamed and desolate, palled in a cloud of smoke.

A factotum in a soiled uniform showed Zorn around. The handsome rooms, their walls covered in rich fabrics, were grimy and unappealing. Rows of chairs awaited a meeting never destined to be convened. As a center intended to relieve the drab monotony of the miners' lives the Hall of Rest and Recreation had certainly not fulfilled its purpose.

In the huge walled garden where a few wan roses bloomed on blackened briars a few children were at play.

In one room at the end of the downstairs corridor a man was lolling in his shirtsleeves with his feet on a table and a bottle of Schnaps beside him. He was the doctor, obviously going to seed like the rest of the establishment.

"What do you think of the amenities provided for the workers?" Valentin asked.

"What amenities?"

"Well—all this."

"Why do tarts paint their faces? To make themselves look more presentable."

"You don't approve?"

"I'm supposed to run a free clinic to which nobody comes. People have no confidence in services they don't pay for."

"Why do you stay?"

"I'm paid more to do nothing than I'd earn working ten hours a day, in a country practice. It's all free; free medicine, free treatment, free advice. The Princess of Piast wants to make herself out to be a good Samaritan. I can't think why she bothers. She's rich enough not to care."

As Zorn was walking back through this necropolis of good intentions he asked the factotum who was shuffling along beside him, "Did you know the Oppeln-Piasts?"

"Worked for them as a footman. I was eighteen when I started here."

"What were they like?"

"I've still got a job here, don't I?"

Disloyally, Zorn tipped him. He had a flat putty-colored face and the drooping mouth of a confirmed grievance gatherer.

"I won't quote you. I'd like to know."

The sour Sudetan looked as if he wanted to spit on the marble floor.

"He was mad and she was a whore." He gave Valentin a sullen, defensive look. "And remember, I never said that."

The foreman of the mines, a harassed Danziger, saw Valentin to the cab that was waiting to drive him back to Breslau.

"It's very impressive," the visitor said politely.

"And expanding all the time."

"Do you have any personal dealings with the Princess?"

"I should say! The company's supposed to be run by a board of directors, but actually she sees to everything. She's very considerate and just, but woe betide you if the accounts are out by a single penny."

Valentin concluded that, despite her efforts to improve conditions, the Princess was no better liked than any other factory owner.

He wrote his article which he called "A Woman Against the World." Max Harden was furious.

"What the hell has happened to you, Valentin? I didn't ask

for a lot of slush that any seventeen-year-old schoolgirl might have written. I want an exposé, not an accolade."

"I wrote what I think is the truth. She's a very remarkable woman."

"Goddamn it, you know very well there's no place for sentiment in journalism!" He tossed the article aside.

He relented later and published it with a few caustic comments of his own.

The Zorns did not receive a return invitation from the Princess. Valentin was not to see her again for some time.

Neither he nor Dolly had any notion that Hugo was in the habit of stopping by at 3 Parisplatz on his way home from school.

It was Dolly who discovered a batch of letters in large lilac envelopes hidden by a shelf of books in Hugo's room.

Dolly had misgivings. It was, on the face of it, unusual for a sophisticated woman in her late forties to carry on a correspondence with a boy of ten. She had the ingrained British respect for privacy and hadn't wanted to bring the matter up before consulting her husband.

"Have you read them?" he asked.

"No. It's not that I mind so much. It's that he has kept them secret."

"You know that she's sent him books. Greek classics. There's surely no harm in that."

"I'm sure there's nothing to it. It just strikes me as rather strange."

Both parents were slightly embarrassed. They didn't want to appear to be early Victorian, but it disturbed them to realize there might be a side to their son that they didn't know.

"I think the best thing would be for me to call on the Princess," Valentin suggested a trifle sheepishly, "and let her know that we're aware."

"I'm sure her intentions are all right," Dolly said doubtfully, "but one hears so many disagreeable things about her, most of which, I grant, are probably not true."

They replaced the letters in Hugo's room, manfully resisting the temptation to read them. He already had seven volumes stamped with the Princess' crest, all bound in the same green leather. Plato, Aristotle, Demosthenes and the Moral Discourses of Epictetus. Although these works were of a sufficiently lofty nature to belie their doubts about the friendship of their son with this controversial woman, a certain suspicion remained.

Valentin collected Hugo from school one day and said casually, "I thought it would be nice to call on the Princess on the way home."

Hugo blushed scarlet. He did not welcome this suggestion at all.

They presented themselves at the side door of the Piast Museum where the old footman greeted "Master Hugo" as an old friend. He went off in search of the Princess and returned to report that she was in the garden and would receive them there.

She was sitting on a stone bench with newspapers strewn around her. Saladin was standing beside her with his head bent over her shoulder.

She greeted them pleasantly. Hugo kissed her hand in the approved fashion.

"Would you like to give Saladin an apple? There are some in the stable."

Hugo hurried off. The affinity between the Princess and her aged horse was touching. Saladin, from his attitude of fond attention, seemed to be reading the papers with her. Valentin was reassured.

"Has Hugo been here before?" he asked.

"Didn't you know?" The Princess' surprise was genuine. "He came by a few days after I dined with you with a bunch of violets. I was flattered. It's years since an admirer brought me flowers."

"I only ask because my wife found some letters from you in his room."

"He's been having trouble with calculus. I tried to help him. I hope your wife doesn't think I'm a bad influence."

"She was a little concerned because he hadn't mentioned it."

"He's an unusual boy. I think only children have more difficulty in making friends. I feel guilty about not asking you back. I enjoyed that evening!"

"I'd like you to know that the disagreeable things in my article were added by my editor. He objected to the generally complimentary tone."

"I thought the article was—extremely tactful."

Hugo returned with the apple which he cut into quarters with his penknife. The old steed was obviously failing, but he managed to chew the apple in a serious, ruminative way.

Valentin observed an easy *gemütlich rapprochement* between these three.

On the way home he asked his son, "Why didn't you tell me you'd been to visit the Princess?"

Hugo looked straight ahead. He said glumly, "She is *my* friend."

Valentin Zorn's work for *Die Zükunft* took him on journeys all over Europe. He was constantly en route for Paris, London or Rome. He would be back in Berlin for a few days when Harden would send him off on another assignment. Dolly complained that she had almost no family life anymore. Valentin sorely regretted this. And Hugo was growing up. He saw hardly anything of his son.

Harden summoned him one day and thrust a paper into his hand.

"You see? You and your sentiment! She's up to her neck in that, your precious Woman Ahead of her Time."

It was a notice announcing that Talaat Bey, the international financier and adviser to the Sultan of Turkey, Abdul Hamid II, had disappeared under mysterious circumstances. There were rumors of foul play.

"What has the Princess to do with this?"

"Plenty, you idiot! He was murdered in her house on the Bosphorus. All part of a scheme to get concessions from the Sultan to continue the Berlin-Baghdad Railway. I have it on excellent authority. Eulenberg was in on it and that means the Kaiser knows."

"Who on earth told you that?"

"I'm not here to give *you* information. That's your job. Get off to Constantinople on the first train and come back with a *story*, you hear? I don't want slush. Give me facts. Facts!"

As he rattled across the Balkans on the Orient Express, Valentin reviewed all he knew about Abbas Talaat Bey.

A cloak of murky mystery hung over the Turkey of Sultan Abdul Hamid II, known to the world as Abdu-l the Damned. His reign had started auspiciously with the promise of wide-spread reforms, but a disastrous war with Russia, which had robbed the Ottoman Empire of most of its European protec-torates, had reduced him to a paranoid recluse who smelled conspiracy everywhere, mistrusted everyone and, in his terror of assassination, cooked his own food over a kerosene stove like a street-hawker. He had immured himself in the Aleysit Palace on the Bosphorus in a labyrinth of false doors, mirrored walls, hidden passages and oubliettes.

Talaat Bey had been the chief of the Mabeyn, the unofficial circle of advisers who supplied information to the Sultan, car-ried out his orders, and took care of liquidating "subversive elements." They were, in fact, undercover agents, henchmen and killers, as well as being personages of great account.

Talaat Bey was well known in government circles all over Europe. He negotiated loans for the Sultan, ostensibly for pub-lic works, armaments, the merchant fleet, and civilizing pros-pects like the building of an enormous opera house, never used because the Turks detested Western music. Most of this money found its way into the Sultan's private coffers and no small percentage into the pockets of Talaat Bey.

Valentin knew him by sight. Imposing and obese like an overfed puma he had an air of corrosive power. His appearance did not belie his reputation for saturnalian excesses. He was reputed to have a penchant for blond European youths. There were dark tales of Nordic seamen snatched from the streets of Pera, oiled and perfumed, subjected to his lusts and then dis-posed of.

He was married to a cousin of the Sultan by whom he had a large family. He was said to have poisoned his eldest son who had joined the Bashnek, a dreaded secret society whose aim was to rid the Sublime Porte of just such officials as Talaat Bey.

Valentin put up at the Pera Palace, the most luxurious hotel in Eastern Europe. Many intrigues had been hatched in those marble halls behind the potted palms.

The first person he ran into was Jacques Pontoise, the ubiquitous correspondent of the Paris *Soir*.

"You don't have to tell me." Pointoise wagged a sagacious finger. "The city's swarming with our colleagues who are all here for the same reason. I can save you a lot of trouble, my dear Valentin. I'll share my secrets. Why not? It's my duty as a fellow scrivener and my pleasure as a friend."

Valentin was leery of Pontoise's confidences. They were generally deliberate misinformation designed to protect his exclusive line.

"He was murdered. Of course you know that. There's no question about it. No one disappears in Turkey. They finished him off, tied him in a sack and dumped him in the Bosphorus. That's the approved procedure. He was murdered in the Princess of Piast's villa—with her connivance. Oh no, I'm not exaggerating. It all had to do with the Sultan's refusal to renew the contract for the Berlin to Baghdad railway. He allowed it to get as far as Ankara and then held out for a further enormous sum which the German government refused to pay. Enter the Princess, very beautiful and mysterious, the ultimate femme fatale. She and Talaat Bey had been thick as thieves for years. They concocted any number of nefarious schemes that netted them millions—under the table. They were both without principles and he was expert at applying a certain pressure. You understand? So the Princess rents a villa. There are midnight conferences. Talaat Bey arranges an interview at the Aleysit Palace. She confers with the Sultan. The Sultan makes certain demands. He agrees to renew the contract on certain conditions, one of which is that she help him get rid of his old friend and confidant, Talaat Bey. Perhaps Talaat had been a trifle too rapacious over the years or perhaps he knew too many things that the Sultan would prefer forgotten. That's how things are arranged in the land of Arabian Nightmares."

"It's too preposterous. I'm quite sure the Princess had nothing to do with it. She doesn't need to resort to such measures. She's already as rich as Croesus."

"It's not money. How can you be so naive? It's power. Once you're infected with the virus of power there's no turning back. Look at Alexander, look at Napoleon. Megalomania! She's obsessed, don't you see, with the orgasmic passion for power."

"How do you happen to know so much about her?"

"I do my homework, my dear Valentin. It's my business to be informed. So—what happens? She makes an appointment with Talaat Bey to discuss developments. He comes to her house, as usual late at night, they have a glass of champagne, she hands over a sum of money, his fee for arranging the meeting. While they're chatting certain gentlemen appear. The Princess excuses herself for a minute and beats a hasty retreat to a boat moored at her dock. She was taking no chances. The Sultan might have had the intention of finishing her off as well."

"You're in the wrong profession, Jacques. You'd have made a fortune writing penny dreadfuls for housemaids."

"You think it's too melodramatic? You're right, it is. But this is the land of melodrama. Turkish politics would drive Jules Verne to drink."

"What proof was there that Talaat Bey was murdered?"

"They found his overcoat in the lobby, the attaché case with the money, two champagne glasses and an amber cigarette holder that belonged to him. There was no question that it was *her* villa. She left all her clothes behind when she fled."

"And the body?"

"You don't think the Sultan would be crass enough to leave a body around! He was very sympathetic. He turned the attaché case over to Madame Talaat to alleviate the anguish of widowhood. The denouement of the whole affair which I'm sure you know, since Berlin is your bailiwick, is that Madame de

Piast got the contract for the railway, that was her commission for the murder, and she has now sold it back to the German government. As you say she has no need for money. But power, my dear boy! What a test of power!"

"Thank you for this illuminating report." Valentin concluded this meeting. "I'm sure I shall read the true story in the Paris *Soir*."

He learned very little more during his few days in Constantinople. There were a number of variations to the main events. What was disquieting was that, give or take the differences in the details, the Princess had undoubtedly played a central role, to what precise extent it was impossible to determine.

Valentin found the villa, a large sugarcake building, screened by palm trees and cypresses, with gardens going down to the Bosphorus, the perfect setting for such a drama. There was a motor launch moored at the dock.

Valentin dropped his report on Harden's desk.

"There are no facts. If you want facts you'll have to invent them yourself. No one knows what happened to Talaat Bey."

As a result of two coincidences that occurred later on Valentin was able to piece together what he came to believe was the solution to this mystery. A few of the details the Princess supplied herself.

A few months after his visit to Turkey Valentin ran into her at the railroad station at Bucharest. He'd been sent to report on the opening of the new Roumanian oilfields at Ploesti.

He recognized the tall, commanding figure at once as he hurried to catch his train. She was swathed in chinchilla with a gray turban that sported two white aigrettes.

She greeted him like an old friend.

"Are you going to Berlin? How lucky! Dine with me tonight. My car's at the back of the train."

She traveled in great style with a chef and two footmen in a suite that would have done credit to the Czar.

After dinner Valentin said, "Look here, Princess, I have to tax you with something because you almost cost me my job."

"How did I do that?"

"I was sent on a wild goose chase to find out what really happened to Talaat Bey. Several people I talked to thought that you'd had something to do with it or, at least, that you knew something about it. My editor was furious because I refused to mention your name."

"How chivalrous, Valentin!" She seemed greatly amused. "Yes, I knew something about it. He arranged a meeting for me with the Sultan. Would you like me to tell you about it? It was one of the wilder episodes of my career."

She was in an expansive mood that evening and settled back with her feet on the sofa and one of those long Russian cigarettes she occasionally smoked, the kind that are wrapped in brown paper.

Seeing her again, in the wavering gaslight, Valentin asked himself how it was that a woman still so beautiful should have so little sexual appeal. Dolly had been right. Some essential element was missing. Perhaps her extraordinary life had stifled her capacity to surrender. She wasn't really a woman, but a sort of high priestess who no longer belonged to the ordinary world where people dreamed and suffered and fell in love. Or perhaps, as Pontoise had said, power had eaten away her heart.

"I wanted the Sultan's signature to a certain contract that no one else had been able to obtain. A great deal hinged on it. Talaat Bey contrived to arrange an interview, almost impossible because Turkish women play no part in business at all. The Sultan sees no one and conducts all his affairs through intermediaries. To put it mildly, he's a very eccentric man.

"I was brought to the Aleysit Palace in the dead of night, heavily veiled and alone. I'm not going to deny that I was frightened. We've all heard tales of Abdu-l's whims and furies and what they result in. I was not on an official visit and couldn't have appealed to the German government if anything went wrong. Besides I would never have had the chance.

"I was bundled in by a side door and led through a network of corridors where every corner was guarded by terrifying bash-ibazooks with scimitars. It was a nightmare from the Arabian Nights. There were a great many passwords given, whispered consultations through panels that slid open and shut without a sound. At last I was shown into a waiting room lined entirely with mirrors, lit by invisible lamps. It was eerie and absolutely silent. I knew that, although I could see nothing, I was being watched.

"I thought that the Sultan, wherever he was hiding, might as well see what I looked like, so I raised my veil. There was no chair or divan to sit down on. I stood there, surrounded by my own reflections. It was one of those occasions when reality fades into fantasy. I didn't know what to expect. I had visions of deadly snakes coiling out of concealed crevices, or the floor giving way and casting me into a pit of starving lions.

"At last a high-pitched voice summoned me. But there was no door. I didn't know which way to go. 'Avancez, Madame,' the voice commanded. I walked straight ahead into a pane of glass which fortunately opened and found myself in another chamber with sofas around the walls and mother-of-pearl furniture that glimmered in a ghostly way. But no Sultan.

"There was a painted screen in one corner and from behind it the squeeky female voice repeated, 'Avancez.'

"I came forward and peered 'round the screen.

"Abdu-l the Second, Sultan of Turkey, was crouching on a stool with his head grotesquely bandaged with a towel. He was a figure of utter misery, small and fat, with tiny bloodshot eyes and swollen, discolored cheeks.

"I didn't know what to do but, after all, he was the Sultan so I curtsied deeply and waited for him to speak.

"His first question was a sort of squeal in heavily accented French. 'Etes-vous bien musclée?'

"I was so taken aback that I didn't know how to answer. I mumbled something about not understanding. He screamed in even worse English, 'Are you strong? Can't you see? I have terrible toothache I'm in agony.'

"He hopped off the stool, gripping his head. He was in a delirium of pain.

"I could only think to ask, idiotic as it sounded, 'Has your Sublime Majesty seen a dentist?'

"'Dentist! Dentist!'" he shrieked like a tortured cat. 'I can't trust dentists. Here!' He darted 'round the screen and snatched up a pair of pliers, ordinary pliers that one uses to cut wire, and thrust them into my hand.

"He opened his mouth, pointed to a back tooth and yelled, '*Eh bien*, pull! Pull it out! I can't stand it another instant.'

"I've been in some bizarre situations in my life, but nothing to compare with being commanded to extract a tooth for the Sultan of Turkey.

"He was jumping about, stamping his feet and uttering cries of anguish. 'Now! Now! Get it out! I'm dying!'

"There was nothing for it. I was locked in with a lunatic in an inaccessible room in a palace bristling with guards.

"I pulled the tooth.

"Luckily it was rotten. One tug, a bloodcurdling howl, and I was standing with an imperial molar between the pliers. I thought the Sultan had fainted. He collapsed on a divan with the towel over his face.

"There was a silver pitcher on a table with goblets. I filled one and brought it to him. He came to sufficiently to take a gulp of water, rinsed his mouth and spat with full force on a priceless carpet.

"After a few moments he peeked out from behind the towel and said in a normal voice, 'I thank you.'"

"And then he signed the contract for the Berlin to Baghdad Railway?" Valentin asked.

The Princess smiled and stubbed out her cigarette.

"'That,' said Scheherezade, 'is a tale for another night.'"

He didn't see her again on that journey. By the time he reached Berlin the Princess' car had been uncoupled from the train.

The following summer Valentin was able to fit another piece into the puzzle.

He had demanded a holiday, well earned after four years of unremitting toil, and decided to gratify Hugo's burning desire to see Greece.

It was a pilgrimage of love for Hugo. He knew the legends and history of every place they visited. The Princess had done her work well. The Zorns had no need for a guide.

They were invited on a cruise through the islands by Nikos

Kafrides, a shipping magnate and a distant cousin of Valentin's mother.

One day of brilliant sunshine as they were sailing through waters as iridescent as a peacock's tail, Hugo, with a cry, ran to the rail.

"Look, there it is! Sunion! Oh, isn't it beautiful!"

It was there on the cliff, pale as ivory, an indestructible statement of man's pride and hope in the face of eternity.

"It's exactly as the Princess said!" Hugo exclaimed as if his soul were flying over the sea to that temple, so white and alone and splendid. It was impossible to believe that there could be evil in a woman who had inspired such enthusiasm.

"A Princess?" Kafrides winked. "Your son keeps fancy company."

"My friend the Princess of Piast is a classic scholar," Hugo said stoutly. "She can recite the *Iliad* by heart."

"The Princess of Piast? You know her?"

"Well, Hugo does. Do you?"

"Oh yes," Kafrides chuckled. "She's sailed with me on this yacht."

Like all Greeks from the islands Kafrides had something of the spirit of Ulysses. He was a rugged dreamer who, along with making a fortune, thoroughly enjoyed his life.

That night, after Hugo had gone to bed, they sat on deck, moored in the little harbor of Samos. The lights of the village twinkled like stars in the darkness and the strains of a zither drifted from a taverna.

Kafrides was in a mood for anecdotes.

"Yes, I know her," he repeated. "A remarkable woman, unique in her way. Mind you, not someone I'd care to tangle with. She's ruthless, I fancy, and utterly wasted. She should have married Philip of Macedon or one of the Caesars or Napoleon. It's a sign of our mediocre times that she was ever involved with a third-rate scoundrel like Talaat Bey."

"You know about that?" Valentin was at once alert.

"Indeed I do." Kafrides chuckled. "It came about in this way. I'd had dealings with her before through one of her agents. She concocted a scheme for building trawlers to carry her coal to various ports in the Levant, impractical because the weather in these parts is too uncertain for the sort of vessels she had in mind. One day I received a message; I should say a command. I was to send a ship at once to one of the islands in the Sea of Marmore and have it ready for immediate departure. Well, you know I have a taste for adventure, so I sailed this yacht through the Dardanelles and anchored at Principo, about half an hour from Constantinople. Sure enough she appeared in the middle of the night in a motor launch with a man I later discovered was Talaat Bey.

"He was shaking in his boots as if the Devil were after him. She was cool as a cucumber. We set sail at once. Talaat Bey remained locked in his cabin. We talked, she and I. I shall never forget those talks. She knew so much about the world, men and politics, but it was a bitter knowledge. I would not describe the Princess de Piast as a happy woman. She's unfortunate."

"Why unfortunate?"

"She's wasted like a great actress in a provincial touring company. I let them off at Corfu. When I got back to Athens the papers were full of Talaat Bey's disappearance. They even said he'd been murdered. You'll forgive me, Valentin, but I don't have much confidence in the press."

"Are you sure it was Talaat Bey?"

"Of course. He lives at Nauplia in a secluded villa with a retinue of young men. I see him sometimes in Athens, so heavily disguised that it's impossible not to recognize him. I fancy he comes in to collect his dividends."

Kafrides tossed the butt of his cigar overboard. It fell with a faint hiss into the black water like a spark from a firework.

"She saved his life, I've no doubt of it. She outfoxed the Sultan and whoever else was after him. She has that kind of courage. Oh yes, an exceptional woman. I must say I can't think why she went to such trouble for that repulsive specimen. He wasn't worth saving, in my opinion."

It was always like that with things one heard about the Princess. One version contradicted another.

Perhaps all along, Valentin thought, only Hugo had known the truth.

In the somnolent heat of the Italian summer Therese was leaning on the balcony of a small hotel on the lake of Garda. The fierce downpouring of light on the enameled water dazzled the eyes and cast over the awning and the walls silver and gold reflections like a shoal of tropical fish.

She leaned, motionless, entranced by the warmth and light, in a lilac peignoir with her hair loose about her shoulders. Time had dulled its burnished brilliance. It was darker now and flecked with gray.

Not a sound rose from the garden. Drugged by the heat the beds of yellow stock exuded their honeyed fragrance.

Vittorio Scotto came out of the sitting room and leaned on the balcony beside her. For some moments neither moved.

"We should have come to live here years ago," Vittorio said.

"I don't recall that you asked me."

"I didn't know you then."

"It took you twenty years in Mexico—?"

"I didn't understand what went on in your mysterious heart."

"I wasn't mysterious. I wanted a man to take over and put an end to all that uncertainty. That's why I married Augustus."

"Only for that?"

"No. I wanted the money too."

She smiled at him with yellow-green eyes, somnolent as a lioness.

"You made a new life for him as you did for me."

"I gave you an opportunity, that's all."

They stayed there, basking for some moments, and then went indoors.

"So here we are twenty years later, two very rich people. We have everything and we're alone."

"You're not alone. You have a wife and four children."

"I'm alone with a family."

"Don't you like them?"

"The boys are handsome, spoiled and selfish. My daughter's

a firebrand and very headstrong. I must have been thinking of you when I engendered her."

She was watching him through half-closed lids. Twenty years of prosperity had transformed the young Brutus into Caesar. He was an impressive figure. The classic features were heavier and the thick black hair was gray.

"Why haven't you remarried?" he asked.

"Independence becomes a habit, too difficult to break."

"Shall I order breakfast?"

"Coffee and fruit for me."

Over their meal Vittorio asked, "Am I to know the reason for this mysterious meeting, in this remote hotel, far from all prying eyes?"

"I wanted to see you again and also we have to talk. There's trouble brewing."

"What about?"

"I think the Baden brothers are going to contest the Prince's will. They've been on my trail for some time."

"After so long? How can they?"

"They've been gathering information. There are things in my past before I met you that could be used against me. Legally there's not a great deal they can do, but they *might* make a case with good lawyers because of who they are and because of my reputation. I'm supposed to be a very evil woman."

"Because you made a success of the mines?"

"In this instance because of my influence over Augustus. As far as you're concerned it would be wise to take precautions."

"I never doubted that my inheriting the mines was your idea."

"That's what they'll say and it won't be so easy to disprove, since I handled all his affairs."

"Did he agree they should be left to me?"

"He didn't disagree."

"Did he know?"

"All that concerned him was that his collections should be preserved intact, and those I saw to."

"Frankly, I was astonished the family didn't do something at the time. After all, they are blood relations," said Vittorio.

"They did nothing for Augustus, except wait for him to die. Fortunately nothing was entailed. What they'll try to prove is that he was senile and that I forced him to sign the will."

"Did you?"

"I didn't need to exert force. He did whatever I told him."

Vittorio finished his scrambled eggs and poured out a cup of coffee.

"I don't want you to be dragged through a lawsuit on my account. I'd rather give up the mines. I'm rich enough as it is."

"I have no intention of their getting anything."

She stubbed out her cigarette. He saw something implacable in her face, a force of will that was disagreeable in a woman.

"Where is your money invested?" she asked.

"In the States mostly, some in Spain. I also have properties in Mexico."

"Would the government be interested if you offered the mines for sale?"

"Undoubtedly. It would take time, of course. Deals of that size entail a lot of palaver in Mexico with bribes up and down the line. As a matter of fact there's been talk of nationalizing companies that are foreign-owned."

She held out her cup which he refilled.

"My advice is to sell the mines as quickly as possible," said Therese. "Once they belong to the Mexican government there's not a great deal the Baden brothers could do. Move all your money to the States and put it in numbered accounts. I'll show you how that's done."

Vittorio lit a cigar.

"You're certain it's going to happen?" he asked.

"Whether it does or not it's as well to be prepared. And don't talk of making a settlement. You gave Augustus nineteen years of your life—six in Paris and Radoom and thirteen in Mexico."

"I know nothing about your life before you married; they

can't say anything about you after. You were a wonderful wife to him."

"Who would ever believe that I really cared about him? We were happier together than I ever imagined possible." She added with venom, "I'll see them in hell before they get a penny."

Suddenly she dismissed the subject, got up and stretched. "Let's go 'round the lake. It's such a glorious day."

An hour later they boarded the little steamer and sat on deck as it chugged 'round the lake, stopping at dreaming villages, passing great villas, painted yellow and pink, with gardens half hidden in trees. The hillsides where the vines were ripening rose to the mountains that, even at this time of year, were powdered with snow.

They got off at St. Germiniano and lunched at a small inn, shaded from the sun by a pergola covered in wisteria. Violet petals floated down and settled in their hair.

She was simple, charming and relaxed and he began to find in her again the young woman who had so dazzled and mystified him and who had remained a haunting enigma throughout his life.

After lunch they strolled, arm in arm, up a lane between workmens' cottages, bright with geraniums and fuchsias. At the top of this incline they turned idly along a road by a cypress hedge and came to an ornamental iron gate. They peered through into the loveliest garden they had ever seen.

"Let's go in," Therese whispered.

A narrow pool in which pink and white waterlilies floated divided a profusion of flowers that reminded her of the garden at the Pavillon. A foam of roses billowed against clumps of early delphinium and rhododendron, clusters of lupins, peonies and white daisies. This enchanted carpet was spread before a square, rose-colored villa with long shuttered windows. Bougainvillea and jasmine wandered across the walls. The air was drowsy with the hum of bees.

A gardener emerged from behind a rose bed. He had a very old face, wrinkled as an apple, and gnarled hands that had absorbed the wisdom of growing things.

"I'm sorry," Vittorio said. "I'm afraid we're intruding. It looked so inviting through the gate."

"Welcome, signori. Welcome. It is a fine old garden, quite famous on the lake. I like to think it belongs to me because we have spent our lives together. Please, look and enjoy. The lady who owns the property is not here now. There are terraces in front with many unusual trees."

"Who lives here?" Vittorio asked.

"An English lady, but she is seldom here. Sometimes in the summer for a while. Please, signori, be welcome."

The perfect garden opened onto a perfect view. The whole panorama of the lake and mountains was spread before them. In front of the villa was a terrace set with urns, profuse with geraniums and petunias. A paved walk led down through a succession of terraces on which ornamental trees were blooming. The air was somnolent with scents and the drone of insects.

On each terrace there were surprises, nooks where flowers bloomed in secret, small statues screened in branches, white seats that invited daydreams. The lowest terrace overlooked a cove where a blue rowboat drifted. Ripples of lazy water brushed against the rocks.

Vittorio looked back at the house, only a glimpse of which was visible through the branches of a white laburnum.

He said suddenly, "This is exactly what I have always dreamed of. If I buy this place will you come and live with me here?"

She was taken aback and laughed. "My dear, how could I?"

"Listen, Therese, and understand. I've had years to think over what happened between us. Granted I made mistakes or perhaps things just happened that way. My relations with my wife are purely formal. She lives for her social round, her charities and her religion. My sons will be going to university soon and my daughter's going to Paris to study singing. I've done my duty by them and I always will. But don't I have a right to some happiness? Don't you? Half our lives are already over. I'm forty-eight. I have perhaps twenty good years ahead. Why should I waste them? I've worked hard. I feel I deserve something. So do you. I'm ready to sell up everything and clear out of Mexico. My wife can go back to Spain which she's always wanted. Get rid of your coal company and all your commitments. Is that all your life is going to be? Business troubles and litigations? We could be happy here."

"Yes," she agreed. "We could be."

"I mean this, Therese. I was never more serious in my life. It only needs one decisive break."

"What makes you think you would be happy with me? I'm not the same woman you knew."

"You are—underneath. I know all you did for Augustus, all you did for me. I'll make up to you for all that. I can make you happy, Therese. I'm wiser now. As to what people will say—I don't give a damn. Let's forget Vittorio Scotto and the Princess of Oppeln-Piast. We'll be two anonymous people living our own life in this garden, by this lake."

He went to her with outstretched hands and as she took them she had the momentary illusion of being back at the Pavillon with Henri. The last thirty years seemed unsubstantial as a dream.

"You don't even know if the owner wants to sell."

"I'll offer so much she won't be able to refuse." He shook her arms as though to awaken her to a decision. "It wasn't by accident that we met again or that we came here."

"It's a beautiful idea, Vittorio, the sort of idea that belongs to this enchanted spot."

"It's not often that one gets a second chance, Therese."

She moved away along the terrace. She was suddenly filled with a longing to experience the youth she had never had. It was astonishing that her heart that had grown so hard could respond to this offer of happiness. What was there, after all, in Berlin? A museum filled with things that were now public property, endless involvements and intrigues to make vaster and vaster sums that had long since ceased to have any personal value. What *was* her future? To own more, amass more, to be stifled by the never-ending struggle to achieve some sort of mythical supremacy?

She turned and looked at Vittorio. He had always been good

and loyal. He had rescued her once before. If she could make a life with Augustus who had never been a man, why not this godlike creature she had once loved and who was offering her happiness across a gulf of time?

She came back and took his arm. "There's no harm in asking the gardener for her address."

"Will you consider it?"

"Why not? It's no madder than most of the things that happen in life."

The old gardener was waiting for them with a bouquet of roses, peonies and lupins which he presented to Therese.

"What is this place called?"

"Belgirate, Signora."

"Belgirate." She savored the name as if it were a magic spell.

"Who is the owner, this English lady?" Vittorio inquired.

"She lives in London, Signor. Far away."

"Will you give me her name and address? I'd like to write to her."

This presented a grave problem for the gardener. He laboriously spelled out the information as Vittorio wrote it down.

"La Signora Dyson-Taylor. Numero Quartordici Il Terrazza Eton, Londra. Inghilterra."

"Thank you. And thank you for letting us look 'round." Vittorio pressed a note into the old man's hand. "I'm glad you're here. You and this garden belong together."

They went back, light-hearted as children who had made a great discovery.

"I feel young again," Vittorio declared, flinging an arm 'round Therese. "As though I were twenty, starting out in life—with you."

The spell was still on them at dinner. Therese was wearing one of her pale green dresses with a stole of gold-thread tulle. She seemed softer, more human, more feminine.

"I remember that ruby ring." Vittorio took her hand across the table. "You always wore it."

"It belonged to my father. This jade necklace Augustus gave me."

"And that barbaric brooch?"

"That was given to me by a man I was going to marry."

"What became of him?"

"He was drowned at sea."

"I'll give you Belgirate. Will you wear it—with all the flowers?"

"And the old gardener, too."

As they lingered over coffee in the hotel lounge where a violinist was scraping out Strauss waltzes, Therese asked, "What does your family look like?"

"They're all good-looking."

"Have you a picture of them?"

"Why do you want to see?"

"No special reason."

He took a snapshot from his wallet.

She examined it closely, holding it under the lamp.

A plump, rather severe matron seated stiffly in a carved chair, flanked by three serious youths with raven hair and proud dark eyes and a wild-looking girl staring defiantly into the camera.

"What are their names?"

"The eldest is Marcantonio, the next one is Allessàndro, the little one is Paolo. The girl is Lucretia."

"She wants to be a singer?"

"She has a fine contralto and a very bad temper, as you can see."

They made love that night. He had not lost his prowess as a lover. Their bodies remembered and found in their embraces an echo of the young people they once had been. All their adventures and misadventures fell away. These were the shadows of their lives.

As they lay together afterward, Vittorio said, "Love never comes in the guise one expects. I think I have always loved you. But you married so quickly, before I could understand."

"It was the wrong time. I was so frightened and insecure."

"You do know that I'm serious, that I meant every word I said. I want this for both of us, Therese. It's a chance that won't come again."

She lay for a long time beside the sleeping man. The past stretched out before her like the path of silver that shimmered across the lake. Her mind went back and back—so many people and places—darkened stages from which the actors had long since fled.

She knew that any woman in her right mind would seize the opportunity that Vittorio had offered her, but she also knew, with a bitter certainty, that happiness is a capacity that has to be exercised like a gift for the violin. Her destiny had been set long, long ago in dingy warren of the Muranov. It dragged her forward to its appointed end.

When he came in to join her for breakfast she had gone.

An envelope addressed to him was propped up against the vase of flowers from Belgirate.

It contained the picture of his family which she had taken from his wallet in the early hours.

These were dazzling times, but dangerous times. Europe danced and the floor beneath it trembled.

The kings and Grand Dukes, the great ladies and the great cocottes, indistinguishable in their furs and tiaras, thronged to Monte Carlo and Biarritz and threw away millions at roulette. American heiresses took over the aristocracy and South African millionaires raced across the Continent in their shining cars. There were more and more strikes, riots and assassinations. Three hundred people were shot down in the snow before the Winter Palace at St. Petersburg and the same night the Grand Duke Serge gave a masquerade party at Venice that cost eighty thousand pounds.

Valentin Zorn had resigned from *Die Zükunft* and was now a roving correspondent for the *London Observer* of which Dolly's brother was the political editor.

As he rattled across Europe in the wake of crisis after crisis Valentin could not suppress the ominous awareness that the great gilded bubble was soon to burst.

The incident at Turnu-Magurela brought Europe one step closer to the brink.

A group of Bulgarian soldiers had crossed the border near

the town of Nicopol, marched into Roumania to the garrison stationed at Turnu-Magurela and surprised the commandant and his officers at a regimental dinner.

Before the astonished Roumanians realized what was happening, the Bulgarians opened fire with Maxim repeater rifles, slaughtered the commandant and six of his aides and then blew up the headquarters with a couple of well-placed bombs.

Unfortunately, in their hasty retreat, one of the Bulgarians was shot and another wounded. The interrogation of this man revealed that these marauders were not Bulgarian soldiers but members of a secret society called the Oltenia, after that province of Roumania which they claimed should be part of Bulgaria, for reasons too complex for anyone but an Oltonian to understand.

Although King Ferdinand of Bulgaria maintained that he knew nothing of this outrage, perpetrated by imposters, King Karol of Roumania demanded an explanation. If the Bulgarian government was not responsible, then who was? Who had provided the uniforms, who had equipped the terrorists with the latest Maxim rifles? Who—followed by a string of thunderous Balkan threats—was behind this act of perfidy and provocation?

By the time Valentin reached the Hotel Metropole in Sofia the bar was already crowded with correspondents, those cognoscenti of disaster. The answer to the riddle of Turnu-Magurela was beginning to emerge.

Jacques Pontoise, who knew everything two days before it happened, cornered Valentin in the bar. It was a perfect setting for Ruritanian intrigue. The Metropole was a tawdry facsimile of the Pera Palace in Constantinople, marble columns, red plush, fake Oriental carpets and a forest of potted palms. In an adjoining room an orchestra was oozing syrupy waltzes while opulent ladies in black silk and pearls waited for assignations.

"It looks as though our favorite Medusa had been up to her old tricks," Pontoise confided. "She's here, you know. Oh, by the merest coincidence! On her way to Constanza for a cruise through the Black Sea! She was forced to break her journey at

Sophia due to the inexplicable carelessness of the Orient Express. You know she always travels with her horse in a special van, tacked on to the back of her private car, so that she can enjoy a leisurely canter whenever the train stops at a wayside station. Due to an oversight the van was accidentally unhooked at the border. She arrives at Sofia. No horse. She is distraught. And what do you suppose was *in* the van along with the pampered beast?"

He sat back with a gleam of triumph in his eye.

At that moment a man entered the bar. His appearance immediately caused a subdued stir among the reporters. He was both impressive and repellent with a sinister hawklike face and an air of mysterious authority. Valentin recognized him as Basil Zaharoff, the representative of Vickers Maxim, already on his way to becoming an armament king.

Pontoise vanished.

Valentin watched Zaharoff as he proceeded with measured tread to the reception desk. A moment later he stepped into the elevator and was borne to the upper regions.

A few moments later Pontoise rejoined his friend.

"As I thought he went to her suite on the second floor."

"And what *was* in the horse car?" Valentin asked.

"A horse. That must be admitted. But, secreted under the hay, was a Vickers repeater rifle, identical to those used in the raid on Turnu-Magurela."

"You have an obsession about the Princess. When I last saw you you accused her of murdering Talaat Bey who I later discovered is living peacefully at Nauplia."

"Gossip! Sheer gossip! Of course he was murdered. But Talaat Bey is child's play to what is happening here. Do you realize what will happen if Roumania declares war? Austria will back Bulgaria. Russia will support Roumania. And if Germany takes sides, so will France and England. We are on the eve, my dear boy, on the very brink, of an international war."

While they sat arguing over the fate of Europe, they heard in the street outside that sound which, of all others, strikes dread to the heart, the tramp of regiments, the clatter of horses and the rumble of heavy wagons.

Someone came into the bar and announced, "Bulgaria is mobilizing."

This was it then! *Der Tag!* Someone had lit a match to the powderkeg. Everyone at once thought of their homes and families and wondered how soon they would be involved.

Valentin sent his card up to the Princess, not for a moment thinking that she would see him. As he was going in to dinner he was handed a note by a pageboy.

Will you dine with me in my suite at seven?
Therese O-P.

She opened the door herself. He was shocked by the change in her. She was painfully thin and haggard. Her eyes had an unnatural glitter.

"What a relief to find someone civilized in this dreadful city!"

"What are you doing in Sofia?"

"A stupid muddle over my horse. It got lost on my way to Constanza. Not Saladin; he's too old to travel. But my beautiful Irish hunter. They unhooked the car by mistake somewhere along the line."

"Can't they find it?"

"They have. It'll be here tomorrow."

She led the way into a sitting room and indicated that he should help himself to a drink.

"Constanza seems an unlikely place to go hunting."

"I heard of an island for sale in the Black Sea. I thought it would be nice to have some place where one could be completely cut off."

"You live on an island now."

"I want a cottage by the sea where I can be at peace."

She lit a cigarette. He could tell from a slight shaking of her hand as she held the match that she was chain-smoking.

"I hate this stupid, uncivilized country. And now these two absurd kings firing off ultimatums. Do you think there'll really be war?"

"I hope the Great Powers will intervene."

She asked abruptly, "How's Hugo?"

"He's at school in England, but I expect you know that. He'll be coming home for the holidays next month."

"I'm very fond of Hugo. Your wife didn't understand that. I suppose she thought I was a corrupting influence. Most people seem to think that."

"I'm sure he'll call on you when he's in Berlin. He thinks very highly of you."

She talked in a staccato fashion as she gulped down a whiskey and soda. He had never seen her in such a state of tension before.

She was listening with one ear to the steady tramp of feet in the avenue outside.

"Hugo wrote me some very interesting letters."

"What about?"

"His studies. At least I inspired him with a love for Greek thought. I hope you don't think that's subversive, too."

She finished her whiskey and peered through the curtains into the illumined, menacing night.

"War—it's inconceivable! All those men—" She turned back abruptly. "Why does everyone mistrust me? People think I'm incapable of honest intentions."

"Doubtless because you make too much money and because of the company you keep."

"Whom do you mean?"

"Basil Zaharoff. Hardly a man to inspire confidence except for people who traffic in arms."

"It's his business. I've helped him occasionally. If governments didn't buy from Vickers they'd buy from some other firm."

"No doubt it's just a coincidence that whenever war's about to break out, he's always first on the scene."

She was moving about the room in a scarcely controllable fever of anxiety, waiting for the news that she both dreaded and counted on.

"Why do they think it's a crime that I make money?" she demanded. "It's what most men spend their lives trying to do."

"It's not that you make money, but how you make it—or how they think you make it."

"What are they saying about me now?"

"That you and Zaharoff engineered the raid on the Roumanian garrison."

She stopped dead, her eyes brilliant with fear and anger.

"That's absurd. I know nothing about military encampments. It was anyway up to the Roumanians to protect their border. They think I run a school for terrorists?"

"They think the arms were hidden in your horse car and that it was lost on purpose."

She laughed in an ugly, strident way.

"They'll accuse me of leading the raid myself, disguised as a Bulgarian officer."

"Did you?"

"Of course. Why else should I travel about with a horse?"

She flung the menu into Valentin's lap. "Order what you want. I'm not hungry."

He let the tension subside a little and then asked in the patient tone one uses with invalids who won't follow their doctors' orders, "Why do you bother with all this, Therese? You're rich enough as it is."

"Would you stop being a journalist if you happened to be rich?"

"If you insist on meddling in Balkan politics, you have to put up with what people say about you."

"I don't meddle in politics. I sell coal and lend money and sometimes I bring people together who are useful to each other. That's my business as writing articles is yours."

Valentin remembered Kafrides. "It seems such a waste of all your potentialities. You don't need to shut yourself off on an island to have a wonderful life."

There was no escaping the insistent tramp-tramp of army boots and the clatter of cavalry horses. The whole of Bulgaria seemed to be marching past the windows, marching to death and glory—if there was any glory in another unnecessary war.

She lay down on a chaise longue and shut her eyes. She had a right to be bitter at the imputations leveled against her, but Valentin had the feeling that in some distorted, perverted way, she relished them. It was part of a deep-rooted disgust for the world and for herself because she was part of it.

"It's different for you," she conceded. "You have a wife and son, a home—a normal background to rely on."

"So could you, if you made the smallest effort. You're a fascinating woman. You have absolutely no need to be alone."

"I've always been alone."

"May I remind you that we offered to be your friends? You never responded."

"Your wife would have grown to mistrust. She did anyway. Hugo understood. He was honest enough to form his own opinion."

"I simply don't understand you. What are you trying to prove? You could buy a villa at Florence like the one you used to rent, gather people around you. You'd be surprised how many there'd be."

"People who wanted favors, people who'd take whatever I gave them and then gossip behind my back."

"There was plenty of gossip I could have written about you. I chose not to do so."

There was no reaching her. She was bent on her own kind of self-destruction.

A knock at the door brought her quickly to her feet. Valentin heard her whispering in the hall. When she came back he saw that she was frightened, terribly frightened, like someone with vertigo looking down from a dizzying mountain peak.

"Something's come up. Would you mind postponing dinner?"

"I'm staying in the hotel if you happen to need me."

"Thank you, Valentin."

In the hall he came face to face with Zaharoff, that Cerberus of doom in whose veins ice water flowed.

As he went downstairs Valentin thought that things had reached a perilous state when the fate of nations hung on the ambitions of two such megalomaniacs.

As it happened war was not declared on that occasion, thanks to the swift intervention of France and England. Indemnities were paid to Roumania and, once again, the Balkans simmered down.

There must have been something to Pontoise's story because the next morning the Princess was escorted under guard to the station and sent back to Germany. Doubtless without her connections in high places she would not have got off so lightly.

The raid on Turnu-Magurela was followed by other incidents that led to the Balkan Wars and these, in turn, inspired a Serbian patriot, Gavril Princip, to take a pot shot at the Archduke Franz Ferdinand in the dusty little town of Sarajevo.

Meanwhile Europe danced and ignored the Day of Judgment.

Hugo was home from Malborough where Dolly had insisted that he be sent to school.

There is a time when parents begin to lose touch with their children. This was especially true with the Zorns. Despite Dolly's visits to England, Hugo was away from them for most of the year. Valentin felt guilty that his peripatetic profession had contributed to Hugo's solitary and undemonstrative nature. He was fifteen already, tall for his age, handsome in a solemn way and very well mannered. It worried his parents that he made no friends.

One evening when Valentin came home from his office, Dolly greeted him with one of the familiar lilac-colored envelopes addressed in the Princess' unmistakable hand.

"Don't you think that this has really gone on long enough?"

"Have you read it?"

"No. It was in his room."

On the face of it, it struck both the Zorns that there was something unhealthy in this persistent friendship between a boy of fifteen and a woman of fifty.

More from curiosity than a sense of parental duty Valentin opened the letter.

My dear Hugo,
   It was so kind of you to send me the two white mice which I find very interesting. I was touched that you should

have thought of me at this time. The loss of Saladin has been a great blow. He was nearly twenty-seven which is very old for a horse. Although I think he was as content as he could be during his last years that isn't much consolation. We were such very close friends.

I have bought a larger cage for the mice whom I have christened Castor and Pollox. You remember who they were, the brothers who loved each other, sons of Leda and the Swan.

The new cage has a wheel and ladders which provide them with exercise. They are intelligent little creatures who are already getting to know me. I'm sure in time they will become quite tame.

I have found it very rewarding to try and understand animals. They have their own sort of souls and thoughts. One must not simply train them to be of use or do tricks. One must try to fathom how they see things and how they feel.

Saladin gave me a wonderful friendship that never wavered throughout his life. When I bought him first in Paris he was wild and unmanageable. He had been badly treated and he was proud. He saved my life once when I was in danger. I shall always consider him to have been my true, perhaps my truest friend, and I mean that in the way that I am friends with you.

Thank you again, dear Hugo, for your thoughtfulness. I am glad that you are enjoying your school in England and that you have mastered calculus. Mathematics is not as dry as we are led to believe. It has its own beauty and its own secrets which it allows us to unlock. And it always gives us the right answers, unlike most things in this world.

My best and affectionate greetings and my warm respects to your parents.

> Always your good friend,
> Therese O-P.

The Zorns felt exceedingly foolish for having read this letter. "We'd better not mention this," Valentin said. "I suppose

Hugo is old enough to make his own decisions. Just put it back."

The news was all over the papers next morning. One might have thought war had been declared.

PRINCESS OF PIAST ATTACKED. BOMB THROWN BY
ANARCHIST. INJURIES FEARED FATAL.

It seemed that the Princess had just left three Parisplatz when a young man had dashed from a group of students who were on their way to the museum and flung a bomb at her carriage.

It exploded under the horses, killing them both, hurling the coachman to a distance of fifteen feet and the Princess into the street.

The coachman was severely wounded. At first it was thought that the Princess was dead. She was covered in blood and one side of her face was lacerated by flying particles of wood and metal.

The assassin was caught by some students who ran after him down the street. His name was Georgi Gionescu. What his motives were was never clearly established. He refused to reveal anything to the police, except that he had nothing personal against the Princess; he was opposed to the system she represented. He made a number of confused statements about injustice and the evils of capitalism. He was ready to die for his beliefs.

Hugo was horrified. Valentin went with him to the Parisplatz. The Princess had been moved to a hospital. There they were told that her condition was critical. It was impossible to say when she would be able to receive visitors.

Valentin couldn't help wondering, since Gionescu was Roumanian, whether this attempted assassination wasn't a reprisal for the raid on Turnu-Magurela.

The behind-the-scenes details of this drama were supplied by Heinrich Twadovsky, the Berlin Chief of Police, an old friend from Valentin's days on *Die Zükunft*.

"She's either a saint or a monster; I don't know which.

Almost as soon as she was conscious, while she was still covered in bandages and could hardly move, she insisted on carrying on business as usual. Secretaries came with papers and, contrary to doctors' orders, she received a number of visitors. Zaharoff came from London and Eulenberg, presumably from the Kaiser. A parade of bankers and magnates called and made tactful inquiries. One had the feeling they were anxious for news that she was sinking. No doubt her death would be greeted by a sigh of relief in financial circles.

"Her strength of will is prodigious, unnatural. She must have suffered appalling pain, but she flatly refused morphine. She had three operations on her hip which was completely shattered. Even while she was still in traction she fired off orders, dictated notes and held conferences. It was admirable, no doubt, but also a bit ghoulish.

"No one knew how much damage had been done to her face. The doctors did what they could. When the bandages were finally removed the results were as bad as they had feared. One side is terribly disfigured. She asked for a mirror and stared at herself. Her only comment was, "Now I look as horrible as everyone says I am."

"Your son came every day, but of course you know that. He always brought her a bunch of violets which she kept in a bowl by her bed. He wept when he first saw her. He's a fine, emotional lad.

"She sent for me one day and announced that she wanted to see Gionescu. I told her that was impossible. It was completely against regulations. She threatened to make trouble in high places if I refused her.

"Gionescu refused to go. He wasn't interested in her. He wanted to shout 'Long Live Anarchy' before a firing squad and die a hero's death. He's a typical dim-witted agitator, a wretched sort of nonentity. She got her way.

"I went with him, handcuffed, to the hospital.

"She was lying in bed. One was forced to see the full extent of the damage. One side of her face was twisted into a lurid Japanese mask. She has a scar down her forehead and another that pulls her mouth down at one side in a sort of grimace. I must say it turned one's stomach. She must have been a very beautiful woman.

"Gionescu stood with eyes firmly downcast. She said sharply, 'Look at me.'

"Her speech was slightly slurred. She kept dabbing her mouth to stop a trickle of saliva.

"He looked and expressed no emotion. He was only sorry he hadn't killed her because her survival reflected on his talent for throwing bombs. And also perhaps he was frightened. I don't blame him. She looked a terrible sort of Nemesis.

"'I hope you're satisfied,' she said.

"He grunted and looked away.

"'I suppose you're able to defend what you did. I should like to know your reason for it.'

"He mumbled, 'It was a blow for freedom.'

"'Did I prevent you from being free?'

"'Not you. What you stand for.'

"'What do I stand for?'

"He was uneasy. She was challenging his whole notion of himself, his chaotic ill-defined ideas of right and wrong.

"'What do I stand for in your eyes?' the Princess demanded. 'I would very much like to know.'

"'I said it's not you. It's the idea.'

"'Because I'm rich? Because I make money while you throw bombs?'

"'I know what I'm doing,' he blurted out. 'And I'd do it again. You're an—an exploiter of the masses. You make millions while millions starve.'

"'I starved at one time, but I learned to do something else.'

"'You—with your factories and your railroads! Revolutions happen because of people like you and as long as you're allowed to live the fight will go on. For justice!' he added, as though he'd forgotten that.

"'You'll lose. You know why? Because old ideas can only be replaced by new ideas. You have no new ideas, only slogans. I thought perhaps you were an idealist with some great vision of the future. I wouldn't have minded so much then. I've known many men like you. Kings, bankers, politicians, beggermen, slaves. You're all the same; mean-spirited opportunists. And stupid, the lot of you.'

"He was stung by the force of her contempt and for the first time recognized in her a genuine enemy.

"'All I have to say is that I'm sorry I didn't kill you.'

"'So am I, in a way. I would have tried to help you, in spite of what you did, if I'd seen some spark in you. But I see that you're not worth helping. They'll shoot you or hang you; it's all you're good for.'

"He let loose with a flood of guttersnipe abuse. I pulled him out of the room.

"He was outraged. 'Who does she think she is? Telling me I'm worthless! It's bitches like her who make the world into a stinking pesthole.'

"He was crying from sheer frustration as I bundled him downstairs.

"I think," Twadovsky concluded, "that was the most bizarre encounter I ever witnessed. But you know something? I believe if she *had* seen something in him, the real spark of an idea, she would have used her influence to get his sentence commuted. She's like that. She hasn't a spark of sentiment but she's just in her own rather brutal way."

Dolly had become increasingly disturbed by what she felt to be Hugo's morbid fixation on the Princess. Valentin was slightly put out because Therese had never consented to see him at the hospital. He had received only a formal note from a secretary thanking him for his flowers. The Zorns were relieved when it was time for Hugo to go back to school.

Two weeks later a card came for Hugo with a picture of a small hotel on the lake of Garda.

> *Dear Hugo, I am here and the sun is healing me. Thank you for all your kindness. You did more than anyone to see me through. With love from the old witch who is still, somehow or other, Therese O-P.*

It was a typical Italian landscape, a pergola festooned with wisteria and the pulsing blue of the lake beyond.

In due course Gionescu was brought to trial. He maintained a morose silence throughout the proceedings and when asked if he wanted to make a statement, shouted, "Long Live Anarchy!"

He was sentenced to twenty years.

When, in the spring of 1900, the famous lawsuit was announced, Valentin was taking a sabbatical in Paris. It was a happy time for the Zorns. They were able to pop back and forth to London and in consequence saw much more of Hugo. He had announced that he wanted to go to Oxford where he would major in Greek philosophy, a decision that came as no surprise.

The trial of the notorious Princess of Oppeln-Piast was the event of the Berlin season, eclipsing royal weddings, military reviews, race meetings and the opera. Valentin returned to Berlin to cover it for the London *Observer*.

The litigants were all socially prominent. Although they were only the sons of a titular monarch, the Princes Sixtus, Maximilian and Otto of Baden-Oldenburg occupied important positions. Maximilian was a commander in the Kaiser's Death Head Huzzars, Otto had married a daughter of the King of Italy and Sixtus was Berlin's most eligible bachelor. He had an outstanding talent for living beyond his means.

Their English cousins, the Hadleys, were less important, though they were members of the English aristocracy. The whole event was as exclusive as the guest list for a court ball.

A crowd had already assembled on the steps of the courthouse when Valentin arrived. He recognized several well-known hostesses, discreetly veiled. There were officials from government and financial circles, including Prince Eulenberg, the Kaiser's closest friend.

The press corps was in full force, including Jacques Pontoise, already scattering exclusive information about like rice after a wedding.

They all had reasons, Valentin reflected, to be against her, the hostesses because she had ignored them, the government officials because she had only dealt with their superiors, the financiers because she had outwitted them, and the journalists because she had never granted interviews. Valentin was one of the few present who was willing to give her a fair trial.

The court was a large gloomy chamber with a north light. It was soon agog with that twittering anticipation that precedes the opening of a play.

The Hadleys were the first to appear. The Marquess was an unconvincing figure with straw-colored hair, bulbous, washed-out eyes and a receding chin. His sister, Lady Honoria Fitz-George was loose-limbed, untidily dressed, with a large unbecoming hat and the abstracted air of a governess who had missed a train.

The Baden princes were more impressive, Otto and Sixtus in perfectly cut suits, with monocles and Maximilian in uniform with a fine display of medals, won not in battle but by fawning on the Kaiser. He had an air of haughty conviction that no court of law would dare to pass judgment against an officer of the Imperial High Command.

The Baden princes were represented by a regiment of frock-coated lawyers, headed by the celebrated Humbert Ratenauer whose court histrionics rivaled any star of the theater, including Bernhardt. He was a commanding personage with a beard trimmed to topiary perfection. With a voice remarkable for its range and resonance, he was a past master at the art of intimidation.

A tremor of excitement swept through the court when the Princess made her appearance. Valentin hadn't seen her since the attempt on her life. The change was shocking. She propelled herself forward with the help of a black cane. She was dressed in black with a long, fur-lined cape and a black hat with a cartwheel brim. The effect she created was demonic.

She was followed by Franz Martens-Stillman and two clerks. Martens-Stillman was not a trial lawyer. He was well known as a representative of industrial firms for whom he negotiated contracts. He worked for the government in matters pertaining to claims and indemnities and had handled the immensely complex problem of reparations after the war with France.

He had the metallic, concentrated manner of a man who

has spent his life doing accounts. A not injudicious choice, Valentin thought, in a case concerned largely with money. Largely, but not entirely, as Ratenauer was soon to show.

As this was not a criminal trial there was no jury. It was to be heard by three prominent judges who, in due course, filed in and, with suitable solemnity, took their places and declared the court in session.

Ratenauer rose and, in a portentous manner, presented his clients' case.

The late Prince Augustus of Oppeln-Piast had inherited a considerable fortune from his father, derived in the main from two silver mines in Mexico, together with extensive holdings in land and other investments. A list of these assets was available to the court. The Prince had had no issue, his only surviving relatives being his sister, the Dowager Marchioness of Hadley and her two children, and the three sons of his younger sister, the late Grand Duchess of Baden-Oldenburg. No other litigants were concerned in the present claim.

"On his death the Prince's estate was disposed of according to the terms of a will which, as I shall demonstrate, was drawn up and signed while he was not of sound mind and entirely under the influence of the woman he called his wife. Under the terms of this will the main portion of the Prince's estate was left to a former valet, Vittorio Scotto. The remainder was utilized by the woman who calls herself the Princess of Oppeln-Piast to finance the Silesian Coal and Coke Company and for many other transactions and investments which have resulted in the accumulation of a fortune estimated to be in the region of ten billion reichsmark."

What the plaintiffs were after, it became clear, was not merely the Prince's fortune at the time of his death, but every penny Therese had made. They wanted the whole damn lot.

"Seldom have I encountered an intrigue of such signal wickedness." Ratenauer's voice resounded through the court, "perpetrated by two people of such deplorable character, an adventuress who for twenty years has been masquerading under an old and honorable name and a servant who, through her connivance, rose to be the owner of silver mines worth millions.

Collusion, perfidy and the ruthless domination of a helpless and trusting man were the cornerstones of this conspiracy, as I intend to show."

The court was shocked to breathless attention. What did Ratenauer mean by "masquerading," by a woman the Prince had "thought of" as his wife?

Throughout this opening peroration Therese remained motionless as a statue in the shadow of her great black hat. From where he was sitting all that Valentin could see of her was one white hand, resting on a sheaf of documents, on which her ruby ring gleamed like a blood clot.

Ratenauer called her to the stand.

By a cruel mischance the witness box was angled so that only the damaged side of her face was visible to the audience. Valentin was horrified by the livid welt that disfigured one cheek and dragged her mouth down in a perpetual sneer. She looked every bit as wicked as Ratenauer was intent on making her out to be.

"In order to understand the full spectrum of the witness's stratagems and deceits, it is necessary to review the main events of her life prior to her meeting with the Prince of Oppeln-Piast.

Valentin thought, "She is going to be crucified." And she was, throughout a merciless interrogation that lasted for two days.

Her name was Therese Lachmann. She was a Jewess, born in the Warsaw ghetto, a fact which did not endear her to a German court. She was illegitimate, her father unknown. Her grandfather, under whose roof she had grown up, was the classic prototype of the scurvy moneylender and receiver of stolen goods.

Ratenauer depicted in broad and lurid strokes the underworld she had grown up in, among whores, thieves and criminals, crowded together in the unrelieved squalor of the ghetto. The thrust of his questioning tried to establish that she and her mother had been prostitutes, a fact she firmly denied.

"My mother was a beautiful girl who had been loved by a Polish nobleman. They would certainly have married if that had been possible. He supported her all her life and she never accepted the attentions of other men."

Ratenauer lingered over the horrific details of her mother's and grandfather's murders as though, in some way, she had been responsible. "You were arrested as a juvenile delinquent, were you not?"

"I was not arrested. I was taken into custody because I had no other relatives and was placed in a convent from which I was rescued by Henri Herz."

Her relations with Herz were debated for over an hour. She admitted to having met him on the street at night. Hadn't she been earning her living in the usual way?

"I was on the street because I was lost. I had only once been out of my grandfather's house before. Henri Herz took me to Paris, cared for me and educated me. When I reached the age of eighteen he asked me to marry him. His treatment of me was always impeccable."

"Are you asking the court to believe that you lived with him in the same house alone for three years without anything occurring between you?"

"That is exactly what happened. He loved me and I loved him."

"Doubtless in the same manner that your mother loved her protector. It was a tradition in your family, was it not?"

"There was no similarity at all. I was fifteen. He thought of me as a child. In fact at first he wanted to adopt me. It wasn't until I grew up that he thought of our getting married."

Ratenauer passed on to the next phase of her career.

"After Herz' death did you return to the only profession you knew?"

"I was nineteen. I knew no one in Paris. Herz' business manager had refused to produce a will and so I inherited nothing. He took me to a woman, a so-called Countess, who made her living by introducing young girls to rich men. I was supported in that manner for a year."

"You had more than one lover during that time?"

"Several."

"Your liaisons did not last long."

"It was a calling I found extremely distasteful."

"You mean the men you met weren't rich enough to satisfy your ambitions? You had set your sites on bigger game?"

"I meant exactly what I said," the Princess snapped.

"Hadn't you determined to ensnare one of the most prominent men in France, none other than the Emperor's brother?"

"The Duc de Morny was not a man whom anyone ensnared. He employed me in an entirely different capacity."

A long argument ensued over Therese's relationship with de Morny. Valentin had to admit that her explanation of having acted as a hostess in order to gather political information did not sound very convincing.

"Weren't you actually running a house of assignation where de Morny and his friends could meet women of a certain kind?"

"Women never came to the Chaussée d'Iena, except for the actress who first introduced us. They were old friends."

Ratenauer's scorn was gathering momentum. Was the witness expecting the court to believe that the Duc de Morny, with the entire French Intelligence at his disposal, would employ a young girl with no experience in the political world to act as—he hardly knew what to call it—a sort of spy?

"He saw something in me that he thought would serve that purpose."

"It seems a good deal more likely that these men gave you information in return for your favors."

"I never gave them what you call my favors. They talked. Sometimes I overheard things that I thought might be useful. De Morny was always anxious to know what was being discussed in Paris, what the Opposition was planning."

"You made a business of betraying confidences?"

"I had become friends with de Morny and the Emperor. I tried to be of use because they had rescued me from a life I detested."

Ratenauer was dumbfounded. "The Emperor of France became your friend, a young woman of no family, whose reputation, to put it mildly, was tarnished, for no other reason than that he liked your company?"

"I was accepted into their circle. The Empress wanted to make me a lady-in-waiting."

Ratenauer laughed outright.

"A Jewess who was being kept by her brother-in-law? I have heard many tales about the Empress Eugenie but never that she consorted with the demimonde."

"She was a fine and generous person. She understood that the circumstances of my life were not of my choosing. She wanted to change all that."

"You must have been, even then, extremely deft at deception."

"Unlike you, she was able to recognize the truth," Therese said sharply.

"I find it increasingly difficult to believe anything you say. And how long did this incredible arrangement continue?"

"About two years."

"Why did it end?"

"Something happened that made it impossible for me to continue."

"What was that?"

"An incident involving a member of a prominent German family."

She let the words drop deliberately like pebbles into a pond.

Ratenauer stepped forward and repeated in the hushed tone in which a death sentence is passed, "A prominent German family?"

The crowd waited on tenterhooks for another scandalous revelation.

"May we inquire his name?"

Therese looked at the presiding judge who started like an actor who has been given his cue.

He picked up his gavel and announced that the court would recess for lunch.

The corridors hummed with conjecture. The more daring whispered that the unnamed German could only be the Kaiser or at least some member of the Hohenzollern clan. Why else was Eulenberg present? Wasn't it to protect the imperial name?

Jacques Pontoise was of another opinion. He cornered Valentin in the lobby. "There's only one other family powerful enough to demand legal immunity: the Bismarcks. Of course she was referring to the Chancellor's nephew. He committed suicide in Paris under very mysterious circumstances at about that time. I tell you if every detail of that woman's life is dragged into the open any number of heads will fall. Did you ever hear such a pack of preposterous lies? She's a high-class tart, nothing else. Ratenauer will demolish her."

The court was agog when it reassembled. They were in for a disappointment. There was no further mention of the German who had ended Therese's career as de Morny's confidante. Instead Ratenauer renewed the attack on other aspects of Therese's life in Paris.

It was a deadly duel between the accomplished lawyer with all the tricks of the trade at his fingertips and the implacable woman with the ruined face, determined not to give an inch whatever impression she made.

"When you were under the protection, shall we call it? of the Duc de Morny, what name were you known by?"

"The Marquise de Païva."

"Was that a *nom de guerre*?"

"No."

"How did you acquire it?"

"I had married a man of that name."

"Oh, you had married. Was that another ambiguous arrangement or was it a legal fact?"

"It was legal, in so far as we signed a register."

"How long had you known this man?"

"I didn't know him."

"You married a total stranger?"

"It was a matter of convenience. De Morny thought it would look better if I were married and had a title."

"So he married you off to a friend of his?"

"They weren't friends. I don't think they ever met."

Ratenauer paused to let the general incredulity sink in.

"Let me understand this—if it is possible. You married a man you didn't know in order to acquire a title? Where did you meet him, on the street where most of your conquests seem to have been made?"

"I met him at the apartment of a mutual friend. He was a gambler who had ruined himself at roulette. He agreed, in return for having his debts paid, to marry me."

Ratenauer put on a great show of stupefaction. He looked 'round the court with a baffled smile that indicated the virtual impossibility of conducting a rational cross-examination with such a witness.

"And did you cohabit with this man?"

"No. After the ceremony I never saw him again."

"You never saw a man who had married, whose name you bore?"

"It was a business arrangement. We had fulfilled the terms."

"And what became of this unfortunate Marquis Manoel de Païva?"

"He went back to Portugal, as far as I know."

"You never corresponded with him?"

"No."

"You have never in all these years had a single word from him?"

"No."

"You never inquired if he were alive or dead?"

"No."

There was a momentous pause.

"Would it surprise you to know that the Marquis de Païva is still alive, living on his family estate at Cintra, Portugal?"

"It would not surprise me."

"You evince no interest, no concern?"

"He was quite a young man when I married him."

Ratenauer stared at her for a long moment in total silence. Everyone in the courtroom stared at her as well.

"Amazing. Truly amazing."

Having brought the court to the tantalizing question of Therese's marital status when she met the Prince, Ratenauer deftly returned to the mainstream of her life.

"When did you meet the Prince of Piast?"

"When I returned to Paris after spending a year in the country."

"That was after de Morny broke off relations because of the scandal mentioned this morning?"

"Yes."

"And because of the nature of that scandal you were no longer received by the Empress or the Emperor Napoleon?"

"I never saw them again."

"They dropped you, as the saying goes, like a hot potato." Ratenauer smiled at the use of this vulgar, if graphic, phrase.

"You might say so."

"Where were you living at that time?"

"In the house I had lived in with Henri Herz."

"How did that come about?"

"A settlement had been made over his will."

"Were you affluent at that time?"

"No."

"Penniless, would you say?"

"I had very little money."

"How did you live?"

"By selling what remained of my jewelry."

Ratenauer made a tour of the central area of the court and stopped before the witness box.

"How did you meet the Prince of Oppeln-Piast?"

"I was knocked down by his carriage."

"Knocked down? On the street? But I was forgetting, all your important encounters seem to take place on the street."

"There was a great crush of people. It was the eve of the declaration of war. I fainted in front of a carriage which ran over me and broke my arm."

"How providential that that carriage should belong to one of the richest men in Germany!"

"I had never heard of the Prince of Piast."

"You found out soon enough, didn't you? with the help of his valet, your lover, Vittorio Scotto."

"You seem to imply," Therese said sharply, "that I slept with every man I met."

"Didn't you?"

"I knew nothing about the Prince or his valet. I fell in front of a carriage that might have belonged to anyone."

"Yes, only it didn't. What happened then?"

"I was unconscious. It was impossible to get to a hospital. They took me back to the Hôtel de Piast and called a doctor."

"Isn't it closer to the truth that Scotto introduced you, without the Prince's knowledge, into his home so that you could carry on your affair?"

"That is ridiculous. I had never met either of them before."

"How long did you stay at the Hôtel de Piast?"

"Scotto and the Prince were extremely kind. They nursed me till I was well."

"And then, just out of kindness, the Prince took you to Germany?"

"It was during the siege of Paris. He had been ordered to leave. He asked me to go with him."

"You mean Scotto persuaded him for reasons of his own?"

"There was nothing between me and Scotto. We looked after the Prince because the other servants had gone. The three of us were alone."

"And so, because they had been kind to you and nursed you, and because you had no money and were already planning how to entrap the Prince, you went with them to Radoom?"

Therese answered disarmingly, "I had nowhere else to go."

The rest of the afternoon was taken up in trying to force Therese to admit that she and Scotto had been lovers. She stoutly maintained that they had never been more than friends. It was impossible to form any clear picture of what had happened between those three strange, disparate people in that half-ruined house in Silesia.

What Ratenauer succeeded in establishing was that Therese was an adventuress and an opportunist whose morals were dubious and whose intentions were suspect. Her appearance added a note of malevolence, of latent evil, all the more tragic to Valentin because it belied the good qualities that had inspired Hugo's devotion. He was infuriated by the silence of Martens-Stillman who never once rose to her defense.

The all-important question that everyone had been waiting

for Ratenauer timed to perfection. At five to five, when the court was due to recess, he suddenly asked, "Did Prince Augustus know when you married him that you had a husband living?"

It was the one moment when Therese, who throughout this long persecution had maintained an iron control, seemed to hesitate. She dabbed her scarred mouth with a handkerchief.

Ratenauer roared like an enraged bull, "Did he know you were committing bigamy?"

In the crash of silence that followed Therese answered, "No."

There was a scrimmage between spectators trying to get out and reporters trying to fight their way to Therese. By indiscriminate elbowing and shoving Valentin managed to break through the barrier. Therese was leaning on the edge of the witness box with a handkerchief over her face.

"Therese, quickly! I'll see you home."

She looked up. She was totally spent and seemed barely aware of where she was.

The reporters were on her like a pack of hounds, bombarding her with questions, demanding that she sit for newspaper sketches. With the help of Martens-Stillman who seemed to have no connection to the proceedings, as though he had strayed into the wrong court, they got Therese out through a side door into a room where lawyers conferred with their clients. Valentin buttonholed a departing clerk and dispatched him to find the Princess' carriage.

She was sitting at a table with her eyes closed, gaunt and pale as a cadaver.

"Why, in God's name, didn't you get proper counsel to defend you?" Valentin demanded. "Martens-Stillman hasn't uttered a word all day."

She looked at him with eyes from which all light had faded. "Their only hope is to blacken my character. I'll need Stillman when we get to the will."

"It was absolute madness to think you could conduct the whole thing yourself."

"This case is about money. I know more about money than Ratenauer. What they say about me doesn't matter. They've said it all before anyway." She took a long painful breath and leaned back. "It was strange, I began to wonder if any of it had really happened, if I wasn't the monster he made me out to be."

The clerk returned and obligingly led them down a corridor to a side entrance where the Princess' carriage was waiting. Valentin helped her in.

"Thank you, dear friend. I'd rather be alone now."

She sank back into the protective shadows.

It wasn't the money, Valentin thought as he walked away, but some burning paranoid need to be publicly brutalized, as though her disfigured face was not the result of a criminal act but retribution for some unnameable sin.

Unfortunately the law did not take into account that exceptional people attract exceptional events. She would be condemned for being what she could not help but be.

Valentin Zorn was not surprised by the morning headlines.

PRINCESS OF PIAST A BIGAMIST
PRINCESS A SPY FOR FRENCH EMPEROR
SCANDALOUS PAST OF MILLIONAIRESS

The press was determined to fan this trial into a cause célèbre.

The court was again crowded. A current of morbid curiosity gripped the spectators, that sickening orgasmic excitement of the arena where blood and brains are to be spilled.

The stage was set. The court rose as the judges filed in. Therese was recalled to the witness box, in the same ill-chosen black outfit, with the same black hat that made her look like the Witch of Endor. Ratenauer resumed where he had left off the day before.

"I want to get this quite clear; you never told Prince Augustus that your husband might still be alive."

"He assumed I was a widow. I saw no reason to disabuse him of that idea."

"You had no compunction at deceiving a man who, as you told us, had shown you so much kindness?"

"I intended to do the best I could for him and I did. We were very happy for thirteen years."

"You cannot deny that you lied? You knew that you had no right to marry the Prince of Piast."

"My marriage to Païva was a business arrangement, as I explained. I only met him on two occasions. It played no part in my life at all."

"But you signed a register?"

"Yes."

"You had a marriage certificate?"

"I may have."

"You were entitled to call yourself the Marquise de Païva?"

"It was an episode I considered over."

"You lied, you deliberately lied because you wanted the social position the Prince's name provided and because you wanted to get your hands on his fortune."

"I wanted security. It was a marriage of companionship. I ran the house, saw to the Prince's needs, helped him with his books. We led a full and rewarding life. It was a true marriage which my other certainly wasn't."

"Rewarding! It was certainly rewarding for you."

Ratenauer hammered away at the illegality of her union to the Prince. One couldn't deny that Therese had been, to say the least, exceedingly cavalier. She had made no attempt to obtain a divorce from Païva and had seemingly never made any effort to get in touch with him at all.

"You felt no compunction in masquerading as the Princess of Piast during the Prince's life and after?"

"The Prince wanted the marriage to insure that I wouldn't leave him. As it happens, I was devoted to him and he was, I think, to me."

"Whatever your highly original way of rationalizing your contempt for the law, I think we have clearly established that your marriage to the Prince was, in fact, no marriage at all."

It was obvious what peril Therese was in. She had had no right to the Piast name on which her fortune had been founded.

Ratenauer passed on to the next phase of her career.

"How soon after your so-called marriage did you start meddling in the Prince's affairs?"

"It wasn't a question of meddling. The Prince had never taken the slightest interest in money. He spent vast sums without ever inquiring how much he had. It did not take much knowledge of business to discover that he had been systematically cheated for years."

"You took it upon yourself to rectify that?"

"I tried to put his financial affairs in order."

"Had you had any previous knowledge of business?"

"None."

"Why didn't you employ a firm of accountants?"

"We were living in a remote part of Silesia. I had plenty of time and I found the work interesting."

"And so you gradually took control of the Prince's money?"

"I never took control of his money. I saw to it that it was properly administered. If you will examine the bank books you'll see that I succeeded in almost doubling his income."

"You made investments on his behalf?"

"He had money in accounts that had lain idle for years. I invested these deposits on his behalf."

"Did you discuss these investments with him?"

"He understood nothing about money. He trusted me to do what I thought was right."

"How convenient! This man you had tricked into marriage trusted you so completely that he allowed everything he possessed to pass into your hands."

"It did not pass into my hands, as the bank books will confirm. I acted as his agent, if you will."

"So that during those thirteen years of domestic harmony you were manipulating his fortune without his knowledge?"

"For his benefit, yes."

"And in what way did *you* benefit from this boundless authority?"

"I benefited to the extent that we lived in a style commensurate to his income."

"You didn't use any of this money you reclaimed to make investments of your own?"

"Never."

"Didn't you, shortly after your bigamous marriage, start to acquire property?"

"Yes."

"A great deal of property?"

"Yes."

"Several hundred thousand acres adjacent to the Piast estates?"

"Yes."

"Property on which you consequently launched the Silesian Coal and Coke Company."

"Yes."

"Did you have any private means at the time of your bigamous marriage?"

"I had a property in Paris which I sold."

"Am I to understand, then, that out of the sums you manipulated for the Prince you appropriated what you needed for these extensive purchases of land?"

"No."

"How did you acquire them then?"

"From loans."

"You borrowed money?"

"Yes."

"From whom?"

"The Prince initially, later from private banks."

"Would you elucidate?" Ratenauer, having brought Therese to the brink of disaster, was purring like a great cat before a saucer of cream.

"I discovered that there was coal on the estates and in the surrounding neighborhood. I realized the potential was enormous. I borrowed money from the Prince and started to buy land. The details of these transactions are all here at the court's disposal."

"Did the Prince object to lending you, the woman he thought of as his wife, such considerable sums?"

"He made no objection."

"Did he know for what purpose you wanted them?"

"He knew that I wanted to make money on my own."

"Did he know that you intended to turn his ancestral estates into a coalfield?"

"The estates were left intact until after the Prince's death."

"Surrounded by smokestacks, mines and factories."

"The estates were not entailed."

"He never objected, never made the slightest demur, to the home of his forefathers, the land that had been in his family for generations, being desecrated in this way?"

"We had gone back to live in Berlin. He never returned to Radoom."

"You saw to that, I am sure. And, after the Prince's death, who owned the Radoom estates?"

"They were bought by the Coal and Coke Company."

"The company you started, the company you owned?"

"I did not own it. I was a shareholder."

"Come, you controlled it, didn't you?"

"I tried to see it was run properly."

"I commend you for your infinite capacity for splitting hairs. So that all through those happy and rewarding years, when you were living with this man who trusted you implicitly, you were carefully feathering your own nest at his expense?"

"As I've already told you, I doubled the Prince's income. I made no money at his expense."

They were circling and circling the pivotal point of how Therese had started the coal mines and how valid her ownership was.

Ratenauer was in for an unpleasant shock.

"However you choose to put it, you cannot deny that you borrowed money from the Prince who thought of you as his wife. He leant you money in good faith because he supposed you to be the Princess of Oppeln-Piast?"

"He lent me money as Therese Lachmann, as all the documents will show."

There was a flurry in the courtroom. Martens-Stillman came to life sufficiently to produce some documents which he handed up to the bench. The judges studied them and they were, in turn, scrutinized by Ratenauer. During this uneasy lull Therese sat motionless in the witness box, shielded by the shadow of her witch's hat.

Ratenauer must have seen at once that his case had received a serious blow.

"I'm afraid I don't understand. Why were these loans made out to Therese Lachmann and not to the name you bore?"

"You have gone to great lengths to prove that I was not legally married to the Prince. I wanted to avoid any future question that the properties I was buying belonged to me."

"Isn't it closer to the truth to say that you cheated the Prince out of a second fortune as you had cheated him all along?"

"I borrowed money in my own name and I repaid it in full, with interest. There was no question of cheating. It was a business deal."

Ratenauer had been hoist by his own petard. Having established that Therese had had no right to marry the Prince, he could not claim that the Prince had had any marital rights over her properties. An individual man had lent money to an individual woman. Just how she had engineered this was a matter of conjecture. Perhaps he had known, perhaps she had tricked him, perhaps, as she maintained, he hadn't cared.

By the midday recess it looked as though, as far as Coal and Coke Company was concerned, Therese was in the clear.

Ratenauer must have realized that, as far as business was concerned, he was not a match for Therese. He now bent his efforts to proving that, having fallen into her clutches, the Prince soon became a puppet whom she manipulated at will and always to suit her ends.

His first witness was Baron Solomon de Rothschild, a legendary figure in Berlin and a senior partner in the financial empire that stretched like a spider's web across Europe—and far beyond.

The Baron had an air of mysterious power. He was Haroun

al Raschid with a veneer of Machiavelli, the guardian of international secrets locked in bank vaults.

"Baron de Rothschild, am I correct in saying that you handled the affairs of the late Prince Augustus of Oppeln-Piast?"

"The family had had an account of long standing at our Berlin branch."

"Did you have dealings with him personally?"

"After he returned from France we took charge of shipments of silver from Mexico which had formerly been handled by the Banque de France."

"These involved considerable sums?"

"They were considerable, yes."

"It is not necessary to remind the court that the House of Rothschild is one of the most highly respected banking firms in Europe."

The great financier directed an impassive gaze upon this mere purveyor of legalities. It was a little like asking Queen Victoria if the British monarchy was respectable.

"Shortly after he returned from France did you arrange a loan for Prince Augustus?"

"Yes."

"A large loan?"

"It could be considered so, for a private person."

"Did the Prince come to Berlin to arrange this matter?"

"Yes."

"Did meetings take place between you?"

"One, I believe. There may have been others with my associates."

"Was the Prince fully aware of the terms?"

"He signed the necessary papers."

"Did he handle the business himself or did he employ an agent?"

"He handled it himself."

"Would you say that, for someone who was not a business man, he was able to grasp the details that were involved?"

"I explained the terms, as I recall, and he accepted them."

"Prior to that time had you dealt with him exclusively in regard to his financial affairs?"

"There was not much for him to do. We collected the silver, disposed of it on the market and credited his account."

"How soon after his marriage did the woman who called herself his wife start to interfere in his affairs?"

"I am uncertain of the date. Perhaps a year."

"In what way did she do this?"

"She requested an audit of our bank statements going back several years."

"On what grounds?"

"She questioned certain of our figures."

"How did you respond?"

"I informed the Prince that it was not our custom to provide audits. They would require a great deal of paper work and consume a great deal of time."

"What happened then?"

"The Princess sent us an audit of her own. We compared the figures and found that there were—minor miscalculations due to the fluctuations in the price of silver."

"On whose authority did she do this?"

"I assume her husband's."

"After that did she exercise control over his affairs?"

"I couldn't say. The Prince's account was closed and his assets were transferred to another bank."

"On his orders?"

"No, on hers."

For the first time Martens-Stillman rose to cross-examine.

In the precise manner of an accountant, he succeeded in getting the great Baron Solomon to admit that the minor miscalculations he had referred to amounted to the goodly sum of two hundred thousand marks which, on the Princess' instructions, had been applied to reduce the capital of the Prince's loan.

This was a second setback for Ratenauer. He redoubled his efforts to prove that Therese had wasted no time in encroaching on every aspect of the Prince's life. Here Martens-Stillman proved his worth. He demonstrated how tirelessly she had worked to set in order the appalling muddle that had resulted from years of mismanagement and neglect. It also emerged that the appointment of Vittorio Scotto as overseer to the silver mines had not been, as Ratenauer insisted, merely the blackmail of a discarded lover. He had succeeded in putting a stop to bribes and misappropriations that had been an accepted custom with Mexican officials. Thanks to these two conspirators the Prince's income had steadily risen, year by year, until it had more than doubled.

The courtroom was dazzled by a pyrotechnic display of figures. Thousands burst into millions and millions into galaxies of marks, pesos, pounds and dollars. It was an Arabian Nights extravaganza with Therese constantly rubbing the genie's lamp.

Ratenauer struggled to keep afloat. He was drowning in a tidal wave of money.

He made a final stand to keep control of the proceedings by announcing, "I will move on to the question of the will."

Unfortunately at that moment the court adjourned.

The afternoon edition of *Die Zükunft* was already on the stands.

Valentin was appalled. A headline glared MERCHANTS OF DEATH. On the front page was a reproduction of Boecklin's famous allegory of the four horsemen of the apocalypse with Therese's face superimposed on the screeching hag who represented Death, while Zaharoff's hawklike features grinned from the figure of Death, brandishing his scythe.

A frenetic article denounced these emissaries of the Devil who made immense fortunes from the indiscriminate sale of arms. Thousands of innocent people were slaughtered, maimed or driven mad, cities reduced to rubble, by these plague-carriers who slipped through Europe in sealed trains in the dead of night.

It was an outrageous violation of the ethics of journalism, deliberately designed to affect the outcome of the trial.

Valentin strode into Harden's office.

"This is a disgrace. You had absolutely no right to publish this during the trial."

"Why not? If those judges haven't the guts to condemn her,

then I will. She should have been driven out of this country long ago."

"She has more right to be here than you do. This third rate scandal sheet you call a newspaper should be shut down."

"Get out my office! You call yourself a journalist! How much did that bitch pay you to be her lackey?"

"A trial is in progress," Valentin shouted. "She has the right to prove she's innocent."

"Innocent!" Harden hooted. "I have a dossier on your Woman Against the World that could get her hanged ten times over. You think she's spoken a word of truth in court—from Bismarck's suicide in her Paris stable to Turnu-Magurela to that pathetic old sodomist's will? You're a juvenile sentimentalist unfit to report anything but ladies' charity teas."

Both men lost their tempers. It was a futile confrontation that did no one, least of all Therese, the slightest good.

When Valentin got back to the courtroom they were still arguing over the will.

"Try and understand this—if that is possible," Therese was saying savagely. "The Prince wanted to leave me everything, the mines, the paintings, everything. All I asked him to do was to sell Radoom to the Coal Company. This he did in lieu of any other financial settlement. That is why I am not mentioned in the will."

"You, with your passion for money, gave up a fortune that ran into millions?"

"I didn't want to inherit money. I wanted to make it on my own. I wanted to be independent."

"You were aware, of course, that his blood relatives had a right to share in what was a family fortune?"

"The Prince had made substantial settlements on his sisters when he came into his inheritance. Their children were well taken care of."

"He felt, according to you, no sense of responsibility toward his own flesh and blood?"

"They had played no part in his life whatever. He had only seen them three or four times; his English nephew and niece he had never seen."

"And whose idea was it that the mines should be left to Vittorio Scotto?"

"He had proved to be an honest and able overseer for nine years. Before that he had looked after the Prince for six years in Paris. The Prince felt deeply indebted to him."

"So he decided, of his own free will, to disinherit his own family, in favor of a former servant?"

"Scotto was to pay one third of the revenue from the mines into the Piast foundation as long as they remained in his possession and this he did."

"Are they still in his possession?"

"I believe he has sold them to the Mexican government."

"On your suggestion no doubt."

"Not on my suggestion. I haven't seen Vittorio Scotto for twenty years."

"And where is Mr. Scotto now? Why has he ignored our subpoenas? Why has he vanished beyond the reach of the law? It's a truly remarkable, a truly incredible conspiracy! But there was a flaw, Therese Lachmann, in your brilliantly conceived cabal. One glaring and fatal flaw."

Ratenauer snatched up two documents which he flourished before the court. "The flaw is that Prince Augustus never signed the deed to the sale of the Piast estates. He never signed the will. They are forgeries, your forgeries, Therese Lachmann, as my experts will now show."

A general hubbub broke out. The presiding judge unavailingly banged his gavel and demanded silence.

It was some moments before order was restored.

For the rest of the afternoon the court was subjected to the testimony of calligraphy specialists who floundered through tedious minutiae about crossed *t*s and underslung *s*s, the significance of upward strokes and downward flourishes. Their consensus was that, granted the Prince's age and the normal deterioration that occurred in the handwriting of elderly persons, the two signatures were not those of the Prince of Piast.

This conclusion was rebutted by an elderly man who resembled a mole and appeared somewhat bewildered at being dragged from his cozy burrow into the light of day. He had been one of the witnesses to the signing of the will, the other two having passed away.

"Were you present when the Prince of Piast signed his will?" Martens-Stillman asked.

"I beg your pardon?" The mole obligingly cupped his ear.

"Did you see the Prince of Piast sign his will?" Martens-Stillman repeated.

"Oh yes, indeed. He was very frail at the time. His hand shook and his Honored Lady had to place the pen between his fingers because they shook so, you see."

"But he did himself sign the will?"

"Oh yes, sir. He gave me a gold coin."

Ratenauer swooped down on this witness. "Are you telling us—and, please try to be accurate—that his wife guided his hand across the paper?"

The old man thought for a moment. "Not exactly. No, I would not say that. But he was very frail. She had to show where to put his name on the document."

"Did she hold his hand when he signed it?"

"I could not say that, sir. No, not precisely."

"You were there. You saw what happened. Remember!" Ratenauer barked. "Did she or did she not help him to sign his will?"

Again the old man hesitated. He didn't want to commit himself to anything that might be a falsehood.

"As I recall she dipped the pen into the inkwell and handed it to him and then we put our names under his and he gave us each a gold coin."

"Did she order him to do what you saw him do?"

"Eh?" The mole, rather flustered now, cupped his ear again. "Ordered? Well—"

"For God's sake, man, can't you answer my question precisely? Did she either push his hand across the paper or did she assist him to write his signature? Did she tell him to sign it?"

"She pointed out the place, I think, the place on the document. But he signed it, oh yes, I'm sure. His Highness took the pen from His Honored Lady and wrote his name."

It was a close shave for Therese. Ratenauer was livid. The spectators were left with the sinister picture of an enfeebled octogenarian deeding away his fortune while his implacable wife stood over him.

The court recessed till the following day.

When Valentin got back to his apartment he found a telegram from Dolly. "Hugo has left school. On his way to Berlin. Is he all right?"

Valentin was startled. What with the trial and writing his reports and his fight with Harden, the last thing he wanted was to have Hugo on his hands. But then he reflected that, although Hugo was only seventeen, he was a sensible, self-sufficient boy who was used to traveling. Presumably he could get from London to Berlin safely. He had obviously read about the trial in the English papers and had decided to hurry to the side of his friend and mentor. It was quixotic and absurd and annoying and he certainly deserved a good dressing down, but Valentin could not resist a certain admiration for his son who had such a strong sense of loyalty and devotion.

He hurried to a nearby post office and cabled Dolly. "Hugo has not arrived yet. Do not worry. Will keep you posted."

He worked on his articles that night with one ear on the doorbell. Hugo did not arrive.

By morning Valentin was worried.

Hugo could have taken the overnight boat to Hamburg. More likely he had gone to Paris and boarded the express to Berlin. It was pointless to wait at the station. There were a number of trains every day from the French capital.

As the trial ground to its final phase the crowd in the courtroom thinned. The society ladies, deprived of the promise of fresh scandals, returned to shredding reputations over their tea tables. The Hadleys had faded into the woodwork. Of the Baden princes only Sixtus remained. The reporters fidgeted over their notebooks. Jacques Pontoise had already sent in a full report to the Paris *Soir*. The verdict was a forgone conclusion in his opinion. The Princess would lose the case, lose everything, and rightly. The weight of prejudice was too strongly stacked against her.

The morning was taken up with Ratenauer's efforts to prove that the Prince had been senile when he signed his will.

The court was subjected to the tedium of a series of professors with unpronounceable names who expounded in terms incomprehensible to the layman the nature of dementia in all its forms. Their testimony could not be more than tangential as none of them had ever met the Prince.

The Prince's publisher testified that, although he had brought out five volumes of the memoirs, he had never met the author. He had dealt exclusively with the Princess who had supervised every detail of the format, binding and illustrations and had personally corrected the proofs.

The architect who had renovated the Berlin house stated that all the plans for the museum had been the Princess', down to the bookcases, display cabinets, even the design for the light switches. He did recall the Prince making one tour of inspection and suggesting how certain paintings might best be hung.

Servants attested to the Prince's forgetfulness, his outbursts of temper, his inability to remember names and dates, his once having thrown a plate of food at a footman. And always, under all circumstances, how dependent he had been on his wife.

A blast of fresh air was provided by a Dr. Stossel, a specialist from Zurich, who, around that time, had been invited to stay at the villa the Piasts rented each year at Florence.

He was large, vigorous and forthright and determined to speak his mind.

"During my stay of a month I formed the opinion that the Prince was in complete command of his faculties, granted the shortened span of attention typical in people of that age. He was visited by a number of collectors and museum curators who wanted his opinion on works of art. He attended gatherings and luncheons and conversed in a perfectly coherent manner. Apart from a degenerative rheumatic condition that severely limited his mobility and caused a tremor of his hands, he was in good health for a man his age. I saw no evidence of mental decline."

Without asking permission Dr. Stossel went on to say, "Much has been said about the domination exercised by the Princess over her husband. It was my observation that quite the opposite was the case." Ratenauer tried to interrupt, but Dr. Stossel went straight on. "It was he who dominated her. She was not only his hostess and companion, but his nurse and secretary." Another interruption overruled. "He was a demanding, difficult and irascible old man. I have seldom seen a woman so dedicated to her husband's welfare. She unfailingly attended to all his needs."

"No one asked you to give your opinions," Ratenauer rapped. "You are here to answer questions."

"I am here to give evidence," Dr. Stossel retorted. "I was in their company for a month which you, sir, I beg to point out, were not."

On that surprising note the court recessed.

When Valentin got home he found Hugo eating a hearty lunch. He was so relieved to see him that he almost forgot to be angry.

"What the devil are you doing here?" he demanded with a suitable show of parental outrage. "How dare you leave school without permission! Your mother has been beside herself. It was a disgraceful, reckless, inconsiderate thing to do."

Hugo swallowed a mouthful of pie. "I felt I ought to be here."

"Why? Because of the trial? It has nothing to do with you. You're a schoolboy—you—you have no right to go careering across Europe—alone—without enough money. Your mother and I have been scared stiff."

Valentin's anger petered out. He couldn't help being overjoyed to see his son.

"Well, you're here, that's something. I must cable your mother at once. Really, Hugo, how could you do such a thing, without a word to either of us?"

Hugo said stolidly, "It was something I just had to do. And I had plenty of money. I hadn't touched my allowance and mother gave me a check the last time she was over."

"That was for clothes and books, things you needed. Not to—oh well—" Valentin rather lamely poured himself a cup of coffee. "How on earth did you manage to leave school?"

"There was cricket practice. I walked to the station and took the train. And I left a note for the Head to say where I was going and not to worry. I knew you were here. I'm sorry if you were upset."

"I was very, very upset. And what was it you thought you could do here?"

"I thought the Princess might need me. How is the trial going?"

"I don't know. All right, legally, I think. They haven't actually been able to prove anything against her. I have to say she's shown enormous courage."

"Will it turn out all right?"

"I don't know, Hugo. I really don't know."

"It's awful the things they said. She never did anything wrong. She couldn't have."

"You've never doubted her for a minute, have you?"

Hugo looked at his father with the clear, unequivocal certainty of youth.

"She's not like other people. That's why they don't understand her."

"You're right there," Valentin agreed. "I only wish she could have avoided this ordeal."

"She had to stand up for what was right."

Valentin loved his son that morning as he had never loved him before.

"I want you to do one thing and I'm going to insist on it. I do not want you to go to the court."

"Why not?"

"It's an ugly, sickening business that you shouldn't see at your age. Also it might upset the Princess if she happened to catch sight of you. It's a bit like seeing someone you know dragged out of a train wreck. Wait till it's over and then go to see her. She'll have need of you then."

He kissed Hugo and fondly patted his cheek.

"Be a good boy. Have a bath and a rest. I'll tell you whatever happens afterward."

Hugo was also seeing his father in a new light. He decided that, after all, Valentin was a decent man who deserved to be trusted.

"Very well. I'll do what you say."

When Valentin reached the courthouse a large crowd had gathered, spreading down the steps into the street. These gray men and women in their gray, shabby clothes had the stolid, sullen look of underdogs grimly determined to avenge themselves on the corrupt Establishment embodied by the Princess of Piast. Harden had done his work well. Several were armed with copies of *Die Zükunft*. Valentin read the signs on that sea of faces. He'd had experience with crowds.

He found a cab and drove to Police Headquarters. His old friend Twadovsky was in conference. He had a string of appointments and couldn't see anyone that morning.

Valentin caught him as he was hurrying downstairs.

"I thought you should know there's an ugly crowd outside the courthouse. Unless I'm mistaken they're bent on mischief. I think you should station some men 'round the Piast museum. Believe me, there's going to be trouble."

"Thanks to your goddamned editor. As though I didn't have enough to contend with without fanatics like Harden screaming their heads off."

"I do not work for Harden and will you please listen! She needs protection."

"She'll be lucky if she isn't torn limb from limb."

It was impossible to get into court. The crowd had swelled to a concourse.

Valentin went 'round to the side door. As he was hurrying down the corridor he bumped into Jacques Pontoise.

"Too late! It's all over."

"It can't be. What about the final speeches, the summing up?"

"It was all fixed. The judges were only out half an hour."

"What happened?" Valentin pinned his colleague to the wall.

"They decided there was no concrete evidence that the Prince was non compos or that the will had been forged. They admitted she was the worst kind of woman in existence, but they said they were not there to pass moral judgments. The money and the estates were not entailed; he was free to leave them to anyone he chose. As to the mines they advised the Baden boys to address themselves to the Mexican government. Wasn't that charming? I never witnessed such a travesty of justice. That bitch got away with the whole damn thing!"

He dashed off to vindicate his gift for prophesy.

The courtroom was almost deserted. A deflated Ratenauer was conferring with Prince Sixtus. Therese and Martens-Stillman had gone.

It was impossible to get out through the front way. Valentin observed that part of the crowd was marching off and that the rest would follow. He had no doubt as to where they were going.

He caught a cab and drove straight to the Piast Museum. The old doorman who knew Hugo let him in.

"Listen to me. There's a big crowd on their way here. I've warned the police. Bolt all the doors and if there are shutters on the downstairs windows shut them. Don't open to anyone until the police get here."

Therese was sitting on a stone bench in the garden beside the red granite slab that marked Saladin's grave. She was drinking champagne with the daily papers strewn around her.

"I've just heard the verdict. Thank God, it's over!"

She looked ghastly. Her pallor accentuated the livid scar on her cheek. She evinced no surprise at Valentin's sudden appearance and stared at him blankly with unfocused eyes.

Victory appeared to give her no elation or even noticeable relief.

"I don't want to alarm you, but there's a big crowd on their way here. There may be trouble. It would be better if you come home with me before they get here. Hugo's come from England to see you."

She looked away with total uninterest. "Let them come. They won't be satisfied till they smash what's left of me.

Therese Lachmann, born in the Warsaw ghetto, killed by a respectable German mob. A fitting end for the wickedest woman in Europe."

She picked up a copy of *Die Zükunft* from the seat, with the caricature of herself as the spirit of war.

"Don't bother with that rubbish." Valentin snatched the paper from her. "Harden's out of his mind. I told him so."

"It's all true," she said slowly. "I sold arms to anyone who would buy them. I didn't care how many people were killed. I tricked Augustus into marriage and I got rid of Scotto because I thought he'd be in my way. I wrote the will and I made Augustus sign it. I even wrote most of his books. It was all true—and yet none of it was true. I wanted him to be admired because he deserved it and I wanted Vittorio to be rich. But what does it matter what my motives were? It all turned into this." She pointed to her disfigured face. "This horror. That's what I am. That's the only true verdict on Therese Lachmann."

"It's over, Therese. Please come with me. We'll look after you for the next few days."

"Why should you care what happens to me?" she said harshly. "You're a journalist. Go and write another article. Write what I told you. Write the truth."

She got up suddenly and lurched over to the red granite slab that bore the single name "Saladin."

"That was the only creature I ever loved, the only one who saw into my heart."

The heavy overcast day, now turning to dusk, was suddenly disrupted by a series of explosions. Rockets soared into the sky and burst, showering the roof of the museum with golden rain. A celebration? For what? Why fireworks?

There rose from around that old mansion the ominous rumble of a human storm.

Valentin grabbed Therese and dragged her toward the house.

In the hall she began to fight, blindly, as if he were trying to abduct her. "Get away! I won't hide from that rabble. This is my purgatory, not yours."

She flung herself at the door into the Museum, unlocked it and passed through.

Valentin ran after her, but at that moment several servants appeared in the hall. They had heard the uproar and were in fear of their lives.

"Go back to your quarters and stay there. I'll wait here till the police arrive."

Meanwhile Therese was going from room to room turning up all the lamps and chandeliers until the whole building was ablaze. It was her last act of defiance against a world that had always conspired against her.

A multitude had assembled in the street outside. They were yelling and throwing stones. The roar of wild beasts was punctuated by the shattering of glass.

And out of that hubbub arose like a killer whale from the deep the anthem that was to haunt the chancelleries of Europe and strike terror into the world that Therese had conquered. Valentin recognized it—the Internationale.

Valentin was thankful when police whistles were heard. The clamor surged to and fro and then started to subside. The revolutionary hymn, more deadly but less heroic than the Marseillaise, submerged, a delayed depth charge. There was a pounding on the door.

It was Twadovsky with the police.

"What the hell are you doing here?" he demanded. "Are you this woman's keeper?"

They found Therese in her living room on the top floor. She had opened another bottle of champagne. The danger and the excitement had restored her spirit. She was exhilarated, even exultant. Valentin wondered if, for a long time, she had been half mad.

Twadovsky apologized for the disturbance. "I'll leave some men outside for the next few days. You'd be well advised to keep the Museum shut for a week or so. I can't answer for vandals."

"I want the Princess to come home with me. Tell her it's a wise idea."

Twadovsky looked at Valentin with a quizzical smile. "Why not? Anywhere away from here."

Therese laughed. "It would make no difference. I have an appointment at Samara. Have some champagne."

"There's no need to tempt Providence," Twadovsky advised her. "You should go abroad for a while. Go to the south of France. You might find another coal mine under the Monte Carlo casino." He raised his glass in a toast.

"What are we drinking to?" Therese inquired. "My acquittal? To the fact that the good citizens of Berlin were deprived of a victim?"

She finished off her glass. She was once again in control.

"Thank you for your assistance," she said in her customary tone. "And now, if you'll forgive, I think I shall go to bed."

She made the final gesture of presenting Twadovsky with a check, somewhat as if she were tipping a headwaiter. "Will you accept this for whatever police charity there is? Your men do an excellent job."

On the way to the door she stopped by a bookcase and selected three books which she handed to Valentin. "Give these to Hugo. He's old enough to read Aristophanes."

"He came all the way from England to see you."

That was the last Valentin ever saw of her, leaning, half drunk against that door, the wreck of a beautiful woman and, what was more tragic, of a superior human being.

"Goodbye, Valentin Zorn," she called after him. "You're a good man. You inherit that from your son."

Hugo called every morning to no avail. He left his violets but received no invitation to see her. One morning the old doorman told him sadly, "I'm afraid, Master Hugo, the Princess has gone away."

"Where to?"

"No one seems to know. She left last evening with some suitcases. I don't think she's coming back. The Museum is taking over the top floor."

Hugo was deeply wounded. He couldn't believe that his dearest friend would leave without even saying goodbye.

He looked ruefully at his violets and asked if he could leave them on Saladin's grave.

He stood for a long time looking down at that granite slab

thinking about the strange, unpredictable woman who had cast such a spell over his life.

To Valentin's knowledge she never returned to Berlin. There were many rumors as to her whereabouts. When hadn't there been rumors about her? Jacques Pontoise had it on good authority that she was living at Petropolis in Brazil and that she had found a surgeon who had operated on her face—with dire results. She was more hideous than ever, had shut herself up, saw no one, and had become a morphine addict.

Dolly had another story. "You'll never guess who I saw coming out of Asprey's on Bond Street," she exclaimed on returning from one of her trips to London. "The Princess! I hardly recognized her. She was completely bent over her cane, a regular old witch."

"Are you sure it was she?"

"Absolutely. I really felt sorry for her," Dolly, who had never approved of Therese, conceded. "She looked so terribly old."

Valentin Zorn had his doubts.

As he traveled about Europe at the dictates of his profession in those years before the First World War, he used to fancy that he would run into her, on some train rattling across the Balkans, on some remote Greek island, in the lobby of some hotel.

He never did. She had slipped off the rim of the world and, like other footnotes in history, was gradually forgotten.

Part Six

Changra Chari

*I*T IS A sad time in the life of any professional man when he is forced to contemplate retirement. It was specially so for Sir Frederick Avondale, KCB, KCMG, ex-Ambassador to China, ex-Governor General of Burma and the Malay States. Most of his adult life had been spent in the Far East. The Orient was in his blood, its grandeur and squalor, its pride and resignation, its infinite complexity and color.

Time had dealt kindly with Freddie Avondale. At sixty-five he still had the slim figure of his early years in Paris. If his blond hair was now gray, his face was remarkably unlined. His mild blue eyes still regarded the world with equable surprise. Orientals liked him. He was trustworthy and unaggressive.

Lady Avondale was already installed in an Elizabethan manor house in Kent and wrote enthusiastically about oak beams and leaded windows, a walled garden and a ruined gatehouse that could be restored to provide Freddie with a study where he could write his memoirs. All ex-diplomats wrote their memoirs. Lingering in India on a round of farewell visits, Freddie thought with foreboding of gray English skies, eternal rain, vicarage teas and evenings on duty at the bridge table.

It came as an act of deliverance, the summons from the Viceroy, Lord Curzon, to discuss "a delicate and private matter."

If Freddie and Lord Curzon had anything in common it was their pleasure in Oriental pageantry and pomp. Grandeur became the Viceroy. He was never more in his element than when, arrayed in the full regalia of his office, he presided at some state reception, bestowing imperial greetings from the King-Emperor on rajahs and nizams, adazzle with jewels and crested turbans. The Indian raj did not feel demeaned to be the satraps of such a sovereign.

Freddie was ushered into an anteroom at Government House, New Delhi, overlooking a garden in which peacocks strutted beside a marble pool. "The old boy does himself proud," Freddie thought and was at once depressed by the mental image of Winifred, his wife, sloshing down the lane to the restored gatehouse to tell him that tea was ready.

An aide emerged from the sanctum sanctorum in which the Viceroy was enshrined.

"Sir Frederick Avondale? His Lordship will see you now."

The Presence was seated at a large desk, polished like glass, on which stood an alabaster vase filled with white orchids.

Lord Curzon had the features of a rare and predatory bird, dominated by strangely elongated eyes, set very far apart, which glazed over when he was angry like those of an owl about to pounce on an unsuspecting mouse.

After an exchange of civilities he came to the purpose of the interview.

"I want to discuss with you something which, if nothing else, may delay the fatal moment of your surrender to the mercies of the P and O. Believe me I sympathize. It has long been my contention that England is a country to die for but not to live in."

"We have received information that the Russians are up to their old tricks in Nepal. As you know a curious situation prevails there. Nepal is a monarchy, but the kings are kept prisoner and only paraded on ceremonious occasions. The country is ruled by the Ranas, a family of hereditary Prime Ministers. It has to be made clear that Russian support is unacceptable to the British government. If they need money we will supply it. If they need arms we will supply those, too. The situation is delicate because the Gurkhas who are Nepalese provide the Indian Army with its finest fighters. Their loss would be a serious blow to our presence here."

It was another phase of what was known to diplomacy as the Great Game, the undeclared war between England and Russia for control over those buffer states that separated the two empires in Central Asia. A vast network of agents and double agents, disguised as merchants, dragomen, priests and scholars, plied their dangerous trade, gathering information, plotting and suborning, and not infrequently killing, in order to prevent these remote countries, Persia, Afghanistan, Nepal, Sikkim and a number of tiny kingdoms hidden in the Himalayas from falling into enemy hands.

"I would like to avoid sending a military expedition as I was forced to when the Dalai Lama was unwise enough to surround himself with Russian advisers. Nepal must remain neutral, but neutral on our side."

By lunchtime Freddie Avondale had agreed to head a mission to Katmandu.

He left a week later with a Gurkha escort, letters of introduction from the Viceroy and gifts from the King-Emperor, Edward VII. These included a handsome eighteenth century clock and the latest of telescopes for the King "so that he may warn us of any approaching Russians," a superb chess set in red amber and chrysophase, and the necessary equipment for croquet—mallets, balls and hoops, "to encourage the Ranas in peaceful pursuits."

It was an expedition after Freddie's heart. He rode at a leisurely pace from Delhi to Benares with his troop, surely the most imposing men on earth, and a covered wagon containing the gifts, tents and supplies, stamped all over with the Lion and Unicorn and emblazoned with the warning: Property of the British Crown.

Freddie could not resist the temptation to linger a few days at Benares on the pretext of giving his Gurkhas a rest. He glided down the Ganges as dawn was breaking and the devout were descending the ghats, carrying their elderly and children, to bathe and pray in the sacred waters, as the first light painted the fabled and ruinous city with pink and gold.

From Benares the mission made its way along the Ganges to Chapra and Barbanghal and then inland toward the foothills of that mountain range that holds up the ceiling of the world.

Freddie was unable to explain the power of this landscape, at once so desolate and so splendid. It was the graveyard of a great race, but also their refuge against Destiny which ignores all men. Brown and bare, it stretched endlessly before him and filled his restless Western mind with a kind of vacancy.

He was impressed, and not a little surprised, by the size of the garrison at the border village and by the excellent quality of their arms, not the usual muskets left over from ancient wars, but the latest repeater rifles such as the British used themselves. Placed menacingly on a bluff above the village was a canon of the Vickers-Maxim type before which two sentries paraded.

After a lengthy perusal of Freddie's passport, the officials examined the contents of the wagon. Their suspicions were at once aroused by the croquet set, the heavy colored balls which they decided must be ammunition of some hitherto unknown kind.

At last, after much parleying and consulting, they stamped the passports and the mission was permitted to proceed under escort to the outskirts of the village. Evidently a new spirit was afoot in the mountain kingdom of Nepal.

"Where do they get their rifles?" Freddie asked Captain Chal, the leader of his band.

"From whoever sells them, I expect, sir," the laconic Gurkha replied.

They rode into a landscape as beautiful as any Freddie had ever seen. A river rushed through this valley, silvery with mica. Groves of fruit trees punctuated a network of jade green fields of millet. Clumps of wild lupin and mallow dotted pastures where the philosophical water buffalo grazed. Tier upon tier, the rice paddies rose to a wall of fir and rhododendron in full bloom. The air became purer and tingled in the veins like a heavenly ozone.

Suddenly, as though in greeting and in warning, the curtain of cloud behind these not inconsiderable heights lifted and behold!—gleaming and majestic, unimaginable in their immensity, the Himalayas towered against an ice blue sky.

They passed through villages blessedly free of the stench and squalor of their Indian counterparts. Bright-faced children with almond eyes ran out to greet the travelers. Stoic, frank-faced women watched them as they rode by and gravely returned their greetings. Sinewy men glanced up from their labor in the fields. Inheritors of an earthly paradise, they felt little interest in strangers.

The mission struck camp by a grove of rhododendrons, a foam of pink and purple. The Gurkhas bestowed themselves in their natural habitat like the great black oxen in the fields. One kept watch by the fire, a rifle across his knees. There were bears and leopards in these parts.

Freddie lay wrapped in his blankets, listening to the silence, and felt singularly at peace.

On the third day the road climbed through gorges bright with a variety of ferns. Clouds of yellow butterflies as big as starlings fluttered about their heads. They passed occasional Sherpas bowed under burdens so enormous they were unable to look up as the foreigners rode by.

There were few temples or wayside shrines though an occasional monastery could be glimpsed, clinging like an eagle's nest to the heights. Once they heard the eerie bellow of the great trumpets, the radongs, echoing from some other consciousness across the sleeping present.

And then great cisterns appeared where the water buffalo bathed, small country houses with market gardens, shops and a long street. The air hummed with human activity and, without realizing it, they found themselves in the busy, thriving city of Katmandu.

It was surprisingly large. They passed a number of extensive residences, set in parks and built in a somewhat amateurish European style. These were the homes of the Rana family.

It proved difficult to find the house of Robert MacGregor, the British resident. They were held up by a regiment of Nepalese troops, very smartly turned out in handsome new uniforms and with equally handsome rifles. They were well drilled and would have done credit to any army.

MacGregor lived in a brick building surrounded by a high brick wall. The jangling bell provoked a clamor of childrens' voices. A doorman peered through a lattice and swung back the gates. Freddie was besieged by a welcoming committee of blithe little creatures all with laughing Nepalese eyes, but with suspiciously red hair.

If you had scoured the moors and glens of Scotland you could not have found a more glorious example of his race than Rob MacGregor. He had bright red hair, red cheeks, merry hazel eyes and a manner as breezy as a gust of wind over the heather and as hearty as a tankard of brown ale.

"Och, I'm right glad to see ye, Sir Frrrrederick," he greeted his visitor with a burr as thick as treacle. "Come in, come in wi' ye. Ye are verra welcome."

MacGregor was married to a large Tibetan lady with jet black hair, lacquered stiff with yak butter, her capacious bosom strung with gold jewelry and necklaces of coral and turquoise.

Having installed Freddie in a guest room cluttered with rickety furniture, but containing a good double bed, MacGregor announced, "Whatever ye require, Sir Frrrrederick, ye have but to command. I shall wait you for a wee drop of Haig and Haig before dinner."

Freddie washed and changed and felt his way through a labyrinth of dusty passages to find MacGregor ensconced in what appeared to be a storeroom. There were shelves and shelves of boxes, spices and dried fruits, tables crowded with brass Buddhas and a group of highly pornographic bronzes on the mantelpiece, disporting themselves under the disapproving gaze of Queen Victoria.

MacGregor's buoyant air was deflated slightly when the envoy of His Brittanic Majesty revealed the purpose of his visit.

"It wasn't you, I take it, who supplied the Viceroy with this information?" Freddie asked.

"Weel, no exactly. In my capacity I'm chiefly concerned with keeping the trade route open."

"It doesn't take much to see that the Nepalese army has some pretty fancy new equipment."

"Och, that they have. They're a proud wee bunch." He scratched his nose thoughtfully. "They had the opportunity of observing Lord Curzon's expedition to Lhasa. It passed through Katmandu."

"They didn't take kindly to that display of force?"

"Weel, I wouldna say so. The Nepalese and the Tibetans are old friends. They trade together and respect each other. It's nae for me to criticize the policies of the government, but in my opinion it was no a wise adventure, no wise at all."

"Tibet was well on the way to becoming a Russian dependency."

"So 'twas said, but I hae me doots. You do no win allies in these parts by sacking a holy city and driving the religious leader into exile."

"What I'm concerned with is the present situation here. Are the Ranas getting their arms from Russia?"

"I wouldna exactly say so." MacGregor took a long diplomatic swallow of Haig and Haig.

They were interrupted by a swarm of children who scrambled all over their father and, between smacks and kisses, imparted the news that dinner was ready.

The following morning, armed with the chess set and two Gurkhas bearing the croquet box, Freddie presented himself at the Rana palace, a vast complex of many stories, balconies and towers.

He was kept waiting a long time in a dim audience chamber, spread with superb Indian carpets. At last a tinkle of fairy bells announced the Prime Minister's chamberlain, an obese and unctuous individual, gorgeously arrayed in embroidered yellow silks.

With obsequious bows and simpers he informed the Viceroy's emissary that regrettably His Highness was away in the country and would not be returning to the capital for some time.

"But it's essential that I see him. I have come all the way from Delhi."

"So very sorry, Sir Avon. Very much regretting. His Highness will be so much upsetted." He bowed and rustled toward the door. "Perhaps when Sir Avon does us much honor by visiting Katmandu again."

"That's not good enough," Freddie said firmly. "You will inform Prince Rana that I have come from the Viceroy to discuss matters of great importance to Nepal. I shall expect to see him while I am here and I will remain here until I do."

The Chamberlain bowed and smiled and swayed his head like a cobra about to strike. It was quite evident that the Prime Minister had no intention of confronting the envoy of His Britannic Majesty, however important the purpose of his visit.

Considerably put out, Freddie proceeded to the smaller palace of the king.

Here his credentials were scrutinized by a Majordomo, a sinister personage with cataracts on both eyes. After peering at the Viceroy's letter of introduction, he shuffled off to consult the hidden powers who controlled the titular monarch of Nepal.

Freddie waited. He was aware of being watched through latticework balconies above. An atmosphere of conspiracy and suspicion hung over this gilded cage where the unfortunate king was held prisoner.

The Majordomo returned and escorted the envoy through shuttered rooms, agleam with gilt and tinsel jewels, to a throne room where a small wizened man, bundled doll-like in orange and scarlet brocades, was waiting under a canopy of gold.

It occurred to Freddie that this must be the Crown Prince who, forty years before, had visited France for the Great Exposition and had evinced such an interest in Parisian beauties.

The mummified monarch murmured a few inaudible words of greeting. He had been well trained by long years of confinement and doubtless lived in daily fear for his life from silken cords or poison.

He was mildly gratified by the clock which he passed to the Majordomo who placed it on a table, but the telescope offered an opportunity which he was quick to seize.

He muttered in oddly accented French, *"C'est très intéressant. Voulez-vous arranger ça pour moi?"*

Before his jailer could stop him, he scurried up a circular stairway that opened into the room. The Majordomo attempted to block the way, but Freddie forced his way past him, armed with the telescope.

The stairway opened unexpectedly onto a wide terrace with a magnificent view over the city with its palaces and temples, built in that highly individual style, a mixture of Chinese and Siamese, but with an intricate, fanciful vitality quite of its own.

The king whispered hurriedly to Freddie, *"Oui. Ici, n'est çe pas?"* As the Majordomo came puffing out to the terrace he managed to add, *"C'est à Changra Chari. L'abbé et la femme Allemande."*

The Majordomo quickly intervened and unceremoniously pushed the king away to a safe distance while Freddie, with some difficulty, set up the telescope.

When it was assembled he beckoned to the king who darted over and applied his eye to the lens.

"Je ne vois rien," he announced.

As Freddie attempted to adjust the focus, the king contrived to murmur, *"Changra Chari. L'Allemande. Vous comprenez?"*

It was too much for the Majordomo. He pulled the king away and said roughly, "No. Is enough. Visit it over now."

"I have come to pay my respects to His Majesty from the King of England," Freddie reminded him with as much authority as he could muster.

But the Majordomo bundled the king away down the staircase and out of sight.

So this was the source of the Viceroy's information, the poor little king whose only hope of rescue was if the British intervened, deposed the Ranas, and restored the monarchy to power!

Freddie found MacGregor in the storeroom poring over his ledgers.

"What do you know about Changra Chari?" he asked.

"Och, it's a wee trading town to the north. A market is held there once a month where the Tibetans and Nepalese do business."

"Is it near the Tibetan border?"

"There's no a border to speak of. It's near the pass over the mountains." MacGregor eyed Freddie with some disquiet.

"Is there an Abbot of Changra Chari?"

"Well, there's a monastery with an abbot. He's a mon of some distinction, being the head of the Lama Buddhists. That's a sect that prevails in those parts."

"Is he important politically?"

"In Nepal politics and religion are much the same thing. And what makes ye ask, Sir Frrrrederick?"

"Do you know anything about a German woman who lives there?"

MacGregor's eyes became quite round with innocent surprise.

"I dinna ken nought of a German woman. There are convents in the mountains. There might be a nun or two from the West, but I never heard of a German."

It was obvious that MacGregor knew a good deal more than he was willing to reveal.

"How far is it to Changra Chari?"

"Och, it's a verra long way," MacGregor exclaimed in alarm. "You're not thinking of going there, I hope?"

"I suppose you wouldn't care to come with me?"

The burly Scotsman squirmed with discomfort. "It's awfu' good of you to suggest it, but I'm a bit long in the tooth for mountain climbing. There's no road after Pokhara. Ye just go oop and ye just come doon. And there are brigands that set upon travelers and a lot of ferocious beasts. Nay, I don't fancy going to Changra Chari and I don't suggest you venture there either."

"I've been sent to find out where the Nepalese are getting their arms and it's clear I am not going to learn much in Katmandu."

MacGregor heaved himself up. His face turned a rich shade of mahogany as he issued a warning that he knew might reflect on his own position.

"Don't go sticking your nose into that hornet's nest. Life is cheap in Nepal. The British should stay out and so should you."

"I have a distinct impression there's a lot you don't want to tell me."

MacGregor's face grew darker. He was the ancient Scot who had driven back the invading English across the moors and through the mists to the wail of bagpipes.

"What I may know is my business. Take my advice; go

back to Delhi and tell the Viceroy everything's just fine in Katmandu."

Two days later Sir Frederick Avondale left with his escort of Gurkhas for Changra Chari. Perhaps in his heart of hearts he was not only motivated by his duty to the Viceroy. He was not beyond enjoying an adventure and this opportunity might not come again.

The three days' journey to Pokhara were uneventful. Beyond this village the road abruptly stopped. The expedition was faced with a sheer cliff down which a race of giants had hurled boulders to obstruct further progress. It was years since Freddie had attempted so arduous a climb. When, pushed and hoisted by Captain Chal, he reached the top, he began to regret that he had not heeded MacGregor's warning.

They entered a haunted wilderness of fog, rushing streams and forbidding forests. A sense of depression and then of dread stole over Freddie as he trudged along. Occasional figures materialized from the milky whiteness and, like specters in purgatory, passed without greeting.

As he lay huddled in his tent at night Freddie could not shake off a feeling of impending doom. His family, country, beliefs, all the elements that made up his identity, drained away into the icy dampness that penetrated his very bones. Blood no longer flowed in his veins, only the slow horror of space and time.

They pressed forward like convicts condemned for some unknown crime, the Gurkhas unapproachable, the Sherpa guides, bent double under their burdens, mere phantoms in a no-man's-land without forms or boundaries.

The only sound was the distant rushing of water through unseen abysses.

As suddenly as they had entered this domain of mists and demons so they emerged into dazzling sunlight. Below them on a carpet of bright green fields lay Changra Chari.

Never in his life had Freddie been so thankful to see human habitations. He stumbled down the long slope like an exile returning home.

The village consisted of a single shabby street that opened

into a market square. It was built on the edge of a ravine across which, seemingly almost within reach, but actually forty miles away, towered the immense rock cathedral of Annapurna.

On a hillside above the village the monastery rose, tier upon tier of walls and roofs, held there, it seemed, by the will of the cliff behind.

The only inn was crowded with pilgrims who had journeyed to this remote spot to celebrate the Feast of the Living Goddess, Annapurna, Mother of Gods and of the Sky.

Captain Chal suggested seeking refuge in the monastery. On their way there they passed a wide tract of turf on which a detachment of soldiers was engaged in military exercises.

"First-rate-looking men," Freddie remarked, "and very smartly equipped. Why are there so many here?"

"To protect the border. Tibet is behind those mountains."

They crossed a river by a swaying pontoon bridge and climbed a hill to the monastery gate. Here Captain Chal explained to the doorkeeper that Freddie was a distinguished foreigner who had come to pay his respects to His Holiness the Abbot.

They were assigned cells whitewashed, bare, but clean.

As depressed as Freddie had been in the fog-bound mountains, here he was equally elated to be sipping hot tea in a safe place and nibbling MacGregor's "Genuine Scottish Shortbread."

Chal made up his bed and Freddie dropped like a stone into blissful sleep.

He was awoken by distant chanting. Night had fallen.

He made his way across the moonlit courtyard, up flights of steps, guarded by glowering stone dragons, to higher and higher terraces, drawn by the mysterious droning dirge and the occasional clang of bells and the rattle of metal clappers.

A dim red glow revealed the chapel. In a long barrel-roofed cavern that extended deep into the cliff, two lines of saffron-robed monks were seated, lotus fashion, heads bowed in the recitation of their liturgy. At the far end on a raised dais, against a mural depicting horrific dieties, the Abbot presided, immobile as a statue and crowned with a strangely embroidered miter.

On either side braziers provided what to Freddie seemed like the glow of hell.

The chapel reeked of rancid oil and incense.

The monotonous chant which fell away into a deep growling sustained on a single half-tone, was now and then broken by the braying of conches, the clash of cymbals and the twanging of strange instruments that sounded like out of tune guitars. Freddie found this ceremony the opposite of uplifting.

It was then that he saw her, seated against the wall with one leg extended, as though a physical disability prevented her from assuming the required position for meditation. She was shrouded in a Nile green sari which revealed the unmistakable profile of a European.

It could only be the German of whom the king had spoken.

There was something vaguely familiar in those chiseled features that Freddie could not place.

His resolve to remain until the chanting ceased so that he could speak to this foreigner wavered after what seemed an eternity. His body ached and his back was knotted in discomfort.

He crept outside into the moonlight that barely disturbed the awesome blackness of the night.

The dim outlines of a conspiracy were becoming clear connecting Prince Rana with the Abbot and this woman. Perhaps this woman was a Russian agent who arranged for shipments of arms to be brought across the mountains. If the training and equipment of a modern army were the initial phase of infiltration then Lord Curzon's apprehension would be justified. It would not be the first time that Russia had provided aid for a native government in order to gain control.

But how did the arms get there? By devious routes across Tibet from Mongolia? Or from India disguised as merchandise? MacGregor had spoken of keeping the trade route open.

Perhaps this monastery was in fact an arsenal, protected by the Abbot's position as leader of the Lama sect.

Debating these questions, Freddie returned to his cell, rolled himself in his blankets, and fell asleep.

He was awoken by Captain Chal who had procured eggs which, splendid fellow, he fried with chepattis. While they were breakfasting the doorkeeper knocked and informed Freddie that His Holiness would receive him as soon as he was ready.

He followed the doorkeeper through interior chambers painted with the terrible gods and demons, up a long flight of steps hewn from the cliff, and was admitted to a large chamber darkened by the overhanging ledge of rock. It seemed to Freddie an unhallowed sanctuary where vile and morbid rites had perhaps for centuries been performed.

The Abbot rose from a commonplace roll-top desk. He was much younger than Freddie had thought, perhaps not more than thirty and obviously part European. He spoke excellent English. He was very urbane, not very cordial and not at all sympathetic.

It was not often that Freddie took an instantaneous dislike to anyone as he did to the Abbot of Changra Chari. He had an inflexible authority that would not shrink from cruelty and was without compassion for those ignorant of the mysteries of his religion.

Directly behind his desk was a tang-ka depicting a grinning demon spurting blood from a hundred wounds and juggling with human skulls.

"I hope you have been comfortable, Sir Frederick. Our amenities are limited, but don't hesitate to ask for anything you need."

He motioned Freddie to a swivel chair that, like the desk, seemed oddly out of keeping in such surroundings. There was nothing about the Abbot that suggested to Freddie a spiritual leader. He had the inflexible cunning of one of those double agents who might well be engaged in the Great Game.

"Forgive me, but you are not, I think, Nepalese," Freddie ventured.

"No, I am half Russian, half Tadzhik. I was born at St. Petersburg. My father was an explorer. He came to Nepal and fell in love with Annapurna, a not unusual hazard for visitors to Changra Chari."

"You were brought up here, then?"

"My father became a monk in this monastery. I was raised by the Rana family at Katmandu."

He had volunteered this information both as a challenge and to put his visitor at a disadvantage.

"Did you have a pleasant journey?" he asked.

"On the whole, except for the days between here and Pokhara which I did not enjoy."

"Visitors find that region of mists disturbing. It is like the tamshin maya."

"What is that?"

"The period after death when the soul wanders between the familiar world of the living and the unknown spheres beyond."

"I know nothing of such things," Freddie answered smugly.

"It is similar to what Christians call purgatory, a stage of nightmare between release and reincarnation."

"You are young to be the leader of such an important sect."

"I was born with certain qualifications which I only realized here."

"And you'll remain as Abbot indefinitely?"

"I go on pilgrimage to pursue my studies. Whatever one learns is only a step to something more."

"To Tibet, you mean?"

"And the Gobi desert. There are centers of ancient learning there. We are all students."

"And that European woman I saw last night, is she a student, too?"

"You might say so. She came here like my father and succumbed to the spell of Annapurna."

"She lives in the village?"

"Part of the time."

"Would it be indiscreet of me to ask who she is?"

"They call her Lalla Nok, the Lady of Kind Intent. She does a great deal of good."

"In what way?"

"Traveling through the mountains with Western medicines. Nepal has a high mortality rate, especially among children."

"Is she Russian, too?"

"I think not," was all the Abbot chose to say.

Suddenly into that shadowed chamber the sun cast a ray of light as blinding as an acetylene flare. Although the Abbot was only a few feet away Freddie could barely see him. He was consumed by a furnace of dancing flame.

"Since you are an adept at mysteries," Freddie heard himself say, "I assume you know why I've come here?"

"Birds bring messages through the mists."

"Birds disguised as Sherpas?"

"We all wear disguises, some more obvious than others."

"What disguise are you wearing for my benefit?"

"Isn't it you who have come here disguised for me?"

The blinding light went out. The Abbot was standing under the grinning demon in the tang-ka.

"You find this painting horrible?"

"Completely."

"What does it represent to you?"

"Satan."

"The King of Hell—but whose?"

"All those who give way to your kind of magic."

"What of those who are forced to give way to yours?"

"We try to bring order to the world and lead people out of centuries of sloth and superstition."

"You solve the world's problems with sewing machines and bills of lading, an empire of commercial travelers. But you, too, stream blood and juggle with human skulls."

"I don't care to talk in riddles. Will you tell me what I want to know?"

"You do not know what you want to know. Tell the Viceroy not to look for simplistic answers to the problems of this nation's destiny."

"He asks one question. Will you answer it?"

"You already know the answer."

"Are you buying arms from Russia?"

"I am not a merchant of death, but a student of life. Can you and your Viceroy say the same?"

Freddie was possessed by an insane rage. He wanted to kill this high priest of deception.

"You are a liar!" he shouted.

"You recognize lies. They are your stock in trade."

Freddie saw him but no longer saw him. The King of Hell

danced. Blood flowed. The smell of unspeakable atrocities burned in Freddie's nostrils. Death poured like black smoke into his brain.

He was alone in that dreadful room, choking for lack of air. He stumbled down the steps, through dark anterooms with obscenely writhing monsters. The sunlight of the courtyard struck him from an alien sky.

What had the Abbot shown him?

Was it a glimpse into himself?

"What is the matter, sir?" Captain Chal asked when Freddie reached his cell.

"I don't want to stay in this place. There is evil here."

Captain Chal was concerned. He had never seen the usually affable and self-controlled sahib in such emotional disarray.

"There is a European woman living here in the village. I want to see her before we go."

"Better rest for today, sir. We can leave in the morning. I'll make some tea."

Freddie lay on his bunk with his hand over his eyes. He felt as though some deadly corrupting virus had entered his soul. He felt unclean.

An hour later they set off down the hill. On the wide greensward by the river the soldiers were drilling, snapping smartly to commands. In the distance they could hear the rattle of firing at a rifle range.

Chal inquired in the village for the house of Lalla Rok. They were directed to a path that led through a grove of jacarandas along the very edge of the ravine.

It was a small house built in the Tibetan style, partially concealed by a well-planted rockery. Cyclamen, gentian and wild orchids bloomed among the ferns.

Freddie rapped on the door and was answered by the screech of a parrot inside the house.

A Tibetan woman appeared. Even for these strange intruders she had the customary smiles and courtesies of her ancient, well-mannered race.

Captain Chal explained that the English sahib was visiting

Changra Chari and would esteem it an honor if he might pay his respects to the lady of the house.

The serving woman bowed and shut the door.

Freddie became aware of an uncanny silence, undisturbed even by the chatter of a distant stream. This house seemed to hang on the edge of eternity, serene and protected.

The door reopened and the Tibetan, with many smiles and little bows, informed the visitors that her mistress could not receive them, but that she wished them a pleasant stay.

Freddie was about to insist when the parrot screamed from within and the door shut.

The silence prohibited further intrusion.

It was then, as they turned away, that Freddie saw through the branches of the jacarandas, powdered with dusky bloom, the dazzling magnificence of Annapurna. Suddenly the horror of his meeting with the Abbot was blotted out by this vision of supernal beauty, the matchless testament of God.

They made their way back to the monastery. It was a pleasant valley of rice paddies, millet fields and shimmering poplars.

"What do you think of all this military activity?" Freddie asked the captain.

"Nepal is a free country. It has the right to defend itself."

"Do they realize the danger of buying arms from Russia?"

The captain's face was inscrutable. "Who says they are?"

Freddie had the disquieting feeling that everyone he encountered was privy to a secret from which he alone was excluded.

Freddie was awakened at four o'clock the following morning by Captain Chal.

"You must get up, sir. The procession has started."

In the pitch darkness a river of candles was slowly winding up the hillside. Some way ahead, Freddie made out the Abbot's palanquin escorted by monks bearing torches. The radongs boomed through the predawn silence. It was very cold.

The procession of pilgrims moved slowly up the road, intent and silent. Small children toddled beside their parents, their faces touched by the magic of candlelight.

After half an hour they came out onto a small plateau, far

above the monastery. Here the company of several hundred waited. There was no moon and not a single star.

The radongs boomed again, the most desolate sound on earth and the monks commenced their subdued, monotonous chanting.

This, too, died away.

They were all waiting.

What were they waiting for, this congregation of believers in the immensity of darkness?

And then the miracle occurred.

A shaft of salmon light shot through the darkness like an arrow and struck the topmost peak of Annapurna. The finger of God reached through eternal night and behold!—there was Life.

The crest of the mountain broke into flame.

A great cheer went up.

Trumpets blared, gongs crashed, the pilgrims cheered and, in a few moments, the lake of candles was extinguished.

In that spellbinding moment Freddie recognized her as she bent forward to blow out her candle.

Time split apart and he remembered a girl he had known forty years before in Paris. Therese de Païva had caused a sensation by riding a black Arabian named Saladin up a staircase to a costume ball.

He had fancied himself in love with her and had been heartbroken when she vanished from the Paris scene. There had been talk of some scandal. A beautiful, enigmatic vision of his youth.

He was certain that it was she.

He tried to elbow his way toward her, but in the crush of people, now laughing and embracing each other, he lost her. He had glimpsed her for a moment as brief as that which had transfigured the mountain.

Therese de Païva, Lalla Nok, the Lady of Kind Intent!

The dawn was breaking and the sky was radiant with iridescence.

The multitude was turning back down the hill toward the village, and Freddie was forced to follow.

On his bunk at the monastery he found a scroll wrapped in

Chinese silk. He knew, without opening it, what it was. The Abbot had given him the ghastly tang-ka of the King of Hell, as a memento or a warning—he wasn't sure.

While Captain Chal was rounding up the other members of the expedition, Freddie went back to the little house on the edge of the ravine.

The smiling Tibetan woman opened the door. Freddie tried to explain that he was an old friend of Lalla Nok, but she shook her head and opened the door wide to indicate that the house was empty. Freddie glimpsed a whitewashed room with a wall of books and a Chinese table with a figure of Quan Yin.

The good woman was shaking her head and pointing. She was trying to make it clear that Lalla Nok had gone away.

"But where?" Freddie demanded. "Where?"

She motioned toward the mountains, to the north, to heaven.

"Katmandu?"

Farther! Farther!

She had gone.

He was bitterly disappointed. It was typical of everything that had happened and not happened on this ill-fated mission.

He looked through the trees at Annapurna. Did it matter? Did any of it matter? The designs of the Viceroy and the Great Game seemed as inconsequential as the games of children, and he seemed no more than a wanderer without purpose or destination.

The King of Hell spurting blood—that was the world he had lived in. Annapurna was the truth he had dimly sought but never found.

They journeyed back into the land of mists. The white desolation no longer depressed him. The tang-ka was his protection against the demons that had tried to drain away his soul. They encountered no one. Therese and the pilgrims had vanished into that other reality he had not earned the right to share.

That night in his tent Freddie thought back over his life to those early days in Paris when he had been so full of absurd ideals and aspirations. He thought of his marriage; a good bargain on the whole. He had had a good life, varied and useful, without outstanding achievements, a Servant of the Crown who had had his day.

He thought of those mornings long ago when he had gone riding with Therese. Had he really loved her or had she been a romantic image of youth? Romance! That certainly faded with middle age. It seemed to him that, somewhere along the way, he had missed an essential element in life. He had followed a prescribed course, bound by conventional ideas of duty, honor, loyalty—to what? Had he really believed in Great Britain's civilizing mission in the world?

This unique and priceless experience, so quickly over, had slipped by as though it had never entirely belonged to him. It was not the Abbot he had so resented, but the challenge to his unknown, unrealized self.

The next morning they resumed their journey through the all-encompassing fog.

They had climbed through a wood of dense and dripping pines when suddenly, following a bend in the scarcely visible path, he saw her, standing alone in a patch of pallid sunlight, in a long, padded Chinese coat, her white hair loosely bound by a green silk scarf.

For a moment he wondered if she were really there or if she were one of the specters that haunted this unearthly region.

He went over to her and said, "Therese? It is Therese de Païva, isn't it? I recognized you last night on the Mountain."

She was unmistakable, despite the scars that disfigured one side of her face.

"Freddie Avondale. I recognized you too."

It was impossible, after such a lapse of time, to go through the usual formalities.

"Why wouldn't you see me when I called?"

"I had work to do. I'm on my way back to Katmandu."

She held out her hand. It was a gesture he instantly recalled, the extension of her arm in an almost military way that was at once a greeting and a rebuff.

"What does one say," Freddie asked, "after forty years, when one meets an old friend on a mountainside in Nepal?"

She smiled. "One says good morning."

She must have been in her sixties, he thought, but she seemed ageless.

"Shall we have some tea?"

Therese's Sherpas were resting on the path among their bundles, squatting like bullfrogs and staring at the ground.

The indispensable Captain Chal made tea.

"How long have you been living in Nepal?"

"Six years."

"At Changra Chari?"

"There and at Katmandu."

"Whatever made you come here?"

"I was traveling. I wanted to see the Himalayas. Once one has seen them it's difficult to leave."

"The Abbot told me that you've become something of a legend in these parts."

"I try to do something for these people because they did a lot for me."

"You intend to stay?"

"I think so. I still have a lot to learn."

They sat nursing their mugs of tea.

"I've so often thought of you," Freddie said, "so often wondered what became of you. I've spent most of my life in the Far East so I never went back to Paris."

"You should have stayed on at the monastery. The Abbot is a remarkable man."

"We didn't exactly hit if off."

"He acts harsh at first to test people, also to wake them up."

"Are you involved in all that?"

"I've tried to understand something about Lamaism. It's not easy when one has always seen things another way."

"It seemed a hellish sort of religion to me."

"It's the world behind the mirror—the hidden side of the moon."

"You study with the Abbot?"

"One learns to ask questions. I spent my life supplying answers. They were never the right ones because I never asked the right questions. I've made some strange discoveries here."

She was quite simple and unpretentious, without that smug self-approbation usually displayed by people who have embarked on a "higher spiritual way."

The Sherpas were stirring and the cavalcade resumed its journey. Therese was carried in a sort of Sedan chair on poles. Freddie walked behind her. They talked at intervals, but for long periods were silent. He was thinking of all the rumors that had surrounded her in Paris, whispers of scandal and intrigue.

"Your Abbot seemed perfectly aware of why I'd been sent to Nepal," Freddie remarked.

"Not many Englishmen come to Changra Chari and you are obviously not a mountain climber."

"I was supposed to investigate a conspiracy. I may as well tell you that you were mentioned as being part of it."

"My days for conspiracies are long since over."

"There does seem to be a lot going on here in a military way."

"Enough to protect themselves. Does your government object to that?"

"Not unless the arms are supplied by people inimical to our interests."

"Perhaps they are not inimical?"

"They were in Tibet."

"I can assure you they're not here."

"Then you have been involved?"

"I had contacts that were useful to the Ranas."

"You know the Prime Minister?"

"Very well. He's a deft and charming man."

She spoke casually as if there were nothing to conceal, as if equipping an army were an every day pursuit that anyone might engage in.

A little later on she said, "You will never find out anything from the Nepalese. They always avoid direct answers. It's considered a point of etiquette. But, if it will set your mind at rest, there is no Russian influence here and no British influence either. That is Prince Rana's policy. He wants to keep the country free of all foreign involvement. And I think he is right."

They were moving along the spine of a hill. The mist had lifted a little. Watery sunlight revealed patches of fern-thick gorges and the glimmer of a river racing through craggy tors.

"These people have a traditional life that suits them," Therese explained. "They need certain things, medicine, practical hygiene, simple technology. In some ways they're very wise. What they do not need are the benefits of Western civilization, either the Russian or British kind. They should be left to develop in their own way. It may not be long before history catches up with them. They'll need to be strong to resist it. We have nothing to offer them in the way of social progress. Europe is on the brink. It will crumble in a series of larger, more terrible wars. The substructure has been rotten for too long." She added, "I know because in a small way I was part of it. I'm like an old leper; I don't believe there's a cure. I can only hope to prevent the spread of the disease."

"You take a very gloomy view, Therese."

"I give the West ten years—perhaps less."

"You say you contributed—?"

"My life was a prolonged act of revenge," she admitted. "I thought I could achieve it through money and then through power and then I simply projected my own bitterness and confusion. You can't avenge the past. You can only outgrow it."

That night as they sat huddled in blankets over a fitful fire, Freddie asked, "What is it precisely you've found here?"

"Precisely? That's hard to say. I used to think I was a victim of circumstance. Things happened to me over which I seemed to have no control. But there was something in me, in my nature, that attracted those events, not in the beginning, but later on. I was both the marksman and the target. It isn't easy to outgrow a lifetime of wrong thinking and wrong ambitions. Perhaps it's too late for me, but I see that it's possible—just. I think that's what the Gospels mean by metanoia."

"What's that?"

"It's a Greek word, mistranslated as repentance. To repent one's sins doesn't free one of them. Metanoia means to transform one's whole way of thinking. Lamaism offers a system for doing that."

She leaned forward so that Freddie could see the damaged side of her face in the firelight.

"When I came here this side of my face was horribly disfigured. There were scars on my forehead, beside my mouth and down this cheek. You can see they've almost disappeared. I'm not being fanciful. I believe that, as I've begun to think differently, the chemical composition of my body has begun to change. I'm not gifted with faith in a religious sense, so that with me the physical changes take much longer. It doesn't seem unlikely to me now that lepers and cripples were cured by a sudden blinding conviction that they could change."

She looked up and smiled at Freddie's incredulous expression. "How old do you think the Abbot is?"

"About thirty."

"He's in his late seventies. He was brought up by the present Prince Rana's grandfather."

They sat for some time staring into the fire.

"You were so beautiful as a girl. Did you never find happiness in love?"

"I don't think I ever understood much about love. For the most part people disliked and mistrusted me. I can't blame them. I got back what I gave."

"You've come much farther than I have," Freddie admitted ruefully. "I feel old and rather inept. I don't seem to have learned much along the way."

"You were always kind. I remember that. Not to have caused pain is also an achievement."

It was time to turn in.

"I'm glad we met again," Therese said. "Don't feel that your trip to Nepal has been wasted. All sorts of unexpected flowers grow in the desert after rain."

Freddie kissed her good night.

"That ring! Didn't you used to wear it in Paris?"

"My old ruby! I've always felt it was my identity. One day I shall be able to do without it. Then I'll be free. Good night."

They moved on steadily the next day. Freddie trudged along at some distance behind Therese, thinking of all she had said the night before. It would be wonderful to be rid of that weary, worn out impersonator, Sir Frederick Avondale, KCB, KCMG, retired!

In the afternoon the fog lifted and they found themselves on the crest of the landslide above Pokhara. It was a lovely sight, the still blue lake with the little temple, sheltered by jacarandas, the cluster of red-roofed houses and the fertile plain beyond.

"Do you know Goethe's poem?" Therese asked as they stood, side by side, looking down. " '*Kennst Du das Land vo die Zitronen blühn.*' "

"Is this the promised land?"

"It may well be." She held out her hand. "We part here. I have things to see to at Pokhara."

"Shall I see you again?"

"Perhaps."

"At Katmandu?"

"There or elsewhere. I'm glad that life has treated you kindly, Freddie."

"I hope you find what you're looking for, Therese."

To Freddie's dismay one of the Sherpas slung Therese across his back and started the perilous descent. Freddie watched with his heart in his mouth. One false step would have precipitated them both to almost certain death.

They reached the ground safely. Therese turned and waved. Freddie watched her as she walked away with a barely perceptible limp. It had been the strangest of all encounters, one he would never forget.

Three days later found him once again installed under MacGregor's disordered but hospitable roof.

That doughty Scot asked no questions. He doubtless surmised that what Freddie had discovered at Changra Chari was not what he had set out to find.

Freddie debated whether to make another attempt at an interview with the Prime Minister, but in a way the whole purpose of his mission was already solved. Instead, after dinner, he set out to explore Katmandu with MacGregor.

It was a lively little city with a charm and vitality quite its own. The streets were thronged with people in their bright costumes out for an evening stroll. They thronged 'round the open stalls where merchants sat cross-legged among bales of silks and cottons, dried fruit and herbs and mysterious condiments. Freddie bought some Chinese brocades for his wife and two ferocious brass dogs from Tibet that would serve as reminders of his visit when he was writing his memoirs in the restored gatehouse, a prospect which no longer filled him with such foreboding.

Everywhere MacGregor was greeted with smiles and handshakes. He was evidently an established component of life at Katmandu.

They climbed the steps into strange temples where the ancient gods performed their ritual dances of Life and Death. They passed the great marble vats where the devout were bathing and praying and scattering flowers on the water. They encountered a wedding procession preceded by a line of youths hidden under the garish trappings of a dragon of fearful mien which made sudden forays into the crowd to screams of laughter and mock alarm.

Indeed they seemed a contented people, well adapted to the traditions of their mountain land.

"There's one last place I've a mind to show ye," MacGregor said. "It's a wee temple that's been here long before anything else. It has one unique feature. Every night a group of musicians gather. They improvise a kind of chant that always picks up where it broke off the night before, so you might say it's the oldest song in the world. Perhaps it goes back to the days of the Lord Buddha who was born in these parts, ye know."

MacGregor led his guest through a maze of narrow streets to a row of dilapidated houses with an arched passageway between.

This opened into a courtyard with a small Hindu temple. The façades of the houses that formed the courtyard revealed lighted cutouts of rooms painted blood red and peacock green in which silhouettes moved like figures in a cryptic shadow play.

Dim suppliants circled the temple, bowing and murmuring prayers and anointing small dieties with scented oil. A few lanterns glimmered in the greenish moonlight. The temple was veiled in a cobweb of mystery, a shrine that, as MacGregor said, predated the dawn of time.

In an alcove near the entrance the musicians kept up a soft, dreaming music with flutes and zithers. Now and then a voice would be raised in a high, wavering melody with many half notes, neither religious nor romantic, the song of lonely men wandering the earth as he had wandered through the land of mists.

Freddie was filled with a peace more profound than anything he had known before.

He followed an aged crone, a mere bundle of rags and wrinkles, as she made her circuit of the temple. She bowed and mumbled and broke off single blossoms from a bunch of flowers clutched in her crippled hand. She laid one before each of the gods with the utmost care as if it were a jewel. Her face, with its toothless gums and cataract-shrouded eyes, was suffused with joy and devotion.

Therese was seated on a broken pedestal, swathed in a gray sari that, with her white hair, blended into the moonlight. She seemed always to have been there. Without greeting her, Freddie sat down beside her. It was not a place for words. In the presence of such ancient sanctity what could there be to say?

How long they sat there in silence Freddie had no idea. The singing, sometimes with the high treble of a boy, sometimes with the resonance of a tenor, seemed like the mountain streams to be very far away.

He was aware that she had risen, and stood beside her. For a moment it seemed to him that he had recaptured the girl he had loved so long ago. She was an old woman now, or rather she was ageless as the temple. Like the Abbot she had outgrown time.

"Did you know that I once almost asked you to marry me?"

"I wish you had. Perhaps in another life."

As they were leaving she paused by the musicians' alcove. The leader, a swarthy Gurkha in a black turban, nodded and smiled. They were acquaintances of long standing.

She listened to the singing for some moments and then, to Freddie's amazement, took off her ruby ring and dropped it into the begging bowl beside a few humble coins.

"Therese, your ring!"

"I don't need it anymore."

Freddie reached to retrieve it, but she restrained him. "Leave it. It's no longer a part of me."

Freddie followed her, shocked and mystified, into the street. Two of her Sherpas were playing knucklebones on the pavement. They shouldered her chair and she climbed in.

"Goodbye, Freddie. Good night, Mr. MacGregor."

They watched her as she was born away.

"A verra great lady," MacGregor said reverently as they started home.

Freddie Avondale left next morning. His host was not altogether sorry to see him go. Only as the family assembled at the gate and the children were waving farewell did Freddie catch on that ruddy countenance the fleeting sadness of an exile who would never again see his native land.

As he rode back through those smiling valleys with their fields of millet, waving poplars and rhododendrons, with the panorama of shining peaks beyond, Freddie wondered how he would explain the outcome of his mission to Lord Curzon, that arch-imperialist. Not that it mattered much. A small flower of acceptance had sprung from a crevice in his heart. It was beyond his power to change like Therese, but he saw his life as it was, without regret or remorse.

Often in the years ahead, as he sat in the gatehouse assembling his memories, he would think of Lalla Nok, the Lady of Kind Intent, in her house on the edge of the abyss at Changra Chari, asking eternal questions of the Himalayas.

About the Author

Evelyn Hanna was born of English and Irish parents, raised in London, educated in France and Switzerland, and has lived mostly in the United States since World War II, with "time off" in the Far East and North Africa. Ten years in television was followed by a stint in Hollywood and a turbulent foray into the theater. Her lifelong passion for history has resulted in her writing of romantic novels, of which *A Woman Against the World* is the second. Miss Hanna is now working on a third, dealing with the fatal love affair between George IV and Maria Fitzherbert. The author currently lives in rural Pennsylvania, where she enjoys gardening, collecting Japanese lacquer, and Chinese dogs.